JOURNEY TO SALVATION

Sam,
Always do the
right thing, like Harrison's!
[illegible]

Journey to Salvation

¤

The Overlords

A Novel

J. Michael Squatrito, Jr.

Journey To Salvation
The Overlords

The Overlords books may be ordered through Internet booksellers or by contacting:

J. Michael Squatrito, Jr.
www.the-overlords.com

Edited by Laura Vadney
Cover design by Patrick Thompson

ISBN: 978-1466245303 (pbk)
Printed in the United States of America

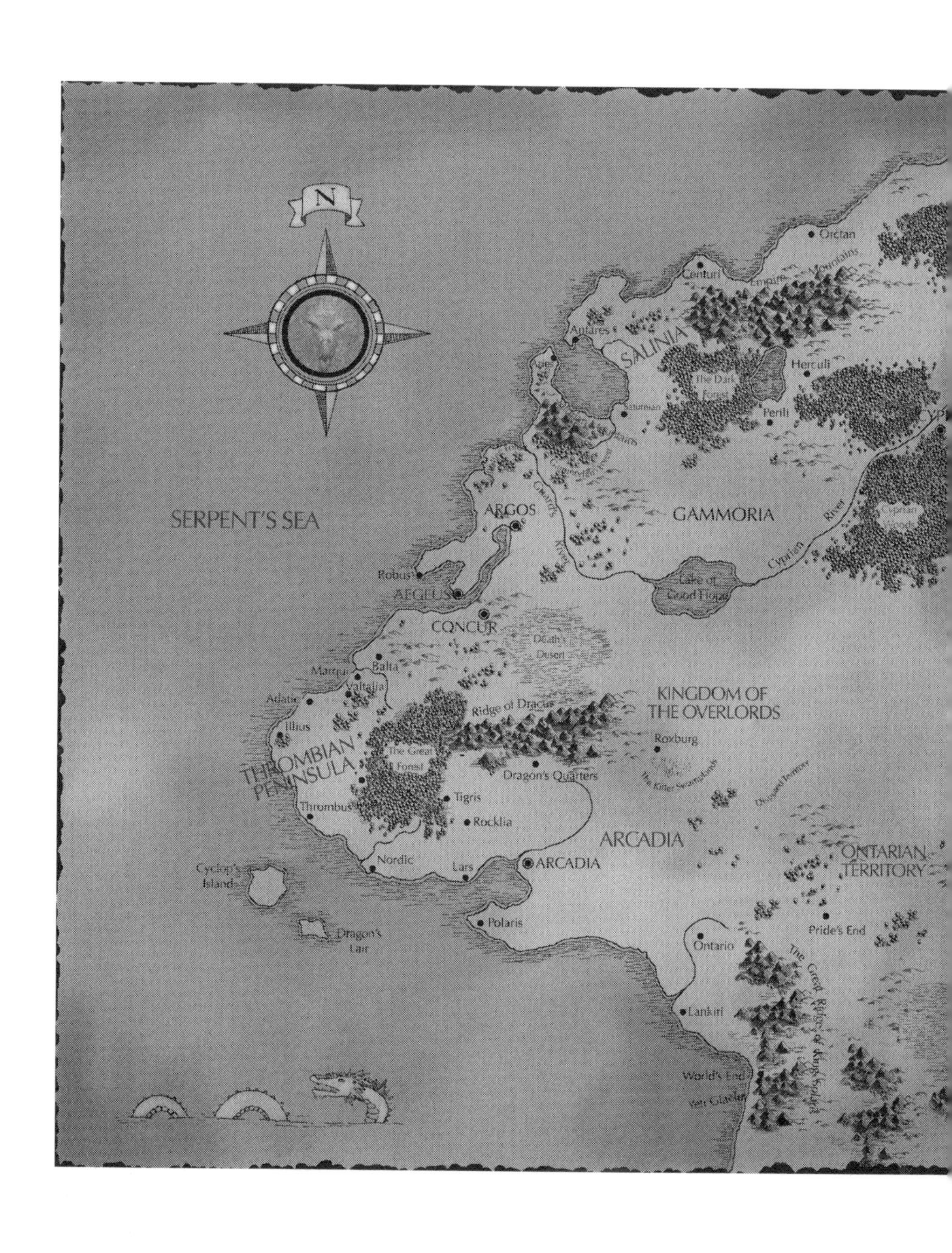
N
SERPENT'S SEA
Orctan
Centuri
Antares
SALINIA
The Dark Forest
Herculi
Perili
ARGOS
GAMMORIA
Cyprian River
Cyprian Woods
Robus
AEGEUS
CONCUR
Lake of Good Hope
Death's Desert
Balta
Adatic
Illius
KINGDOM OF THE OVERLORDS
Ridge of Dracus
Roxburg
THROMBIAN PENINSULA
The Great Forest
Dragon's Quarters
Tigris
Rocklia
Thrombus
ARCADIA
Nordic
Lars
ARCADIA
ONTARIAN TERRITORY
Cyclop's Island
Dragon's Lair
Polaris
Ontario
Pride's End
Lankiri
World's End

Prologue

The ancient warlock heard faint, distant screams of anguish and terror. Rather, he felt them rattle his frail bones. Taking purposeful steps to his work area, the ancient mage used long bony fingers to grab numerous magical items, stuffing them into his tattered backpack. When he completed that task, he collected a black cloak, slung it over his shoulders, and clasped its golden hook around the base of his neck.

A cobweb-covered mirror hung on the wall next to the door. The elderly man took a moment to gaze at his image, using his one good eye to stare at his ghastly reflection, almost turning away in shame. A faint visage of his former self gazed back at the warlock; the past thousand years had not been kind. Long, unkempt gray hair fell to his shoulders and his left eye was nothing more than a white mass, the unfortunate result of an intruder wielding a razor-sharp blade many years ago.

Age had redrawn the warlock's facial features, his skin barely covering his skull. Gazing deeper into his sunken eye sockets from his side of the mirror, a flicker of hope began to burn inside his otherwise grotesque body, for he knew his upcoming journey would provide purpose to his life once again.

Slinging the knapsack over his shoulder and closing the door behind him, the wretched soul trekked down the muddy path leading away from his home. The steady rain did nothing to hinder his advancement; instead, he pulled a hood over his head to keep somewhat dry. A half hour later, he reached his destination.

The wind and rain blew into his face as he gazed at the boats in the harbor. Tied to a dock close to him bobbed a vessel that would satisfy his needs, along with an unfortunate captain. Taking slow, shuffling steps, the warlock traversed the slick pier.

Reaching the slip, the ancient being stared at the unsuspecting man. "Is this your boat?" the warlock hissed.

The innocent captain tightened the rope to his mooring, then turned to face his intruder. An utter look of shock crossed the younger man's face as he gazed into what he thought was an image of death. Taking a step back, he tried to gather himself.

"Yes. Yes, it is," the frightened man managed.

The caped figure leaned closer to the captain. "You will take me to Dragon's Lair."

A profound look of surprise raced across the younger man's face. "What? I'll do no such thing!"

The warlock paused, the whipping wind and pounding rain becoming the only sound. "I say again, young man, you will take me to Dragon's Lair."

The captain swallowed hard, trying his best to control his fear. Using a more diplomatic approach, the younger fellow said, "Please understand, sir, I have a wife and family and I can't just leave on a whim." The man looked around the harbor, motioning with his head to another vessel.

"Maybe that person over there can take you."

The warlock remained motionless, staring. Not wanting to continue the conversation, the ancient mage mumbled, then spread his arms wide.

Noticing something wriggling in the caped man's pack, the captain's eyes grew round. At lightning speed, a rope sprung from the backpack and wrapped around the anxious soul.

The warlock pointed an elongated, bony finger at the young captain. "I grow tired of your act. Prepare this boat to sail."

As the mage twirled his finger in a slow, deliberate motion, the twine constricted ever tighter around the captain's torso with every revolution of the warlock's digit.

The captured chap's face turned red and he gasped for air. "I can't breath," was all he could muster through ragged breaths.

The old wizard waited an extra second before breaking his spell. The captain dropped to his knees as the rope uncoiled and slithered back to its hiding place.

Huffing, the poor man nodded reluctantly. "I'll take you wherever you wish. Please, don't hurt me any more."

With the slightest of nods, the warlock boarded the wooden vessel. The captain watched the gangly figure shuffle out of the rain before entering the ship's cabin.

The seaman could see the old man gazing out at him. "Dragon's Lair is a good day's journey, and I'm a bit unsure of the weather."

Without a word, the wizard motioned with a flick of his wrist for the captain to ready his boat for departure.

A gust of wind blew cold rain across the nervous man's face. "I don't like the looks of this one bit," he mumbled to himself as he uncoiled a rope from the mooring. A few moments later, the unlikely couple set sail for the misty island.

All night long, the storm rocked the small boat across the body of water that separated the mainland from Dragon's Lair. By mid-afternoon the next day, the vessel approached a dock on the east side of the island.

The warlock, already with his backpack in tow, raced to the ramp as fast as his frail body could take him. The captain, in the midst of securing the moorings, felt a cold hand grab his shoulder. Gazing upward from his position, the seaman stared into the wizard's dark, sunken eyes.

"You will wait for my return."

To insure that his guide would not try to escape, the warlock performed another spell. The old mage retrieved a vial containing a sludge-like black substance, which he poured into his hand. Next, he mumbled to himself before spitting into the mixture. After a final word, he threw the concoction to the ground.

At first, nothing happened, but then the captain witnessed the substance transform from a dark mass into a snarling, slobbering dog. The beast's coat was jet black and its left eye resembled the white matter of the warlock's. The menacing canine stared at the shaking captain, then barked ferociously, saliva flying in all directions.

The warlock held a firm gaze on the seaman. "If you entertain any thoughts of fleeing, Samokan will not stop attacking until he leaves no part of you undigested."

Nodding in compliance, the younger man dared not test the older man's resolve. The warlock, satisfied that he had convinced the captain to wait for him, turned and stared at the muddy path ahead of him. Using a hand to shield his face from the rain, the old wizard took his gaze upward to the top of the hill, where a massive castle rested.

The ancient man held his stare on the fortress. Many years had passed since he had left his exiled king and ventured off to the mainland in obscurity, biding his time. However, the screams of terror he had sensed the previous day told him that he must not delay, for all would be for naught if he arrived too late.

Proving treacherous for the battered soul, the mountainous trail took longer to traverse than he had expected. After an hour of trekking in the soaking rain, the warlock reached the gated entranceway of the castle. To his surprise, no guards manned their post. Without anyone to stop him, the old wizard engaged the mechanism that allowed the gateway to rise.

Waiting, the old man let the gears churn and grind as the metal gate lifted. Before the portal reached its apex, the warlock scampered through the opening. The ancient soul panned left to right, each image bringing back memories from a distant past.

The wizard finally came to a stop in front of a set of large, wooden doors. His mind churned with delight, recalling what rested behind the secured portal. The warlock peered about the deserted fortress before grasping the iron handles. With a mighty pull, the frail wizard opened the doors.

He gasped; his mouth dropped open. Panning the room in shock, the old mage muttered, "How can this be?"

Where fine tapestries had once hung, now there were none. Glass exhibits that had contained the best armor and weaponry in the land now stood empty. A fire ignited deep inside the old man and he ground his teeth with anger.

Departing the room with disgust, the ancient warlock ascended the spiral staircase that rose from across the hall of the treasure chamber. A moment later, he reached the top.

The old mage stared at the closed entranceway to the king's royal bedroom. After a moment, the enraged soul took purposeful steps toward the doorway, then threw open the double doors. What he saw next astounded him.

Dressed in black, the corpse of a man rested in a pool of cold blood. The poor person's head lay facing away from the wizard and five feet removed from the rest of the body.

The ancient warlock rushed to the motionless corpse. Bending to one knee, he began to examine the body when he heard a weak voice.

"Who is here?"

The old mage sprung to his feet in surprise. The voice had come from the severed head!

"Please, help me!"

Taking cautious steps, the ancient wizard approached the body from behind and craned his neck to get a better look at the face. His eyes widened as he recognized the poor soul.

"King Holleris! I had sensed something awful had happened, and now it is true."

The king looked upward at the old face, squinting in an effort to recognize the intruder. After a moment of thought, a wry smile overtook his face.

"Finius Boulware! You have returned!"

The old mage nodded, an uncharacteristic smile showing chipped and jagged teeth.

The king's expression turned grave. "You must help me! There's not much time!"

"That is true, my lord." Finius grasped the king's severed head and walked over to the lifeless body that lay on the floor. "I must perform the most dangerous of spells if you are to survive, but I cannot complete my work here. We must go back to the mainland."

"Do what you must, but my betrayer and his men left more than a day ago and I fear that at any moment they will break the spell that has allowed me to live for so long."

The old mage nodded. "I fear the same. What I must do now will keep you alive, regardless if the spell is broken or not. But I warn you, your immortality will cease after I complete my work."

"That doesn't concern me now. I don't want to live forever in this condition."

The old mage gazed deep into the king's eyes. "The pain will be unbearable, but you will survive."

The king closed his eyes in an apparent reflexive motion to nod his head, which he could not do in his current predicament. "Nothing can hurt more than the pain of disloyalty."

Finius carefully placed the king's head on the royal bed, then turned and approached the corpse. Being careful not to step in the pool of semi-dry blood, the old wizard dragged the body next to the bed. With a heave, the ancient warlock propped the torso up, placing it in a sitting position on the floor.

Next, Finius tossed his backpack on the bed and rummaged through it, before pulling out another burlap sack. Fishing through his pack again, he retrieved a jar containing gray worm-like slugs that slithered over themselves in the container.

Still not uttering a word, the ancient warlock continued with his task. Reaching into the smaller pouch, Finius removed six rust-covered, two-sided hooks that resembled those used by a fisherman. Grasping the king's head, he took care in aligning the spinal column with the base of the neck.

"The person who attacked you was a skilled swordsman," hissed the wizard. "He sliced your head off cleanly."

"The traitor was the best swordsman I had ever seen. Now hurry!"

Finius grabbed the first hook. "Ready?"

The king closed his eyes. "Ready."

Using his left hand to hold the head in place, the ancient warlock used his other to pierce the skin on the king's neck, bringing the barb completely through to the other side. The king's eyes widened and he wailed in pain.

"Stay still!" yelled Finius. "You will rip your skin to shreds!" The king gritted his teeth, trying his best not to move.

The ancient warlock then took the other side of the barb and forced it into the base of the headless corpse's neck. He completed his task by pushing the hook through the skin, exposing the sharp edge again. Squeezing the two tips of the hooks together, the wizard managed to get the rusty pieces of metal to lock in place.

An eerie toothy smile graced the ancient warlock's face. "One down, five to go."

Finius performed the same sequence of steps, securing the hooks at equidistant points around the front and sides of the king's neck, allowing a small area to remain open in the back. After he completed that task, he stepped back to examine his work.

The king sported an expression of excruciating pain and tears welled up in his eyes. Forcing the words out of his mouth, King Holleris asked, "How much longer do we have to go?"

The old mage stared at the bones teetering between the king's spinal column and the base of the skull. "A few more minutes."

Finius snatched the jar from the bed and unscrewed the top. The slimy creatures raised their heads and gazed at the sudden opening. In one swift motion, the ancient wizard smeared the oozing slugs around the king's exposed neck and spinal column.

The tiny beasts levied a multitude of pinpricks with their sharp teeth, causing the king to wince. The grey slugs gnawed at the king's bare bones, then regurgitated a sticky film upon filling their bellies, creating a seal between the severed vertebrae and spinal chord. After the worms finished that task, they burrowed under the king's flesh and began clearing away the caked blood from the major veins and arteries. Upon completing their internal chore, the creatures came back to the surface where they sealed their entry point to the king's skin, and were returned to the jar.

Fifteen minutes had passed when Finius asked, "How do you feel, my lord?"

The king carefully moved his head from side to side, the rusty hooks stretching his skin, causing him great pain. "I feel awful, Finius. When do I get better?"

"Once your blood starts flowing again."

The king squinted, skeptical. "How are you going to manage that?"

The old mage whirled around and snatched more items from his bag of tricks. When he turned to face the king, he held a transparent orb in his right hand and a metallic wand in the other. Without uttering a word, Finius plunged the wand into the orb, creating electric sparks that enveloped the globe.

Seconds later, he removed the magical stick and held a sparking, gelatinous sphere. Gazing at the king with his sunken eyes, Finius said, "Now it's time to bring you back to life!"

The ancient wizard hurled the orb at the king's chest and, upon its impact, waves of electricity coursed throughout King Holleris's midsection. The king wailed in pain as the jolt jump-started his heart and began to push blood throughout his body.

King Holleris moaned with each pump of his cold heart as the coagulated blood flowed to his vital organs. His body began to warm in the same way an athlete's muscles would at the start of an event. Over time, feeling returned to his extremities and his muscles came alive. The black-clothed man drew a deep breath, then buckled over awkwardly and coughed.

Finius watched the king with great anticipation. "Good! Good! The spell is working!"

"I still feel awful," said the king from his hunched position.

"I'll take care of your physical situation when we get back to the mainland," said the ancient wizard before grasping the king's arm and jerking the transforming man to him.

King Holleris winced. "What are you doing?"

Finius drew a dagger from his belt, then slit his forearm. As the king watched in horror, the ancient mage said with a hiss, "The time has come to join together completely."

The warlock sliced King Holleris's arm in a similar fashion, then pulled him closer. Joining both limbs at their wounds, Finius allowed their blood to mix.

"Now we are one, both in mind and soul," said the old wizard. "Our greatest feats are yet to come."

The king's expression changed from fear to understanding. Smiling, he said, "Is this your way of telling me that the next phase of our operation is commencing?"

Finius nodded. "Yes, but first we must restore your health to its fullest. Only then can we utilize our combined powers."

King Holleris squinted and cocked his head. "What do you propose?"

A toothy grin overtook the ancient being's face. "A creation that will instill fear over all. You will be highly revered when we are done."

The regal man smiled. "Very well." The king extended his arms to show that his pasty, gray body had begun to return to its natural pinkish hue. "I'm feeling better already. What is our next maneuver?"

"Back to my workshop." Finius motioned to the doorway. "A boat is awaiting you, my lord."

King Holleris took a final moment to gaze about his royal bedroom. "I shall restore this castle to the power it once was! And I shall take my revenge on those who turned their backs on me! They will rue the day they left me here to rot alone for eternity! My day of reckoning starts now!"

The two men then left the chamber and commenced on a mission the likes the land had never seen before.

CHAPTER 1

¤

The great vessel, VENTURE 3, rocked gently on the unusually calm sea during its late night voyage to the mainland. Inside one of its cabins, Harrison Cross and his friends paid their last respects to the young warrior's twin, Troy Harkin.

Troy had fought the better part of two weeks to combat the devastating injuries he sustained while helping his brother defeat the evil dragon Dracus. In the end, his wounds were too severe and, on this tranquil night, Troy succumbed to the inevitable.

Harrison, a single tear rolling down from his right eye, turned to his close friend. "Swinkle, is there a prayer you can say for him?"

The young cleric, flanked by Murdock, Pondle, Gelderand, and the ship's captain, Portheus, nodded and stepped forward. "I know just what to do."

Swinkle took a moment to gather one of his holy books from his backpack. Lance, Harrison's faithful canine companion, and Rufus, Gelderand's feline pet, both sat next to the pack and felt the obvious pain that permeated throughout the group. The young cleric patted the dog on the head and moved the cat out of his way, then rejoined his friends. Finding the appropriate passage, the holy man raised his head to speak.

Using the dim candlelight that illuminated the room with a soft yellow glow, he read. *"A life's end is only the beginning of a far grander journey. Rewards beyond imagination await those who sacrifice their wholesome lives for the benefit of their lesser brothers, for those people will remain with me, Pious, in paradise for all eternity.*

Grieve not for your fallen friends; rather rejoice in knowing that I will watch over them now. Keep their memories close to your heart and use them to embolden yourself as you continue your journey to me."

Swinkle closed his book and approached Troy. Taking a hand to the young general's forehead, the lad sprinkled holy water over the body while saying, "Rest, Troy, your job here is done."

When he finished administering the sacred solution, the young cleric closed the dead man's eyes, then turned to face his friends. "What shall we do now?"

Harrison stared into nothingness, vaguely hearing his friend's question. The young warrior took a moment, recalling the events of the past few days. After their fierce battle with Dracus and their confrontation with King Holleris, Harrison and his friends had decided to sail to Arcadia with the hopes of finding someone who could save Troy's life. Now that the young general had passed away, the group's situation had changed.

With tears welled in his eyes, the young warrior answered, "Continuing to Arcadia is pointless now that Troy's gone." Harrison raised his head, staring at his friends. "We need to reclaim the Treasure of the Land from Gelderand's home."

Murdock nodded in concurrence, as did the rest of the men. "I agree one hundred percent. That treasure has been stashed there for too long."

"And bringing two ships of this stature to Arcadia might raise suspicions," added the young warrior, alluding to the second vessel that carried the bulk of Troy's soldiers and supplies.

"Where should we sail to?" asked the ranger. Harrison pondered the question and drifted off in thought.

Portheus also heard Murdock's query and offered his solution. "We can sail to Nordic. The harbor is smaller, as is the village. We won't draw as much attention there."

The adventurers all looked at each other, agreeing with the stout captain. "Alter course to Nordic, then," ordered Harrison. "How will the other ship know of our change in direction?"

"My captain on VENTURE 5 will see our maneuver and adjust accordingly," said Portheus.

"Good." Harrison brought his gaze back to his friends, while Lance sprawled next to his master. "After we get the treasures from Tigris, I think we should figure out the last piece of the Talisman puzzle before we go back to Aegeus."

"We have accumulated everything we set out to find," added Swinkle, recalling the jewels, artifact, book, and container of Dracus's blood that they possessed. "The ancient manuscript instructs us to position the jewels in the appropriate position before lighting the candle."

Gelderand added to the conversation, doing his best to remain focused while Rufus twined around his legs. "Remember, a gateway should open if we do everything correctly."

Harrison scanned his friends' faces. "Where should we perform this act?"

All eyes turned to the mage. "Well, I'm not an expert on gateways," began Gelderand, surprised that the group felt he harbored untapped information, "but I have heard of phenomena ranging from translucent entry points to violent explosions." The older man shrugged and clasped his hands together. "We need to do this as inconspicuously as possible. I say we open the gateway inside of my home."

"Inside your house?" said Murdock with an incredulous look on his face. "What if this explosion occurs? Don't you think that'll attract some attention?"

"Without sounding condescending, who would care?" Gelderand raised an eyebrow. "We'd all be dead if that happened."

Murdock cocked his head and appeared as if he wanted to say something, but instead he nodded, agreeing with the older man's assessment.

Harrison raised a hand. "I agree with everything we've said, but there's another problem." The young warrior panned over to the motionless corpse. "Troy needs a proper burial."

"Harrison," started Murdock, "we can't cart him to Tigris with us."

"And he can't rot on this boat!"

The ranger raised his palms. "I agree; let's think about this."

"I think I know what we can do." Gelderand took a hand to his face, stroking his beard in the process. "I can perform a spell that will keep his body in stasis for ten days. With a little luck, we will be finished opening the gateway and gathering the Treasure by then."

Harrison had additional concerns. "I want Troy to be buried with our town's heroes in Aegeus." The young warrior looked up at the captain. "How long will it take to sail from Nordic to Aegeus?"

Portheus took a moment to make some mental calculations. "If everything goes well - normal seas, no obstacles - then we should reach Aegeus in four days." The captain panned the adventurers. "How long will it take for you to travel to Tigris, retrieve your things, then return?"

Harrison did not waver. "Six days; less if it's possible."

"We'll be in Nordic by sundown tomorrow," affirmed Portheus.

The young warrior nodded. "Very well." Harrison took his gaze to Gelderand. "When can you perform this spell?"

"I need to study an ancient scripture and gather some ingredients. I should be ready in an hour or so."

"Do what you must," said the young warrior. "I'll be waiting here."

"I'll stay with you," said Swinkle before taking a seat in a bedside chair.

Murdock gazed over to Pondle, then said, "There are more than enough people in this cabin. We'll rejoin you when Gelderand's ready. Let's go, Pondle." The two men then left the room.

Portheus followed Murdock and Pondle's lead. "I have a ship to sail. I'll keep you posted on our progress." The captain departed as well.

Gelderand waited for the men to leave before speaking. "I won't be too long," he said in Harrison's direction. The mage took a closer look at the young warrior and could see the pain the young man harbored. "He was a good man, Harrison. You learned much from him."

"I can't believe I lost my brother." The young warrior shook his head, still in disbelief. "I've known him for what, three weeks, and now he's gone."

"You need to cherish the little time you had with him." Gelderand let out a heavy sigh. "I need to prepare for this spell." The mage scooped the orange tabby into his arms, then left

Harrison and Swinkle alone in Troy's cabin. Lance, sensing his master's anguish, sat beside him and nuzzled Harrison's leg with his snout.

The young warrior rubbed the dog's neck. "Everything will be all right, boy."

Swinkle took the opportunity to speak with his friend alone. "What do you think the elders will say when we arrive in Aegeus?"

"I haven't really thought about that." The young warrior's blue eyes gazed at his friend. "I hope they'll be pleased."

"How could they not?"

Harrison shook his head. "Anything's possible with them. But I'll tell you one thing – they're expecting Marcus to return the kings' bounty, not us."

Swinkle's eyes widened. "I never thought of that! What do we tell them?"

Harrison did not flinch. "The truth."

The young cleric nodded, knowing that a detailed explanation of their journey should be enough to gain the trust of the town's dignitaries. "I suppose we wait for Gelderand now."

Harrison turned to face Troy, tucking the blanket up to his brother's neck. "Yes, we wait."

Gelderand finished his research an hour and a half later, then went about finding Murdock and Pondle before heading to Troy's cabin. The three men found Harrison and Swinkle right where they had left them, beside the young general's side.

Harrison lifted his eyes to the men entering the cabin. "Do you have everything you need to perform the spell?"

The mage nodded. "I think so." Gelderand gestured to the young warrior. "Please, give me some room to operate."

Harrison, Swinkle, and Lance moved out of his way, giving the older man direct access to Troy's body. Gelderand carefully removed the blanket that covered the young general. The wizard reached for ingredients in his pack, while Rufus scooted away from the scene. With the correct components for the spell in hand, Gelderand brought his attention to the fallen hero.

The mage took a white powdery substance and smeared it over Troy's broken body. When he finished that task, Gelderand closed his eyes, outstretched his arms, and began to chant. A moment later, a bright white glow enveloped the dead man, remaining around him for ten seconds before dissipating. Gelderand lowered his hands after the light ceased.

The magician took his gaze to his friends. "The spell is in place. We have ten days to lay Troy to rest."

Harrison gazed upon his brother yet again. "I say we leave this room now and don't enter it again until we reach Aegeus, out of respect for Troy." All of the men nodded in agreement.

The young warrior stood from his seat. "It's late and we should get some rest. Thank you for your efforts, Gelderand and Swinkle."

The two men accepted the young warrior's gratitude, then turned to leave the cabin along with Murdock and Pondle. Rufus and Lance scooted out of the room as well. Harrison, the last to leave, grasped the door handle and gazed back one last time on his brother.

He looks so peaceful, thought the young warrior. Without looking back, Harrison closed the door, sealing Troy's makeshift tomb until the great vessel reached its destination.

CHAPTER 2

¤

Less than twenty-four hours had elapsed since Harrison and his friends docked in Nordic. They wasted no time in proceeding to trek for the next two days, reaching Tigris without incidence. Along the way, the young warrior pondered what the Talisman of Unification would produce for them, but another thought had clouded his mind as well.

Tara had no idea that Harrison, her uncle, and a contingent of soldiers advanced on her unsuspecting little town. The young warrior had wondered how she was doing during his adventures across the land and had longed to see her again. With the small village nestled in front of him, he knew he would have his answers in a matter of moments.

The young warrior called over to his wizard friend. "Gelderand, I think someone is going to be very surprised to see you."

A wide smile overtook the mage's face. "Tara will be most happy, I am sure."

The group descended on a house situated at the far end of the town. Bewildered townsfolk gazed at the small group of armored men, wondering what business they had in their quaint village.

Gelderand approached his property, and before he walked to the doorway, he removed his backpack and took Rufus out, caressing him in his arms. The wizard gazed back at his friends, then knocked on the door.

The older man heard movement from behind the portal, then a latch unlocking. A second later, a set of nervous blue eyes behind radiant golden locks peeked through the crack in the doorway.

It took Tara a moment to process the faces that stared back at her with wide smiles, but when she did, the young girl threw open the door and leaped into her uncle's arms.

"Uncle! I've missed you so much," she exclaimed, the emotion evident in her voice. "I'm so happy to know you're safe!"

"We've been on quite a journey," said Gelderand, kissing his niece on the cheek. "Someone else has missed you, too." The mage handed Tara the little orange fur ball.

"Rufus! You're alive as well!" Tara hugged the cat as he meowed with delight.

"We need to come inside, Tara. There's still work to do." Gelderand waved his friends forward.

Harrison leaned over to Murdock. "I'm going to give the soldiers their orders. I'll meet you inside in a minute."

The ranger gave Harrison a sly look. "Don't keep the girl waiting," he said before flashing him a mischievous grin. The young warrior nodded, then went to address his contingent of men.

"Everyone remains outside until we secure the Talisman," said Harrison, while twenty-five fresh faces stared back at their leader. "Your job is to protect this house. Under no circumstances should you allow anyone inside."

"Yes, sir!" barked the soldiers in unison.

Harrison, a little taken aback at the soldiers' exclamation, nodded to them before entering Gelderand's home. As he walked through the doorway, he saw Tara waiting for him, stroking the cat in her arms.

The young warrior took a step toward the girl. As he did, Tara dropped the animal and embraced Harrison with all her might. "I missed you so much!" The two then met with a passionate kiss.

"I've missed you, too." Harrison gazed into Tara's big blue eyes and an incredible feeling of happiness raced throughout his body. "And, we all made it back alive."

Tara's expression changed from joy to concern. "Harrison, a man that looks just like you came by this house a short time ago." The girl peeked over the young warrior's shoulder and gazed at the soldiers who positioned themselves in the front yard.

"Those men were with him." Tara shook her head. "And then they found poor Thomas in the woods with his leg broken." The girl gazed into Harrison's eyes. "I had sent him off to warn you that these people asked about Gelderand and the treasure."

Harrison nodded slowly. "Tara, that man was my twin brother."

Tara's brow crinkled. "You have a twin brother?"

The young warrior's heart sank as he thought about Troy and how he lay dead on the ship docked in Nordic. "I never knew about him." Harrison cast his eyes down to the floor. "He died on our way back from Dragon's Lair."

Tara felt sorrow for Harrison's loss, but she still did not understand the whole situation. "You'll have to tell me all about this another time."

Out of the corner of his eye, Harrison noticed that his friends had started to move furniture away from the carpet that covered the trap door that led to the hiding place of the Treasure of the Land.

"I will, but right now I need to help my friends."

Tara peeked at her uncle, who gave her a caring glance. "By all means. What do you need me to do now?"

"Take care of the animals." Harrison motioned to Lance and Rufus. "They've been through a lot, too."

Tara smiled. "I'll make sure they have plenty of food and water." The young girl gazed longingly at Harrison. "I really missed you, you know."

Harrison smiled and kissed Tara on the lips again. "We'll have plenty of time alone later."

By the time the young warrior approached his friends, Pondle had already descended the ladder leading to the basement. Murdock brought his gaze to Harrison.

"Nice of you to join us," he said, his voice thick with sarcasm.

"Is everything still intact?" asked the young warrior, brushing aside his friend's remark.

"It appears so." Murdock called down to his friend. "Pondle, do you see anything unusual?"

"Nope, just stacks and piles of treasure!" The soft glow of the thief's torch became brighter as Pondle headed back to the ladder. Peering up at his friends, he said, "Looks like everything is just as we left it."

Harrison gazed over to the ranger, who smiled and nodded. "You know what we must do next," said the young warrior to his friend.

"That I do." All eyes turned to Swinkle. "Let's see what that book says again," said Murdock in the young cleric's direction.

Swinkle fumbled through his backpack, trying to find the elusive item, while Pondle climbed the ladder and rejoined his friends. A moment later, the young cleric held the leather-covered scripture in his hand.

Swinkle scanned the pages that revealed the clues to finding the pieces of the Talisman, before stopping in the section that described how to use the artifact. "I need to gather the other parts of our prize."

The young cleric took a moment to retrieve three jewels, the holding structure, and a candle filled with Dracus's blood. After Swinkle spread all the ingredients pertaining to the Talisman of Unification on Gelderand's kitchen table, he stepped back and placed the book down.

Like a chef peering at a recipe while preparing a meal, Swinkle repeatedly gazed at the sacred book as he placed the pieces of the treasure in their appropriate position. When he finished, he turned to face his friends.

"Everything is in place. Now, it says we need to light the candle in order to open the gateway."

Harrison gazed at the contraption that rested harmlessly on the table. A brilliant diamond sat in one of the cup-like placeholders of the triangular-shaped artifact. Just as dazzling, a ruby and emerald secured the other two positions. The foot-long gold canister, filled with dragon blood, rested in the artifact's center, the redness resembling the vile creature whose heart once pumped the liquid. Last of all, the ancient manuscript leaned against a slanted piece of wood that protruded away from the rest of the relic.

The young warrior gazed at his friends, whose faces reflected their anticipation. "Are we ready to light the candle?"

Gelderand raised his hands. "No!" The mage then turned to his niece. "Tara, I want you out of this house before we open the gateway. For safety's sake."

The young girl gave her uncle a quizzical look. "Why? Is something bad going to happen?"

"That's exactly the point – we don't know. I would feel more comfortable if you stayed away from the scene."

Tara did not back down. With a forceful tone to her voice, she said, "I spent the better part of a month worrying about you, Harrison, and everyone else. I'm not afraid if the house blows up. At least we'll all be together, unlike when you left me here alone."

Gelderand smirked, recognizing his sister's stubbornness in his niece. "The more you grow up, the more you are like your mother."

The young girl crossed her arms and looked away, dismissing the comment. "I'm not leaving."

The mage glanced at the rest of the men before answering. Gesturing to the entranceway, he said, "Close the door and secure the shutters." Tara did as her uncle instructed, then returned to the table.

"I think we are ready to light the candle." Gelderand motioned to Pondle, who retrieved his flash and tinder. A moment later, he held a harmless lit match next to the candle's wick, its flame awaiting its task.

The thief gazed at his friends, noticing the mixed looks of apprehension and excitement. "Here goes nothing," he said, before lighting the candle.

The tip of the wick sparked as it accepted the flame, then stood on its own. The candle remained lit, flickering harmlessly.

Murdock huffed at the slow course of events. "I suppose we should all start singing happy birthday," he said in a snide tone.

Gelderand waved his hand at the ranger, not bothering to look at him. "Give it a minute, magic takes time."

Harrison also felt Murdock's anxiety. He and his friends had traversed the countryside, battled countless foes, witnessed scores of men die, and for what? To watch some contraption's soft yellow glow?

Before he could add his thoughts to the conversation, the flame made a quick descent down the wick, the way a firecracker would ignite before exploding. As soon as the heat touched Dracus's blood, the container's four gold rods burst from their hinges and fell to the floor, along with the glass pieces engraved with the dragon's emblem. However, instead of watching the beast's blood splatter over the table, the red liquid began to rotate and hovered about eight inches above the tabletop.

The young warrior gazed at the scene with wide eyes. The sphere revolved faster and faster, and as it did, energy began to flow between the three jewels. Arcs of static electricity zapped from the precious stones to the sphere, causing the object to spin faster.

The men took a collective step back, giving the artifact ample room to perform its task. A second later, with the red globe spinning at its fastest, a bright white flash erupted from the sphere, lighting the entire room. Next, a translucent gateway, eight feet tall and four feet wide, appeared in the middle of the area.

Harrison stared at the newest phenomenon. The young warrior could gaze through the portal and see the back wall of the room, but images of the fireplace, desk, and chairs were distorted, the way they would appear if someone was peering through a waterfall. The gateway rippled slightly, allowing the amazed adventurers to see it better.

Tara approached Harrison, clutched his arm, and held him close. "I'm scared."

The young warrior fixated on the scene. "Don't be. This must be the way it's supposed to happen."

The young girl gazed up at Harrison. "What are you going to do now?"

Harrison gave Tara a caring glance. "Don't worry. I have a feeling that things will be all right." The young warrior looked over to Gelderand and Swinkle. "What does the book say to do now?"

The young cleric swallowed before answering. "All the book says is to light the candle, which will open the gateway. I'm thinking we are supposed to enter it."

Gelderand nodded. "I agree. It only makes sense." The mage gazed at the strange scene. "But we better move quickly. We don't know how long that gateway will remain open."

Murdock scanned the group. "I think you're right. How do you want to proceed?"

The mage stood tall. "We enter one at a time. I'll go first."

"Wait a second!" The ranger spread his arms wide. "Shouldn't somebody stay outside?"

Gelderand looked to his niece. "Tara will. It's time to go."

Tara gave her uncle an exasperated look. "I want to see what's in there, too! What am I supposed to do out here?"

"No," said Gelderand in a stern voice. "Someone needs to remain outside the portal in case something happens. At least you can explain what you saw."

The young girl shook her head, then turned away and gave the men a flick of her wrist. "Do what you must."

Gelderand smirked, finding his niece's feigned indifference amusing, and headed for the strange doorway. The older man stopped just before entering. Taking a finger, he touched the portal. Ripples reverberated across the gateway, mimicking the effects of a stone cast into a calm puddle of water. With a smile back to the men, the wizard stepped through the gateway and disappeared from view.

Pondle moved forward. "I'll go next."

Murdock nodded and motioned to his friend. "I'll follow you."

Swinkle teetered from one foot to the other while tapping his fingers in front of himself as he anxiously watched the halfling enter the gateway, followed close behind by Murdock. After the ranger disappeared, the young cleric heard Harrison's voice.

"You're next, Swinkle." With a nod, the nervous cleric approached the portal. Closing his eyes, he stepped through, leaving Harrison alone with Tara.

Harrison pointed a finger at Lance, who sat next to the girl. "Stay, boy! You need to protect Tara." The small dog whimpered, but obeyed his master. The young warrior brought his gaze to the maiden. "I'll be right back."

Tara leaned over, kissed Harrison, then said, "I'll be waiting. Now, hurry."

The young warrior turned and walked over to the translucent doorway. Harrison looked back at Tara one last time, nodded, then disappeared like the rest of his friends.

The young warrior stepped out of Gelderand's home and into what appeared to be an ancient castle. The surroundings, though, looked vaguely familiar to him. Taking his gaze about the room, he noticed that fine tapestries and artwork adorned the solid stone walls, pristine furniture sat arranged in a comfortable setting, and brilliant rugs lay on the floor.

Murdock, Pondle, Swinkle, and Gelderand stood before him, but beyond his friends, three figures glared back at the group. Harrison took a closer look at one man in particular and instantly recognized him. Taking a step forward, the young warrior approached the middle-aged man.

"You're King Ballesteros, aren't you?"

The short, sturdy figure nodded. "And you are Harrison Cross, correct?"

Harrison's eyes widened. "Yes, I am. How did you know my name?"

King Ballesteros glanced back at his counterparts before answering. "We've watched you for a very long time and we are most impressed."

The young warrior shook his head, confused. "Watched me? How?"

The royal man stroked his dark goatee, which had grown sprinkled with white hairs over time. "I think you know that answer, too." When Harrison continued with his puzzled expression, the king decided to elaborate.

"My fellow lords, King Solaris and King Nicodemus," Ballesteros motioned to each man, who nodded when he heard his name, "saw you reading the book your friend Philius gave to you. Just as you watched us in our world, we watched you in yours."

The young warrior's face beamed. "I knew it! Even though a piece of me always thought that the book was nothing more than some kind of magical spell that Philius had cast on me, I never doubted that it meant something more."

Ballesteros pointed to the mage who stood behind Harrison. "You need to listen to your friend Gelderand a bit more. Magic is a very powerful thing indeed."

Pausing a moment, the ancient king said, "We have not all been formally introduced. Nicodemus, Solaris, and I are the kings that you read about in your manuscript." The three regal figures approached the band of adventurers.

Harrison took a moment to introduce the group. "My friends, Murdock, Pondle, and Swinkle helped me uncover the Treasure of the Land." The men and the kings shook hands. "Gelderand joined us later and assisted in finding the pieces to the Talisman of Unification." The mage exchanged pleasantries as well.

The young warrior fidgeted, unsure of the situation. "How long will this sanctuary remain intact?"

Ballesteros waved a hand. "Fear not, my boy. Maligor would not have created something that would destroy the next leaders of the land, would he?"

Harrison glanced back at his friends, finding the same puzzled expression on their faces. Cocking his head, he reiterated, "Leaders of the land?"

King Solaris interlocked his hands near his waist, resting them on his long gray beard. "You are destined to be the new Overlords. You have proven your worth." The tallest man in the room gazed down at the men, gauging their response.

The young warrior shook his head. "Forgive me, but we set out to find the Treasure of the Land to help the people of our communities. We never dreamt about ruling over the land."

"However, your destiny says otherwise," said the third king, Nicodemus, youngest of the three. "You have a long way to go from here."

"Why don't you explain the reason we have journeyed to this point," said Gelderand, hoping for clarity about the grueling adventure they had embarked on.

Ballesteros nodded. "We've been waiting for this day for almost a thousand years." The king looked up in thought.

"Where to start," he began. "As you all know, a millennium ago forces from King Holleris's underground army kidnapped and removed us from power. Before all was lost, Maligor the Red cast a spell over Holleris, which teleported him to Dragon's Lair and rendered him immortal as long as he stayed on his isle of banishment."

Solaris stepped forward and continued the story. "We were left in this in between state, another dimension you might say. We could look into your world, but you could not see ours."

"Until you began reading the scripture Philius gave to you," added Nicodemus, pointing to Harrison. "Maligor made sure the manuscript would follow the Prophecy."

"And that is where you come into the picture," said Ballesteros, staring at the young warrior.

Harrison acknowledged the kings' praises, but he still had a nagging question. "You've mentioned this 'prophecy'. What does this really mean?"

Ballesteros closed his eyes and nodded slowly. "Before Holleris had us abducted, we knew of the growing tension he had about our vision of rulership. Years before he put his plan into action, we laid the foundation for our heirs to rule the land as proudly as we had in our day." The king gazed at Harrison, waiting for his response.

The young warrior played back Ballesteros's comment in his mind. Crinkling his brow, he said, "Your heirs?"

The king flashed Harrison a wide smile. "You and I are distant cousins, Harrison. Our bloodlines are one and the same."

The young warrior shook his head, perplexed. "How can that be? I don't understand."

"Harrison, this is what the Prophecy stated, that our heirs would rule the land once again. You being here today is just another step to attaining that goal."

Harrison did not allow himself to believe the words spoken to him just yet. "This all seems very surreal. Is it me, or does this whole prophecy talk seem a bit too convenient?"

Ballesteros raised his palms to the young man. "Don't mistake coincidence for fate, Harrison. Not all things can be explained."

"Can you at least tell me how we're related?"

The king let out a heavy sigh. "That's not as easy as it sounds," said Ballesteros. "You see, Sir Jacob, my trustworthy knight, hid my sister and her family from Holleris. We had felt that my royal bloodline should be intact and we hoped for this day to come."

Ballesteros could read the uncertainty on Harrison's face. "We never groomed an heir; we allowed the forecasts from the ancient Scrolls of Arcadia to take shape. You are living proof of their prognostications."

Harrison remained skeptical. "If what you say is true, how do you explain my twin, Troy Harkin, and his allegiance to King Holleris?"

The regal man took his gaze to the ground. "An unfortunate twist of events." The young warrior waited for more.

"Holleris knew of the prophecies written in the Scrolls of Arcadia and understood how we could return some day to reunite the land. He made sure that we could never come back by having his wicked warlocks cast an evil spell, suspending us here for an eternity. However, he also groomed a lineage, one that would be ready to fight for him and stop the forecasts from coming to fruition." Ballesteros paused. "Harrison, the scrolls mention that brothers would reunite the land."

Harrison let the king's last words sink in before answering. "Troy was supposed to rule with me?" The young warrior shook his head, visibly shaken. "That can never happen - he's dead now!"

"And the Prophecy is now fractured." The king's expression turned grave. "Time is of the essence, Harrison. With Troy gone, Holleris's lineage is also broken, and he will do whatever he can to stop you."

Harrison crinkled his brow. "Troy severed his head - the king is dead."

Ballesteros slowly shook his head from side to side. "No, he is immortal until the spell is broken."

"I saw his head on the ground. He's incapacitated and will never move from his spot ever again."

"Don't be so sure of that, Harrison. Evil always has a way to perpetuate itself." Ballesteros turned and removed an article from a desk that rested behind him, then faced the young warrior again, holding a small chest in his hands.

"You still have a long way to go before your mission is considered a success." The king opened the chest and took out a pure silver piece of curved metal. "Behold, the Talisman of Unification."

Harrison, along with his friends, gazed at the unimpressive artifact. Murdock pointed to the object in the man's hand. "We've ventured all this time in search of that worthless junk?"

Ballesteros let out a little laugh. "I must admit, it is not an awe-inspiring treasure. However, when joined with the other three sections, it becomes the symbol of unity."

Harrison asked the obvious question. "Where do we find the other three pieces? Are you going to send us on yet another quest?"

"Yes and no." The king handed the silver metallic object to Harrison, who inspected its consistency. "The elves hold the second section and they will instruct you how to attain the third."

The young warrior continued his questioning, while his friends listened with anticipation. "Would these be the elves that live in the Dark Forest with Moradoril as their leader?"

The regal man nodded. "That they would." Ballesteros held his palms up toward Harrison before he could ask another question. "However, you need to do some work first before you bring the elven race into the fold."

"What must we do?"

"Reunite humanity; only a unified force will sway the elves to align with you."

"Align with us?" Harrison sensed a greater fear from the expression on the kings' faces. "What's going on here?"

Ballesteros stared with intent at the young warrior. "Harrison, Holleris will strike back hard, with unknown fury. We created the Talisman to prevent this wicked man from ruling for an eternity. The elves will honor their agreement once they see that piece of metal in your hand."

Harrison gazed at the unimposing object. "Who else possesses the last two pieces?"

"Don't worry about them now. They will be revealed in time." The king took a step toward the young warrior. "Harrison, look, with this fracture in the Prophecy everything becomes much more complicated. You must gain the allegiance of all humanity. Only then can you move forward against Holleris."

Ballesteros brought his gaze to the entire group of adventurers. "You must succeed or all will be lost. We know what Holleris is capable of and whatever it is, it will be evil; we just don't know to what degree."

Harrison returned the man's glare. "Then we will succeed."

The king smiled, knowing the lad did not fully understand the task ahead of him. "You must use all of your resolve to convince others of your position. Make no mistake; your crusade is a mission of goodwill. Did we not send you all across this land to find the pieces of the Talisman? Did you not see the despair on the peoples' faces? Now go back to your hometown and take our bounty with you. Distribute the riches among the people and you will gain their trust. Good luck."

Harrison gave the kings a nod, knowing what needed to be done, and gestured for his friends to depart the sanctuary. As the adventurers started to leave the gateway, the young warrior looked back at the royal men and noticed that they had not moved from their spots.

"Wait!" he shouted to Pondle before the thief exited the area. Taking his gaze to Ballesteros, he asked, "Aren't you coming with us?"

The king cast a somber eye toward his fellow lords. "I fear that our lives' journey ends here. As soon as you leave this place, the sanctuary will dissolve and we will no longer exist."

"What?" Harrison's jaw dropped and his eyes opened wide. "We need your guidance! This can't be true!"

"I'm afraid that it is." The king attempted to calm the young warrior. "Our time had passed long ago. Our family and friends have been dead for a thousand years. Knowing that you have made it to this point is closure for us." Ballesteros stood tall. "Now go and fulfill your destiny. Just remember, the Prophecy can change at any time - don't allow that to happen again."

Harrison, though saddened at the thought of the kings' fate, understood Ballesteros's rationale. With reluctance, he nodded and said, "Thank you for instilling your trust in us. We won't let you down."

The young warrior then motioned again for his friends to exit the sanctuary. One by one, each party member departed. Before Harrison left the magical room, he looked back and gave the three kings a final nod, then he left them forever.

A moment later, Harrison found himself back inside Gelderand's home with his friends standing in front of him and Tara sporting a look of surprise on her face. The spherical globe of dragon's blood stopped rotating and turned to a fine red dust before spilling onto the tabletop. The gems stopped producing electricity and rested harmlessly in the cup-like holders of the artifact.

Tara continued to hold Rufus with Lance sitting by her side. "You're back so soon!"

Harrison gave her a quizzical look. "So soon? We've been gone about fifteen minutes."

"Fifteen minutes?" Tara shook her head. "Try less than ten seconds!"

The young warrior gazed over to his friends, each one shrugging as well. "Are you sure of the timeframe?"

"Of course I'm sure," said Tara. "I didn't have time to move from this spot before you all reappeared."

Gelderand approached his niece. "Time seemed to pass slower inside the sanctuary. It is the only rational reason why the kings still looked relatively young despite having disappeared almost a thousand years ago."

Swinkle nodded in concurrence. "I have to agree with Gelderand. It is the only logical assumption." Changing the subject, the young cleric asked, "What do you make of what we heard?"

Murdock let his feelings be known. "Reunite humanity? Approach the elves after this? What have we gotten ourselves into?"

Harrison rubbed his temple with his left hand. "The kings are asking us to take on a monumental task, but we must succeed. We can't let them or our people down."

"Our people?" Murdock's brow cringed. "Forget about succeeding in this ludicrous adventure; where do we even start?"

"This whole quest commenced in Aegeus," began Harrison, "and that's where we need to go now. We possess the Treasure of the Land, control a small army, and have the burden of bringing all people together."

The young warrior panned and read his friends' faces. They all accepted what Harrison had said, but each one silently harbored their own anxiety.

"The elders in Aegeus will help us with our task," continued Harrison. "I say we gather the treasure now and leave immediately; Troy still needs a proper burial."

Gelderand approached the young warrior, resting a hand on his sturdy shoulder. "Instruct the soldiers to help cart the riches back to Nordic and secure them on the ship. Make sure they are as discreet as possible."

"We've already marched through the main street, but I'll give them their orders." Harrison was about to leave when he gazed upon Tara, her bottom lip quivering ever so slightly.

The young girl alternated her gaze between Harrison and her uncle. "You just arrived! You can't leave again!" Tara's eyes began to glisten with tears.

Harrison took a step toward Tara, then held her in his arms, with the young girl hugging him back. "This journey's going to get a bit more difficult. I couldn't even begin to tell you when we'll back in Tigris."

Tara pulled away from the young warrior's embrace. "Oh, I'm not staying here this time. I'm going with all of you to Aegeus."

The young warrior frowned. "What? No, it's too dangerous."

"Do you honestly expect me to wait here while you all gallivant across this countryside again?" Tara read the adventurer's blank expressions. "I'll answer that for you - I won't."

Tara's uncle approached the excited young girl. "I think it would be wise for you to accompany us. I don't like the idea of you being too far away from me."

The young girl raised her eyebrows, expecting more of a fight from Gelderand instead of acceptance to her outburst. "I'll gather my things and be ready to travel before the soldiers have finished packing the hoard." Tara rushed out of the room.

Harrison stood in his place, mouth agape. Turning his gaze to Gelderand, he said, "What are you thinking? Tara shouldn't be put in harm's way."

"You heard the kings; they want us to reunite humanity, then gain the allegiance of other races." Gelderand drew a heavy sigh. "I don't like the sounds of this and I want Tara close to us in case we run into some mishaps."

Harrison let Gelderand's words sink in. We're about to embark on something big, he thought. *Bigger than all of us.* The young warrior took his stare to Tara's room where he saw the young girl rummaging about. It will be nice to have her around, but I must protect her at all times, he said to himself.

"All right, but we must take special care of her," said the young warrior.

"I know you will," said the mage before moving closer to Harrison. "Don't let the special bond between you and Tara cloud your judgment."

Harrison furrowed his brow, fumbling for words. "Special bond?"

"It's all right, Harrison." Gelderand smirked. "You're of good stock and I approve of you." The mage wagged a finger at the young warrior. "Just treat her well, understand?"

The young warrior turned a slight shade of red. "Of course I will." Harrison brought his gaze once again to Tara's room. The young girl moved so elegantly, causing his heart to skip a beat. "I'll take excellent care of her."

Gelderand nodded. "Let's get moving; we have a lot to do."

Over the course of the next three hours, Harrison and his friends helped the soldiers cart weaponry, armor, chests of coins and rare jewels, and various magical staffs, scrolls, and artifacts from Gelderand's safe haven to the awaiting carts outside of his home. When finished with the mundane process of packing, the men requested Gelderand to make a final sweep of his premises.

The wizard went about his home one last time, making sure he and Tara did not leave anything behind that they would need. Satisfied with his inspection, Gelderand approached Harrison and the others.

"It's time to go," said the mage, securing his front door. "Believe it or not, I'm going to miss this little place."

Tara came to her uncle's side. "I will, too, but we have so much more to look forward to."

"That we do." Gelderand looked over to the young warrior. "Let's go."

Harrison nodded. "Murdock and Pondle will lead the way with the advance scouts. The rest of the soldiers will flank the carts and protect us from a sneak attack." The young warrior brought his gaze to Tara. "You stay close to Swinkle, Gelderand, and Lance – I won't be far from you either." Harrison smiled.

Tara nodded, holding Rufus in her arms. "I'm not as frail as you think. I'm ready to journey."

Harrison motioned to Murdock and Pondle. "Whenever you're ready!"

The two men nodded and waved the soldiers forward and in a matter of minutes the procession of adventurers, soldiers, carts, and treasure began their short journey to Nordic.

CHAPTER 3

¤

The small army made a successful three-day trek to Nordic and loaded the Treasure of the Land onto the great ship, *VENTURE 3*. Without wasting another minute, Portheus guided the vessel out of the harbor with their sister ship, *VENTURE 5*, following them to Aegeus.

Harrison knew that they had only a few more days before Gelderand's spell would no longer keep Troy's body in stasis. The young warrior approached the familiar cabin. Hesitating for a second, he turned the knob and entered the room. Inside he found Troy just as he had left him – in bed, eyes shut, resting peacefully.

"You'll be laid to rest in honor soon enough, brother," Harrison said. The young warrior noticed that the candle he had lit days ago had melted away to its base, and he replaced it with a new one.

"I'll check on you again once we reach Aegeus." Harrison left his brother behind and attended to the needs of his men.

Harrison proceeded to the lower deck where the massive treasure rested. His friends had hung candle-lit lanterns throughout the vast belly of the ship, providing ample light to digest the riches. Lance, upon seeing his master, scampered over to greet him.

The young warrior acknowledged his canine companion with a pat on the head, but his eyes remained transfixed on the hoard. Finding a pair of stools, Gelderand and Swinkle sat down to examine ancient scrolls and books. Rufus played among the piles of treasures, never straying too far from the magician.

Panning to the left, Harrison found Pondle rummaging through chests of coins, the thief barely able to contain the wide smile on his face. Murdock allowed his friend to inventory the loose treasure, while he set his sights on the weaponry and armor associated with the riches.

However, the most beautiful sight of all was neither the countless shimmering jewels nor the glistening blades of the weaponry. Tara, intent on helping the group with their cause, sat near her uncle, a fancy feathered pen in her hand and a large leather-bound volume on her lap.

Intrigued with what she was doing, as well as yielding to an unstoppable urge to just be near her, the young warrior passed rows of swords, axes, and other assorted armor and weapons to stand behind the fair maiden. Clasping his hands behind his back, Harrison leaned over her left shoulder, his chest lightly touching her body, and peeked at the book that rested on her lap.

"What do we have here?" he said softly in her ear, before giving the girl a peck on the cheek.

Not flinching, Tara said, "We found this manuscript with the rest of the Treasure." The young girl swiveled in her seat to look toward him, their faces dangerously close to one another.

"The ancient kings provided us with a list of everything associated with the Treasure of the Land, and we're checking off every item." The couple's lips hovered only a few inches apart from one another.

Gelderand cleared his throat. "We do not want to miss a single thing," said the magician, playing the part of the concerned parent. The mage's simple ploy worked; his statement caused Harrison to pull away from his mate. "The book also relates what village shall receive which gifts."

"That makes our job a whole lot easier," said Harrison, regrouping.

"And it will allow the townspeople throughout the land to understand that our mission is for the benefit of all," added Swinkle, taking a moment from reading an old parchment.

Harrison could not contain his curiosity any longer. "What has everyone uncovered so far?" The young warrior looked at the mage, who made eye contact with his niece.

Tara flipped a few pages back, then ran her finger to the top of the left page. "Swinkle and my uncle have found Scrolls of Wisdom that belong to Robus, a Scroll of Battle Unity for the army," the young maiden shook her head, having no idea on how to use that parchment, "spell books for magicians throughout the land, and staffs and wands to be handed out to each town. Furthermore, my uncle has taken a liking to a rather unique item." Tara gazed over to Gelderand.

The mage took his cue and reached behind him for a large staff that leaned against the wall. Holding the wooden object, Gelderand gazed at its lacquered finish before speaking.

"I think that this staff contains hidden secrets," said the mage. He pursed his lips before continuing. "Secrets that I am sure will reveal themselves at another time." Gelderand peered over to his niece. "Continue, Tara."

The young maiden turned to the next page in the manuscript. "Murdock has counted over two hundred types of weapons – swords, battle-axes, maces – you name it, and he's nowhere near done with his chores. And Pondle said that there's so many coins that every town would be rich a hundred times over, whatever that means."

Harrison stood tall, a smile gracing his face. The Treasure of the Land had been more than he could have imagined, and all of mankind would benefit in the end.

"I think what Pondle means to say is, everyone's life is going to get a whole lot easier once we distribute the Treasure," said Harrison, full of pride.

Gelderand was not so quick to agree. "Riches also bring out the worst in people, just remember that as well."

The young warrior nodded, agreeing with the older man. "I know. That's why we must make sure that no one gets more than their share."

"People's lives cannot be made so simple that they would strive to do nothing at all," continued Gelderand. "Things can be made easier for them, but they must also have a purpose in life." The mage leaned on his staff, saying to no one in particular, "A life without a purpose would be wasteful indeed."

Harrison took the older man's words to heart. Wasn't his purpose to bring happiness to everyone in the land? He knew that he still could succeed on that mission, or he would die trying.

Swinkle raised his hand toward Harrison, signaling that he had something to add. The young warrior broke out of his trance, asking, "What is it, Swinkle?"

The holy man unfurled an ancient parchment. Scanning the document, he said, "I think I found a very important scroll."

"Is it magical?" asked Gelderand, intrigued.

"No," said Swinkle, his brow crinkling. "I think it is a treaty of some sorts."

The small group huddled around Swinkle, each member wiggling closer together to get a better look at the parchment.

"Its title reads Unification Agreement," said the young cleric, pointing to the top of the page. "Sections of text that follow state the signatory binds his or her town to the pact. Any village then becomes part of the New Kingdom."

Harrison's eyes lit up. "This only makes sense! The kings have given us another means to reunite all peoples. And if we restart the Legion of Knighthood, the person who signs the document can appoint their town's representative."

Swinkle began to roll the parchment. "I am going to keep this in a safe place, away from the rest of the Treasure."

"Good idea," said Harrison, as the rest of the group began to disperse and continue with their inventorying. "Be sure to bring that scroll to our planning meeting with the elders." Swinkle nodded in affirmation.

The new discovery behind him, the young warrior took a look around the immediate area and still found more than enough items that needed to be counted. Wasting no time, he began to rummage through the loot, staying close to Tara whenever possible, and helped inventory the greatest treasure the land had ever seen.

Another three days passed before the great harbor of Aegeus came into view. Harrison and his friends stood on the deck of the ship, taking in the scene before them.

The young warrior noticed Tara gazing toward the shoreline and approached her from behind. Sensing his advancement, she said, "It looks like a beautiful city." The girl turned and faced Harrison, a flirtatious smile stretching across her face.

"I have bittersweet memories of this town," he answered, leaning against the railing. "I grew up here, but without my parents." The young warrior gazed into Tara's eyes. "I want to take you to a special place after we visit with the elders."

Tara nodded and took hold of Harrison's hand. "Of course." The moment went no further, as Swinkle and Lance approached the two.

"We'll be bestowing a monumental gift to this town in less than an hour," said Swinkle, while Lance nuzzled up to his master. "I hope the townsfolk understand the importance of this treasure."

"They'll have no choice," said Harrison, petting the dog. "We'll keep everything on the ships and report to the elders as soon as we dock."

Swinkle agreed. "Perhaps we should bring the dignitaries on board to see what we have recovered."

The young warrior pointed at his friend. "That's an excellent idea. That way no one will know the specifics of the treasure and we wouldn't be carting the loot down the main street."

Tara added to the conversation. "What do you think the people will do when they see the riches?"

"Some will be gracious, other greedy," said Harrison. "The kings said that we must disperse this treasure appropriately. That's what I intend to do."

"And one of Troy's last wishes was to give back the treasures he stole from the mainland," Swinkle said as he brought his gaze to the other ship.

Harrison looked down and let out a sigh. "Great wealth can bring out the best and the worst in people." The young warrior made a point to look both Swinkle and Tara in the eye.

"Both of you must promise that you will watch over me and make sure my decisions are for the good of all. I don't want these treasures to be used to make anyone powerful."

Tara snuggled up to Harrison. "You can count on me."

"Me, too." Swinkle rested a caring hand on Harrison's shoulder. "It's time to get ready to reveal our secret to the world."

Harrison brought his gaze to the advancing shoreline. With a slight sigh, he said, "I feel the days of innocent adventuring are coming to a close. Let's find the others and prepare ourselves for our departure." The three young people left the panoramic view of the Aegean harbor and searched for the rest of their friends.

Tara went back to her cabin, allowing Harrison and Swinkle to locate the three missing party members. The two men found Gelderand in his chambers and Murdock and Pondle below deck. Finding an empty room with a long table and chairs, the five adventurers made themselves comfortable.

Harrison invited Lance into the room with them before securing the door. "The time has finally come to tell everyone what we know," he began, taking a seat at the table with the rest of his friends. "How do we want to go about telling the elders?"

"They're going to be expecting Marcus, you know," said Murdock, referring to their deceased leader.

The young warrior cocked his head, having thought about that very thing before drifting to sleep the night before. "All will go well as long as we tell them the truth."

"I agree." The ranger shifted in his seat, then leaned forward, staring at Harrison. "How well do you know the Aegean elders?"

With all eyes focused on him, the young warrior took a moment to answer. "They gave me free room and board at the Fighter's Guild after my parents died, trained me to be an ultimate fighter, and allowed me to be part of the team to search for the Treasure of the Land." Harrison glanced away from his friends. "I think they're of good stock."

"You think?" Murdock noticed his friend's discreet loss of eye contact. "Do you believe in your heart that you can trust them with all of these riches?" Gelderand, Pondle, and Swinkle hung on Harrison's every word.

"I don't know!" The young warrior huffed. "Deep down I feel we should be the ones telling them how to disperse the treasures we've found."

"I completely agree!" Murdock scanned the group. "So, what do we do?"

"Allow them on board this vessel, but you must control the situation," said Gelderand, wagging a finger at Harrison. "You have the knowledge of this land's history, which the ancient kings reinforced in you. They believe in you and so do I." The mage paused. "Don't let the elders take your future away from you."

Harrison thought hard about what Gelderand said. Part of him wanted to show the elders that they were right in choosing him to be part of the group to find the Treasure, but he had a nagging feeling that kept telling him to remain cautious. Suddenly, a thought sprang to mind.

"Philius!"

"Philius?" The mage looked at the other men. "Who's Philius?"

"He's the mage that gave me the magical manuscript before I left Aegeus," exclaimed Harrison. "Remember? I told you about him."

Gelderand took a moment before recalling hearing Harrison's familiar tale. "Yes, I do remember, but what does he have to do with anything?"

"He's the only one that I have absolute trust in. He must be present when the town's dignitaries board the boat."

"If you feel that strongly about him, then I suggest you summon him right away." Gelderand took his gaze around the room. "People will start to get suspicious of these two ships sitting in their harbor."

Murdock added to the conversation. "Harrison, if you tell us where he lives, Pondle and I will go fetch him."

The young warrior nodded. "All right, but don't scare the man. He's very old, you know."

"Just let us do our job and everything will be fine."

"I suggest we wait until nightfall," said Pondle. "That way we can maneuver without as much activity."

Harrison frowned. "Won't that just raise everyone's suspicions?"

Gelderand focused on the young warrior. "Again, this is our situation to control. Fetch Philius, then send someone to gather the elders to our ship."

Harrison lowered his head in thought, clasping his hands in front of him. "All right, we'll proceed as you both have suggested. Once Philius is on board, I'll send three of the soldiers into town to gather the dignitaries." The young warrior gazed over to Swinkle, who pursed his lips and nodded in concurrence.

Murdock moved away from the table. "Great. Nightfall is about an hour or so away. Where's Philius's residence?"

The young warrior took a moment to gather his bearings. "Let me see, if we go from the docks to the main road —" Harrison closed his eyes, imagining the route in his head. "Then take a left after the first shop, go two blocks further before taking a right —" Harrison opened his eyes. "His house is the third one on the left."

Murdock glanced at Pondle, who nodded. "Got it. We'll be off soon and we'll let you know when Philius is on board." The ranger slapped his friend on the shoulder. "Let's go, Pondle. We got some work to do." The two men left the table and headed out of the room.

Swinkle waited for his friends to leave before speaking. "Is this the best course of action? Sneaking around your hometown, covertly bringing people on these vessels?"

Harrison drew a heavy sigh. "I wish we could just walk down the main street and parade the riches by the townspeople. But it's just not that simple."

The young cleric crinkled his brow. "Why?"

"I'm just being very cautious. I don't want to announce to the world what we have just yet. In due time, everyone will come to appreciate the struggles we went through for them."

Harrison's answer satisfied his friend. "And we'll do everything for the benefit of others, right?" asked Swinkle.

"Absolutely." The young warrior pushed his chair away from the table. "I suppose now we wait and see what unfolds. I have a feeling we're in for a very interesting night." The three men silently concurred, then left the cabin to await the evening's visitors.

Two hours later, Murdock and Pondle returned to *VENTURE 3*, escorting a frail, elderly man. The cloak-wearing being took care in navigating up the plank before stopping on the ship's deck.

As the man pulled down his hood, his eyes widened as he saw the ranger and he asked, "Where is he?"

Murdock motioned with his finger. "Follow me."

The three men went deeper into the vessel before coming to a cabin with its door closed. The ranger knocked on the portal. "Enter," said the voice from the other side.

Murdock opened the door and gestured for the old man to cross the threshold. Inside, Philius found Harrison and two other men seated at a table. Upon seeing the ancient wizard's face, the young warrior sprung from his seat and greeted his old friend.

"Philius! I'm so happy to see you again!" Harrison shook the old man's hand with vigor.

Philius clasped the younger person's hand. "I am so proud of you, son, if what these men have told me is true."

Harrison smiled, nodding. "It's true, all right. We have the Treasure of the Land on this boat as we speak."

The old mage gazed around in astonishment, secretly wondering where his friend hid the bounty. "Is it everything they spoke of?"

"And then some." The young warrior motioned for the old man to sit at the table. Harrison sat down as well, flanked on either side by Swinkle and Gelderand. Murdock and Pondle remained standing near the doorway. "I wanted to consult with you before bringing the elders on board."

A look of disdain crossed the man's face. "A wise move on your part. Tread lightly with them."

Harrison was about to say something else when he heard Gelderand clear his throat. The young warrior took his gaze to the wizard, his eyes widening. "Where are my manners? These are my friends Gelderand and Swinkle," said Harrison. "You've already met Murdock and Pondle."

The older man nodded in the direction of both men. "A pleasure to meet you all."

Gelderand leaned forward. "What do you know of the dignitaries of this town?"

"They discredited me years ago," huffed Philius with a wave of his hand. "Just because someone ages doesn't make that person senile."

"I agree one hundred percent." Gelderand brought his gaze to the faces staring at him. "And just because someone is young does not mean he lacks experience."

Philius panned the room as well. "How true."

"I think we're really looking for some kind of direction," began Harrison, "and I had hoped that you could help us with our first step."

"What direction has been given to you?"

"The ancient kings told us to reunite humanity. That starts here."

Philius nodded, rested his elbows on the table, and interlocked his fingers. "I see. And did they give you any other clues on what to do?"

Harrison nodded. "We are to approach the elves after the land is united. They also mentioned that King Holleris might be planning something sinister."

Philius raised his eyebrows. "Holleris? Sinister plan?" The wizard shook his head. "What were they insinuating?"

The young warrior sighed. "They said a lot of things - a fracture in the Prophecy, reuniting all of humanity, Holleris and his evilness - too much to keep repeating." Harrison leaned forward. "We must tell the elders and begin our next quest."

Philius sat back in his seat with a vacuous stare. "Enough talk. Summon the elders and I will help your cause."

Harrison looked over to Murdock and Pondle. "You two can handle this task. Also, find three soldiers to carry out this mission with you."

Murdock looked at Pondle, who shrugged. "Sure. Any three in particular?"

Harrison was unsure of who to send, not really knowing the members of the army Troy had handed over to him. "Tell them of their mission and ask them who they feel should go with you. Troy trained them very well."

The ranger nodded. "We'll be back."

Two hours later, under the cover of darkness, Murdock and Pondle returned with representatives of the town's elders — two middle-aged men and one woman. The small entourage boarded the awaiting vessel, and the two adventurers, along with three soldiers, escorted their guests deep below the ship's deck. After several uncomfortable minutes of speechless following, the small party stopped in front of a cabin door.

Murdock knocked once, then opened the portal. Inside, Harrison, Gelderand, Swinkle, and Philius rose from their seats on the opposite side of a long table. One by one, the Aegean elders entered the room, nodded to the standing men, and positioned themselves across from their hosts.

A heavy-set man, the only member of the elders not adorned in a cloak, spoke first. "Is it true what these men have told us? Have you secured the Treasure of the Land?" asked Governor Rollins, his voice rising with excitement.

Harrison, not wanting to start the conversation with a lie, answered, "Yes, we have. It's on this ship as we speak."

Governor Rollins opened his mouth to talk again, but another member of the elder's group cut him off.

"Where's Marcus?" asked a tall, bearded man.

Harrison did not waver. Many had regarded Gareth Tyne as a very stubborn man, but one who carried great influence. A seasoned warrior like Harrison's mentor, Marcus Braxton, Gareth always took a straightforward approach to everything he put his mind to. The young warrior knew this and began his tale with caution.

"Lord Nigel Hammer of Concur murdered Marcus in the catacombs leading up to the Sacred Seven Rooms."

Gareth's dark eyes focused on the young warrior, burning a hole through his skull. In a condescending tone, he responded, "And you survived?"

Harrison knew Marcus lobbied hard for his selection as a member of the party that represented Aegeus in their search for the Treasure of the Land. Listening to the tone of the current conversation, he determined who had caused his deceased leader the most grief.

"We all survived," said the young warrior, "and we succeeded in returning the sacred prize here."

"We must alert the townspeople," said a jubilant Governor Rollins, a smile gracing his face while he unwittingly played with his black moustache. "The people of Aegeus deserve to know!"

"They will hear of no such thing!" scowled Gareth. "I want to see this hoard for myself before I believe anything I've heard tonight."

"All in due time," said the elderly man across from Gareth. Philius motioned for everyone to sit. "Make yourselves comfortable."

Gareth glared at the old wizard. After a few seconds, he nodded toward the empty chairs facing the table, signaling to his equals to sit.

With everyone situated, Philius continued. "This is better, no?"

"I don't see where you come into the picture, old man," said Gareth. "You were not selected as part of the original group, as I recall."

Harrison felt his blood simmer. Had he not returned with the land's ultimate prize? Who did this man think he was anyway?

"I don't like your tone," blurted Harrison, staring at Gareth.

A frozen gaze met the young warrior's. "What did you say?"

"I think you heard me. What's your agenda here? To bully us into handing over the Treasure to you?"

Gareth shifted in his seat, then moved forward. "I'm leaving this ship with the Treasure. You are not capable of even comprehending its importance."

Harrison could not believe his ears. His disbelief turned into anger, but before he could rebuke the elder's last statement, a smoother, soothing voice added to the conversation.

"Enough, Gareth," said Fallyn Tierany, placing a soft hand on the man's forearm before applying a firm grip. "This bickering is senseless." Fallyn focused her radiant green eyes on Harrison and smiled.

"We should be commending this fine young man and his friends for a job well done." The woman fixed her gaze on Harrison, putting him at ease. "Tell us about your adventure."

Harrison felt a slight burden lift and a gentle calmness began to overtake his body. The sweet aroma of Fallyn's perfume swirled about the room, helping the young warrior's senses return to normal. As he spoke, he made sure to focus on the forty year-old woman.

"As you know, we left Aegeus with Marcus several months ago and started trekking across the countryside in search of clues for the Treasure of the Land. After completing a quest for Silas and escaping from Concur, we found ourselves deep in the Dark Forest seeking help from the elves that live there.

"Moradoril, their leader, provided trackers to help us find the Sacred Seven Rooms, which we successfully navigated through." Harrison cast his eyes to the table. "Nigel Hammer murdered Marcus in the catacombs, and we lost Aidan Hunter and Jason Sands along the way, too."

Fallyn reached over and took hold of Harrison's hand. "I've lost many a friend to the rigors of battle. Be thankful you survived." The woman removed her hand from Harrison's. "Continue, please."

The young warrior gazed at the auburn-haired elder. "My friends and I gathered the Treasure and intended to return to Aegeus immediately. But we found ourselves in Tigris with a magically encrypted book that spoke of a greater treasure, the Talisman of Unification."

Gareth interrupted Harrison's story. "Are you saying that you took it upon yourself to leave the sacred bounty behind and search for another treasure?"

"We felt that would be the best course of action."

"Leaving a priceless hoard unguarded was a foolish act!" Gareth panned to the other elders. "Am I not right?"

Governor Rollins nervously fiddled with his hands while Fallyn took a deep breath. "I'll admit," started the female, "Harrison and his friends took a big gamble leaving the Treasure behind, but they did succeed on their next quest."

Harrison jumped at the chance to continue. "We traversed the countryside in search of pieces to the Talisman – and we found them all!"

Philius felt the need to interject at this point in the conversation. "Gareth, Fallyn, Governor," the old man nodded in the direction of each person as he said their name, "I know that we've had our differences in the past, but we must come together at this moment in time for the benefit of all." The eldest person in the room held a firm gaze on Gareth before speaking again. "And I'm talking all of mankind, not just Aegeus."

Gareth drew a heavy sigh and ran a hand across his brow. "All right, now that we have the Treasure of the Land and the Talisman of Unification, what do you propose our next step should be?"

Philius looked at Harrison. "I believe the boy should answer that question." All eyes in the room shifted to the young warrior.

Harrison felt the stares of the people in the room. Now was the time to open his heart and let everyone know how he felt about all he had learned from his adventures of the past several months.

With a nod, he began. "The ancient kings said that we need to reunite humanity. We can only accomplish this with an army, starting with Aegeus. I have seventy-five seasoned soldiers who accompanied me from Dragon's Lair and are under my command."

The young warrior thought for a moment, then continued. "As I recall, the Aegean army consists of about a thousand soldiers, not counting the youngsters at the Fighter's Guild. This is a good start."

Gareth's mouth fell agape. "Soldiers? Army? What are you proposing? That we overtake all the villages in the land by force?"

Harrison shook his head. "No, but we are going to overthrow Nigel Hammer of Concur." The young warrior hedged his bet that the older warrior would love a chance to depose the ruthless leader. "Can we gain the allegiance of Argos and Robus?"

Gareth sat back in his chair, then looked at Governor Rollins and Fallyn before speaking again. "Harrison, we all know that Nigel Hammer has always lusted about ruling the land, but attacking that city is not a simple task."

"And what makes you think we could overtake him?" asked Fallyn, her green eyes full of concern. "Even with the help of Argos and Robus, Lord Hammer's army is large and talented. It's a fight we might not win."

Harrison flashed a smile. "We'll fight him from the inside." The young warrior glanced at Murdock, who pursed his lips, knowing what was coming next.

"An underground resistance movement is taking hold in Concur. We need to alert them of our intentions before we strike. Furthermore, if we can liberate their First Lady, Meredith, who the residents adore, we'll gain the allegiance of almost all of the populace."

Fallyn shook her head. "How do you know of this underground movement?"

"An illusionist, Thoragaard, helped us escape from Concur and told us about the Resistance." The young warrior pointed a finger at the elders. "If we find him, we can plan our attack."

"And what about Meredith?" asked Gareth, knowing full well who this woman was.

"That's a bit trickier," started Harrison. "We'll need to get word to her about our actions, but we need to talk this through with Thoragaard. He'll know how to reach her."

Gareth took both his hands and rubbed his face. "Let's say your little plan works, where do we go from there?"

Harrison had prepared for this question. "Just as the ancient kings did, we'll march our army from village to village along the coast, informing them of our conquests and asking them to join the new kingdom. To help entice them to accept our offer, we'll give them their rightful possessions from the Treasure of the Land."

Fallyn nodded. "That just might work."

"And I feel we should rekindle the Legion of Knighthood," added Harrison.

The woman cocked her head and squinted. "How so?"

"The current town's leader will appoint someone to represent their village. And, we'll leave a contingent of soldiers behind to ensure a smooth transition to the new kingdom." Harrison had studied the leaders of the past and knew his history well. "This is what the Ancient Kings did with great success and we should repeat their actions."

Gareth took another deep breath. "This is all happening very fast. I suggest we digest everything we have heard today, sift through the Treasure, and come up with a strategy before we alert any other cities of our intentions." The elder warrior gazed at everyone in the room. "Agreed?"

Everyone present nodded.

Gareth brought his gaze to Harrison. "Is there anything else tonight?"

The young warrior nodded. "There is one last thing. I wish for my twin brother Troy to be buried in our fallen heroes cemetery."

The elders all looked at each other with blank stares. "Twin brother?" asked Fallyn.

"King Holleris abducted Troy when he was an infant and took him to Dragon's Lair. He learned too late that he carried out his deeds for a wicked man, but he helped us secure the Talisman and he should be buried with honor."

"We'll take that into consideration as well," said the female member of the group.

Harrison leaned in Gareth's direction, his eyes showing the pain he tried to hide. "Sir, my friend here," Harrison pointed to Gelderand, "placed his body in stasis ten days ago, but his spell will be broken by the end of today. We must bury him as soon as possible."

"We'll have an answer for you shortly." Gareth rose from his chair. "Take us to the Treasure."

Gareth did his best to hide his lifelong injury, but he winced as he hobbled away from the table. Fallyn and Governor Rollins also rose from their seats, nodded to the men, then followed Gareth out of the conference room.

Harrison gestured to Murdock and Pondle, who then escorted their guests away from the cabin and to the great bounty. The young warrior and the rest of his friends followed close behind.

The elders took their time inspecting the treasures, impressed with the massive hoard. Swinkle showed them the manuscript that they had used to inventory the riches, making sure not to keep anything from the dignitaries.

Satisfied with their examination, Gareth summoned his cronies. "This treasure appears to be legitimate. Now, we must ponder the transgressions that occurred tonight. We'll convene in private for two hours, which should give us enough time to make our decisions. Join us at the Elder's Council at that time."

The young warrior nodded, eager for this man to leave so that he could speak with his friends alone. "I'll have my soldiers escort you off the ship."

Harrison summoned the same three soldiers to guide the elders off the vessel, while the young warrior and his friends returned to the cabin.

After the door closed, Murdock waited an additional moment before speaking. Glaring at Harrison, he said, "What in the world were you thinking?"

The young warrior raised a palm to his friend. "Before you go into a tirade, I said what I felt we need to do and I stand behind my statements one hundred percent."

The ranger flashed a sly smile. "Isn't that noble of you." Murdock spread his arms wide, gazing at the other party members in the room. "Harrison's going to save the world all on his own."

Harrison shook his head. "We're all in this together. We must band as one and reunite the land, just like the kings said." The young warrior panned his friends for reassurance.

Knowing that he was the eldest member of the group, Gelderand felt compelled to add his thoughts. Sitting tall and using a soothing voice, he said, "Harrison, we don't doubt that your intentions are just, but enacting a battle plan as sophisticated as you explained to the elders is a monumental task. We cannot simply rush into this."

The young warrior nodded in understanding. "I agree, this must be thought out." Harrison gazed back at his disbelieving friends with wide eyes. "Look, if we don't take the actions described by the kings, we'll lose control of everything we struggled to find. This is the next step we must take. *We must!*"

"Though I despise bloodshed and battle," started Swinkle, placing a caring hand on the young warrior's arm for reassurance, "I feel Harrison's ideas are a perfect start. We will need to hash out the details, but it is a just beginning."

"Attacking Concur is a just beginning?" chimed Murdock. "And this coming from someone who can't wield a weapon!"

"You know we should take this opportunity, Murdock," said Harrison. "Overthrowing a ruthless leader is one way of bringing all of the people together."

"You're just using us to help rescue poor little Meredith," said the ranger, thrusting a finger in his friend's direction. "Don't try and tell me that you haven't thought about liberating her the minute we escaped from Concur."

"The idea has been on my mind and it grows stronger every time we see or speak of Nigel Hammer. But that's not why I feel we should eliminate him. Tearing down those walls will show all the people of the land the importance of our crusade; that and the distribution of the treasures to their rightful owners. I'm sure Nigel pilfered more than his share of riches from hard-working Concurians."

Murdock folded his arms. "Things are moving too fast, Harrison. We haven't even gained the complete allegiance from the elders. Gareth will want to direct the actions, you know."

Harrison let his friend's comment sink in, which sparked a memory. The young warrior drifted off for a brief second, finding himself back at the elven village in the heart of the Dark Forest, just before they set off for the Sacred Seven Rooms. At that time, Briana, the beautiful elven queen, had told him something that caught the young warrior off guard.

"When you reach your destination, be sure you can recognize your enemies," she had said. "Those who seem to be friends may turn against you."

Harrison focused on Murdock's statement about Gareth. "We'll need to keep a close eye on him. I'm not sold on his intentions."

"Especially considering the way he demanded the Treasure at first," added the ranger. "No one takes that from us; we distribute the riches."

"I agree." Harrison was about to say something else before a frail voice interrupted.

"This has all been very enlightening," said Philius. "I suggest we spend the rest of our waking hours hammering out the finer details of Harrison's plan. Does everyone agree?"

Murdock and Pondle shrugged, Swinkle and Gelderand nodded, and Philius took the gestures of all the party members as a sign of agreement. "Fantastic! I say we begin right now."

With that, the small group set out to plan how they would bring happiness to all.

Gareth, Fallyn, and Governor Rollins followed the three soldiers off the vessel and headed toward the main meeting hall in the center of Aegeus.

After they maneuvered out of earshot of the fighters, Gareth turned to the Governor and said, "You should meet with your sorcerer. He might be able to provide some enlightenment on our current situation."

The heavyset man's eyes lit up. "Ryno the Prognosticator?"

"If that's what you call him."

The Governor nodded with a gleeful grin. "Excellent idea! I will go to him right now!" The big man nodded and bid his equals goodnight, then left to meet with his fortune teller.

Fallyn watched the man leave. "He's a fool."

Gareth gazed at the man who waddled away into the night. "Who, Terrence or that buffoon, Ryno?"

"Good question," she answered with a smirk.

The two people continued their trek, with Gareth doing his best to keep the pain that shot through his left leg to a minimum. "We cannot let those people plan the fate of Aegeus," said the limping warrior in reference to Harrison and his friends.

The auburn-haired women concurred. "I agree wholeheartedly." Fallyn looked over at Gareth, her brow crinkling, concerned. "You really should use your walking stick. It will help take the pain away from your leg."

The older warrior brushed her comment aside with a wave of his hand. "I'm fine." Gareth then turned and smiled at Fallyn. "You had an award-winning performance tonight, I might add."

A wicked grin graced the woman's face. "The boy just needed to hear affirmation for his actions. You always come on too strong."

"That's why I make sure you're with me in times of negotiations." Gareth stopped and grabbed the woman's arm, spinning her toward him. "We make an excellent team."

Fallyn's green eyes melted her counterpart. "That we do." She stretched up and accepted her lover's kiss.

"You know what we need to do next, right?" asked Gareth.

"That I do," said Fallyn, moving away from the man and giving him a stern stare. "And we shouldn't be seen like this in public. Understood?"

Gareth smirked. "But of course." The couple then continued on their way to the elder's compound.

CHAPTER 4

¤

The small group of humanity savers had spent the better part of their time discussing, arguing, and planning the plight of their race. Harrison leaned on the wisdom of the elder members, Philius and Gelderand, to help shape a very muddled picture.

Caressing his temples with his right hand as he leaned his elbow on the wooden table, Harrison asked to no one in particular, "And the rationale again for not heading to Concur first?"

Murdock huffed. "What don't you understand? Concur is a fortified city with legions of soldiers! The only time we try to neutralize that place is when we have the backing of all peoples."

"Again, Harrison, I agree with Murdock," said Philius. The old man drew a heavy sigh. "Attacking Lord Hammer without the appropriate resources could cripple your noble plan before it even starts."

The young warrior continued to rub his head, eyes closed. "Nigel will hear about our plan well before we reach his city if we don't surprise him up front."

The ranger folded his arms and said, "Better to have enough men for a long fight than losing momentum from the outset."

Harrison had tried in vain to hammer across his point, but all his friends, including Swinkle, his most trusted ally, disagreed with his strategy. The young warrior felt his judgments were sound – attack Concur first before trying to convince the coastal villages to join their new empire. If Harrison's army could liberate the great metropolis, the other smaller villages would fall into place and everyone would be united.

Harrison's friends felt otherwise. A loss in the battle of Concur would deter others from joining their cause, and attempting multiple attacks on the city could trigger dissention in the ranks of the townspeople.

Lifting his eyes to meet the gaze of the ranger, the young warrior said, "So, you think it would be better to unite the coastal villages, culminating with Arcadia, then bring the entire army back to face Concur?"

The ranger nodded once, his arms remaining folded.

"What about the supplies needed for the men, horses, ships ..." the young warrior looked away, thinking about the magnitude of the battles that lay ahead.

"Harrison, no one said that this would be easy," said Philius, "but we can distribute the Treasure of the Land to each and every village. The townsfolk will be overjoyed to hear that the ancient kings' bounty has been uncovered."

"And even if Nigel saw us coming," said Murdock, "we'd have legions of soldiers trekking through the countryside together, learning each other's ways and moves, their battle strategies, their way of life."

"A means to bring all the people together," added Swinkle. The young cleric had patiently waited for a point to add to the conversation. Knowing that his close friend was almost at the point of accepting the rest of the group's rationale, he did his best to drive the final point home.

"Is this not what Ballesteros, Nicodemus, and Solaris told us we must do?" asked Swinkle. "Our adventure has always been about bringing joy and happiness to all of mankind. And this new journey will be one of true salvation."

Harrison gazed back at his friend and could see the conviction in his eyes. The young warrior thought hard about all of the ideas that had bandied about a small cabin, on an insignificant ship, which rested in a modest harbor. From this apparently inconsequential place in the land, a small group of men were about to approve the most important battle plan of the ages.

Sitting tall in his seat, Harrison said, "I think we've done our due diligence over this matter and I agree with your strategy. We'll move against Concur only after we have a sizeable army to match their strengths."

The young warrior smiled. "As Marcus used to say, the time has come. Let's draw the battle plan on a map before we announce our new line of attack to the elders."

All the party members drew a sigh of relief.

"We need to finalize our inventory in regards to that great treasure so that we do not start arbitrarily handing out the riches to the villages," said Swinkle.

"I agree," said Harrison. "Why don't you, Murdock, and Pondle handle that chore, while we," he nodded at Philius and Gelderand, "meet with the elders to discuss Troy's burial plans."

"You won't talk about what we discussed until we're all present, right?" asked Murdock with concern.

"No one will know what went on in this room before it's time. Let's finish that plan."

The men all took their seat around the table while Swinkle retrieved parchment and writing utensils from his pack. A moment later, they began putting the land's master plan down on paper.

After an hour of more intense thinking, the adventurers completed their strategy. Harrison yawned and stretched, then said, "I know it's getting late, but we need to contact the elders." The young warrior looked over the group of tired, older men.

"We might as well go now," said Gelderand. "And we can escort Philius back home afterwards."

"Do you really need all of us to accompany you?" asked Murdock. "You know how much I love politics."

Harrison raised his eyebrows, a bit surprised. "I figured that we all would want to meet with the elders."

"You can fight for your brother's rights," said the ranger. "The rest of us can finalize the Treasure list." Murdock peered at Pondle, the thief's eyes glazed with the thought of running his fingers through countless coins once again.

"And I can help them with the inventory," said Swinkle. "Too many people at this meeting might portray an attack on our part."

The young warrior, though he felt more comfortable with larger numbers, understood his friends' rationale. "I suppose you're right." Harrison leaned closer to Swinkle, squinting.

"You're really all right with helping Murdock and Pondle finish cataloging the Treasure?"

His friend nodded. "Yes, I am. Good luck on your brother's behalf." Swinkle rose from his seat, along with Murdock and Pondle. "We will see you later tonight."

"I'm taking Lance with me," said Harrison. "If Tara asks for us, let her know we'll be back in awhile."

The young cleric nodded, then proceeded to leave the cabin with his friends. After they left, Harrison turned to the older men. "Time to go." With that, the three men and dog departed to discuss Troy's fate.

The trio and Lance walked down one of Aegeus's main streets with the young warrior pointing out familiar places from his youth. Being later in the evening, Harrison had the luxury of explaining the finer points of his village without the bustle of townspeople in his way. The young warrior gazed about his hometown with mixed emotions; part of him felt overjoyed to be back, but another piece kept reminding him that his parents, his mentor, and many of his friends no longer resided here.

Putting the negative thoughts out of his mind, he said to no one in particular, "Do you think the elders will allow Troy's burial with our town's heroes?"

Philius huffed. "Maybe."

"Why wouldn't they?"

The elderly man drew a heavy sigh. "Harrison, Troy did not grow up here. He's not really a hero of Aegeus."

"But he was born here," the young warrior lamented. "It wasn't his fault that the king abducted him."

"I'm sure that plays into his favor," added Gelderand, trying to give his friend some hope. "The elders must take that into account."

The men then approached a large, grassy area, the square marketplace, which acted as a meeting ground for the townsfolk; a place where vendors sold their wares and Aegeans haggled for their necessities.

The young warrior pointed to the many tents that sat upon the grounds. "My parents would erect tables and spread their findings on them."

Harrison recalled distant memories of assisting his parents with the set up, mingling with townspeople, and helping friends with their displays. Gazing at the tents that lined the perimeter of the marketplace brought a pang of sadness to his heart.

"I am sure that you spent many fun days with them," said Gelderand, breaking the lad's somber recollection.

"Some of the best days of my life," said the young warrior.

The mage brought his gaze to the two-story edifice that loomed beyond the square. "Is that the Town Hall?"

"Yes, that's the place," said Harrison, maintaining his forward stare.

The Aegean Town Hall housed all business activities for the seaport. The elders congregated there to discuss everything from simple taxation to complex battle plans. Harrison knew that a meaningful meeting would take place here tonight.

After traversing the market square, the group ascended a stone staircase that culminated in front of large wooden double doors. Harrison took the initiative to open the portal but found it locked. With a shrug and a look back to his friends, the young warrior knocked on the door. A moment later a person his age opened the left portal a crack.

The young man squinted. "What's your business?" he asked in a huff.

"We're here to see the elders," responded Harrison.

The door remained open only a sliver. "Your name?"

Harrison's eyebrows arched and he shook his head. "Harrison Cross. They should be expecting us."

The lad let his gaze linger. "Wait here." He then closed and latched the door.

Harrison turned to his older friends, an incredulous look on his face. "What was that all about?"

Philius shook his head. "Harrison … these people …" The old man's voice trailed off, his head still shaking. Lance nuzzled his master's leg, offering support the only way he knew how.

"We're going to talk about the Treasure again, you do realize that," said Gelderand, pulling his cloak tighter. "Stick to your beliefs and do not waver."

"That's not what we're here for!" protested Harrison.

At that moment, the door swung open, the young man holding the portal to its maximum. "Straight ahead, first room on the right."

The three men and dog entered the building and followed the directions given to them. Harrison gazed at the paintings of past Aegean dignitaries, images that peered back at the trio from their position on the wall.

Reaching their destination, the men found Gareth and Governor Rollins seated at a large table. A younger man, about five years older than Harrison, sat next to the governor.

Governor Rollins stood and gestured toward the person. "This is my personal advisor, Ryno Vatemule." The paunchy man nodded upon hearing his name.

The town's lead dignitary extended a hand toward the table. "Please, have a seat." Harrison sat first, followed by the older men.

"We've been discussing your brother's burial arrangements," started the Governor, before taking his gaze over to Gareth. "Why don't you take it from here?"

"This committee does not feel your brother has any merits to Aegeus," said Gareth with a cold stare.

Harrison's blood simmered. "He was born in this town, just like you and me. The least we can do is lay him to rest here in dignity."

"Harrison, the town's charter specifically states that the only people to be buried in the Cemetery of Honor are those individuals who have demonstrated extraordinary feats in the name of Aegeus." Gareth waved a dismissing hand in the young warrior's direction. "Troy did not fulfill these criteria."

"But he helped us secure the Talisman of Unification!" Harrison pointed to Gelderand. "He did likewise! I would assume that Gelderand would be laid to rest in Aegeus when his time comes."

Gareth let out a deep breath. Locking his gaze on the magician, he said, "On behalf of the town of Aegeus, we all thank you for what you have done. However, you don't qualify for hero status either." Facing Harrison, he said, "Rest assured, you will be buried with our town's greats."

Harrison had heard just about enough from this old war veteran. Panning the room, he asked the next obvious question. "Where's Fallyn? Has she agreed to this line of reasoning?"

Gareth glanced at Governor Rollins. The dignitary sported a nervous expression and began to sweat; the repeated tapping of his fingers together only compounded his anxiety level.

"Fallyn did not feel well after talking with you earlier this evening and decided to rest for the night," said Gareth. "She wanted me to tell you that she also feels the same way this council does."

The young warrior was not finished just yet. Glaring at Governor Rollins, he said, "Do you also believe that my twin brother doesn't deserve to be buried with our heroes? Even though mercenaries abducted him from my parents as an infant, but upon learning the truth of his life's story, he decided to help my friends and I recover the Talisman of Unification and return the Treasure of the Land to Aegeus?"

The governor's mouth opened, but uttered not a sound. He then glanced at Gareth for support.

"Don't look at him!" barked Harrison. "I want to hear your own words, not his!"

Again, the Governor tapped his fingers together, trying not to make eye contact with anyone. Before speaking, he turned to his fortune teller beside him, hoping for an answer. The man gave him a simple nod.

Governor Rollins sighed, then slumped, as if someone had suddenly laid a great burden on his shoulders. "I ... we ... do not agree with Gareth and Fallyn, but they have outnumbered us two to one. There's nothing I can do, the decision is final." The large man lowered his eyes to the table.

Harrison maintained his stare on the heavyset man, who refused to look up at the young warrior. Taking a wicked glare to Gareth, Harrison said, "That's it? There's no debate, just a final answer?"

Gareth raised his palms toward the young warrior. "Harrison, we've debated this issue enough. You have to abide by our decision."

The young warrior was about to launch into another tirade when he felt a hand squeezing his forearm. Philius sat forward. "Let the record state that I feel a great injustice has been bestowed here tonight." The old man shook a finger in the older warrior's direction. "Shame on you, Gareth."

Gareth raised his eyebrows. "Shame on me? I'm only following the guidelines of our town's charter."

"You can do the right thing. The charter can be amended."

Gareth crossed his arms and sat back. "This issue is dead. Let's move onto the next one."

"Which is?" asked Philius, mimicking Gareth's actions.

"Celebrating the Treasure of the Land with our people."

Harrison squinted and shook his head. "My brother has about an hour left before his body starts to rot, and you want me to help plan a celebration?"

Gareth waved his hands in front of him. "You're right, Harrison. That was insensitive of me. Why don't you let the Governor and I handle this matter. You can tend to your brother's needs."

"How understanding of you," said Harrison in a condescending tone. Facing his friends, he said, "Let's go."

As the men rose from their seats and began to leave the room, Gareth said, "We'll alert you about the festival."

"You do that," said Harrison. A moment later, the three men and dog departed the building and stood outside of the government complex.

Gelderand approached the young warrior. "What are you thinking?"

Harrison lowered his head, dejected. "I don't know what to think. We have no resolution on my brother's burial, they're planning to announce to everyone that we've recovered the Treasure and will probably mention our intentions to reunite the land." The young warrior shook his head. "We need Gareth out of our way."

Philius rested a frail hand on the lad's shoulder. "You can't mean that."

Harrison gazed up into the starry sky. His warrior pride shattered, he shook his head, knowing eliminating Gareth went against all of his core beliefs. Taking his eyes to the older man, he said, "No, I don't mean that. I'm so angry and confused."

The young warrior stood motionless, trying his best to take in everything that had transpired since they allowed the elders on their ship. All of his good intentions seemed to have disappeared in front of his very eyes — all the journeys, the lost men, the death of his only brother — all for naught.

At the height of his self-dejection, Harrison felt Lance's warm muzzle rub against his leg. The young warrior gazed down at his canine friend.

The small dog sat next to his master, the animal sensing the great anguish and turmoil that coursed through his master's body. He then yapped, "Fight."

Harrison squinted, taking in the most simple of words. From that insignificant one word phrase, a frenzy of thoughts rocketed inside his head.

Fight. Isn't that what I've done my whole life? Did I give up when I learned of my parent's death? No, I became the best warrior I could be.

Fight. Did I back down when Marcus fell to Lord Hammer's sword? No, with the help of my friends, we pressed on and secured the land's ultimate treasure.

Harrison grew stronger with every answer to his own questions.

Fight. Did I back down when Troy lay helpless on the ground, all but dead? No, we destroyed the wicked dragon and completed our journey to gather the Talisman of Unification.

And now, with my hands tied by the bureaucracy of an arrogant man, will I let him make the wrong decision for me, for my friends, for my people, even though we all know he's wrong? No! It's time to fight.

Harrison patted his furry friend on the head, then faced Gelderand and Philius with confidence. "We're going back to the ship and tomorrow we'll partake in the town's celebration with our townsfolk."

Philius and Gelderand exchanged curious glances. "Did you not just say how unfair Gareth's decisions were?"

The young warrior smirked. "I have a plan." With that, he and his friends headed back toward the harbor.

CHAPTER 5

¤

The small convoy returned to *VENTURE 3* a short time after their meeting with the town elders. Congregating in the same cabin as before, the group of adventurers closed the door and began a most important meeting.

Murdock took the initiative. "What did the *dignitaries* have to say?" he asked, sarcasm dripping from the word.

"Basically, no matter what we do, we're wrong," said Harrison. "That's why we must do things our way."

The ranger grinned. "I like the sound of this already. What do you have in mind?"

"First, we'll bury Troy in the Cemetery of Honor, then we'll partake in the festivities planned for tomorrow."

Gelderand and Philius gave their friend a look of surprise, their mouths agape. "Harrison," began Gelderand, "Gareth and the Governor both told you that Troy was not to be buried in that cemetery."

"I know, but we'll dig the grave, have our own ceremony, and be gone before the break of day." Turning to Swinkle, he added, "I'm hoping that you'll perform the service, but I'll understand if you can't break the law."

"Some laws should be broken." The young cleric smiled. "Performing Troy's service would be an honor."

Harrison smiled back. "Good. We need to start this task first, but before we begin, did you find anything unusual with the Treasure?"

"Aside from more wealth than this land has ever seen?" started Swinkle. "Not really. We completed updating the scripture that itemizes what each town and village should receive from the great bounty." The cleric took a moment to fumble through his backpack. "And here it is."

The young warrior's eyes widened with anticipation at the sight of the old, green-covered book. "What does Aegeus receive?"

Swinkle flipped through several yellowed pages before stopping. "The book states that Aegeus will take scores of enhanced weaponry and armor, enough to begin the arduous task of reuniting the land."

"How much weaponry and armor?"

"The book does not get into specifics. I assume we distribute the goods as we see fit."

"How do we supply Aegeus's fighters?" asked Murdock. "Especially since All Mighty Gareth is so against us?"

"We'll let the townspeople decide that," said Harrison.

Murdock closed his eyes, shook his head, and waved his hands in front of himself. "What are you talking about? How will they know about us?"

Before Harrison could answer, Lance raised his head and began to sniff in earnest. Pondle noticed the dog's actions, just as he had so many times in the wilderness.

The young warrior, oblivious to Pondle and Lance's actions, answered Murdock's question. "I know what I need to do. You're going to have to trust me on this one."

Murdock laughed. "Oh, like nothing has ever gone wrong in the past when you've uttered that phrase!"

"Just don't worry!" Changing the subject, the young warrior said, "We need to tend to Troy. The cemetery is several blocks away from here, on the outskirts of town. We'll get Troy's soldiers to set up a horse drawn cart, something to transport him there."

"We should do this as fast as possible," said Gelderand. "My spell is almost over."

Pondle stood up, placing a hand on his stomach. "I'm going to the deck for a few minutes."

Murdock crinkled his brow, gazing at his friend. "What's the matter with you?"

"It's this ship. My stomach's queasy."

The ranger laughed. "I figured all this sailing would have gotten to you days ago!"

The thief proceeded to the door. "Well, it has now. I just need to clear my head." Pondle left the room, leaving the door open.

After the thief departed, Harrison said, "It's time to get started. Murdock, gather the soldiers. Swinkle, join me, Gelderand, and Philius in Troy's room. Let's go." With that, the men scattered in different directions to complete their tasks.

The cabin door next to the adventurer's was open a sliver, just enough for Pondle to watch his friends disperse from the room. The thief waited an extra moment, making sure that the corridor remained devoid of people. Pondle then reached for the small sack that he had secured to his belt after he had left his friends behind. He poured a powdery substance into his hands and waited for an opportune time.

No human could hear the sound of the faint creaking the ship's floorboards made, but Pondle was not only human. His elven heritage granted him the pleasure of hearing much better than his human counterparts, which benefited him at this very moment.

Pondle used his shoulder to burst though the doorway, sending the portal flying. The thief glanced down the hallway. Nothing was there, or so it seemed. Taking the gray substance, he tossed the powdery solution into the air where it then transformed into a sticky consistency that eventually landed on the invisible body of a middle-aged woman. The material clung to the startled figure, giving her the appearance of a sand-covered statue, albeit a living one.

Fallyn recoiled from Pondle's sudden actions, shocked that anyone would know she were there at all. The thief unsheathed his short sword and took a step toward the surprised woman.

"A magician on the elder's council," he said. "A wise move indeed."

"What are you going to do with me?" asked Fallyn, frightened at the sight the weapon.

"You have some explaining to do. I'm taking you to my friends."

Fallyn dropped her hands to her waist, interlocked her fingers, and lowered her head in shame. "I'm so embarrassed. This was not my idea."

Her statement did not faze Pondle. Taking a step toward the gray-colored woman, he said, "I don't care."

Before the thief could get any closer to the female, Fallyn's eyes turned a dark green and her feminine form morphed into that of a hawk. Pondle stopped in his tracks, astounded at the woman's transformation.

The bird flapped its wings hard in an effort to rid itself of the gray matter that covered its body. With the substance all but gone, the hawk screeched, flew past Pondle, and proceeded down the narrow corridor.

Shaking his head in disbelief, the halfling gathered himself and raced after the bird of prey. Pondle could hear the faint sound of flapping wings ahead of him as he dashed deeper into the vessel's underbelly. A second later, the noise ceased.

The ship's hallways employed glass-encased candle holders to provide enough lighting for the human eye. Pondle instead utilized his infravision to better see down the dimly lit corridor. Taking cautious steps, the thief moved closer to the end of the passage. Straining to differentiate between the vessel's subtle noises and a flying bird, Pondle did his best to focus on the latter.

The halfling reached the doorway. Peeking inside, he could see stairs that led deeper into the ship's cargo bay. The thief knew the steps led to the holding area of the land's ultimate treasure. He then heard something he did not expect — the patter of feet, and they were getting closer.

As the sounds grew louder, the thief raised his blade in a defensive posture. Pondle then saw the blurry image of a wolf charging up the staircase, making a rapid ascent toward his position. Grasping the hilt of his weapon with both hands, the thief readied himself to strike the beast.

Three feet before the wolf intercepted Pondle, the canine let out a high-pitched howl. The thief recoiled and slashed his weapon at the oncoming animal, but instead of striking the beast he swung at air.

The canine transformed again into a bright green lizard, which jumped to the wooden ceiling and scurried past Pondle unscathed. The thief took a moment to gather his bearings, but by the time he registered what had happened, the gecko dropped to the floor and morphed once again into a majestic tiger.

The large feline stopped in its tracks and stared down the confused thief with its brilliant green eyes. Growling, the tiger showed its dagger-like teeth. Pondle, unsure of what to do next, remained motionless, his weapon ready for attack. The tiger took a step toward the nervous halfling, then turned, ran down the corridor, and ascended the stairwell at the opposite end of the hallway.

Pondle lowered his weapon and raced after the feline. Upon reaching the end of the passageway, the thief stopped and listened for the sound of heavy feet. He heard nothing. Taking an anxious breath, Pondle entered the stairwell, brandishing his short sword in front of him. The tiger was nowhere to be seen.

Pondle dashed up the stairs, which led to the ship's deck, and panned the area in earnest for the elusive beast. Being ever so cautious, the thief recollected his time in the catacombs searching for the same treasure that sat in the belly of the vessel and the many lions and tigers that hunted him and his friends. The thief understood that he could not match the strength of the striped feline, and seeing no trace of the beast caused his heart rate to quicken.

Taking a silent step out of the stairwell and onto the deck, Pondle crept into the openness. A crescent moon shed very little light, even less so when one of the many clouds in the nighttime sky passed in front of the heavenly body.

The halfling relied on his infravision to scan the area, but at this moment in time, his acute hearing became his strongest sense. A raised cabin stood to his right, and the soft sound of shuffling feet emanated behind it.

Pondle brandished his weapon in the direction of the subtle noise, waiting for the beast to show itself. To his surprise, one of Troy's soldiers walked by, oblivious to Pondle's presence, as well as the missing animal.

In a shallow whisper, the thief called to the sentry, "Hey, you!"

The young man's eyes widened, startled at the sound of someone calling for him. Gathering himself, he said, "Who goes there?"

"It's me, Pondle," said the thief, making sure to remain as quiet as possible. The halfling swiveled his head from side to side, confused at finding no sign that the tiger even existed.

The soldier noticed Pondle's peculiar antics. "What seems to be the matter, sir?"

"Have you seen a tiger up here?" Had there been more light, the young man would have seen the thief's face turn red.

The soldier furrowed his brow. "A tiger? On the ship's deck?"

"I don't have time to explain," said Pondle, knowing just how ridiculous his question must have sounded to the sentry. "Fallyn is a shape-changer and she's morphed into a tiger right now."

The soldier's mouth fell open. "A shape shifter?" The young man panned wide-eyed, scouring the area for the hidden feline. "I've heard of magicians being able to change into animals, but I never saw one for real."

"Maybe you have and didn't realize it," said Pondle. "Stay focused, but don't aim to kill this person. We want her alive."

Both men tiptoed about the deck, but after several minutes of uneventful searching, they stopped their investigation, dumbfounded.

"Where could she have gone?" asked the young man.

Pondle sheathed his weapon, placed his hands on the ship's railing, and gazed at the buildings in the distance. "If I had to venture a guess, I'd say she morphed again into an animal that could fly and is watching us right now from over there."

The young man stood alongside Pondle and peered in the same direction. "What happens now?"

Pondle drew a heavy sigh. "That's a very good question."

"She changed into a what?" exclaimed Harrison.

While Pondle hunted down Fallyn, the rest of his friends had taken the time to move Troy's body to a horse drawn cart. Now, Harrison, his friends, Philius, Portheus, Tara, and a contingent of twenty soldiers stood on the mainland, torches in hand, and ready to trek to the town's Cemetery of Honor.

"She changed from a hawk to wolf, then to a lizard, and again into a tiger." Pondle shook his head. "I wouldn't have believed it either, but I saw it with my own eyes."

"A doppelganger," huffed Philius, shaking his head as well. "This is not good. Not good at all."

"Can she change into a person?" asked Harrison.

Philius glanced over to Gelderand, who gave the elder a subtle nod. "It appears so," said the elderly man.

"Then she could be standing among us right now," said Harrison as everyone took a closer look at the people in the general area.

"I don't think so," said Gelderand, trying to put everyone at ease. "If she morphed into all those creatures, she's exhausted right now. I'm thinking she needs at least a good day's rest to get back to full strength."

"I agree," said Philius. Wagging a finger at the group, he said, "We must come up with a phrase, right now, that only we know. Consider it our password."

"That's a great idea," said Harrison. "What should the password be?"

Philius shrugged. "Make it something subtle, something only we will know."

Harrison thought hard. A moment later he said, "Teleios." All the men, save for Philius, recognized the name immediately. The young warrior faced the old man.

"Teleios was Troy's loyal advisor," he said and the old man nodded in understanding. "If we're ever unsure of each other, we can be certain that no one but us knows of Teleios."

The young warrior gazed about the fresh faces staring back at him. "Does everyone understand?"

All of the men nodded in concurrence. "Good," said Harrison. "If someone doesn't know the answer, consider that person to be from outside of our group." With the business of the secret code behind them, Harrison focused on the next matter at hand.

"It's time to get Troy to his resting place." The young warrior stood by the wooden cart and motioned to the sentries in front. "The Cemetery of Honor is on the other side of town. Keep to the outskirts and we'll run right into it."

The wagon creaked as its wheels began to move. The solemn procession had barely commenced when Tara approached Harrison.

"Can I walk next to you?" she asked, her blue eyes melting him.

"Of course," said Harrison. "I would prefer it."

"How does it feel being back in your home town?"

The young warrior thought for a moment. "Very strange. I don't like the way everything has started — the elder's reaction to us, sneaking Troy's body to the cemetery, and now this shape shifter." Harrison shook his head, wanting to say something else, but he could not find the right words.

Tara took hold of the young warrior's hand. "Have faith, Harrison. Things will get better."

Harrison smiled. "I suppose they have to."

Fifteen minutes later, the small group of adventurers arrived at Aegeus's hallowed Cemetery of Honor. Grand headstones carved with ornate drawings of warriors on horses, brandishing weapons against their downtrodden foes, littered the area. In all, Harrison recalled about 150 or so fighters, warriors, and mages had been laid to rest in the graveyard. And deep in his heart, he knew one more warrior of worth would be buried there tonight.

One of the soldiers who led the procession came back to speak to Harrison. "Sir, where shall we lay General Harkin to rest?"

The young warrior gazed about the area. To his left rested an empty, flat section of earth, about twenty feet away from a grand oak tree. Without hesitation, Harrison knew he had found his brother's eternal resting place.

Pointing to the spot, he said, "Right there."

The soldier nodded and motioned for his counterparts to maneuver the wagon to the specified location.

"It's such a peaceful place," said Tara, clutching Harrison's arm and snuggling her petite body as close to him as possible.

"That it is." Harrison gazed over Tara's head and locked his gaze on Swinkle. "What needs to be done to make this right?"

"I know just what to do," said the young cleric. "I will instruct the soldiers where and how to dig the grave." Swinkle then left the couple to begin his religious duties.

Twenty minutes later, two piles of fresh earth flanked an empty six-foot hole, while the grave diggers awaited Swinkle's ceremony. The young cleric ordered two of Troy's men to lay the deceased general's blanket-covered body alongside the tomb. The soldiers then placed Troy's sword in his hands. Upon completion of that task, Swinkle gestured for the group to encircle the holy site. The flickering glow of the men's torches provided ample lighting for the ceremony.

The young cleric rummaged through his backpack, retrieving a holy book and a vial of water. Mumbling a prayer to himself, Swinkle sprinkled holy water on the dirt, in the grave, and on Troy's body. He then said another prayer and, taking his index finger, he dipped it into the holy liquid and traced it along Troy's brow. When he finished, he stood tall and positioned himself at the forefront of the gravesite.

Flipping to the appropriate page in his scripture, he started, "It is with both pain and honor that I stand before you today. The pain comes from the untimely death of a brilliant warrior, loving brother, and great friend in the making. The honor comes from knowing one of this town's greatest warriors is receiving the burial he deserves.

"Pious, ever the god of diplomacy, looks with favor upon those who perform good and righteous deeds. Troy, though misguided by an evil man most of his life, realized his mistakes of the past and made atonement for them by helping us on our journey. His long awaited reunion with the brother he never knew, all but assured his fate as a great warrior and human being who hailed from this modest town."

Peering at the manuscript, Swinkle read, "*A warrior will be held accountable for his deeds. War and fighting are vehicles of evil, but even a righteous man must answer this unfortunate calling at times.*

Pious holds those in the highest rankings to be true leaders of good, the ones that must set the example for his men. Never shall a life be destroyed for naught; never shall children, the innocent, the sick, or the elderly be persecuted without mercy; and all combat must end at the soonest possible time, even if continued fighting will bring personal gain.

"Those warriors who heed this calling are true men of honor and deserve a place beside me, for on that last day, they will help shepherd the righteous to their eternal resting place. Their sacrifice will bring life to them forever."

Swinkle closed his book and stared at the group. "Troy understood the rigors of battle, and he exemplified the traits of a true leader. I have no doubt that Pious will take him under his wing for the righteous deeds he performed at the end of his life. May he rest in eternal peace."

Swinkle tucked his scripture under his arm, then administered holy water and oils over Troy's body again.

Rising a final time, the holy man said, "That concludes my service."

Harrison stepped to the forefront. "On behalf of everyone, thank you, Swinkle, for another fine ceremony." The young cleric nodded once in affirmation.

The young warrior took a deep breath, staring at his brother who lay on the ground. "I didn't have much time to know Troy, but from the moment I met him, I knew we'd have a special bond. I learned so much from him in the short time that we were together and I hope that I can lead my men the way he led his.

"We all have a monumental task ahead of us, and I wish that Troy could venture alongside me. I for one feel that his life's journey doesn't end here – he'll be in my heart everywhere I go. But now we must lay him to rest and allow his spirit to flow through each and every one of us." Harrison's eyes watered. "Our parents would have been so proud."

The young warrior stepped back from his position, then motioned for three soldiers to lower their deceased general's body into his grave. Swinkle went over to the lifeless form one last time, mumbled a final prayer, then covered Troy's face with part of the blanket that wrapped his body.

"It is time to move away from the burial site," said the young cleric. The small group of mourners left the gravesite, allowing the soldiers to bury their fallen leader.

Harrison, with Tara and Lance by his side, called to Murdock and Pondle, "Can you lead the men back to the ship? I want to take Tara to a special place before returning."

The ranger rested a caring hand on his friend's shoulder. "Don't stay out for too long," he said under his breath, not wanting to alarm the young maiden. "I know this is your hometown and all, but there've been strange things happening ever since we arrived."

Harrison nodded. "We won't be long."

Murdock pursed his lips and squeezed Harrison's shoulder before leaving to guide the crowd back to their awaiting vessel.

With the others departing, Tara took hold of Harrison's hand again. "Where are we going?"

Harrison gazed down at the young girl. "I want you to meet my parents."

With Lance scampering up ahead, the young couple strolled along the empty streets. The moon hung low in the nighttime sky, telling Harrison it was well past midnight and getting late. In the distance, the two young people could see several small rolling hills that led away from the residential part of Aegeus.

Harrison pointed to a set of moss covered mounds to the right. "We need to go that way."

Tara clung to her man tighter as they began to walk on the uneven ground. Headstones, sprinkled amongst the many large trees that would have provided ample shade had it been daytime, littered the area. Large clumps of grass jutted up from the bumpy landscape, causing the young girl to lose her balance more than once, but Harrison was always there keeping her from falling down.

After passing five gravesites, Harrison faced a pair of small tombstones. Tara gazed at the memorials; they appeared no different than any other that she had passed in the cemetery. The passage of time had faded the etchings, rendering them barely legible, but she knew that they held great importance to the young man who stood beside her.

"Tara, these are my parents," said Harrison with pride. "They've rested here in peace for the last eight years."

The girl sensed his great sorrow, as did Lance who nuzzled up against his master's leg. "I know that they meant the world to you, Harrison," said Tara. "I'm so happy that you brought me here with you."

Harrison gazed at the young maiden. "I just wish you could've met them before they died."

Tara gazed at the young warrior with teary eyes. Harrison recalled the first time he saw her and how her glance melted him like no others ever had.

The maiden held Harrison's hands, squeezing them. "I'm sure they were beautiful people and I know that they're looking down upon us right now."

The young warrior nodded. "I know they are, too." Harrison brought his gaze back to the headstones. "Now Troy's with them and I'm sure that they have a lot of catching up to do."

Tara gripped Harrison's hands tighter. "You've made them so proud already. Now it's time to show everybody else who you really are, Harrison."

Harrison nodded, taking in Tara's words. "Indeed, it's time." The two locked eyes on each other. Without hesitation, he lowered his head and gave her a passionate kiss.

After a long moment, the young warrior pulled away and gazed at Tara again. "I wish nothing more than to be with you, but the time is not right."

Had there been enough light, Harrison would have seen Tara's face turn a lovely shade of red. "I've been hoping for the same." The young maiden stood on her tiptoes to entwine her arms around his neck. "Waiting isn't always a bad thing." The couple kissed yet again, this time with more passion than ever.

They parted a moment later, with Harrison saying, "It's time to get back to the ship. We need rest and there's a lot of work yet to do." The young warrior smiled at his mate. "I'm truly falling for you, Tara."

Blushing again, the young maiden answered, "I already have." The couple allowed their lusty stare to linger a moment longer.

"We really need to go," said Harrison. The pair gazed upon the young warrior's fallen parents one last time, then turned and headed out of the cemetery hand in hand.

CHAPTER 6

¤

Harrison, Tara, and Lance retuned to their awaiting ship and found their own cabins where they soon fell fast asleep. At sunrise, while the vessel gently rocked in the harbor, two frazzled men approached the craft, demanding to board.

A repeated pounding on Harrison's cabin door startled the young warrior, causing him to jump from his bed and instinctively clutch his battle-axe.

"Who is it?"

One of Harrison's soldiers spoke from the other side of the doorway. "Sir, the Governor and his sorcerer are here and they wish to meet with you."

Harrison opened the portal a crack. "They want to see me now?" The young warrior sensed something amiss. "Are Gareth and Fallyn with them?"

"No, sir, just the two men I mentioned. What shall I tell them?"

Harrison did not hesitate. "Take them to the conference room. Round up my friends and have them meet me there."

"Yes, sir!" said the sentry, who went off to fulfill his task.

Harrison shook his head, trying his best to combat the sluggishness from his lack of sleep. What does Governor Rollins want with me, he wondered. And where are Gareth and Fallyn? I don't like this one bit.

Pulling on his clothes, the young warrior left his cabin and proceeded to the other end of the ship. Just as he commanded, his friends all congregated outside the large room and lingered in the hallway.

"What's going on, Harrison?" asked Murdock. "Can't we even get a little bit of rest?"

"I don't know what's happening either. But it's time to find out."

The young warrior entered the room, his friends following close behind. In front of him sat Governor Rollins and his sorcerer. Harrison gazed upon the fidgeting, heavyset man, but found the pointed hat that Ryno wore even more peculiar.

Taking a seat across from the town leader, Harrison asked, "What brings you to us so early in the morning, sir?"

The Governor tapped his fingers together, his nerves getting the better of him. He then glanced at his fortune teller. Using his right hand to play with his mustache, he said, "Ryno, why don't you tell him what you saw?"

The young man nodded. "As I lay in bed last night, I had a vivid vision."

Harrison crinkled his brow. The prognosticator's pause lasted so long that he had to ask, "What did you see?"

"I saw Gareth and Fallyn in a hazy woodland setting," started the fortune teller, before his eyes became round. "Grand treasure chests surrounded them and they were throwing coins up in the air – laughing all the while!"

Harrison cocked his head, then glanced over to Murdock, who stood beside him. The ranger took a hand to his forehead and shook his head in disbelief.

The young warrior noticed the obvious nervous state of the gentlemen who sat before them and he tried his best to soothe their uneasiness. "Ryno, are you telling me that you had a dream?"

The soft-bodied man sat tall in his seat. "All my visions come to me in dreams. I interpret them from there."

Maintaining his calming voice, Harrison said, "All right, can you decipher what you saw for us?"

Ryno began to wring his hands in front of him. "What this dream means is that Gareth and Fallyn will partake in a great treasure. And, by throwing coins around at will, it further tells me that the bounty is so vast that they don't care if some of it gets lost."

Harrison took a hand and covered his chin and mouth, nodding all the while. "Have you seen either of them since last night?"

The Governor's eyes widened. "No! They're gone!"

"Gone?" The young warrior leaned forward with wide eyes. "Where did they go?"

"Ryno told you — they're off in some part of the woods!"

Harrison closed his eyes for a moment, pondering how this man ever became the de facto leader of his hometown. "Ryno, what does this dream tell you about their current whereabouts?"

Ryno shrugged. "I have no idea. But like the governor said, they're gone."

Harrison thought about saying something else before he heard a throat clearing behind him. Gelderand stepped forward, holding Rufus in his arms, and said, "If what you say is true, that Gareth and Fallyn are gone, does that mean you make the decisions now?"

Governor Rollins raised his eyebrows. "I suppose so."

"Then why don't you finalize plans for the celebration today. We'll cart the treasure off this ship at noon and parade it to all the townsfolk." Harrison turned to protest, but Gelderand nodded in assurance.

"That's a wonderful idea! We'll continue with the preparations immediately."

"Good, Governor. We'll see you in the town's square at high noon."

Governor Rollins rose from his chair. "Yes, high noon." The big man gazed at his counterpart. "Ryno, let's go!" A moment later, the two large men waddled out of the room and off the ship to commence with the day's festivities.

After the town's dignitaries left, Harrison swiveled in his seat to face Gelderand. "Why did you tell them to start the celebration so soon?"

The mage patted the young man on the shoulder. "We have spoken enough about what and how to do things. It is time for action. Today is going to be a most important day, not only for Aegeans, but for all of mankind."

Harrison let the older man's comments sink in. It was time. "Then let's prepare for this day as well. A few hours from now, the whole town will see the land's greatest treasure and I'm sure the stories about it will spread across the countryside like wildfire."

"That I am sure of," said Gelderand, stroking the feline's furry coat.

With the time for talking over, the small group of men went about preparing the Treasure of the Land for all to see.

Several hours later, horse-drawn carts transported the ancient bounty from the ship to the mainland. Harrison watched as seven wagons, loaded with chests of coins, weapons, armor, and rare artifacts made its slow procession into the awaiting town.

The young warrior, with Tara, Lance, and his friends flanking him, led the small group up the main avenue. One by one, townspeople saw the adventurers, some recognizing Harrison and his friends, others astonished at the sight of the riches. With each passing step towards the town's marketplace, a larger and larger following of Aegeans trailed their new heroes.

The town center rested seven blocks from the harbor. Vendors hurriedly erected their displays around the perimeter of the grassy marketplace, hoping to make big sales during the upcoming event. Trees provided ample shading all along Aegeus's dirt roads, save for the town square. With the Town Hall looming in the distance, Governor Rollins had done all that he could to prepare a celebration for his beloved village, but the lack of time limited him to a makeshift platform with a canopy to shade the warriors. By the time Harrison's group arrived at the festival site, throngs of townsfolk swarmed about the area.

Harrison waved to the heavyset man on the staging. "Governor, what shall we do with the treasures?"

Governor Rollins put a finger to his lips, thinking. "Arrange them in front of the platform in a way for all to see."

Harrison directed his soldiers to do just that. After completing that task, he motioned for his friends to walk with him onto the stage. Tara tugged at Harrison's arm just as they prepared to climb the makeshift stairway.

The young maiden had a worrisome expression on her face. "Harrison, I don't belong up there."

"Nonsense! I want you with me."

Tara crinkled her brow. "I know you do, but this is your big event. I'm going to stay here in front of everyone else. You'll see me from the stage."

Harrison was about to protest again, but the young girl moved away and positioned herself at the forefront of the growing crowd. Lance witnessed her actions and scurried over to her side. The young warrior knew he could not change his woman's mind, and his canine friend's maneuvers solidified that belief.

Before Harrison could proceed to the staging, a familiar person wandered toward Tara.

"Would it be all right if an old man stood with you?" asked Philius to Tara.

"By all means!" she exclaimed and intertwined the elderly man's arm with hers. The young maiden cocked her head, smiling at the young warrior.

Harrison smiled back, happy to see that Philius had joined the celebration and furthermore that Tara had someone she knew to keep her company. With the issue of his woman's plight settled, the young warrior gestured again for his friends to mount the staging.

Governor Rollins could hardly contain his enthusiasm. "Look at all the excitement," he said, spreading his arms out toward the crowd. "And to think, it was just a short time ago that you left on your journey, from this very spot!"

The young warrior reflected back to that infamous day, some four months ago. Scanning his friends, he realized that only Murdock and Pondle remained from that initial group. Gone were Marcus Braxton, his leader and mentor, Jason Sands, and Aidan Hunter, replaced with Swinkle, Gelderand, Lance, and Tara.

Harrison looked the governor in the eye. "We lost some very good men along the way. Please remember that in your speech."

Governor Rollins nodded with emphasis. "By all means! Their sacrifices have enabled Aegeus to stand on the threshold of a fortune, with everyone to benefit."

The town leader then walked to the center of the stage, faced the crowd, and began to wave his hands over his head. "Attention! Attention, everybody!"

After several minutes, the throngs of people heeded their leader's command. Clearing his throat, Governor Rollins began, "Less than a season ago, these fine men left our little town in search of the Treasure of the Land. Today they return with the great bounty!"

The crowd erupted in thunderous applause, cheering, whistling, and even cries of happiness. The governor raised his hands again, signaling for quiet.

A moment later, he continued. "They fought many battles along the way to exotic places, and not everyone returned home. Let us not forget our fallen comrades, Marcus Braxton, Jason Sands, and Aidan Hunter. Please let us have a moment of silence for their sacrifice."

The governor lowered his head to his chest, as did Harrison and his friends. The crowd of people turned eerily still, sensing the great hurt their new heroes must have endured to secure the sacred prize.

After an appropriate amount of time, Governor Rollins continued. "I feel now is the moment to introduce to you the finders of the Treasure." The chubby man pointed to the young warrior. "My fellow Aegeans, it is my pleasure to introduce to you, Harrison Cross!" The mass of townspeople roared with delight.

Harrison took a step forward upon hearing his name called. He panned the area, taking in the throngs of people, realizing just what lay ahead for him. Only a few months earlier, he stood on this very stage with his mentor, but now he was the leader. And with his newfound position, he understood its awesome responsibility.

The ecstatic, smiling faces that cheered for him, for his friends, drove home the point to Harrison that he must succeed in reuniting the land, just as the ancient kings had declared. Before speaking, he recalled his studies from the Fighter's Guild. It was his duty to make the righteous decisions for those who could not fight. The townsfolk looked up to warriors like him to bring order and stability to their lives. Now he understood why his teachers painstakingly instilled these beliefs in him. Standing tall, he knew he was no politician, but these townspeople deserved to hear the truth, and far be it from him to let them down.

Harrison waved to the crowd, then used both hands in an attempt to silence their exuberance. After a few moments, he was ready to speak.

"My fellow Aegeans, we have succeeded in finding and returning the most sacred prize of the land. And we intend to disperse the riches to everyone."

The crowd roared, with the people envisioning personal wealth and contentment. Harrison also knew that they would feel this way, and he needed to clarify his position at once.

"By everyone, I mean all the peoples of this great land, not just Aegeus." The townspeople appeared stunned by Harrison's remark, as murmurs whisked throughout the crowd. "The great kings of this land have instructed us that our journey is not yet complete. We found a scripture within the bounty that states how to distribute the riches, so that all of mankind can share the wealth."

The young warrior could feel the confusion from the crowd. Random people then started shouting.

"Why must we share what is ours?" asked a middle-aged man.

"Don't you represent Aegeus?" asked another. "Doesn't that mean we all own it?" People began to agree with their fellow townsfolk as emotions started to rise.

Harrison raised his palms to the crowd again, trying to stop the onslaught of negativity. "There's more than enough here for everyone," he started, recalling how he had told Swinkle and Tara that a great bounty can bring the best and the worst out of people. "We must abide by the kings' decree."

"The kings are dead and this treasure is for Aegeus!" bellowed another younger man, as the tide began a dangerous turn away from Harrison and his friends, and toward the angry masses.

The young warrior could feel the tension in the air, and as he pondered what he would say next, he noticed the crowd parting toward the back. The mob separated further, and Harrison could see another set of people advancing toward the stage.

When the new group, which contained over one hundred armored warriors, stood about ten yards from the staging, a broad smile stretched across Harrison's face. "Brendan!"

Brendan Brigade, the warrior master of the Aegean Fighter's Guild, stepped to the forefront. "Harrison Cross, it is an honor to welcome you back to your hometown."

The young warrior could hardly contain his excitement. Brendan, with the watchful eye of Marcus always on him, had helped to hone Harrison's fighting skills. Because of the warrior's teaching efforts, Harrison learned the art of righteous combat better than anyone in the history of the Fighter's Guild.

Harrison rushed off the stage and greeted his one-time mentor. Clasping his hand, he said, "Brendan, am I glad to see you!"

The warrior smiled, recalling the days he spent countless hours training the raw teenage fighter. "I expected Marcus to return, but I'm not at all surprised to see you here."

"Marcus was right," said Harrison, shaking his head. "Every single thing he told us was true. He should be here addressing the crowd, not me."

The older warrior glared at his former pupil. "Nonsense! You proved your worth and now you can reap the rewards."

"There's so much more you don't know."

"I know more than you think," said Brendan, resting a hand on Harrison's shoulder and leading him back to the stage. "We'll talk later, but now you must control this mob."

The young warrior nodded as he climbed the stairs to the staging, Brendan following close behind.

"What do I tell them?" asked Harrison.

"Keep telling them the truth."

Harrison took his spot on the platform, while Brendan made sure to introduce himself and thank every member of the young warrior's team. When finished with the introductions, the older warrior faced the crowd, resting a hand on Harrison's back.

"Let it be known to all that Harrison Cross has the complete and total backing of the Fighter's Guild." The warrior looked at Harrison. "We are ready to follow your lead."

The crowd, silent at first, began to clap their hands. Sensing a change in attitude, more and more townsfolk began to applaud until the sound became deafening.

Brendan leaned closer to Harrison. "You see, we have the backing of the people, too."

"There's much to do. Will you honor your pledge after the crowd disperses?"

"You have my word."

Harrison nodded once, then looked over to the crowd. Again, he raised his palms, signaling for them to settle down. When they did, he addressed them one last time.

"Like I stated before, with the help of Aegeus's best fighters, we will reunite the land and disperse the riches to their rightful owners. I know giving away wealth might seem foolish to some, but in the end all of mankind will benefit. You have my word that we will do the right thing."

Harrison peeked over at Governor Rollins, who took his cue to intervene. "Thank you, Harrison. We all await your next move, and we all stand behind you one hundred percent." Facing the crowd, the heavyset man continued.

"I declare today a holiday — go, enjoy the rest of the day with your friends and family! Long live Aegeus!" The crowd erupted in cheers as the celebration continued.

Harrison took the opportunity to speak with Brendan. "Have you heard about Gareth and Fallyn?"

Brendan's demeanor turned dour. "He's a jealous man, Harrison. I'm sure he would have treated Marcus with a little more respect."

"If I might ask, how did you find out about this?"

"Governor Rollins sent an envoy to the Guild last night as soon as you sent your men to fetch him." Brendan peeked over to the large man. "He might be dim-witted at times, but he has good instincts for the most part."

The young warrior nodded in concurrence. "What can we expect from you and your warriors?"

The older warrior's eyes lit up. "My warriors? I trained them for this day, Harrison. They're yours now. Do with them as you deem fit."

The young warrior looked at the hundred men who stood beyond the stage, knowing that a thousand more waited in the barracks. "Brendan, I'll need your help."

"I know you will, son. You're not going into this alone."

Harrison drew a heavy sigh. "There's so much to do and we need to get started."

"Let's convene at the Fighter's Guild and we can strategize from there. I'm sure your friends want to be included in all discussions."

Harrison glanced at his friends, who watched their new leader converse with the decorated town hero. "And they will be. I'm nothing without them."

The young warrior gazed about the marketplace, at the bustling townspeople, the soldiers, the hope that everyone left the festivities with. Not only was it his duty to do the will of the ancient kings, it was his honor.

The young warrior waved his friends over. With them encircling him and Brendan, Harrison said, "We're going to the Fighter's Guild. The reuniting of the land begins today."

Harrison's friends all nodded in assurance. Before they departed for the military installation, a beautiful figure appeared from the bustling crowd. Tara had encouraged her man to handle his leadership duties, but now she commanded his attention.

The young warrior raised a finger in his friends' direction, signaling for them to wait. Harrison approached Tara, saying, "We need to go to the Fighter's Guild. I don't think it would be wise for you to go there."

Tara, saddened to know that she would have to wait to see Harrison again, understood the young warrior's position. "You need to do this, Harrison. Go with your friends, I'll return to the ship after I let Philius escort me about town."

"I will be sure to point out all of Aegeus's sights," said the beaming gentleman.

Harrison smiled, growing more in love with the beautiful girl with each passing day. "I'm glad you understand." The young warrior peered down at the little dog sitting next to him. "Take Lance with you. He's probably hungry and he'll keep an eye on you for me."

"I'll see you on the ship," said Tara. She then kissed Harrison on the cheek. "Come on, Philius, Lance! Let's go!"

The young maiden then held out her arm, allowing Philius to hook his around hers, and stepped away from Harrison. After a few paces, Tara swiveled her head, winked at Harrison, then left him behind. Lance trotted alongside the site seers.

The young warrior took a long second to watch Tara's petite frame wander away from him, secretly wishing that he could show her the landmarks of his hometown. Instead, he glanced at the awaiting convoy of men, and with a wave of his hand, they left the staging area behind and proceeded to the fortified training grounds.

The Aegean Fighter's Guild resided four blocks to the east of the town's center, just far enough away to allow soon-to-be warriors the proper arena to hone their skills. Harrison walked with Brendan and his friends toward the complex with the horse-drawn wagons carting the Treasure of the Land behind them. With each step, the young warrior recalled memory upon memory of his training behind the doors of the fortified building.

Though only a few short months had elapsed since Marcus called for him to begin his famous journey, it seemed like Harrison had been away an eternity.

The young warrior stopped in his tracks in order to take in the familiar structure. Resembling a fort, the creators of the complex had constructed the walls with twenty-foot tall wooden stakes. Along the wall tops patrolled sentries, who now peered from their positions to see the new visitors.

Upon recognizing Harrison, Brendan, and the rest of the convoy, the two sentries who guarded the Fighter's Guild entrance grasped the wooden handles of the large double-doors and swung the portal open. Just as they reached their widest point, a loud roar burst from the horde of fighters who greeted the men from the other side of the entryway.

Harrison's eyes widen with surprise, for in front of him cheered platoons of excited instructors and would-be soldiers. The young warrior looked over at Brendan, a wide smile beaming across his face.

"This is a proud day indeed," started the older warrior. "Today one of our very own has returned a hero."

Harrison continued to stare wide-eyed, while the youthful fighters encircled the group to greet their champion.

Brendan leaned over to the young warrior. "Now would be a good time to say something," he said, raising an eyebrow.

Harrison tried to corral his emotions. "Thank you all for this unexpected warm welcome. I'm so proud to be able to come back here with my friends, knowing we succeeded in what we set out to do." The young warrior extended an arm toward the carts. "I bring to you, the Treasure of the Land!"

The men erupted in cheers and applause, just as the townspeople had. Beneath the noise of the affirmation, Harrison said, "Brendan, would you have them find a place to stow the bounty and make sure nothing happens to it?"

"Would you expect anything else?" Brendan pointed to a platoon of seven fighters. "Take the wagons to the repository and lock the doors behind them. When you have finished that task, set up a guard rotation — I want sentries watching over that treasure every second of the day."

"Yes, sir!" said the men in unison before rushing past their leaders and taking hold of the horses' reins.

Harrison and his friends watched the carts disappear deeper into the fortress, each one realizing that this marked the first time that they had let someone else willfully take the Treasure.

The young warrior then brought his focus to the training grounds where inexperienced fighters practiced hand-to-hand combat, while others engaged in agility drills. Further to the back of the complex, he could see would-be soldiers training on horseback in the jousting fields. Harrison recalled the times he participated in the same drills and how they prepared him for his journeys. With fond memories in his heart, he continued his trek behind his old mentor.

As Brendan brought the men to a small building, Harrison recognized the place; Marcus had summoned him to the leader's headquarters many times, usually to point out the flaws he had made during the course of his training sessions. Though he felt the sting of Marcus's comments then, he now understood that they helped mold him into the successful warrior he was today.

The elder warrior offered chairs and benches to the men. Harrison gazed about the familiar dwelling and noticed that all of Marcus's mementoes sat where he had left them, awaiting his return. He felt a pang of sorrow in his heart, knowing that the keepsakes' owner would never come home again.

Brendan's voice broke the young warrior out of his trance. "Harrison, tell me what you feel our first move should be."

Harrison took a moment to respond. Marcus would ask him similar questions from behind the same desk, but now a different person occupied the seat. Harrison shook the cobwebs from his head and focused on the information that he and his friends had discussed the night before.

"We need to reunite the land in the same manner that the ancient kings did." The young warrior shifted in his seat, hunching over and resting his arms on his legs. "We need to disperse the treasure to the coastal towns from Balta to Polaris, then everywhere in between."

"Have you thought about Argos?"

"We feel that we should join forces with them so that the other towns and villages won't feel as if we're trying to overtake them."

Brendan nodded in concurrence. "What does the scripture say we should offer them?"

"I'm not sure," said Harrison, before peering at Swinkle. "Can you tell us what Argos gets?"

The young cleric made haste to extract the ancient manuscript from his backpack, then flipped to the appropriate page.

"The city of Argos is to receive," Swinkle squinted, then read verbatim from the book, "*Swords and axes forged from the finest metals shall accompany scores of body armor and shields to the people of Argos. Maligor himself chanted over the equipment rendering them even stronger than they appear.*"

"Magically enhanced," said Brendan with a smile. "The Forge brothers will be most satisfied."

"That they will," responded Harrison, recognizing the names. Octavius and Caidan Forge were very skilled warriors and loyal allies, and the weapons and armor offering would only make their bond stronger.

"How do you foresee utilizing the Argosians?"

"We'll need both of our armies, plus all of the fighters who join us from the towns in the land," Harrison lifted his eyes, "if we're going to topple Concur."

Brendan frowned and leaned forward in his seat. "Topple Concur?" The warrior shook his head, folded his arms, and sat back in his chair. "Why in the world would we want to do that?"

"The kings said we must reunite the *whole* land. Concur is part of the plan, is it not?"

The older warrior shook his head and looked away, focusing on a battle-axe that hung on the wall. Harrison watched his expressions and could not help but notice the similarities between Marcus and Brendan's mannerisms.

"We'll need to plan this out very, very carefully with the backing of all the people in the land."

Harrison had more to tell. "I know where we need to start."

Brendan raised an eyebrow and cocked his head. "Oh, really? Where's that?"

"Before we start any attack on Concur, we need to notify the head of the Resistance movement. I know who he is, and he must alert Meredith about what is going to happen."

"Lord Hammer's woman?" The Aegean shifted in his chair. "What good will that do?"

"She's part of the Resistance. The Concurian townspeople adore her and will do anything she asks. We need to liberate Meredith so that she can direct her people."

Brendan took in Harrison's information, but was not at all convinced. "And this person of interest inside their Resistance movement – is he reliable?"

"I believe so. He helped us escape from Concur before, and I feel we can trust him again."

The decorated warrior looked away for a moment before saying with a smirk, "Nigel will be most agitated."

"To say the least."

"Is there anything more I should know?"

Harrison continued to push his agenda. "We found an old parchment with the bounty that details terms of a Unification

Agreement. Aegeus needs to sign this treaty as well as every other town in the land."

Brendan continued to accept the younger man's way of thinking. "As long as the terms of this agreement are sound, I see no reason not to sign it." Cocking his head, he asked, "Anything else?"

Harrison was not finished yet. "We'll need to reestablish the Legion of Knighthood."

Brendan pursed his lips. "Not a bad idea. That way we can have representatives for every city."

"Precisely. And that person can be appointed by the one signing the treaty." The young warrior did not wait for another comment from Brendan. In a bold move, he added, "and I think Aegeus's delegate should be Philius."

The older warrior crinkled his brow. "What? That old man? Why should he represent our town?"

"He might be old, but he's very wise. Without him, we might not have found the Treasure. I agree that it's a token gesture, but not a foolish one."

Brendan flipped a hand in Harrison's direction. "Fine, but if he falls asleep during a crisis, it's your head not mine."

Harrison smirked. "Deal."

Brendan kept his stare on the young warrior for a moment. "Before we head to Argos, we must secure the allegiance of the clerics in Robus. They are a very intellectual crew and having them agree with our plans would be a symbolic move of great importance."

Swinkle's eyes widen at the mention of his hometown. "Sir, if I might say, I am one of those clerics you speak of."

Brendan extended a finger toward Swinkle. "You're from Robus?"

"I am indeed."

"Then I suggest you interface with your people." The elder warrior brought his attention back to Harrison.

"You will lead a platoon of men to Robus and outline our intentions. We'll visit Argos upon your return."

The young warrior frowned. "It sounds like you're not coming with us."

"That's because I'm not."

Harrison still appeared confused. "Don't you think you should join us? To show unity?"

Brendan understood the young warrior's concern and he tried to put him at ease. "Harrison, Robus is a very religious village and not accustomed to having warriors trudge through their town. The smaller the group, the better. You and your friends will be able to deliver this treasure's message just as well as an army from Aegeus could."

"I suppose that does make the most sense." Feeling better about the situation, Harrison said, "We can leave tomorrow morning, and we should be back within the week."

Brendan concurred. "That will give me enough time to hand pick the men to bring to Argos." The Aegean rose from his seat. "Do you need a place to sleep tonight?"

"No, we'll remain on the ship. We have some preparations to take care of before we embark on this journey. We'll be back in the morning."

Two soldiers escorted Harrison and his friends from the Fighter's Guild. After the small group strolled far enough out of earshot from the walled structure, Murdock took it upon himself to approach their leader.

"Harrison, I think I speak for everyone when I ask, what are your plans for us?"

The young warrior gazed into his friend's dark brown eyes and could see a look of genuine concern. Stopping in his tracks, Harrison did his best to put his friends at ease.

"I know everything's happening very fast, and that there are a lot of new faces to contend with, but all of you will be part of the inner circle." Harrison scanned the group, reading the anxious faces.

"Murdock, Pondle, you two will lead the way on all of our missions, like you always have, as well as being in charge of any other platoons of soldiers that might accompany us." The young warrior took his gaze to the group's eldest member.

"Gelderand, I'll need you to help me comprehend all of the mystical things that come our way, things I know I won't understand."

Harrison rested a firm hand on Swinkle's shoulder. "And I'm hoping that you will continue to be my personal advisor and spiritual guide. I take to heart the wisdom you convey to me." The young cleric smiled.

"All of you are more important than anyone else we'll ever meet. We've come so far together, sacrificed so much. I would never turn my back on you, and I know you wouldn't do that to me either. When I said we would save the world some day, I meant it. Now's the time."

Harrison's friends took in their leader's words. Murdock held a firm gaze on the young warrior. "I'm with you, Harrison, and I know the others are, too." The ranger checked the group and saw each member's subtle nods. "Let's get back to the ship. Tomorrow's going to be a busy day."

The small group of adventurers heeded Murdock's advice and proceeded to their awaiting vessel.

CHAPTER 7

¤

A cloudless sky brought warm sunshine to Aegeus's bustling streets. Unbeknownst to the local townsfolk, Harrison and his friends had spent the morning securing their gear for their short trip to Robus. The young warrior knew that the people of Robus were vastly different than those of his hometown – religious, intellectual, and passive. Nevertheless, Harrison also knew that Swinkle would relay their very important message to his kindred and felt confident that his friend would convince the high clerics of their noble cause. Today, Harrison and his friends would begin their journey to bring hope to the towns of the land.

Before leaving, though, the young warrior searched for his new love. Tara had kept to herself, allowing Harrison to handle his responsibilities, and remained in her cabin for the time being.

The young warrior knocked on the girl's door. "Who is it?" said the soft voice from the other side of the portal.

"It's Harrison."

The door swung open, and upon seeing the young warrior, a beaming smile stretched across Tara's face. The young maiden threw her arms around her man, hugging him tightly.

"I've missed you!" Tara gave Harrison a quick kiss. "I know how busy you've been and I wanted to stay out of your way until things settled down."

Harrison squeezed the girl. "I've missed you, too." The young warrior pulled back from Tara, gazing into her eyes with a sly look.

Tara cocked her head and furrowed her brow. "What?"

"I want you to come to Robus with us. This is a very important diplomatic mission and you being with us will drive that point home."

Tara frowned. "Is that the *only* reason you want me to go with you? I thought you said you missed me."

Harrison's mouth fell agape. "I, um, yes, of course, I've missed you! I want you as close to me as I can. The thought of leaving you behind again is killing me."

Tara smiled. "That's more like it." She then reached up and kissed Harrison again. "I better pack," she said, wriggling out of the young warrior's embrace and beginning her search for her necessities.

Harrison stepped deeper into the room. "I don't want you to stray too far from me, though. I'll be sure that Lance is with you all the time. Swinkle, too." The young warrior took a moment to think further. "Maybe I'll assign a soldier or two as well," he said, while gazing off into nothingness.

The young girl wheeled around, placing her hands on her hips. "Do you think that I'm some frail flower that will snap if a stiff breeze blows?"

Tara took a step in Harrison's direction, holding a frozen stare on her mate. She snapped her fingers and, in an instant, a soft flame hovered just above her fingertips in the same manner one would sit atop a candle.

Harrison's eyes widened in amazement.

"Do you think I just sat in my uncle's house and knitted sweaters? I'm going to be a very powerful mage some day. I can handle myself."

The young warrior's eyes remained round. "I guess you can. What else can you do?"

A mischievous grin graced Tara's face as she blew out the soft yellow glow, her warm breath spreading over Harrison's red face. "You'll see when the time's right."

The young warrior let out a little laugh. "I suppose so." Gathering himself, he said, "We'll be leaving soon. Do you want me to come back in a little while to carry your things?"

Harrison did not have to look up to see Tara's exasperated expression; instead he waved his palms toward his mate and said, "Never mind what I just said! You can handle that yourself." He then walked over to Tara and gazed into her blue eyes.

Pulling her close, he kissed her once again. "I'm so glad you'll be with me. You have no idea how much that means to me."

Before Tara could speak, he added, "I have to go now. I'll see you upstairs in a few minutes."

Harrison turned to leave, and as he did, he heard Tara say, "Thank you for asking me to join you on this trip. It means a lot to me, too."

The young warrior flashed the girl a heartfelt smile, then left her to tend to her things and proceeded to the ship's deck.

Before joining his friends, the young warrior sought *VENTURE 3*'s captain. Upon locating Portheus, he said to the big man, "Captain, I know you served under my brother and earned his utmost respect. I feel the same way about you, and I'd be honored if you would serve as the captain of our new fleet."

Harrison's remarks came as a surprise to Portheus. "I don't know what to say, sir, other than, yes I accept! But what fleet do you speak of?"

Harrison gazed about the ship he stood on, then looked over at the other one that swayed in the harbor. "We'll start with these two vessels and I'm sure we'll grow from there someday."

Portheus smirked. "I've sunk more ships than that."

"Let's hope that doesn't happen anytime soon!" Changing the subject, he continued, "Remain in Aegeus until we return. I'm not sure what our next course of action will be until we return from Robus."

"As you wish, sir." Portheus saluted his new leader. "I'll be here awaiting your return."

"Thank you, Portheus." Harrison extended his hand, the captain accepting it with a vigorous shake. "I must go now." With that, Harrison left the captain behind and joined his friends on the ship's deck.

The young warrior found the familiar faces huddled together, awaiting their leader. Harrison noticed Tara first; the young maiden holding Rufus in her arms, swaying slightly. The girl flashed Harrison a smile upon seeing him.

"We're ready to go," she said, stroking Rufus's fur.

The young warrior scratched the cat on the head, saying, "Portheus is all set as well." Harrison gazed past his mate, finding Murdock close behind.

"Let's find some more men to join us," said the young warrior.

Murdock gave him a single nod, then motioned for everyone to follow his lead. After summoning ten soldiers, the small group of adventurers began their trek to the Fighter's Guild. By the time they arrived, Brendan had already convened a convoy that consisted of two large, horse-drawn carts that contained Robus's share of the Treasure.

The Guild's leader approached its once star pupil. "Good morning, Harrison. Everything is stowed and ready for travel."

The young warrior nodded in approval. "Great. We're anxious to get going." Harrison noticed a subtle look of concern on Brendan's face. "Is something the matter?"

"It's probably nothing, but I think your mage should take a look at this."

Gelderand's eyes lit up at the mention of his name. "What have you found?"

Brendan waved the older man over to one of the carts. The soldiers had covered the contents of the wagon with a heavy covering, which they peeled back to reveal twenty or so avian figurines.

"They're clay falcons or so I gather." The fighter summoned one of his soldiers, who handed him an ivory tube. "This parchment accompanied them. Do you know what they are?"

Gelderand smiled as he gazed at the strange statuettes. "That I do," he said.

The mage leaned his large staff against the cart, then accepted the container from Brendan and uncorked it, allowing a rolled, ancient scroll to fall into his hand.

"This will be our first time using a part of the great treasure." Gelderand looked over to one of his friends. "Swinkle, I think you should be here for this as well." The young cleric joined the mage, his excitement level rising at being included in the event.

Gelderand unrolled the scroll, revealing magical text. The mage gathered ingredients for his spell, then mumbled to himself, all the while sprinkling silver granules over the parchment. Immediately, the scroll's text appeared legible to the wizard as he read the words it contained. The older man's eyes widened in surprise as the manuscript's intent became clear to him.

Swinkle, anticipating an explanation that had not come yet, blurted, "What does it say?"

The mage stood mouth agape, then shuffled to the back of the cart where the bird-like figures stared back at him. The young cleric, along with Brendan, Harrison, and the rest of the party, followed.

"It seems these clay falcons become a messenger system of some sort," said the mage.

Swinkle shook his head, his brow crinkled. "How?"

"We will find out right now." Gelderand motioned for Swinkle to pick up one of the light brown, bird-like statues. "Hold it in your hands."

The young cleric grabbed one of the clay figures. Swinkle inspected the two-foot tall statuette with a meticulous eye, admiring the intricate details the statue's creator had used in constructing the figurine. Had he not known that the artifact was made from clay, he would have sworn a live bird rested harmlessly in his hands.

Gelderand began to read the scroll's text. *"Behold the Messenger Falcon, the conduit for the New Kingdom. Each bird of prey will be loyal to its master and its instincts will never lead it astray from its course. Recite the following for each winged creature and forever shall it be bound to that town."*

The mage lowered the scroll and looked at the figure that rested in Swinkle's hands. With a forceful voice, Gelderand read from the parchment once again. *"Breathe, o courier of Aegeus!"*

A split second later, the brownish coloring of the clay falcon morphed into the majestic markings of a bird of prey. The bird's large eyes blinked and it opened its beautiful wings in an attempt to stabilize its position in Swinkle's hands. With a hop, the falcon gripped the young cleric's forearm and pierced his skin with its talons in order to gain better footing.

"Ouch!" yelled Swinkle as the bird's claws drew blood. The falcon screeched, signaling to all that it was alive and well.

Brendan witnessed the scene transpiring in front of him and summoned one of his soldiers. The young man knew just what his leader wanted and brought Swinkle a leather gauntlet. The soldier then gestured for the bird to rest on the protected forearm, which it did.

Harrison had stood back and watched the spectacle with his friends, but now he walked over to the living bird. With a gentle touch, he stroked the animal's head in a calming manner, the same way that he would put Lance at ease.

"I'm honored to have you as part of our new army," said the young warrior. "I know you understand me."

The bird ruffled its feathers and squawked. "At your service, Master."

A wide smile graced Harrison's face. "You and your friends will be very useful to the peoples of this land." The young warrior cocked his head. "What is your name?"

"Aegeus," squeaked the bird.

Harrison turned to his friends. "He says his name is Aegeus, just like our city."

"That will make things easier when it comes to distributing these creatures to the other towns," said Gelderand.

The young warrior nodded, then said to Gelderand and Swinkle, "Be sure you bring to life a bird for every village of this land. We'll give one to each town leader as a gift for joining our cause."

"That we will do," said Gelderand, clutching his staff. "Come, Swinkle, let us finish our task." The two men, with the aid of the soldiers, went about bringing to life each and every clay falcon, being careful to recite a different village name in the process.

Brendan, along with Murdock and Pondle, approached Harrison. "We'll leave once they're finished," said the ranger. "Is there anything else to do before we depart?"

"Everything's in order," said the young warrior. "Our trek to Robus begins now."

Brendan extended his hand to the men. "You have made our humble village proud. Now go out and spread the word." The three men shook hands. "I'll see you back here in a week."

A short time later, the small convoy consisting of Harrison and his friends, Tara, Lance, Rufus, and twenty soldiers, ten from the Fighter's Guild and another ten from Harrison's new army, left the familiar city of Aegeus behind.

The young warrior worked with Murdock and Pondle to set up a marching formation. The ranger and thief led the way with scouts and trackers from the integrated platoon, followed by Harrison, Tara, Swinkle, and Gelderand, with another convoy of soldiers bringing up the rear. Lance, mindful of making sure all was well, darted back and forth from the front line to the two horse-drawn carts carrying the treasures specific to Robus, which trekked between Harrison and the end of the procession. Rufus remained snuggled in his keeper's backpack, enjoying the trek in relative safety.

The small group had hiked for half a day, finding nothing but quaint woodlands, clear skies, and most importantly, no trouble. Harrison, finding Tara busy talking with her uncle, sought his good friend Swinkle. The young warrior then realized that the cleric had kept to himself on the short trek, remaining unusually quiet along the way.

Approaching his friend, the young warrior asked, "What's on your mind?"

Swinkle shook his head, his face flush. "I am not sure what to tell the High Priestess when we arrive in Robus."

"Just explain what you've seen, what we've all done together, and what we hope to do."

"That's easy for you to say." Swinkle brought his stare to the muddy ground. "My people are very interrogatory. They will ask me question after question, just to see if I will break from my beliefs."

Harrison had not heard about this practice before and wanted to learn more. "Why would they interrogate you as if you had done something wrong?"

The young cleric's face reflected the anxiety that coursed through his veins. "My people will not help a militaristic cause. Never. And our crusade, noble that it may be, also employs a war-like strategy."

"Sometimes you have to fight for what is right."

Swinkle nodded, knowing full well how much bloodshed he had witnessed through the course of his journey. "I agree, but they will still need convincing."

Harrison put his arm around his friend's shoulder. "I'll be there to pick you up if you start to stumble."

The young cleric smiled at his friend's sincerity. "I know you will."

Murdock and Pondle's rapid approach halted the pair's conversation. Harrison, his warrior instincts always on high alert, gripped his battle-axe's handle.

"What's the matter?" asked the young warrior.

"What?" said Murdock, crinkling his brow. "Do you always expect bad news whenever you see me?"

Harrison eased a bit. "You do tend to bring your fair share of gloom."

"It's getting late," added Pondle, "and we think this is a safe area to rest for the night."

The young warrior searched for the sun, fighting the thick branches that covered the vast woodlands. Shards of sunbeams scattered low to the west.

"I suppose you're right. Find us a good place to set up camp."

Murdock and Pondle did just that, and within the hour, the small army had strategically placed soldiers and scouts around the encampment, protecting their leaders.

Harrison and his friends enjoyed a hot meal cooked over the campfire, resting their tired bodies after a long day of traveling. Tara sat alongside Harrison, enjoying their first night together in the wilderness. Lance accepted handouts from the couple, as well as the discarded foods that Swinkle tossed over his shoulder as a sacrifice to his god, while Rufus picked at meat that Tara offered to him. When finished, the group found places to sleep for the night.

The young warrior arranged his backpack on the ground, while Lance curled up near him. Before he could look for her, he found Tara approaching him from behind.

"Can I lay my pack next to yours?" she asked. The young maiden did not wait for her man's answer; instead she placed one knee on the ground and placed her pack alongside Harrison's.

"By all means," said the young warrior.

Tara retrieved a blanket from her sack, then smoothed out the earth beneath her, removing any sticks and small rocks. When finished with that chore, she laid herself down on the ground and waited for Harrison to join her.

The young warrior mimicked Tara's actions and placed his body next to hers. The couple snuggled under the blankets, keeping each other warm.

Tara wrapped her arm around Harrison's midsection, then reached over and kissed him. The young warrior peeked toward the campfire, noticing that his other friends congregated in close proximity to the couple.

"I'm a little uncomfortable with us lying like this while everyone else is so close," said Harrison.

"You should have brought a tent," whispered Tara in his ear before giggling. "Relax, Harrison, it's time to go to sleep."

The young warrior pulled the girl closer to him, their bodies seemingly melding into one. "We'll be in Robus tomorrow."

Tara closed her eyes and rested her head on Harrison's chest. "Is Swinkle ready for his big day?"

"I think he's very nervous."

"Then you'll have to keep him calm." The young maiden yawned. "He looks up to you, Harrison. Make sure he's safe."

Harrison took his mate's words to heart. Swinkle would need him tomorrow, and he vowed to be there for his friend. Harrison lowered his head and kissed the top of Tara's golden locks. He could feel her breath against his chest and knew she had fallen asleep.

Harrison took the time to watch the beautiful girl that he held in his arms sleep. He knew she had some spunk in her, a trait he found incredibly attractive, but she was also very vulnerable to the rigors of the wilderness, and he feared what might happen to her if they ran into an encounter. He had to be her protector, as well as her loving companion.

Swinkle on the other hand, had been through more battles with Harrison, and had seen more than his fair share of death on this journey. The young cleric had a very strong will, and he respected the fact that he would never waver in his beliefs, no matter what the situation. However, like Tara said, Harrison needed to protect him as well.

He yawned. Night began to fall and his body, relaxed next to Tara, begged him to sleep. Panning the campsite, he found his friends already in a slumber, with various soldiers keeping watch over them. Over to his right, Lance lay curled in a ball with Rufus snuggled next to him. The young warrior closed his eyes and yawned again, then fell into a deep sleep. All was safe.

The next morning brought clear skies and bright sunshine. Everyone in the encampment enjoyed a cool, dry night, devoid of Scynthian activity and natural woodland predators.

Murdock and Pondle had gathered the trackers and soldiers, and readied them for their short trek to Robus. The rest of the group broke camp, and by mid-morning, the convoy from Aegeus was ready to travel.

Harrison, with Tara by his side, knew his good friend would be ready for the return to his hometown. Not knowing what to expect, though, gnawed at his warrior instincts.

With the young cleric trekking a step ahead of him, Harrison called to his friend, "Swinkle, how do you want to proceed once we get to Robus's outskirts?"

Swinkle let out a sigh, his friend seeming to read his mind. "I must lead the convoy toward the enclave. I would like all of us to enter together." The young cleric shook his head, not finishing his statement.

Harrison waited for additional information, but Swinkle had nothing more to offer. "Is there something that we should know?"

"My people will not like all the armor and weaponry that the men carry," said the young cleric. "It goes against our core beliefs."

"That might be true, but this is how we must proceed." Harrison rested a hand on his friend's shoulder. "I'll be here for you."

Swinkle gazed into his friend's blue eyes. "You have no idea what you are in store for."

After two more hours of travel, Swinkle asked Murdock and Pondle to halt the small platoon's advancement. The twenty-plus people stood on the outskirts of Robus; behind them rested the lush forest and before them stood several small buildings. Beyond the structures loomed a great body of water, the Serpent's Sea.

"My people already know we are here," said Swinkle, gazing at the edifices before them.

Murdock scowled. "How so? I haven't seen anyone try to intercept us. As a matter of fact, we haven't seen anybody, period. I bet we could walk right down the main road and no one would do anything to us."

"You would be right about that," said the young cleric, "but we are standing in a very holy place. Pious will protect us."

The ranger rolled his eyes. "If that's what you want to believe." Murdock took his gaze to Harrison. "How do you want to proceed?"

The young warrior left that decision to his friend. "Swinkle?"

The cleric did not remove his gaze from the horizon. "Like Murdock said, we walk right down the main street."

Harrison could tell that Swinkle had a plan in mind, which he trusted just as much as if it were his own. Mimicking his deceased leader, the young warrior extended a hand and said, "Lead the way."

Before taking the point, Swinkle addressed all of the men. "Everyone please sheath your weapons and follow me."

The men did as instructed and marched behind the unlikely convoy leader. Harrison walked a couple of steps behind Swinkle, giving his friend complete control of the situation. As they marched into Robus, Murdock leaned over to speak with Harrison.

Trying not to let the young cleric hear, the ranger said, "Are you sure it's a good idea letting him take charge?"

"He's the only one these people will listen to," said Harrison. "I have faith in him."

"You have faith in a bunch of people who wield no weapons, wear no armor, and throw their food over their shoulders?" The ranger shook his head in disbelief, making his opinion quite clear.

"We really have no choice," said Harrison. "This is the way it must be and we'll all support him." Tara pulled the young warrior's arm closer, signaling her support for her man.

Murdock panned the area, taking in the circular design of all the buildings. "It feels too 'religious' here for me."

Harrison smirked. "It might do you some good."

"Don't bet on it."

Ahead of the group loomed a large circular building with a tall cathedral-like spire rising upwards towards the sky. Swinkle stopped the procession fifty yards from the edifice's entrance.

"That's the Holy Sanctuary. It's where we come to worship Pious, as well as hold our sacred meetings."

A breeze blew through Harrison's hair as he gazed about the building. Constructed of smooth blue-gray stone, the walls curved around the structure, creating a perfect circle. The spire rose high into the sky, with three bells hanging in the tower, and before them stood two double doors, closed shut for the time being.

Tara tugged on Harrison's arm, disturbing his warrior's examination of the new place. "Where are all the people?"

The young warrior had been thinking the same thing. "That's a good question." All of a sudden, Harrison's warrior training took over and he gripped the hilt of his battle-axe.

"Something's wrong," he started to say before a foreign energy coursed through the bodies of all party members. The young warrior tried in vain to raise his weapon, but found that he could not move his arm. As a matter of fact, his whole body remained motionless and he stood frozen in his tracks.

Harrison lifted his eyes in Tara's direction; she was too unable to move, save for the anxious expression on her face. To his surprise, a familiar cloaked figure passed in front of him.

"This is not right!" said Swinkle, his eyes wide, his head swiveling in all directions. "This is not right!"

The young cleric bounded about the motionless platoon, shocked that all members had fallen under the spell of one prayer, albeit a powerful one. Swinkle knew that his friends would not be in any peril, but he needed to protect them now.

A creaking sound permeated the group, followed by a soft shuffling of feet and low murmur of chanting. Swinkle spun around to see the double doors open and eight hooded figures appear from the depths of the temple.

The young cleric recognized the leader instantly, and upon seeing her, knelt to one knee. "High Priestess Miriam, it is I, Brother Swinkle."

The high priestess spoke in a firm, yet flowing voice. "Rise, Brother." Swinkle did as instructed and waited for his leader's next move.

Miriam Wynd pulled down the hood of her dark green cloak, revealing raven-black hair and green eyes. The forty-five year old woman had striking features, comparable to Tara's beauty that hid her age well.

"Who are these armed people that you have brought into our humble cloister?" Miriam stood tall in waiting for the lad's answer. Her fellow monks continued to chant, holding Harrison and his convoy at bay.

"My Lady, we have come to you with plans of a righteous journey." Not wavering, the young cleric added, "I intend to ring the temple's bells."

Miriam's eyes opened ever so slightly, an uncharacteristic eyebrow arching as well. "You must truly believe in your mission, Swinkle. No one sounds the bells without understanding the consequences."

The young cleric swallowed, hoping that his nervous reaction would go unnoticed. It did not. "I assure you, Madam Priestess, this undertaking will change the lives of everyone in the land. I am willing to place my standing in our order on its success."

The high priestess subtly cocked her head. "You will as soon as you tug on the bells' rope." Miriam stared at the stationary platoon. "Are these people trustworthy?"

Swinkle extended an arm toward his friends. "I would trust each and every one of them with my life. I pledged to help their cause and dedicated my Mission of Goodwill to them."

"I also sense a feeling of goodness from them, outside of their obvious current state of fear." Miriam waved her hand to the chanting monks, who stopped their mantra. All members of the group regained control of their bodies as soon as the religious people ceased their actions.

Immediately, all the soldiers and trackers reached for their weapons. Miriam noticed the maneuver and pointed in their general direction. "I would advise against that."

Swinkle swiveled and waved his palms toward the men. "Please, put your weapons away!"

Murdock, always reluctant to listen to anything the young cleric said, called over to Harrison. "I'm not going to take orders from him after what just happened!"

Harrison released the grip on his battle-axe, then gestured to the ranger. "Murdock, let's give these people their due. Do as he asks."

The ranger gritted his teeth, knowing that he should heed Swinkle's command, but he did not want to give the young cleric the satisfaction. Hearing the plea from Harrison, he grudgingly obliged.

With Murdock taken care of, the young warrior addressed his cleric friend. "Swinkle, you have our support. We'll listen to you."

The holy man nodded, then turned his attention to his superior. "I suggest that we commence with the ceremony right now."

Miriam appeared unfazed, knowing that Swinkle had learned all of their customs long before he went off on his mission of goodwill. "If that is your wish." The high priestess motioned for the monks to move away from the temple's entranceway.

Swinkle took that as his cue, and after the clerics repositioned themselves, he entered the sacred site. A minute later, the sound of clanging bells permeated the area.

Harrison could not believe his eyes. Thirty seconds after hearing the bells ring, the seemingly empty town teamed with life. Robed figures of all ages exited from the circular homes and congregated in the temple.

The group from Aegeus watched person after person filter by their platoon, heeding them no attention. Murdock did not care for the current course of events.

"Harrison, just what's going on here?"

The young warrior shook his head. "I have no idea."

Miriam overheard the conversation. "Your friend is putting his commitment to his faith on the line for your cause. You may enter the temple, but you must stay in the back." She then pointed to the weapons and armor. "All vehicles of war must remain outside of this sacred place."

Harrison nodded as his soldiers began to remove their belongings. Gazing down, the young warrior noticed both Lance and Rufus waiting patiently for their orders.

Pointing to the animals, he asked, "What about them?"

Miriam smiled. "They are pure of heart and are more than welcome to roam about the temple." Sensing that the religious building was near capacity, she said, "I suggest that you enter now."

The high priestess then entered the holy place, followed closely behind by Harrison and the rest. The young warrior looked from side to side, taking in all of the sights inside the shrine. What he saw surprised him.

Harrison felt Tara's small hand tug on his arm. "Why is Swinkle standing up there?" The young maiden motioned with her head toward the center of the building.

Harrison looked there as well, finding his close friend standing alone in the middle of the auditorium at a podium raised a few feet above everyone else, which allowed his fellow townsfolk to see him with ease.

Besides the young cleric positioned at the podium, the rest of the congregation took seats on benches that encircled the center staging area. From his vantage point, the young warrior deduced that the area was carved into four equal pie-shaped wedges containing ten rows of benches apiece.

Miriam and three other clerics sat behind individual tables, each one strategically placed in front of one of the four sections. Swinkle fidgeted, taking his watchful eye all about the area while the arena filled.

The young warrior brought his gaze to his mate. Answering her question, he said, "I don't know what they have in store for Swinkle, but I get the feeling he's going to have to defend our actions."

Even though the temple had filled with people, no one spoke a word. An uncomfortable aura radiated from the Aegeans who were filled with genuine concern for their friend. Before the young warrior could dwell on Swinkle's possible plight, one of the clerics seated in the front row across from them rose from his bench, headed to the opposite side of the room, and grabbed a thick rope that hung from the ceiling. With a mighty tug, the robed figure pulled the cable, causing the bells to ring once. The man waited ten seconds, then performed the operation again. He replicated the action one last time, then went back to his original position.

Harrison and his friends sat glued to their seats, anticipating the cloister's next move. They did not have to wait long.

Miriam, remaining seated, spoke first. "My fellow members of Pious's community, I welcome you today to listen to Brother Swinkle's dissertation."

Motioning in the direction of the other high clerics who sat behind their own tables, she said, "Aside from me, Brother Lester Platius, Sister Umbra Memnok, and Brother Benjamin Laramie will preside over this counsel. Let it be known, Brother Swinkle's fate in our community hinges on his testimony, for he did ring the temple's bells, calling for the assembly of this emergency meeting."

Harrison's eyes widened. Whispering in Tara's ear, he said, "Swinkle should have told us how dire this meeting would be! Why didn't he say so?"

"Because you would've tried to stop him," said the young girl. Harrison shook his head, crossing his arms, upset.

Miriam started the proceedings. "As everyone knows, we will employ the number system when directing questions to the main podium."

The number system mimicked ten equidistant points around the circular temple. The person standing at the pedestal faced position one with position five directly behind them. Members of the cloister sat on benches that encircled the staging area and would have the opportunity to ask questions at will.

Pausing a moment, the high priestess said, "Now, Brother Swinkle, why have you summoned us here today?"

The young cleric took a moment to gather himself. Gazing right at Miriam, he started, "High Priestess Miriam, after finishing my studies here at our sanctuary, I made preparations to leave our cloister and preach the good word of our people, in the way Pious had taught us.

"I left Robus with the intention of finding a cause worthy of my two-year Mission of Goodwill. I met a group of adventurers who had set out to discover a treasure that would bring peace and happiness to people all over the countryside."

A female voice came from behind Swinkle's podium. "Position Five. How long after you departed from Robus did you meet these people?"

The young cleric swiveled to address the person. "Two or three days."

A male voice hailed from the opposite side of the room. "Position One. Were these the first people you encountered on your journey?"

The young cleric turned to face the man. "Yes."

"Position Two," said the next female voice. "It appears that you made a hasty decision and did not give yourself the benefit of choosing the most worthy cause."

The young cleric maneuvered to face the next questioner. "I did not make my decision on the first day I met these people." Swinkle looked over to the Aegeans who were crammed into the arena to his left. "I asked for safe passage to Valkala and in return I would help their cause. I learned that these adventurers, my friends, were searching for the Treasure of the Land."

"Position Seven," said a man with a deep voice. "You joined yourself with a group of treasure seekers? How does this align with Pious's teachings?"

Maneuvering again, Swinkle said, "The treasures that they searched for did not intrigue me; it was their cause."

The same man spoke again. "Did they carry weapons?"

"Yes."

"Did they use them on your journey?"

"Yes." Whispers and murmurs permeated the temple after Swinkle's answer.

"Lead Position Six," said Brother Lester, seated behind the young cleric. "I want to hear about the cause these people were on before we delve into the use of weapons."

Harrison squirmed in his seat, hating the fact that his good friend had to answer repeated questions about his noble quest.

"I don't know if I can sit still for this," he muttered in Tara's direction.

"Harrison, it's not your place to say anything! Not now!" For the first time, the young warrior saw the seriousness of the situation in Tara's deep blue eyes. The maiden pursed her lips and crinkled her brow, further hammering her point across to Harrison.

"All right," he said. "I'll be good."

Swinkle faced one of the lead clerics. "I do admit, these Aegeans are a group of strong warriors, but I learned that their cause was a noble one. They sacrificed their lives to find the Treasure, which they intend to disperse amongst the peoples of the land.

"We have been to all corners of our small world, have seen the despair on the faces of the townspeople, and now we can make a difference. Commencing in Robus, we can start to bring joy and happiness to everyone."

Brother Lester continued. "How do you intend to do that?"

"There is a scripture that contains a specific list of items that are to be passed to all the towns. Each village will be given their rightful share of the Treasure."

A female voice spoke next. "Position Nine. The thrill of riches will drive some to greed. How do you intend to stop that?"

"I have inspected this list and examined the treasures myself. Though the total treasure is great, no one village will have it all. This should curb the sense of greed you speak of."

"Lead Position Three," said Umbra Memnok. "How can you be sure that the town's dignitaries won't keep the loot for themselves?"

Swinkle faced the blonde-haired lady. "We intend to resurrect the Legion of Knighthood, holding each village responsible for nominating someone from their town to represent them."

"And this will ensure their compliance?"

"It will be a step in the right direction."

"Lead Position Nine," said the elderly man to Swinkle's left. "Let's resume the discussion on weapon usage." Benjamin paused, shifting in his seat. "Did you use a weapon at any time on your journey?"

Swinkle did not have to think long on this question. "No."

"Did you witness death on this trip?"

"As I stated before, yes."

Brother Benjamin leaned forward. Wagging a crooked finger in the young cleric's direction, he asked, "Did you witness any unnecessary killings?"

The already quiet room seemed to grow even quieter. All eyes focused with intensity on the young man who stood at the podium.

Swinkle gambled and asked a question himself. "When you say unnecessary killings, do you refer to humans only?"

Harrison hoped no one saw him cringe after hearing Swinkle's rebuttal. Murdock tapped his friend on the shoulder and whispered, "He was doing fine until now."

"Give him a chance," said the young warrior, eagerly awaiting his friend's response.

Brother Benjamin did not waver. "*All* humanoid races."

Swinkle paused, thinking how to best answer the question. "Our group encountered humans, elves, and Scynthians alike. I can assure you, the only humans or elves who died at our hands attacked us first. We avoided potential conflicts at all costs. And, if we had to fight, we tried diplomacy first, just like Pious taught all of us."

The old man continued his questioning. "You mentioned Scynthians in your last statement, but failed to discuss how you handled them. Elaborate, please."

The young cleric exhaled, knowing that the fate of his future most likely hinged on his next answer. "The Scythians we encountered exhibited no redeeming qualities. We were attacked for no reason, we were imprisoned for being human, and we were beaten for their amusement. Without a trial to state our case, we were sentenced to death. The Scynthians were going to sever our arms and hurl us into a raging inferno while we were still alive.

"We found these beasts everywhere — in the Dark Forest, the Great Forest, the Ridge of King Solaris, everywhere, and in every instance they tried to eliminate us."

Swinkle shook his head, recalling the bad memories he witnessed at the hands of these beasts. Staring into Brother Benjamin's eyes, the young cleric's voice wavered as he continued.

"I defended these beasts, being sure not to allow the atrocities of a few to cloud my judgment of the whole race. Even after my good friend had his arm severed at their bloody hands."

The young cleric paused. "All that changed after we ambushed a convoy of Scynthians on the Arcadian plains. These filthy monsters had dismembered fifteen people – men, women, and children alike. We had to sift through a wagon filled with body parts, only to find a young girl, Larissa, clinging to life under them all.

"The girl had one arm severed and multiple broken bones. I prayed and prayed over her, trying to heal her and hoping that Pious would somehow make things right. As we traveled to Ontario on horseback, I took it upon myself to hold the girl in my arms, where she ultimately died before reaching our destination.

"From that day forward, I cannot treat these beings as equals to our race. I will understand if you feel that this goes against our code, and I will accept the consequences."

Every being seated in the temple felt for Swinkle. Things changed a moment later. In an unprecedented move, Sister Miriam rose from her seat.

Fixing her stare on the young cleric, she said, "You have given unwavering testimony, Brother Swinkle, and I commend you for your actions." The dark-haired woman took her attention away from her fellow Robusites and searched the crowd of seated patrons for an outsider. Her eyes stopped on Harrison.

"Young man," she called, "please stand."

The young warrior's eyes opened wide and his mouth fell agape. He looked toward Tara as he rose, the girl sporting the same stunned expression.

"Yes, Sister Miriam?" Harrison answered, sounding more like a scared student in a strict teacher's class.

"Brother Swinkle has spun a very elaborate tale, one that is full of promise and truth, but I need to know from you if what he said truly transpired."

Harrison did not hesitate to answer the high priestess. "Every word that Swinkle has spoken did indeed happen." The young warrior seized this opportunity to further back up his friend's words. "And, he made sure that we did the right thing every step of the way.

"Many times Swinkle stopped us before we did something that we would regret later. He pointed out the possible consequences of our intended actions, forcing us to rethink our strategies many times." The young warrior nodded to his friend.

"We didn't always agree with what he said, but that young man stood by his word, never wavering. And he healed our wounds and buried our fallen friends along the way." Harrison lowered his head. "Most important of all, he helped me lay my twin brother to rest and to deal with his loss."

Sister Miriam smiled and appeared impressed with Harrison's remarks. "I can feel the love you have for your friend. Is your cause as dear to you?"

"Reuniting this land is of the utmost importance, and possessing this treasure will assist everyone. That is why we came here today, and that is why Swinkle took the actions that he did."

The high priestess pointed at Harrison, then motioned for him to sit back down. The young warrior obliged.

The raven-haired woman brought her gaze back to Swinkle. "My brother, your testimony today is in keeping with the teachings of Pious. However, you have taken unprecedented liberties by aligning yourself with a band of weapon-wielding warriors." Sister Miriam paused, the tension building within the temple with every passing second.

"My final verdict is this: we will allow you to continue your two-year mission of goodwill with these men. Their cause, though chaotic, is noble and not misguided, and because of that, we will join them."

A huge smile stretched across Swinkle's face upon hearing Sister Miriam's last statement. The high priestess was not finished, though.

Pointing at the young cleric, she said, "However, I hold you personally responsible for all the actions this group performs. You must provide guidance, preach the teachings of Pious, and be sure that your journey does not stray into the world of death, destruction, and despair."

Sister Miriam held her stare for a final second. "We shall meet in my chambers, along with the other high priests, and go over the finer details of your plan." The cloaked woman raised her voice for all to hear. "This council is adjourned. Everyone may go back to their duties."

Upon hearing their leader's last command, all the robed figures began to evacuate the temple, leaving Harrison and his friends behind. The young warrior wasted no time in seeking out his good friend.

Swinkle stepped down from his raised platform, only to receive a big hug from Harrison who picked him clear off the ground. "You did it, Swinkle!" he exclaimed, laughing.

The young cleric also felt the joy, but knew he had to restrain his feelings more so than Harrison. "Your words sealed my fate. Thank you."

Harrison put Swinkle back on the ground. "You really did it all yourself." A throat-clearing sound stopped the young warrior from adding more to his thoughts.

"Follow us," said Sister Miriam, along with the other members of the high council. The clerics brought Harrison and his friends away from the temple's main area and through a doorway that led to an enclosed courtyard.

The young warrior scanned the general vicinity, noticing yet another circular sanctuary. The ivy-covered stone walls mimicked the ones found in the temple, while evenly-spaced trees provided ample shade for all. The roofless enclosure sat no more than fifteen people, and acting before being told, Harrison ordered his soldiers to remain outside the sacred area.

Sister Miriam gestured toward the many soft mats that lay on the grassy flooring. Harrison guided Tara to one of the oversized pillows, while everyone else found a mat to their liking and took a seat.

Brother Lester placed a couple of logs into the fire pit that rested in the middle of the circle. He then added a fine powder to the wood before lighting the fire. Within seconds, the heavy smell of incense filled the area.

The high priestess, sitting cross-legged, looked in the young warrior's direction. "Now that your friend has passed his test, what do you expect Robus to contribute to your master scheme?"

Harrison took care in choosing his words. The young warrior knew that the clerics detested warfare and his new journey might be full of just that. "Trying to reunite the land will be a daunting task and we wish all of the peoples in the land to participate. The ancient kings relayed that message to us and provided direction via an ancient manuscript. It's our hope that you will provide us with clerics to aid our cause."

Sister Memnok spoke next. "Will our people be put in harm's way?"

Harrison drew a heavy sigh. "I can't say that they won't. We're all hoping that the bloodshed will be kept to a minimum."

"So there will be warfare?" continued the fair-haired woman's questioning.

The young warrior shrugged. "I have to believe there will be."

Harrison knew that he had initiated the talks about toppling Concur, but felt that mentioning those plans now would jeopardize the support from Robus.

"We all need to sacrifice," said Sister Miriam. "It would be foolish to believe that everyone would agree to reunite the land under your terms, and that none would fight to keep things as they are.

"That said we all understand what must be done. Robus will allow twenty clerics to join your cause, but I stress this; my people will not fight for you, but they will aid in helping those who are hurt and the ones that need guidance. And, if your noble journey turns into a crusade of evil, our clerics will not provide any more assistance and will return home."

The high priestess turned to address Swinkle. "Brother, I am directing you to personally assign your people their duties. I trust your judgment and believe that you will do the right thing."

The young cleric, though very happy with his new position, tried not to smile. "Thank you, Sister Miriam. I will not let you down." Swinkle then took it upon himself to relate what Robus would receive from the great Treasure.

"In return for Robus's support, there are several ancient scrolls that will be given to our village. And there is a messenger falcon that will remain behind. I'll show that to you later."

Harrison waited for Swinkle to finish before speaking. Addressing Sister Miriam again, he said, "I guess that settles it then. Before we can leave, we would like you to sign this treaty with us as a symbol of Robus's allegiance to the land."

The young warrior retrieved an ivory tube from his backpack, uncorked the stopper, and let the parchment fall into his hand. He then passed the scroll to the high priestess.

"Where did this agreement come from?" asked Miriam, raising an eyebrow. "Did you create this on your own?"

"No," said Harrison. "The ancient kings gave us this scroll to share between all villages. It was part of the great Treasure."

Satisfied with the young warrior's answer, Sister Miriam accepted the land's new treaty. After reading its contents, she used a quill pen to sign the parchment.

Harrison took his cue to add his signature to the agreement as well, but before he could pen his name to the scroll, he felt a tug on his arm. The young warrior swiveled his head to find Tara gazing at him.

Crinkling his brow, he asked, "Is there something wrong?"

Tara shook her head, then placed an object in the young warrior's hand. Harrison opened his palm to find a handmade seal. Making a closer examination of the object, he found that it depicted an image of a dove.

Harrison locked his gaze on his mate, understanding the seal's hidden meaning. "Where did you get this?"

"I bought the necessary pieces when I took in Aegeus's sights with Philius, then created the outline of a dove, just like the one your mother gave to you," said Tara, smiling. "I thought you might want to use it when signing important documents like this one."

"This was so thoughtful," said the young warrior. He leaned over and kissed the maiden on the cheek. "Thank you so much." Tara beamed.

Harrison brought his attention back to Miriam. "I'm sorry for the interruption."

"Your friend has made a wonderful gesture," she said, smiling.

"More than you know," responded the young warrior. He then signed his name to the treaty and affixed his newly acquired personal seal. With the ceremony complete, Harrison had officially secured Robus's commitment.

"And one last thing," he said. "Robus will need to nominate a representative for the Legion of Knighthood."

The high priestess did not hesitate with her nomination. "I will represent Robus and partake in all proceedings of this council."

Changing the subject, she said, "I suggest that you remain in our village for the night so that we can prepare our monks for their journey. Brother Swinkle will see to it that you are given everything you need for your stay."

The young warrior nodded. "Thank you, Sister." The clerics rose from their seats, followed by Harrison and his friends, and left the sanctuary behind.

As the parties departed, Murdock approached Harrison. Under his breath he said, "Twenty clerics and no weapons?" Murdock jerked his thumb in Swinkle's direction. "And I thought watching over him was a treat."

"We're going to protect them, too?" asked the ranger.

"I'm sure they can handle themselves," said Harrison. "But to answer your question, yes, we'll watch over them in times of battle."

Murdock shook his head, visibly agitated. The ranger glanced about the area and found nothing but circular residences and the religious site.

"What do you suppose we do tonight?" he asked.

Harrison smirked. "I hope you brought your own ale. I don't think you'll find a suitable drinking establishment here."

The ranger scowled, realizing that neither he nor Pondle had bothered to fill their tankards with alcohol. Murdock then gestured to the thief. "Let's go, Pondle. We might as well settle in with the troops tonight."

The young warrior agreed. "Keep them away from the main part of this village. I don't think the clerics appreciate all the armor and weaponry."

"Fine with me," said the ranger. With that, Murdock and Pondle left the small group and guided the platoon of men away from the center of town.

Harrison brought his attention back to Swinkle. "Now that they've gone, what shall we do?"

A smile graced the young cleric's face. "I want to show all of you something."

Swinkle escorted Harrison, Tara, and Gelderand through the reclusive cloister, away from the quaint village and toward a marvelous view. Harrison held Tara's hand as the small group left the lightly wooded area and walked through a grassy field that overlooked the Serpent's Sea.

"Look at this view!" exclaimed the young warrior, staring in marvel at the endless blue water. "I've never seen anything like this before!"

Tara stopped in her tracks, squeezing Harrison's hand tighter. "That's close enough for me!" The young couple stood about twenty feet from Robus's most revered landmark.

"Don't worry, Tara, I won't let go of you!" said Harrison.

The young warrior craned his neck forward in an attempt to see over the steep cliff that loomed before them. Everyone could now hear the sound of waves pounding the rocks below.

"Swinkle," said Gelderand, also concerned at the group's proximity to the drop, "how far down does the slope go?" Unbeknownst to himself, he clutched the orange tabby a little tighter to his chest.

"About five hundred feet," said the young cleric, watching Lance carefully inspect the ledge. "Many times I would come here to pray and meditate. It is a most sacred place to me."

"I can understand why," said Harrison, keeping a careful eye on Lance. "Thank you for bringing us here." He then turned and focused on his friend in earnest.

A prideful smile stretched across the young warrior's face. "I just want you to know how proud I am of you today. You really came through for us, but most importantly, you came through for yourself."

"You did such a good job," added Tara.

Swinkle flashed a sheepish smile. "I have prepared my whole life for this day. Every cleric here knows that they must address the high priests at some point in their life. I suppose my time came earlier than expected."

"Well, you were more prepared than I ever would've been," said Harrison. The young warrior then returned his gaze out at the open sea. His demeanor changed, becoming much more serious.

"Swinkle, will your people be able to handle the rigors of trekking through the countryside?" asked Harrison.

"We might not look like a physical bunch, but we can handle our own in the wilderness."

The young warrior turned his head and focused on his friend. "How about during the heat of battle?"

Harrison knew Swinkle's reluctance in agreeing with many of their battle plans in the past and wanted to be sure that he could count on the clerics who would be journeying with them.

"I will counsel them in what to expect on this trip."

"I'm sure there'll be some decisions made that go against your core beliefs."

"I know," said Swinkle with assurance. "I will make sure that they are well prepared."

Harrison gazed out at the sea again. "Good. We should find a place to settle in. We'll be leaving in the morning."

Swinkle, along with the others, let their gaze linger a moment longer before leaving the beautiful vista. A short time later, the small group followed their cleric friend and settled in for their one night stay in Robus.

CHAPTER 8

Harrison felt someone watching him, causing him to stir from a sound sleep. Opening his eyes, he found Tara staring back at him.

"Good morning," she said, a smile stretching across her face, happy to see him awake.

The young warrior leaned over from his cot, kissing the maiden. "How long have you been watching me?"

"Long enough to know that you talk in your sleep," she said with a giggle.

Harrison frowned. "No, I don't!"

"Yes, you do!" said the young girl, trying to keep her voice low.

The young warrior squinted, continuing to play his mate's game. "No, I don't!"

"Yes, you do!" shouted a voice from the other side of the room. Gelderand, lying in his own bed with his back turned away from the couple, pulled the covers up to his chin.

Harrison and Tara allowed the older man's comment to linger for a moment before breaking out into laughter. The mage sat up, crossed his arms across his chest and said, "I didn't come along this journey to baby sit! I suppose it is time for us all to rise for the day."

Gelderand rose from his bed, stretched, then started to go through his belongings. Harrison took the older man's actions as his cue to start his day as well.

In a whisper, he said to Tara, "Next time we'll have a place of our own; I promise."

"Promise?" whispered Tara back, showing him her white, flawless teeth.

Tara's smile highlighted her perfect, high cheekbones. The young maiden's intense beauty stunned Harrison, melting his heart as he stared into her eyes. It took all the restraint within the young warrior's body not to jump in bed with Tara and release his passion. In lieu of the circumstances, he thought of the next best thing, leaning over and kissing her again.

Gathering himself, he said, "Let's get up." The young couple rose from their respective beds and began readying themselves for their journey back to Aegeus.

The platoon of warriors, clerics, and adventurers left the city of Robus behind and trekked to Aegeus without incidence for the next three days. Once in town, Harrison gathered the fighters he had obtained from Troy's army and advanced to the Fighter's Guild. The young warrior sought Brendan Brigade and introduced the Robusite clerics to the decorated warrior.

After the introductions, the older warrior said, "I was beginning to wonder if you were ever coming back."

"We had a very trying time convincing the high clerics of the worthiness of our quest," said the young warrior. "At times I didn't think they'd accept our offer."

Brendan stared at the twenty robe-clad clerics. "What skills can they offer us?"

Harrison took a subtle look to the religious folk as well. "If they're anything like Swinkle, they can heal wounds, provide sanctuaries, and give counsel to anyone who might need it."

The older warrior raised an eyebrow. "Provide counsel? Our warriors won't crack under pressure."

"Maybe not ours, but who knows what the other towns and villages have to offer."

Brendan nodded once. "Good point." Gesturing with his sword, he continued, "Let's prepare to leave."

"I'll get everyone together. We can start our trek to Argos whenever you're ready." Harrison paused, then said, "I feel that we should equip ourselves with our portion of the Treasure."

Brendan squinted slightly, asking, "What will that prove?"

"Showing off the new armor and weapons will only entice the Argosians to join our cause," said the young warrior. "I know

I'd want to unite with them if they gave us the treasures we're going to offer them."

The decorated leader pondered the young warrior's opinion and with a subtle nod said, "Equip the army as you see fit, but don't overdo it. We don't want to create the perception that we're gloating."

Harrison summoned his friends, then went about the task of equipping the group. After the men supplied the soldiers with magically enhanced body armor and weapons, they went about resupplying themselves with updated equipment.

The young warrior replaced his own tattered chain-mail armor with a stronger, lighter, banded-mail body covering. When done with that chore, he rummaged through the scores of weaponry.

Murdock watched Harrison pick up a sword or axe, examine it, then place it back into the pile. "Are you really going to take something new?"

The young warrior held up his battle-axe, inspecting the scratches, chips, and gouges that littered the weapon's blade and hilt. He recalled the repeated blows he had inflicted on countless enemies, each one responsible for creating the marks on his weapon.

"Maybe I'll just sharpen the blade," he said with a smile.

"I didn't think you'd replace that axe," said the ranger. "I'm taking a couple of quivers of arrows." Murdock swiveled the container so Harrison could see. "I don't know if they have any special properties, but they're the best constructed arrows I've ever seen."

"What about Pondle?" asked Harrison. "What did he find?"

"Daggers, short swords, light armor, you know, things he likes."

"And I'm sure Gelderand and Swinkle have plenty of magical scriptures to work with."

"You'll have to ask them," said Murdock. "I have no idea how half of that stuff works." The ranger motioned toward the soldiers. "I'll get these guys ready. Find the rest of our party."

Harrison furrowed his brow, realizing that he did not see Swinkle in the immediate area. "Where's Swinkle?"

Murdock shrugged. "Last I saw him, he was with his cleric friends." The ranger then continued his task.

Harrison nodded, then went about gathering Gelderand and Tara, who had spent the time filling their backpacks with parchments and scrolls. The young warrior found his mate on one knee near a chest filled with ancient manuscripts.

Bending over to inspect the loot, Harrison placed a light caress on Tara's back, saying, "What are you bringing?"

Tara smiled upon seeing him, then said, "I'm just gathering a couple of scrolls that my uncle wanted for our trip." The young maiden then nodded toward the man ten feet behind the couple. "Take a look at what my uncle's doing."

Harrison turned in the mage's direction and found the older man holding his staff out in front and away from his body. Bringing the rod up to eye level, the magician inspected the object's knotty grain. Curious, he approached Gelderand.

"Find anything interesting?"

The mage had a confused look on his face. His brow crinkled, he said, "I think this is a very powerful item, but I am a little perturbed that I have not determined how to use it just yet."

"We'll have plenty of time on our journey to figure that out," said the young warrior. "Come on, it's time to go."

Harrison and his friends joined Murdock, Pondle, and their soldiers. Lance darted about the groups, making his presence felt in his own way. Just then, Swinkle led the collection of monks to the forefront.

"My people are ready for their journey," said the young cleric.

Harrison rested a hand on Swinkle's shoulder, smiling in the process. "You'll be a great leader."

Swinkle sighed. "I hope it does not become a burden."

"Remember what our cause is all about and it won't be."

Harrison then sought Brendan to alert him that the convoy was ready to leave. The decorated warrior gave last minute instructions to his men staying at the Fighter's Guild, then joined the young warrior and his friends.

Brendan checked the ranks of soldiers, finding scouts, fighters, the Robusite clerics, and — Tara. Keeping his gaze fixed on the girl, he muttered to Harrison, "Is it a good idea to take her with us?"

"Absolutely! I want her with us when we visit all the villages of the land," replied the younger man.

"She's your sole responsibility, Harrison." The elder warrior raised an eyebrow, making his point. "Just remember that." He then assumed his position in the ranks.

The young warrior took Brendan's message to heart and remained near Tara. With everyone set to leave, the growing convoy began their journey from Aegeus.

The large group of adventurers spent many hours traveling through the lightly wooded forest, the bright sunshine creating a pleasurable trek. Harrison gazed about the landscape, taking in the pristine scenery. Birch trees, with their white trunks and small deciduous leaves, littered the countryside. Peering to the left he watched Lance lap water from a clear stream before an image blocked his view.

Tara smiled, her blonde hair radiant in the sunlight. "When did you visit Argos last?"

"A long time ago," said the young warrior, maintaining his march to Aegeus's twin. "I was a young boy then."

A disturbing thought entered Harrison's mind and his demeanor turned dour. Gauging the length of time the group had traveled, he figured that they had ventured about halfway to Argos – the same distance his parents had trekked before the Scynthians surprised and killed them.

Tara noticed the sudden change in the young warrior's mood. "Are you all right?"

Unaware of his reactions, Harrison began to sweat and clenched his jaw. "This is where it happened," he said, tightening his grip on the hilt of his battle-axe.

"What happened?" asked the young girl.

Harrison felt the adrenaline course through his body. "They killed them here!"

Tara took a cautious step toward the young warrior, confused. "Killed who here?" She touched Harrison's bicep, causing him to flinch and pull away.

"My mother and father!" Harrison swung his head with wild abandon, looking for the beasts that murdered his beloved parents. "This is the place!"

The young warrior then stared into Tara's nervous blue eyes. "I'll never let them get you!"

Swinkle and Gelderand noticed Harrison's strange antics. "Is everything all right?" asked the cleric. Swinkle took a closer look at his friend, noticing his sweat-covered body.

"Harrison?" asked Swinkle, beginning to worry.

The young warrior rubbed his bicep. "They're here!"

Swinkle knew firsthand what his friend meant as he watched him knead his arm, recalling how the beasts had severed that very limb in a brutal ceremony. The holy man looked ahead at the other men in the platoon, but found them marching along, oblivious to Harrison's antics. He even noticed Lance trotting in the distance, playing with one of the soldiers.

Swinkle stared into Harrison's eyes, and with a forceful voice, he said, "There are no Scynthians here."

Gelderand, using his new staff for balance, walked over to Tara and guided her away from the young warrior. Using a soft, gentle approach, he said, "Harrison, you are recalling a very traumatic moment from your childhood."

The warrior took his gaze to the magician, his breath becoming heavy, yet he did not say a word.

With a soothing voice, the mage continued, "Pull yourself together, son. People will be looking up to you, and episodes like this will make it difficult for others to follow your lead."

The young warrior took his gaze from Gelderand to Swinkle, then to Tara. He read the looks of worry and concern on their faces, and knew he needed to put this incident behind him — now.

Channeling the teachings from the Fighter's Guild, Harrison recalled how to calm himself in a tense situation. Using deep cleansing breaths, he cast the image of Scynthians butchering his parents and their friends out of his mind. He then focused on Tara.

The poor girl had witnessed the whole scene and now stood trembling before him. Caressing her hands, he looked deep into her soul. "No one will ever harm you. I make that my solemn vow to you."

Tears welled up in Tara's eyes, and she pulled the young warrior close to her. "What did those beasts do to you?"

"I'll be all right," Harrison said, trying to put her at ease and the situation behind him. "We must keep moving."

"No!" Tara moved away. "I want to know, what did those beasts do to you?"

Harrison shook his head, lowering his gaze to the ground. "They murdered my parents, slaughtered innocent people, and cut off my arm." The young warrior lifted his head. "I hate them with all my soul."

Tara felt his deep, repressed pain. Nodding, she said, "That's more like it. I need to know how you feel, no secrets. I can help you." She again held Harrison's arm. "Now we can go."

Before the pair began their march, Swinkle mumbled a prayer. "I sense an aura; pain, anguish, violence. Your parents indeed perished here."

Harrison took a deep breath, but continued to stare forward. "I have unfinished business to take care of, but not today. We must save our people first."

The young cleric agreed. "There's much to do."

"Beginning with Argos, and we're almost there." Harrison gestured for his friends to quicken their pace and catch up with the soldiers around them.

Satisfied with his friends' movements, the young warrior thought back to his parents. Saying a silent prayer to himself, he promised to never forget his loved ones or to forgive the race that took them away from him.

Argos, like its sister city, benefited from resting at the end of a large inland bay. Unlike Aegeus, Argos sat many miles away from the Serpent's Sea, nestled deep in the wilderness. Boats and ships would follow the natural waterway and sail far inland, where traders would sell their wares that they had uncovered on their adventures through the Valkaline and Gammorian forests.

Harrison's convoy had marched two miles shy of the city before they encountered the first scouts of the Argosian army. The two towns had shared a common alliance for centuries, and when the sentries from Argos saw the men from Aegeus with their flags lowered, they knew that diplomatic missionaries had trekked to their town.

Brendan Brigade motioned for Harrison and his group to join him at the head of the convoy. Murdock and Pondle had already recalled the advanced scouts and stood by the Aegean warrior's side.

The young warrior escorted Tara, Gelderand, and Swinkle to the older fighter's position. Lance stayed close to Harrison, while Rufus remained tucked in the mage's pack for safety.

Harrison focused on the magician. "Gelderand, I think it would be best if you stayed close to Tara." The young warrior gazed at the girl, nodding at her. She obliged, knowing the fighters had to handle the situation now.

"I'll let you know what's happening later," Harrison promised her.

"They're waiting for you," answered Tara, shifting her eyes between the awaiting men and Harrison. The young warrior smiled, then joined the other soldiers.

"Nothing out of the ordinary," said Brendan to Harrison, who nodded in concurrence.

Though he did not expect any surprises on this short trip, Harrison had learned at the Fighter's Guild to never let your guard down. Terrible outcomes can happen under otherwise calm situations.

"Let's proceed with caution," said the young warrior.

The Argosian men informed the Aegeans that they would be escorted into the city, and a short trek later the small platoon entered the waterfront village of Argos.

The young warrior looked ahead, into the town, past his men and the Argosian guardians, and to the contingent of soldiers who waited on horseback some twenty yards away. Octavius and Caidan Forge, the decorated warrior brothers from Argos, sat on their steeds, flanked on either side by ten armored men also perched on large war horses. After a brief moment, the two leaders dismounted and strolled toward the Aegeans.

Harrison's brow furrowed. "Brendan, you know these men better than I," started the young warrior. "Why don't you take the lead?"

"How noble of you," said Brendan with a wry smile. An oversized bumble bee danced about the older warrior, who swatted it away. "Don't let this leadership thing go to your head."

Harrison felt foolish. He knew he needed to assert himself as a leader, but giving orders to a man of Brendan's stature broke lines of protocol.

"I'm sorry, Brendan, I was just ..."

The older warrior raised his palm to his former pupil. "There's no need to apologize. Just don't forget who trained you in the past."

Harrison flashed Brendan a sheepish grin. "I won't."

"Follow my lead." The older warrior spoke from the side of his mouth in a hushed tone. "And keep your guard up without looking like you're keeping your guard up."

Harrison frowned. "What do you mean?"

"You'll see. Just don't start an unnecessary fight."

Brendan approached the Forge brothers, Harrison following close behind. The young warrior waved his close friends over as well.

Gelderand handed his pack to Tara, Rufus meowing from inside, unsure of the situation. The mage then gestured for Lance to remain close to the young maiden. The dog barked once in affirmation and raced to the girl's side. Tara patted Lance on the head, watching the men with anxious eyes. The four adventurers then advanced past their lead scouts and joined the small group.

Brendan led Harrison and his friends to the forefront of the platoon. "Octavius, Caidan," said the older warrior, extending his hand. "It's always a pleasure."

Octavius, the older of the Forge brothers, took Brendan's hand and gave it a firm shake. Cold blue eyes that burrowed deep under his brows and a face almost hidden behind a thick brown beard searched for a reason for his counterpart's surprise visit.

"Indeed, a pleasure it is," responded the Argosian leader. Without warning, Octavius unsheathed his broad sword and, with a roar, took both hands and swung it toward Brendan's midsection.

The Aegean appeared to anticipate his counterpart's action, deflecting the attempted blow with ease. Brendan then held his ground in a defensive posture. Octavius flailed again, hacking at the Aegean warrior, but not doing him any harm.

Harrison stood wide-eyed, shocked at the sudden act of violence from this sword-wielding maniac. In one smooth motion, he slung his battle-axe into his hands and prepared to help his leader.

Caidan Forge, standing behind his brother and watching the action, reacted to Harrison's movement. Unsheathing a sword of his own, he pointed the weapon at the young warrior and shouted, "Back down!"

Harrison recalled Brendan's words of advice and instead of joining the melee he brandished his weapon and stood his ground.

Octavius gave the junior fighters little heed; instead he focused on Brendan once again. He took another wild swing at the Aegean's head, which the warrior deflected, before slashing toward the fighter's legs. Brendan again prevented the weapon from hitting his body, but did not anticipate Octavius's next move.

The Argosian leader feigned a blow to the midsection, causing Brendan to lower his blade for protection. In an odd maneuver, Octavius dropped his weapon and threw a punch aimed at Brendan's head. His fist smacked Brendan's chin, snapping his opponent's head to the side and dropping the Aegean to one knee.

His foe defeated, Octavius offered a hand of assistance. "It's been a long time, my old friend."

The Aegean's jaw throbbed and he spit blood to the ground. Taking Octavius's hand, he allowed his counterpart to pull him up. "A pleasure, as usual." Brendan rubbed his chin, paying attention to one tooth in particular.

"I think you've loosened one of them."

"Sorry about that, Brendan, but you know how I am." A wide smile stretched across the Argosian's face.

Brendan nodded and smirked at the comment, then turned his attention to Octavius's younger brother. "Caidan," he said with a smile as he sheathed his sword. The younger Forge took a step toward the Aegean, offering his hand, which Brendan received.

Turning to Harrison and his friends, Brendan said, "Ocatvius, Caidan, this is Harrison Cross and his band of advisors."

Harrison, still unsure of the scene that had just transpired before him, lowered his battle-axe and stepped forward, shaking hands as well with the Forge brothers. The young warrior introduced his friends next and, after the pleasantries concluded, turned to Brendan.

"You're probably wondering why we're here," said the elder Aegean warrior.

"The thought had crossed my mind," said Octavius with a slight smile, securing his weaponry. "It's not every day that decorated warriors show up on your doorstep unannounced."

"Why are you here, Brendan?" asked Caidan, his voice deep and rough. Both brothers thrived on battle and had the scars to prove it. "Is Aegeus in some kind of trouble?"

Brendan shook his head repeatedly. "Oh no, on the contrary we're fine. We're here to offer something to you." The older warrior whistled, signaling to the soldiers to bring the cart of treasures forward. "A most precious gift from the town of Aegeus."

Octavius and Caidan glanced at each other, their eyes squinted with uncertainty. "A gift? What do you mean?" asked the older brother.

"These fine men have uncovered the Treasure of the Land," said Brendan, pointing to Harrison and his friends. "They returned the loot to Aegeus, which in turn directed us to Argos."

The Forge brothers took a closer look at the five men who stood with Brendan. Both men knew the legend behind the Treasure, the myths of underground catacombs, clues dispersed throughout the land, and the countless armies that had spent centuries searching for the bounty, all failing. Now, this modest group of men were about to willfully bestow on them a piece of the prize.

"If what you say is true," started Octavius, "why were you sent here?"

"It's part of the unification process," said Harrison, feeling the time was right to speak. "Unifying the land is the ultimate goal of the Treasure. Everything that comes with it leads up to this."

"Unification process? Ultimate goal? What are you talking about?"

"We really should find a place to talk," said Harrison. "I can explain further at that time."

Octavius pointed to the forty-plus Aegean men, the anxious clerics, and the cart full of treasure. "We'll talk now. I won't let you parade through the streets of Argos with all this. My people will look to me for answers and I want to know your intentions."

Over the course of the next fifteen minutes, Harrison explained in detail how he and his friends found the Treasure of the Land, their journey through the countryside to obtain the Talisman of Unification, the teachings of the ancient kings, and their quest to unite humanity. The young warrior's perseverance and tenacity impressed the Forge brothers, as he left no element of his tale untold.

Harrison finished his story with the following. "We'll need to plan a strategy to take down Lord Hammer and Concur."

Octavius smiled. "I've wanted to bring that bastard to his knees for years now. You won't have to convince us to join you for that battle."

"Does that mean you'll help us?"

Octavius glanced at his brother, who nodded his approval. "The people of Argos have always helped their Aegean brethren in times of need. We will join you on your noble quest."

"Fantastic!" exclaimed the young warrior in obvious joy. Harrison knew securing Argos's allegiance was of the utmost importance. Recalling how his brother would formulate meticulous battle plans, he employed the same strategy, saying, "Like I mentioned before, we should map out our route, culminating with the Battle of Concur."

Octavius raised a palm in the young warrior's direction. "Not so fast, Harrison." Squinting, he peered over to the wagon full of loot. "I want to see what you have brought for us first."

The young warrior looked at the horse-drawn cart, noticing that the tarp covering the falcons rippled as they moved beneath it.

"By all means." Harrison gestured to Swinkle. "Bring them their messenger bird."

The young cleric went to the back of the wagon, called for the bird named Argos, then returned with the falcon balancing on his covered forearm. He then presented the bird of prey to Octavius with a wide smile.

The Argosian leader did not share the same enthusiasm. With a scowl, he said, "You ask us for our allegiance and all you give us in return is a bird?"

Harrison motioned toward the bird of prey. "This is no ordinary falcon. Its primary purpose is to relay important messages from Argos to any village in the land. The bird will be most useful in due time."

Octavius did a bad job trying to hide his disappointment. Unsheathing his sword, he pointed it at the falcon. "Be that as it may, but how will this animal help us in battle?"

Harrison shook his head. "It won't." He then gestured for four of his soldiers to bring the rest of Argos's prize. "But this will."

The fighters made multiple trips to the cart, carrying as much weaponry and armor as they could, placing them in front of the Argosian leaders.

Caidan reached down into the pile of weapons in front of him and grasped the hilt of a long sword. Raising the blade to his face, he examined its razor sharp edge, as well as the craftsmanship of the hilt, which was encrusted with fine gemstones.

"This weapon is flawless," he said in awe.

"And there's a magical signature radiating from the sword," added Gelderand, taking it upon himself to further divulge their findings. "Everything we have brought to you is enhanced with magical properties."

Caidan gazed at his brother, a sly smile gracing his face. "You should have shown us these before the bird."

Harrison's face flushed. I should have known that warriors would appreciate weapons and armor more than magic, he thought.

Nodding, the young warrior said, "Perhaps. I'll keep that in mind for the next village we visit."

Octavius, who had squatted to get a better look at his bounty, stared at Harrison from his position. "Are you telling us that every town and village will be getting gifts as prestigious as these?" The older man cocked his head, never removing his fix on the younger fighter.

"Not all aspects of the Treasure of the Land are in the form of weapons and armor." Harrison pointed to the Robusite clerics. "We handed over ancient scrolls to the clerics from Robus."

Octavius glared at the robed figures. "What are we to do with them?"

"They're an asset, trust me, with one of their many strengths being able to heal battle wounds. We'll discuss their responsibilities later." Harrison figured he would have to defend the clerics' role at every step of the campaign.

The Argosian leader returned his gaze to the weapons that lay in front of him, nodding. "I suppose a treasure that had remained so elusive for so long would have unthinkable qualities." Octavius stared at Harrison again. "We'll have more allies than we can count."

"We'll need them if we're going to neutralize Concur."

"You can say that again," said Octavius. "Come, let's work on our strategy."

The leader of Argos waved his men forward to collect the bounty that Harrison's soldiers had spread before them. When they completed that task, the Forge brothers escorted their guests to the town hall. Harrison took the opportunity to introduce Tara, Lance, and Rufus to their new allies, who seemed both surprised and intrigued to see such an unlikely trio as part of a military convoy. Once the group reached the large building, they took no time in beginning their strategy session.

Inside the Grand Hall of Argos, Harrison and his crew, as well as the Forge Brothers, positioned themselves around a large map of the land that they had spread across a sturdy wooden table. The young warrior had detailed their route to the southern villages before Octavius interrupted.

"Why not just take on Concur now? Combining all our men will provide us enough fighters to give Lord Hammer the battle of his life."

Harrison nodded, understanding Octavius's reasoning, but he had thoughts of his own. "That might be true, but imagine the size of the army we can assemble by gaining the allegiance of all the other towns and villages across the countryside. The Treasure of the Land can bring everyone together."

Octavius knew Harrison meant well, but he felt that the young warrior's strategy had its fair share of flaws. Staring at Brendan, he said, "We'll lose our element of surprise. Nigel will hear about our maneuvers and he will prepare for us."

Brendan nodded in concurrence. "I agree, but we'll need as many soldiers as possible. There's no way that we can simply knock those walls down."

"And he will secure them before we step foot in his countryside," added Caidan.

"That's why we have to work from the inside out," said Harrison.

Bewildered, Octavius crinkled his brow. "Work from the inside out? Explain yourself, son."

Harrison recalled his pledge to Meredith, Lord Hammer's woman, that if circumstances arose, he would do everything in his power to liberate her.

"There's a resistance movement within Concur," he said.

The elder Forge sat back, crossing his arms. "I'm sure there's great unrest there, but what makes you think that there's a movement to overthrow Lord Hammer?"

Harrison remembered his imprisonment at the hands of Nigel's men. "When I was there, I was foolish enough to let my guard down, and Lord Hammer's henchmen beat me and tossed me in prison. But I managed to meet Meredith and Thoragaard, and they told me about the Resistance."

Octavius glanced at Caidan before turning his attention to Harrison again. "Thoragaard has been in contact with some of our people. It's funny that you mention his name."

The young warrior frowned. "Funny how?"

"Thoragaard approached us over a year ago, asking for our help. We refused."

"Why didn't you help him?"

Octavius glared at the young warrior. "Were you not imprisoned there? Nigel has an army that would have destroyed us. And, his mage is very powerful as well. Keeping Argos's best interests in mind, we decided to steer clear of Concur at the time."

Harrison nodded in understanding. "The time is right now."

The older warrior agreed. "I'll send a few scouts to our people in the woods. They'll relay Thoragaard our intentions."

"You know where he is?"

Octavius stroked his beard. "Not quite, but he told us what to do if we needed to reach out to him."

The young warrior nodded, showing approval for the Argosian leader's plan, but there was something that he needed to know. "Who are these people of yours you speak about?"

"I'd rather not say." Octavius shifted in his seat. "Having you people here today answers a lot of questions for us."

"How so?"

"We've been keeping a close eye on Concur. In the past two years, Nigel has maneuvered his army all about the countryside, and we kept our forces ready in case of a conflict.

"Now that you've brought Argos a piece of the Treasure of the Land, I can understand his actions."

Harrison finished Octavius's thought. "He was searching for this very treasure. We encountered Nigel in the catacombs, as well as in Cyprus. He's not happy with us."

"You think?" Octavius cocked his head with a slight laugh. "That egomaniac probably has a bounty on your head. This was his treasure, you know, and you took it from him."

Harrison chuckled, having heard that exact statement from Nigel himself. "You can say that again." The young warrior went back to his original question. "So, you're not going to clue me in on your people in the forest?"

Octavius stood firm. "No. They'll seek you out when the time comes. However, they'll set the plan in motion in regards to Concur. I'm sure Thoragaard has a strategy of his own in mind."

Harrison knew where the illusionist would start first. "He'll begin with Meredith. She's the top person in the Resistance."

"Meredith?" Caidan threw his arms wide. "How can Lord Hammer's woman be in any position to overthrow him? He would know her every move."

"That might be true," Harrison wagged a finger in the younger Forge's direction, "but she made sure Thoragaard would set the plans in motion." The young warrior rested his elbows on the table. "We need to get a message to Meredith."

"Well, you can forget Thoragaard," said Octavius. "He's been on the run ever since ... ever since you showed up in Concur!"

Octavius had put the pieces together in his mind, realizing that the mage's disappearance from Concur coincided with Harrison's imprisonment in the same city.

Harrison could read the connection on Octavius's face. "Like I said, Thoragaard will set any plans in motion to overthrow Nigel. But in order to do that from inside Concur, Meredith must be notified. She's the only person who can start the Resistance."

Octavius turned toward Caidan. Both men stared at each other, appearing to share a common thought. Harrison noticed the subtle maneuver.

"What is it?"

Octavius turned to face the young warrior, then pursed his lips and gazed up in thought, stroking his beard once again. "Thoragaard mentioned something that didn't make much sense at the time, but hearing you speak today, I think I might understand what he meant."

Harrison waited anxiously for the Argosian to continue. "He does tend to speak in general terms," said the young warrior.

"Yes, he does," responded Octavius, recalling the frustrations he encountered with the illusionist. "He said something about Meredith needing a new handmaiden when the time came."

"A new handmaiden?" Harrison glanced at Swinkle, both men picturing the sweet young girl, Catherine, who tended to Meredith's every need. "What happened to her old one?"

"How should I know?" said the older warrior with a shrug. "But I think we're missing the point. This new handmaiden can carry an important message to the first lady of Concur."

Harrison's eyes lit up. "An anonymous person would be the perfect cover to get a message to Meredith!" The young warrior then crinkled his brow, taking his gaze to the table. "Who could we get to be Meredith's new servant?"

The Forge brothers both looked in the direction of the blonde girl seated behind the men from Aegeus. Harrison used his own eyes to follow their line of sight, which ended with Tara.

The young warrior spun his head back to the Argosians. "Absolutely not! Tara is not going on a mission such as this! It's way too dangerous!"

"Harrison," started Octavius in a soothing manner, "she's the perfect decoy. No one else in this room fits the description of a female helper, now do they?"

Gelderand pivoted to see his niece. Tara, her blues eyes wide and mouth slightly agape, held one hand to her chest, her breath short, nervous. The mage, quiet until now, twisted back in his chair to voice his protest as well.

"My niece will not be the person for this mission. Pick someone else."

Octavius wrung his hands together, while he pondered who else could take on the proposed assignment. "Though I have some female warriors who could fill the role, they have encountered Concurian soldiers before. They might be recognized."

"Tara's not doing this," said Harrison. There was no wavering in his voice.

Octavius was just about to concede defeat when a soft, yet firm voice spoke from behind the men.

"I'll do it," said Tara, rising from her seat, her heart pounding. "I'll go to Concur and signal the beginning of the Resistance." The young maiden clutched Rufus tighter, unconsciously stoking the cat's little head.

Harrison pivoted in his seat, staring at Tara for a brief moment before getting up and approaching the girl. The young warrior lightly laid his strong hands on her arms.

"Tara, you don't have to do this." The young warrior shook his head, fumbling for words. "We'll find another way."

Tara noted the legitimate concern and worry in his eyes. "My going to Concur makes perfect sense. I've never visited there, no one will know me, and I'll be sure to relay the message to Meredith."

Harrison shook his head. "It's not that easy," he started. "So many things can go wrong."

Gelderand listened to the young couple. "He's right, sweetheart. This is not a mission for you."

"But I can do this, uncle," protested the young girl. Tara peeked around Harrison to get a fix on Octavius. "I'm sure you'll have your soldiers escort me to a rendezvous point, correct?"

Octavius interlaced his fingers, resting his arms on the table. "Um … of course. Our men are very seasoned and know the terrain."

"And they can get you in touch with Thoragaard," added Caidan. "Harrison, we can do this."

The young warrior gazed deep into Tara's blue eyes. He could read the concern on her face and feel the anxiety course through her, but he also perceived an undeniable sense of purpose.

"Harrison, let me do this," she whispered with conviction.

The young warrior maintained his fix on her, and against his better judgment, said, "I want one of my close friends to accompany Tara to Concur."

Octavius knew the sensitivity of the situation and did his best to reason with the young warrior. "Harrison, you said that all of you went to Concur. You all might be recognized."

Harrison's head dropped, agreeing with the older warrior without saying a word. Just then, another person voiced an opinion.

"I did not accompany you when you went to Concur," said Gelderand. "I'll take her to Lord Hammer's city and escort her into the metropolis as my daughter."

"That won't work," said Octavius. "It's not believable."

Harrison, his head still hung low, suggested, "We need someone my age to act as her husband. They can pretend to be a young couple looking for work."

The elder Forge nodded. "That sounds better. Do you have anyone in mind?"

While the young warrior racked his brain in thought, he noticed a person shuffle closer out of the corner of his eye.

"Sir, I will take on this mission for you," said the young man.

Harrison looked up and focused on one of the soldiers from Troy's army. The young warrior recognized the fighter, but realized that he did not know the boy's name.

"That is noble of you," said Harrison. "This will be the most important mission of your life. Failure is not an option."

"Harrison, you cannot be seriously considering this?" Gelderand stared at the young warrior. The mage shifted his focus to his niece. "Tara?"

"Uncle, I can do this." Tara moved away from Harrison and approached the magician. "We won't stay in Concur a second longer than we have to."

"That's not the point," said the mage. "This mission is very dangerous. You could get hurt or worse."

The young soldier hoped to put the older man at ease. "Sir, your niece will never be out of my sight; that I promise you. She'll be safe with me."

Gelderand squinted. "What is your name?"

"Justin Wolfskehl, sir."

"Justin, Tara is no trinket you need to keep an eye on. She is a living, breathing treasure that cannot be lost." Gelderand pointed a finger in the young fighter's face. "How do you intend to battle Concurian soldiers?"

Octavius intervened before the young man could answer. "Thoragaard must harbor those answers. We need to escort these two to him."

Harrison looked at Tara, then turned to his canine friend. "Lance, come here, boy." The small dog quickly scampered to his master's side. "He'll go with you, for protection."

Tara smiled. Softly, she said, "He doesn't have to come. I'll be all right."

"Lance won't let anything happen to the ones he loves, just like me."

The maiden's eyes watered at Harrison's last comment. "I'll take good care of him for you."

The young warrior, sensing that the discussion was over, said in a loud voice, "I'll go along with this plan, but I don't like it one bit."

Then he whispered to Tara, "We'll talk later, but I need to finalize things with these men now."

The young maiden nodded, knowing she would have Harrison's undivided attention after this important meeting. The girl kissed him on the cheek, then returned to her seat.

Harrison let his stare linger on his mate for another long second before turning to face the Forge brothers.

"We'll discuss this part of the mission in more detail later." Changing the subject, he said, "Getting back to our original plan, I think the first town we need to visit is Balta, and we'll proceed along the coastline until we reach Polaris."

"That seems the most prudent course of action." Octavius pointed to Harrison. "Your group will go back to Aegeus where you'll sail a vessel along the coast to Balta. March to each village from there."

The young warrior cocked his head, squinting. "My group? What about you and your men?"

Harrison had agreed that they could not simply march with their army from Argos through the Concurian countryside without being seen, but he did not envision embarking on this journey alone.

Octavius read the look of confusion on the faces of the Aegeans. "We need to ready an attack on Concur from here. Surely you must understand that. Right, Brendan?"

"When Harrison concludes with his goodwill mission, he should have quite a large army advancing from the south. And we'll have a combined force of soldiers from Argos and Aegeus from the north."

Brendan stroked his moustache, strategic battle plans racing through his mind. "Attacking from two fronts instead of one will force Nigel to make hard decisions." The older Aegean nodded in agreement. "I like this tactic."

Harrison had listened to the more experienced leaders converse, but the time had come to add his comments. "Who's going to lead this force from Aegeus if we're heading down the coast?"

His mentor from the Fighter's Guild pivoted to face him. "I will. You will take your men on the ship and visit the coastal towns."

The young warrior, still reeling from the news that Tara would be embarking on a mission into the heart of the enemy's stronghold, could not believe his ears.

"I figured that we would all go on this mission, to show the other villages of our commitment to each other and the unification of the land."

Brendan closed his eyes, raised his palms to the young man, and slowly nodded once. "Your noble mission will not go for naught." The older warrior fixed his gaze on his one-time pupil.

"Harrison, you have an incredible amount of goodwill and righteousness. That alone, and the signatures from Aegeus, Argos, and Robus on the Unification Treaty should be more than enough to persuade the others to join our cause."

Harrison took Brendan's comments to heart. He had hoped that the others would notice all his sacrifices and that validation came from one of Aegeus's finest leaders.

The young warrior examined the faces of his closest friends. Everyone had heard Ocatvius's rationale for sending troops to the north while letting Harrison handle the goodwill mission. Murdock nodded in the young warrior's direction, signaling what he felt they should do.

Harrison, satisfied with all of the explanations, said, "I suppose that this course of action is best for all parties involved."

"It is, Harrison," said Brendan. "All will work out well." The elder Aegean took his gaze about the room. "Are we all in agreement?" Everyone nodded in concurrence.

"The plan is approved," said Brendan to the elder Forge.

"Good," said Octavius. Pointing to Harrison, he said, "You should leave in the morning for Aegeus, but we'll spend the rest of today going over the finer details of both plans."

"Agreed." Before anyone could leave, Harrison added, "You also need to appoint someone from Argos to be part of the Legion of Knighthood."

"What?" shouted Octavius, thinking that the statement had just popped into Harrison's head.

"Part of the ancient kings' instructions was to reassemble the Legion of Knighthood," said the young warrior. "Aegeus and Robus have nominated people; Argos must do the same."

"I nominate Caidan," said the elder Forge, never giving another person a second thought. "He deserves this honor and he will handle his responsibilities well."

Caidan stared wide-eyed at his brother, his mouth open, but remaining speechless. Regaining his composure, he said, "This is a monumental honor, my brother."

"Argos deserves someone like you to represent them. I know you won't let them down." Octavius gripped his sibling's shoulder, giving it a firm squeeze.

The Argosian leader then turned his attention to Harrison and his friends. "You and your men are probably hungry. Let's find some food and good drink. This is a very glorious day in both of our towns' history; we should celebrate."

"I couldn't agree more," said Harrison who glanced at his friends, witnessing their look of contentment as well. "Let's join these fine men and get something good to eat."

While the group of decorated warriors left the confines of the Great Hall, Harrison turned his attention once again to Tara.

"I need to discuss the finer details of your mission with the Forge brothers," he said, before taking his hand and lifting her chin. "I can't bear the thought of losing you."

Tara stood tall. "You won't." She then reached up and gave him a long kiss. "We'll all succeed, for the benefit of everyone."

Harrison smiled, recognizing the sentiment he had preached over and over again. Still holding his beloved, he responded, "That we will."

A moment later, they separated with Harrison saying, "Let's join the others." The young couple then held hands, proceeded out of the Great Hall of Argos, and followed their hosts for a well-deserved meal.

CHAPTER 9

¤

Harrison, Gelderand, and the Forge brothers mapped out their strategy for Tara and Justin, working until late into the night. The young warrior agreed that a small convoy of Octavius's men would escort the couple, along with Lance, to an undisclosed meeting place. From that point, the Argosian men would hand over the faux married couple to undercover scouts, who would then lead them to Thoragaard.

In the morning, Harrison and Gelderand counseled Tara and Justin during breakfast on the particulars of their mission, informing them that no one but Meredith should hear what they had revealed to them. The young maiden listened with great intent as her man explained in meticulous detail what to say to Concur's First Lady. Harrison further explained that Thoragaard harbored the remaining details of their mission, which he alone would relay to them, including a contingency plan if things happened to go wrong. Satisfied that Tara fully understood her assignment, the small group enjoyed their fresh food in what would be their last meal together for quite some time.

Later that morning, Harrison stood outside the Great Hall of Argos, along with Octavius and Caidan, his friends, and about one hundred combined Aegean and Argosian soldiers. More on his mind, though, were the people congregated to his right.

A few of Octavius's soldiers were conversing with Tara and Justin. Harrison squinted, trying to overhear their conversation, but he stood too far away. A deep voice interrupted his thoughts.

"It looks like you're ready to start your trek back to Aegeus," said the elder Forge. Octavius had noticed the young warrior's obvious concern directed toward Tara.

"Go talk to her, Harrison," he said. "Put your mind at ease."

The young warrior fastened the straps on his backpack, nodding in the process. Without saying a word, he approached the group of twelve people.

"Are you ready to go?" asked Harrison toward one of the scouts.

"Yes, sir, we were just going over the final details of our mission."

Harrison nodded his approval. "Might I have a word with these two?" he asked, pointing to Tara and Justin.

"Of course. We'll be leaving when you finish." With that last statement, the young fighter joined his fellow soldiers.

Turning his attention to Tara and Justin, Harrison said, "I can't tell you how important it is to do everything these men say." Facing Justin, the young warrior continued, "I'm putting my trust in you. Don't let Tara leave your sight."

"She won't, sir. You can count on me." Sensing that Harrison wanted a moment alone with Tara, Justin said, "I'm going to check my things one last time. Excuse me."

Harrison and Tara watched Justin walk away, before focusing on each other. The young warrior took a step closer.

"Deep down, I know you can do this, but I won't stop worrying about you until I have you in my arms again."

Tara flashed a nervous smile. "I trust these men, but I'd rather have you escort me to Concur."

Harrison caressed the young maiden's hands. "I wish I could, too." Pulling Tara close, he whispered in her ear, "I'll be thinking about you every second of the day."

"So will I," she whispered back. Tara then pulled back and gazed into Harrison's eyes before reaching up and giving the young warrior a passionate kiss. "I'm going to miss you so much."

"Me, too." Harrison then looked down at the little dog that sat beside Tara. Bending to one knee, the young warrior addressed his faithful friend.

"Make sure nothing happens to her, Lance." Harrison scratched the dog behind his ears. "You need to protect her."

"Yes!" yapped Lance in affirmation.

Harrison stood tall again. "He says you're all set." The couple both let out a nervous laugh. Taking a more serious tone, the young warrior said, "It's time for both of us to go. Do you have everything you need?"

Tara nodded. "Yes, I've checked my things a hundred times."

"And remember, no magic tricks; we don't want you to draw attention to yourself."

Again, the young girl nodded. "I know, I know." Tara hugged Harrison again, then they kissed for the last time before separating.

Harrison noticed tears beginning to well in Tara's eyes. "Be careful," she said.

"Don't worry about me," said the young warrior. "I'll see you again before you know it." Harrison noticed Justin returning.

Clearing his throat, the fighter said, "Sir, we need to leave now."

The young warrior nodded. "So do we." Harrison then leaned over and kissed Tara once again, as tears rolled down her cheeks. "Don't cry; now go."

Justin lightly took the young girl's arm and guided her away to the small group of Argosian soldiers. The men gave her their final instructions, then arranged themselves in their marching formation.

Harrison stood his ground, watching their actions, making sure nothing went wrong. Just before they started to depart, Lance darted over to Harrison.

"Tara. Safe," barked the little dog, before scampering to the young maiden's side.

The young warrior smiled, sensing that Tara's mission had commenced with success. The couple's eyes met a final time, with Harrison giving her a wave good-bye. She waved back, and before too long, the small platoon disappeared from view.

Harrison turned his attention to the large gathering of fighters and soldiers. Gelderand approached the young warrior first, planting his staff in the ground.

Sounding like an anxious father, the mage said, "I'm assuming everything is all right."

"Tara will be fine," said Harrison. "I just wish I could go with her."

Gelderand harbored the same feelings. "Let us just hope that her mission finishes soon. I do not like the fact that she will be in such a hostile city."

"Concur is not as bad as you think," reassured Harrison. "Nigel might be a ruthless leader, but he wouldn't know Tara from any other girl in that place."

"Let's hope so," agreed Gelderand.

"It's time for us to leave as well." The two men then joined the rest of the group before heading back to his hometown.

The growing convoy of united warriors and clerics trekked for two days through the woodlands that separated the two towns. Upon reaching Aegeus, Harrison sought Portheus, who readied the two-vessel fleet for their trip to Balta.

A day and a half later, the two ships anchored off the rocky coast. Six smaller boats left the larger vessels, accompanied with soldiers, treasures, and Harrison's hopes of a unified land.

The young warrior peeked at Swinkle, who nestled the falcon named Balta in his arms. His thoughts then drifted to Tara, just as they had for the past two days and he wondered if she were all right. Of course she is, he convinced himself.

Attempting to keep his woman from occupying his thoughts, Harrison asked the man seated in front of him, "What was the name again of the Baltan leader we're visiting?"

"Nora Leffingwell," said Murdock, maintaining his gaze on the stony shoreline. Turning to face the young warrior, he added, "I've never been here before."

"Neither have I."

Murdock took a more serious tone. "This is our first real test, you know."

Harrison had thought the same thing, ever since they had agreed to head to Balta first. "Aegeus and Argos were always allies – close allies," said Harrison. "If we couldn't get them to buy into our plan, no one would have."

The ranger nodded. "It'll get harder with every village we go to."

"I know. I don't want to intimidate anyone either. These towns and cities need to join us willfully, not because a bunch of soldiers stroll into their town."

Murdock raised an eyebrow. "What would *you* think if you saw us coming into *your* hometown?"

Harrison pondered the question. "I'd be afraid of being overthrown."

"Me, too."

The young warrior shook his head. "We have to do this right."

Thirty minutes later, the six smaller watercraft delivered their human cargo and treasure to the Baltan shores. After a few minutes of assembling, the group started their march into the town.

Harrison took in the sights of the open-air village. Docks lined the shore, boats large and small tethered to their moorings. Various bait shops and fish markets slowly gave way to more traditional stores and establishments. In the distance, the men could see a small cluster of residential buildings. Just by making a simple visual sweep of the seaport, Harrison understood the importance of the open ocean to these people's way of life. Furthermore, he had a feeling that the Baltan leaders would appreciate their share of the Treasure.

The young warrior had wondered how the citizens of Batla would react to their convoy entering the small town. In less than five minutes, he received his answer.

Townspeople came out of their shops to take a look at the men who had invaded their village. Harrison read the looks of worry and concern on their faces. The young warrior scanned the storefronts until his eyes met those of a woman with her small son.

Recalling how his brother Troy commanded his men, Harrison raised a hand in the air, then barked, "Everybody, halt!" The convoy stopped upon hearing his command. The young warrior handed his battle-axe to Murdock, who had taken position next to him while still focused on the nervous woman.

The lady watched this stranger come nearer. As he did, she maneuvered her boy behind her. The little child peered around his mother's legs in order to get a better look at the man who approached them.

"Ma'am," Harrison started, using a soothing tone, "we would like to speak with your town's elders. Do you think you can find them for us?"

The woman took quick peeks to the platoon of men. "I suppose." Holding her head high, she asked, "What do you want with us?"

Harrison did not expect the woman's question, figuring she would scamper off with her child to find her leaders. Speaking the truth, he answered, "We wish for you and your people to join us in uniting the land."

The woman raised an eyebrow, skeptical. "You and your little group of friends are going to bring this world together?"

The young warrior tried not to sound foolish, knowing that if he could not convince a simple person of their cause, he would never be able to persuade hardened leaders. Harrison spoke from the heart.

"I know what you must be thinking, but all we ask is for you and people like yourself to believe in our cause. We've uncovered this land's most sacred treasure, and we intend to share it with everyone. But we can't do this without the support of people like you."

The woman listened to everything Harrison had to say and believed him. With a simple nod, she said, "I will find our dignitaries for you." Taking her little boy's hand, she quickly left the group of soldiers and headed away from the men.

Harrison returned to his friends, with Swinkle being the first one who was waiting for him. The cleric had heard every word the young warrior had spoken.

"If you can maintain that level of sincerity, you will be able to gain the trust of every good person in this land."

Harrison smiled, knowing he had done well. "That's why I need all of you to keep me in line. Our cause is too important."

"What do we do now?"

"We wait for their leaders."

Tara's white horse stopped its trek through the Concurian countryside. The small convoy of ten soldiers, Tara, Justin, and

Lance had traveled for two days without incidence. Today, things would change.

Justin and the other scouts dismounted their horses.

"Miss, let me help you off your steed," said one of the Argosian scouts.

Tara allowed the young man to help her dismount, before standing beside Justin. Lance scampered between the maiden and the soldier.

"We're going to set up camp here," started the armored guard. "While we do that, two of our scouts are going to find the contacts who will lead us to Thoragaard's people."

"How long will they be away?" asked Justin.

"Hopefully only a day or so, but it could be as long as a week."

Tara's eyes grew wide. "A week? Why so long?"

"We're standing in enemy territory." The Argosian motioned with his right hand, pointing to a grove of oaks as he continued speaking. "These trees mark the end of the forest cover. Beyond them start the rolling hills that lead to Concur. With sentries manning the walls of the city, they can see a convoy approaching from miles away.

"Thoragaard's people are in the area keeping an eye on the actions within Concur. If what Harrison said is true, he'll be able to start the resistance movement."

"Harrison would not lie!" said Tara, taking offense. "How do you think we'll proceed to Concur?"

"We'll leave that to Thoragaard. For now, make yourselves comfortable, we might be here for awhile."

Tara and Justin nodded, understanding their predicament for the time being. "I'll set up your tent, Miss Tara. I suggest you stay close to all of us for now."

"Thank you, Justin." The young girl placed her small pack on the ground, patting Lance on the head in the process.

Tara retrieved a few strips of dried meat from the bag's inside pocket. Holding them out to her furry companion, she said, "You've been a brave bodyguard, Lance." The little dog barked with delight, accepting the food.

The young girl gazed about the landscape, taking in the soldiers setting up camp, Justin erecting her shelter, and the scouts securing the area. She looked toward the daytime sky with its white, puffy clouds before her thoughts drifted to Harrison, wondering how his mission was going. She missed him.

Looking at Lance, she said with a sigh, "I suppose we should get comfortable." With that, she found a place to sit and pulled out a spell book to study, while her canine protector nestled alongside of her.

Harrison felt the butterflies swirl in his stomach as he watched the Baltan leaders approach him. Far be it for a warrior to be nervous about trying to get others to accept his agenda, or so he thought. The young warrior had not worried about gaining the allegiance of Robus since he knew Swinkle would be instrumental in helping there. However, he had not anticipated that Brendan and the Forge brothers would remain behind to strengthen the battle plan against Concur. Trying to project an air of confidence, the young warrior stood tall as Balta's leading lady and her entourage positioned themselves before him and his men.

Flanked on either side by three armored guardians wielding spiked clubs, Nora Leffingwell was not a woman to be taken lightly. Fair and compassionate at times, she insisted upon clear intentions, which she sought from the band of men who stood before her.

"I understand that you and your army are here to heal the world," said Nora, a hint of sarcasm in her voice. The light breeze ruffled her dark blue garment, similar to the apparel of the men who accompanied her.

"I wouldn't put it quite that way, but we're hoping for your support," said Harrison.

Squinting, the woman said, "Elaborate your position, young man." The Baltan leader's guards squeezed the hilts of their weapons a bit tighter.

The young warrior took his cue from the female leader and reiterated his dialogue about what the Treasure of the Land entailed, the plight of the Ancient Kings, the reuniting of the land, signing the Unification Treaty, and the resurrection of the Legion of

Knighthood. After he finished his speech, the young warrior motioned for Swinkle, who brought Balta's gifts to their leader.

The middle-aged woman craned her thin, six-foot frame to accept a messenger falcon from Swinkle, as well as to graciously receive three magical nettings. The young cleric explained how the bird of prey would operate, then waited for Gelderand to explain the next treasure.

Harrison nodded to the magician, who read from a scroll that described the mesh to be Nets of Plenty, which when cast into ocean waters would always yield an abundance of fish. Satisfied with the mage's description, Nora now waited for her final gifts.

Five of Harrison's soldiers dragged two small chests of gold coins, all with the same dragon markings, as well as assorted weaponry and armor, then presented them to the Baltan leader.

Standing tall, the woman spoke. "You say you come in peace and to help restore unity to the land, yet you present us with weapons. If what you say is true, why would we require them?"

Harrison nodded, figuring that he would need to explain himself and his cause many times along this journey. "The Treasure of the Land listed what each town would receive. I don't know why your town got what it did, but rest assured we did not hold anything back."

Nora did not miss a beat. "What if we asked for more?"

The young warrior tried to suppress his look of surprise. "You'll only get what's listed; no more, no less."

The woman stared back, her dark eyes appearing huge due to her high cheekbones and pale face. "And what if I decided that I want to nominate myself to be part of the Legion of Knighthood that you spoke about? I feel that I should represent our town and no one else."

"That would be all right, too," said Harrison, recalling that Miriam Wynd also nominated herself to represent Robus. "There won't be any problems as long as you fulfill your duties like all the other members of the Legion."

The woman's dark blue clothing rippled with the sea breeze as she pondered the young warrior's request. Nora craned her neck forward and pointed a bony finger at Harrison.

"Balta will join your alliance, but mind you, we will not compromise ourselves if your plan fails. Do I make myself clear?"

"Absolutely," said Harrison. "How many soldiers can you afford to travel with us now?"

Nora knew she did not have many warrior types in her village. "Most of our residents are fishermen, not fighters like you." Taking another moment, she said, "I can sacrifice one hundred; that is all."

Harrison nodded, though he had hoped for more men. The one hundred troops from Balta brought his new army to just over three hundred members.

"Thank you, ma'am." The young warrior then gestured for Swinkle to retrieve the land's treaty. "The last step for you is to sign this document."

Harrison had already explained the parameters of the treaty, showing Nora the signatures from the town leaders of Aegeus, Argos, and Robus, further convincing her to grant Balta's allegiance.

The Baltan leader reread the parchment, making sure it clearly stated her town's commitments and nothing more. Satisfied, she took an ink pen and signed the treaty, then affixed her personal seal next to her name.

The young warrior waited for the woman to finish her task, then rolled the scroll and handed it back to Swinkle. Addressing Nora again, he said, "We'll be leaving tomorrow for Marqui and would like to gather more food and supplies for our journey."

"Take what you need," said the woman leader. "Balta is here at your service." Nora gestured to her entourage. "Assist these men as you see fit. Provide them with supplies and soldiers." The woman nodded once in the young warrior's direction, then waved her people along.

Harrison thanked Nora one last time before gathering his friends. "Let's integrate whoever she gives us with our new army."

"Let me and Pondle handle this," said Murdock. "We'll be able to explain their role since we'll be with them the most."

"That would be great," said Harrison. "And we'll concentrate on supplying the troops."

The ranger gave the young warrior a mock salute before bellowing at the soldiers, "Let's go, men! We have work to do!"

Harrison watched Murdock and Pondle follow the Baltan fighters and go about their task before turning his attention to Swinkle and Gelderand. "How do you think things went today?"

Swinkle shrugged. "Fine, I suppose."

The young warrior frowned. "Only fine?"

"The Baltans accepted our request," added Gelderand. "Did you expect more?"

Harrison was not sure how he truly felt. "For some reason I thought we would be treated differently. We're doing a great thing for all the peoples of the land."

Swinkle understood how his friend felt. "Did you expect them to sing our praises? As if we came to save them somehow?"

The young warrior sighed. "Part of me did. Nora was just skeptical, like she doesn't fully trust us."

"Would you?" added Gelderand, cocking his head. "Think about it. If a convoy of soldiers marched into your town, demanded to meet with your leaders, and claimed to be on a mission to save humanity, would you not be skeptical, too?"

The mage witnessed the young warrior lift his eyebrows, signaling to the older man that he did concur. "Expect this reaction from every town and village we encounter throughout this land. It is just human nature."

"I know," started Harrison, "but we *are* here to do good!"

"I understand," said Gelderand. "You must relay that message clearly and concisely each and every time."

"And we will be here to help you do just that," said Swinkle with a smile.

Harrison grinned, his friends reinforcing his core beliefs. Even though they relished in the success of the first day, the young warrior felt a sudden pang of loss. Many times during situations like these, he would gaze down at Lance and see him wagging his tail in delight. Today, his furry friend was in the midst of an important mission, safeguarding the love of Harrison's life.

"How do you think Tara's doing?" asked the young warrior, her beautiful face focused in his mind.

Thoughts of his niece swirled about Gelderand's head. "I am very concerned about Tara, but deep in my heart I know she will succeed."

"So do I," added Swinkle. "I have been praying for success on their mission every minute of the day. I hope that puts your mind at ease a little bit."

"It sure does," said Harrison. Doing his best to put Lance and Tara out of his mind, he then said, "We better make sure we have what we need for the next few weeks. There are a lot of stops to make along the coast." The three men concurred, then left to join the newly integrated army.

CHAPTER 10

¤

Tara, her back resting against a large log, sat on the ground with her spell book, trying in earnest to memorize the text that stared back at her. She had just begun to recite the magical words to herself when Lance sprung to his feet, breaking her train of thought.

The young maiden closed the scripture and focused on the little dog. Lance sniffed the air, then growled under his breath. The canine's actions did not go unnoticed.

"What is it, Lance?" asked Tara, her heart beginning to pound.

Still growling and unable to understand the girl's words, Lance gazed back at Tara. The dog sniffed again and seemed to identify the scent, yet he kept growling and whimpering, all the time gazing back at Tara.

The young maiden began to worry. "Lance, I don't understand. What's out there?"

Tara thought she saw the little dog sigh. In his own way, Lance realized that he and Harrison possessed a unique bond, and not being able to convey his message to Tara had begun to frustrate him.

The fallen leaves behind a small tree began to rustle, causing both Tara and Lance's head to swivel in that direction. The canine growled, staring at the tree. Just then, a little squirrel with large green eyes peeked around the trunk before scurrying to another tree.

Tara let out a nervous exhale, a smile gracing her face. "It's only a squirrel," she said, pointing to the rodent. "And to think, I let you get me all worked up over him!"

Lance did not share Tara's enthusiasm. The dog glared at the creature, showing his teeth and growling.

The young maiden gave the dog a little smack on his hindquarters. "Don't be such a bully, Lance! You don't need to protect me from him."

The dog turned to face Tara, whimpering. The young girl furrowed her brow, still unsure why Lance was getting so agitated for seemingly nothing.

Rising to a standing position, she darted toward the squirrel and shooed it away. The rodent scampered to another tree, then climbed up as fast as its tiny legs would take it.

"There, now he can't harm either of us," said Tara, gazing high in the tree, watching the squirrel scratch its underbelly. "Come on, let's go."

Tara went to see what the soldiers were doing, while Lance reluctantly followed. The dog gazed up at the squirrel, whose green eyes glared down at the canine. The rodent then hopped from limb to limb to get a better view of the humans below.

The young girl noticed Justin adding another log to their campfire and walked over to join him. The soldier then began to prepare meat over the flames for dinner.

Tara's soft steps did not go unnoticed by the young man. "Would you like some food, Tara?"

The young maiden nodded. "Sure, when you're finished cooking." Changing the subject, she added, "Where did those three scouts go?" Tara had observed the sentries leave the campground over an hour ago and had yet to return.

"They're scouring the area for their contacts." Lance trotted over and sat next to Tara, then lifted his head and stared at the squirrel that watched over them.

Justin glanced at Lance, then gazed upwards. "What's he looking at?"

"Are you still bothering that poor critter," huffed Tara, patting the dog on his head, causing him to break his concentration. "Just leave it be!"

The soldier skewed a piece of fresh meat and placed it over the fire. "He's just being overprotective." The juices from the beef dripped into the flames, causing them to crackle.

Suddenly, Lance focused on something from the other side of the camp. The little dog then scampered across the site. Justin stood from his position, gripping the hilt of his sword in the process.

Both people watched Lance greet the three sentries, who escorted another three fighters into the makeshift campground. Justin released his grip and motioned for Tara to follow him to the newly arrived group.

Before them stood three female warriors, clad in armor, weapons ready at their side. "These are the contacts we've been waiting for," reported the lead Argosian soldier.

The first woman stepped forward to greet Justin and Tara. Standing at eye-level with the six-foot tall soldier, she offered her hand and said, "I'm Kymbra, and these are my partners, Marissa and Adrith." The two darker haired fighters nodded when the leader called their names.

Justin acknowledged the two other females with a nod of his own. Gesturing toward the young maiden by his side, he said, "This is Tara, the person who will be the focal point of our mission."

Kymbra shook her long blonde hair, making a point to look Tara over, determining right away that she was not the warrior type. "You'll be in good hands, Tara. Thoragaard has told us to pass along his assurances."

The young maiden tried not to let the other women intimidate her. "Thank you. I'm sure he has everything planned out."

Kymbra gave Tara a polite nod, then turned her full attention to Justin. "We'll be leaving soon. Thoragaard understands the importance of timing our mission with that of the Resistance."

The female fighter's comments caught Justin off guard. "I'll have to disassemble the campsite, but we should be ready to go when you say."

"Marissa, Adrith," shouted Kymbra to her cohorts, "help with the dismantling of the area." The lead woman gazed at Tara. "You, too."

With the help of Kymbra's colleagues and the Argosian men, the small platoon of mixed fighters stood ready and waiting to leave within thirty minutes of the female warriors' arrival.

Before disembarking, Kymbra gave orders to the men from Argos. "Marissa and Adrith will lead the way, followed by your scouts." In one smooth swivel of her head, the tall blonde then brought her focus to Justin. "Stay with Tara; we'll keep you all safe."

As the small convoy readied themselves to leave, Lance heard something that grabbed his attention. High in the treetops rested the squirrel in the same spot as before. The little dog growled under his breath.

Tara heard Lance's sounds and took her gaze upwards as well. With a sigh, she looked down at the dog and said, "Lance, I think you need to concentrate on getting us to Thoragaard and leaving that creature alone."

The canine heard Tara's words, but what happened next caused him to sport a look of shock on his furry face. The rodent jumped from its perch, morphed into a raven, and flew off into the cloudless sky.

Lance yapped repeatedly, trying in vain to convey his important message, but instead he received a scolding for his actions.

"Keep that dog quiet!" barked Kymbra in Tara's direction.

The young maiden pointed a finger in the dog's face. "Quiet, boy! We're about ready to go."

Lance yapped a final time, waiting for a response in the way Harrison had always reacted to him. Tara crinkled her brow instead.

Sensing that the dog's theatrics had a deeper meaning, she asked, "What's the matter, Lance?"

The dog gazed upward yet again. Tara, unimpressed with Lance's outburst toward the harmless squirrel, said in a firm voice, "Enough, Lance! Let the squirrel be." Pointing toward the moving convoy of people, she ordered, "Let's go!"

Lance dropped his head and whimpered, acting in the same manner that a child would when his mother does not understand the message he is trying to convey. Huffing, the little dog trekked beside Tara, feeling stronger than ever that he indeed needed to protect her.

Marissa and Adrith led the convoy on an elaborate route through the Concurian countryside, being mindful of enemy soldiers who patrolled the vicinity. Lance maintained his vigil of staying by Tara's side.

Nightfall had not taken grip of the land just yet, but the ensuing twilight started to make it hard to see. Concerned about the lack of light, Tara called to her designated escort from the comfort of her steed.

"Justin, shouldn't we light some torches?"

Kymbra, trekking alongside the Aegean soldier, heard the young maiden's request and answered her question before Justin had a chance. "Absolutely not! Don't you think someone else might see them, too?"

Tara did not care for the female warrior's condescending tone. "I suppose you're right." The young girl then took the conversation in another direction. "Do you have a problem with me?"

Kymbra maintained her march through the countryside, but managed to take a quick glance at Tara riding atop of her white horse. "I'm not used to escorting princesses on elaborate missions."

Tara shot Kymbra a look of surprise. "Princess? Is that what you think I am?"

"Are you not?" The warrior did not bother to make eye contact with the young maiden.

"Hardly! Whatever gave you the idea that I was some kind of royalty?"

"Oh, I don't know, maybe the white horse, your warrior boyfriend, and your obvious lack of fighting skills for starters."

The darkening sky hid Tara's reddening face. With a forceful tone, she said, "I may appear to be a harmless person, but I'm a mage in training."

Kymbra flashed a mock smile. "A mage in training? That's sweet."

The young girl huffed, then clenched her teeth. "I don't need to take this from you. I wouldn't have accepted this mission if I were as frail as you believe me to be."

"I'll give you credit, this assignment's not an easy one. Maybe you'll change my opinion of you in time."

"Don't worry — I will."

Kymbra squinted into the distance, sensing something lay up ahead. "Stop this horse," she said to the girl. Tara pulled on the steed's reins, bringing it to a halt.

Four figures approached from the woods ahead. Marissa and Adrith advanced to Kymbra's position, along with two Argosian soldiers.

"We've reached the point," said Adrith.

"All right," said the lead female, nodding. "You know what to do from here."

Marissa and Adrith both nodded back, before returning to the cover of the underbrush. Justin and Tara watched the scene unfold, neither understanding the current situation.

"Can you fill us in on what's happening?" asked Justin.

"We're standing on the outskirts of Thoragaard's compound. Marissa and Adrith are going to make contact with his people."

Tara gazed about the area, using the fading twilight and the rising moon to aid her sight. No matter how hard she tried, all she could spy were trees and underbrush.

"I don't see anything that resembles a compound," said Tara in Kymbra's direction.

"You do know that Thoragaard is a master illusionist, don't you?"

"A master illusionist?" Tara shook her head, not recalling that important bit of information. "No one told me that."

"He's the best this land has ever seen." Without warning, three illuminated pink balls danced about a hundred feet in front of them.

"Thoragaard is up to something," said Kymbra, keeping a close eye on the dancing lights.

"Works every time," said a monotone voice from behind their position.

Kymbra and Justin both unsheathed their weapons and spun to face the intruder. A tall man in a hooded robe stood before them, signaling to put away their weapons.

Thoragaard pulled down his hood, revealing his bearded face and dark eyes. "I thought you would be more careful than that, Kymbra."

The female warrior secured her weaponry. "I recognized your handiwork, Thoragaard. We weren't in trouble."

"When you start taking things for granted is when you will be surprised the most," said the mage, not pleased with the answer he just heard. "Do not let that happen again or you will be replaced."

Kymbra knew she had to atone for her mistake. "It won't. You have my word."

Thoragaard cocked his head once in acknowledgement. Taking his gaze to the girl on the horse, he said, "You must be Tara."

"Yes, I am," she answered, trying to get a feel for this strange person.

"It's time for you to get down."

Justin steadied the animal while Tara dismounted the steed. Thoragaard walked over to the horse. "Such a beautiful animal," he said, petting its long nose. The illusionist then took his gaze to the dog standing by Tara's side.

"I remember you too, Lance." Thoragaard reached down and scratched behind the little dog's ear. "We had quite an adventure, didn't we?" Lance wagged his tail, recognizing the dark figure as well.

Changing his tone to a more serious one, Thoragaard said, "It's time to leave this area and start you on your mission." The illusionist pointed to a rock formation that rested about three hundred feet beyond their current position.

"My compound is over there."

Justin did his best to see past the stone barrier in the darkness. "Are we going to go around that hill?"

Thoragaard smirked, pleased at the question, but more so to validate his handiwork. "On the contrary, we're going through it."

"Through the rocks?" asked Tara.

Removing a torch from his pack, the magician lit it. "You'll see. Light your torches as well."

Justin helped Tara with hers, while the female warriors teamed with the Argosian soldiers and escorted the couple to the rocky configuration.

Upon reaching the natural barrier, Tara crinkled her brow and asked, "Why have we stopped here?"

Thoragaard advanced to the jagged rocks that jutted out from the formation. With a simple push of his hand, one of the larger stones easily slid back into the mound, triggering the next phase of the spell. Before the group's very eyes, a six foot-by-six foot section of the rocks morphed into the entrance of a dark tunnel.

The illusionist waved everyone forward. "Follow me."

Lance scurried to Tara's side as the small group guided their horses into the passage. Tara waved her torch in front of her, revealing a solid stone corridor, similar to that of a dwarf's mineshaft.

The young maiden estimated that they had traveled a good three hundred feet into the hilly structure before she saw a light in front of them. Lance scampered up ahead, racing past Thoragaard in order to investigate.

The little dog stopped about fifty feet in front of the group, barked once, and wagged his tail. Tara witnessed Lance's actions and breathed a small sigh of relief.

Thoragaard approached the area first, patting Lance on his head as he passed the dog. Waiting a few extra seconds for the rest of the party to catch up to him, he said while sweeping his hand from right to left, "Welcome to my home."

Tara peeked in from the tunnel and gazed upon a rather large compound. Large tents and campfires littered the area, as well as stockpiles of used armor and swords.

The young maiden, surprised to find such an area inside a pile of stones, asked, "How come no one has discovered you yet?"

Thoragaard laughed under his breath, amused at the girl's lack of knowledge of his powers. "I'm very good at what I do." Looking at the rest of the group, he said, "Everyone, exit the corridor and enter the main area of the sanctuary."

The mage waited until all members of the party left the passage, then mumbled something. He spread his arms high before slowly bringing them together. As he did, a black cloud formed around the opening, filling the entranceway. A few seconds later, the haze dissipated, revealing a solid stone wall.

Tara, impressed with Thoragaard's skills, said, "No one will be able to get in, right?"

"That is correct. And, no one can get out."

"No one can get out?" responded the young maiden, with a slight tinge of nervousness in her voice.

"Don't worry; we have everything we need here, and," Thoragaard pointed upwards at the view of the starry sky, "we're not entirely encapsulated."

Tara was still coming to grips with their surroundings. "How does this place work?"

"From an outside observer, the area appears to be nothing more than just another rocky formation that people must travel around. No one would think to enter into its center."

Thoragaard had planned to elaborate further, but heard a throat-clearing sound from behind him.

"We should let them settle in," said Kymbra. "Then we can go over their mission in detail."

The illusionist nodded. "I agree. Find a place to rest and drop off your things. We'll meet in about a half hour."

Tara and Justin peered about the vicinity, looking for a comfortable place to relax for the night. Thoragaard's people had arranged their sleeping quarters around a large central gathering place, which made it easier for everyone to congregate and work together on strategies.

"Miss Tara, let me take your things and I'll set up your shelter," said Justin.

Tara placed her backpack on the ground. "Thank you, Justin, but I'm more than capable of doing my fair share of work. And please, stop calling me Miss all the time." The young maiden smiled.

"Very well, Tara. We'll have this place set up in no time."

After the couple erected their shelters, Tara fumbled with her pack, searching for food for Lance. As she did, two of her female escorts took the opportunity to speak with the young maiden.

"Tara, do you know the whole story of this adventure?" asked Marissa.

The young girl frowned. "I'm not sure what you mean."

Marissa closed her green eyes and shook her head, her dark hair swishing from side to side. "Um, what I mean is, do you know all the members of the group that left Aegeus a few months ago?"

Tara realized that the warrior was trying to step around a pointed question. "Yes, I do, for the most part. Why?"

Adrith, her light eyes full of concern as well, answered next. "Marissa wants to know how Aidan and Jason are doing."

"Aidan and Jason?" Tara's eyes widened just a bit, recalling that Harrison and his friends had mentioned that the two had perished during their quest. Her subtle gesture did not go unnoticed.

"Do you know something?" pressed Adrith.

Tara rose from her crouched position. "Why do you ask?" The young maiden moved her gaze between the two women, searching their faces for answers.

Marissa's shoulders slumped as she nervously bit her bottom lip. "Aidan's my brother and Jason is his best friend." The female warrior placed her hands on her hips, looking away from Tara. "Last I heard they were joining a group to find the Treasure of the Land."

"Harrison and his friends uncovered the Treasure," said Tara. "They brought it back to Aegeus and now they're distributing it across the countryside."

Marissa nodded several times. "Yeah, I heard that from the Argosian soldiers."

Tara could sense the deep emotions welling inside this otherwise intimidating fighter. Softly, she said, "Marissa, Aidan helped secure this Treasure. I know that for a fact."

The warrior heard Tara's words, but her gut feeling told her something else. "He's dead, isn't he?" Adrith placed a caring hand on her friend's arm, both women beginning to put the pieces together.

The young maiden cast her eyes downward. "Yes. So is Jason."

Marissa brought a trembling hand to cover her mouth, trying not to cry. Adrith rubbed her friend's back.

"He was a great man, Marissa," said Adrith, consoling her friend. "They both were."

The lithe fighter's body heaved as she tried to control her sobs. Lifting her head, she sniffed and wiped her eyes. "I had a bad feeling when no one mentioned Aidan's name."

Marissa gave in to the inevitable and started to cry. Adrith pulled her close, holding her fellow warrior, sharing her pain. Tara also felt the deep anguish within Marissa's soul, comforting her by rubbing her back.

"People will write about your brother's role in this journey's legacy some day, Marissa." The young maiden's eyes welled with tears. "No one will ever forget him or Jason."

Marissa nodded, doing her best to stop crying. A moment later, she spun away from Adrith and faced Tara. Exhaling and averting her eyes, she said, "All right. Thank you for telling me what you know."

Before both warriors could leave, Tara lightly grabbed Marissa's forearm, gaining her attention. "If you ever need someone to talk to, you can talk to me."

The female fighter tried her best to regain her composure, again wiping tears from her eyes. "I may take you up on that offer some time." Marissa and Adrith then left Tara to tend to her things.

With the female warriors gone, Tara went back to finding Lance some dried meat. Offering the food to the dog, she said, "That poor girl is very sad, Lance."

The little dog gobbled the food out of Tara's hand, then turned and looked in the female warrior's direction, before gazing back at Tara. The young maiden witnessed the dog's actions.

"It's almost like you know what I said, Lance." At that moment, Tara understood why Harrison's little friend meant so much to him and how much it must have hurt to allow him to protect her.

Tara hugged Lance, giving him a vigorous rub on his side. "I'm glad you're here with me, boy." Lance nuzzled his snout against the girl's leg, thankful for the young maiden's affection.

Justin, finished with getting their area situated, approached Tara and Lance. "I think it's time to regroup with Thoragaard."

Tara nodded. "I agree."

The young couple, along with Lance, meandered through Thoragaard's camp. Tara looked at the people, male and female alike, who were focused on their individual tasks.

The young girl leaned closer to Justin and spoke in a soft tone. "What are they doing?"

"Preparing for their battle with Concur."

Tara took a closer look at the men sharpening their weapons and arranging their armor. Some women worked with their own swords, while others filled flasks with water and wrapped individual packages of dried meats and food.

"Can they really defeat Lord Hammer and his army?"

"Not if we don't do our job." Justin pointed to a larger tent on the other side of the encampment. "Thoragaard's over there."

Two sentries protected the shelter's opening. The young couple approached the illusionist's sanctuary, but before Justin could utter a word, both guards pushed back the covering to the entranceway.

"Thoragaard has been expecting you," said the soldier on the right. "Enter."

Justin allowed Tara and Lance to go in first. The young maiden's eyes took a moment to get used to the soft illumination provided by the strategically placed candles. Taking her gaze about the fifteen-by-fifteen foot enclosure, Tara found the place littered with incense, books, scrolls, and scriptures.

The young maiden stepped with care on the fine carpet that lay on the ground and took further caution about breaking the meditation of the man that they came to see.

Thoragaard, his hood draped over his head, kneeled on a large green pillow that rested before a low table. An open scripture sat in front of him.

Tara hesitated to say anything; instead she remained motionless next to Justin, the sweet smell of incense circling around the two. The young couple locked gazes on each other just before the mage spoke.

"Please, make yourselves comfortable," said Thoragaard, who remained kneeling. Tara and Justin gazed about the shelter, but found no chairs.

Sensing the apprehension emanating from the young people, a voice from behind the robe said, "Find yourself a pillow." Tara found a soft red one, while Justin grabbed a blue cushion. The young maiden patted the ground, signaling for Lance to sit next to her.

Thoragaard took a deep, cleansing breath, before turning to face the two. Lowering his hood, he nodded to both young people, then said, "You must never be that unsure of yourself. Figuring out where and how to sit in a room is the simplest of tasks." Both Tara and Justin nodded, taking the illusionist's words to heart.

"Kymbra, Marissa, and Adrith have arrived and will partake in our discussions," continued Thoragaard. No sooner did he speak those words than the three women entered the tent.

The magician extended his hand toward the floor, signaling to the warriors to take a seat as well. The female fighters found pillows to sit on and formed a semi-circle around Thoragaard, along with Tara and Justin. The young maiden peered at Marissa, making eye contact and nodding once, acknowledging the fighter's fragile emotional state. Marissa cracked a slight smile, appreciating the girl's gesture.

With everyone situated, the mage addressed the young maiden. "It is time to talk about your mission. The first thing we need to do is establish your cover."

"What did you have in mind?" asked Justin.

The illusionist cast his eyes to Kymbra, who unfastened a small sack from her belt. She opened the pouch and allowed two rings to fall into her hand, which she then gave to Thoragaard.

The magician examined the bands of gold, then handed one each to Justin and Tara. "You will arrive at Concur a married couple —"

"Married couple?" exclaimed Tara. Her thoughts had drifted to Harrison and it took a moment to reorient herself.

"Let me rephrase; an apparent married couple," clarified Thoragaard. "The story goes that the both of you are recently wedded and are heading to Concur to start your new life together."

Thoragaard took his gaze to Tara. "You are to inquire about the position of Meredith's new handmaiden."

The young maiden felt unsure of her role. "Isn't Meredith the First Lady of Concur?" The illusionist nodded.

"Then how would I ever know about this so-called opening if I've never been to Concur?"

Thoragaard smirked. "I'm glad to see that you have good insights. There will be a guard posted at the East Gate. You will tell him that you have arrived for that specific position. That phrase will signal the beginning of the Resistance."

Justin needed to hear more about Thoragaard's plot. "Will this sentry relay the information to the Resistance army."

"Not exactly," said the mage. "There is no way that a guard will have access to our underground leader, but a handmaiden will. When Meredith finds out that her new helper has arrived, she will start the movement." The mage motioned to the couple. "Put on those rings."

"Who do we talk to once we've passed this guard?" asked Tara, placing the ring on her finger. She took her gaze to the gold piece of jewelry, secretly wishing that Harrison had given it to her and not Thoragaard.

"I am not privy to that information," said the illusionist, a slight scowl gracing his face. "Meredith and I agreed that the chain to the Resistance must be kept in complete secrecy. Only a handful of people know the succession to Meredith, and that sequence changes every two weeks.

"I have lost the luxury of knowing this procession ever since I helped Marcus and Harrison escape from Concur three months ago."

"What does this guard look like?" asked Justin.

"His hair is as blonde as hers," said the illusionist, pointing to Tara. "Not many of Lord Hammer's men share that quality."

Justin waited for more information from the mage, but none came. Shaking his head in disbelief, the fighter exclaimed, "That's all? Blonde hair?"

"Everything will work as planned," said Thoragaard, sure of his strategy.

"And I suppose we will be led to where we need to go by people on the inside."

"You, too, have good instincts."

Justin drew a heavy sigh, knowing that a person of his stature should not question the actions of his superiors. "You're leaving a lot of this plan to chance. What if there are two guards with blonde hair and we choose the wrong one?"

Thoragaard leaned in the couple's direction. "You must be very convincing and play your parts well. If you choose the wrong guard, ask the other one about the position. Either way, you will start the process for the overthrow of Concur. Trust in the people I have put in place."

"Say we do everything right," started Tara, "and I meet Meredith and relay this information, how do we get out of Concur?"

"You simply walk out the gate where you arrived," said the mage. "Kymbra and her colleagues will be watching for you and will escort you to Aegeus via another route."

The young girl sighed. "You make this sound so easy. Where will you be?"

Thoragaard sat back. "In the shadows, waiting for Harrison and his army to return."

Justin still felt a need to express another concern. "What are we to do if something goes wrong? Say we get intercepted before reaching Meredith, what do we do then?"

The illusionist scowled. "There is the possibility of unforeseen situations, no matter how solid the plan. If you fail in your mission to reach Meredith, under no circumstances are you to reveal who sent you to Concur."

The Aegean needed to hear more. "Will anyone come to save us?" Justin glanced at Tara, who eagerly awaited the mage's response.

"There are many people within Concur who are part of the Resistance and they will be watching you." Thoragaard pursed his lips. "I cannot say for sure how or when these people will come to your aid, but I assure you that they will try."

Both young people glanced at each other again, neither one happy with the illusionist's answer.

Tara stroked Lance's fur, burning off some nervous energy. "When do we start this mission?"

The illusionist locked his gaze on the young couple. "Tomorrow." Thoragaard gestured to Kymbra and her friends. "They alone will escort you to Concur. You will also be resupplied with provisions for your trip."

"I want Lance to come with us," said Tara, still petting the animal. Thoragaard nodded his approval.

The mage had one more question. "Do you possess magical capabilities?" he asked Tara.

The young maiden brought her hand to her chest. "Me? Umm, well, I do know a few spells, but I can't do the things you can."

Pointing at the girl, he said, "You are *not* to perform any magic. We do not want to draw any undo attention on you. Understood?"

Tara nodded. "Yes, I'll refrain from any magic."

Thoragaard smiled. "Good. Rest tonight; a very important day in this land's history begins tomorrow."

Kymbra rose from her position, along with Marissa and Adrith. "We'll take you to your shelter and get you more supplies," said Kymbra.

Justin and Tara stood up as well and followed the women out of Thoragaard's sanctuary. With the meeting over, the first steps towards Concur's overthrow had commenced.

CHAPTER 11

¤

"This one's mine," said Murdock, crouching beside Harrison, ready to fire.

The ranger, in one swift motion, rose from his position behind the fallen log and fired an arrow at the unsuspecting Scynthian. The projectile hit its mark, entering the beast's chest and dropping him to the ground.

"My turn," said Harrison, sprinting from his location. The young warrior hovered over the wheezing creature, blood spewing from its mouth. Harrison brought his battle-axe to an attack position. The Scynthian, seeing the sharpened blade, tried to maneuver away from the human, but in his haste to flee he rolled over, forcing the arrow deeper. With a final gasp, his life expired.

Harrison watched the scene with his axe raised over his head. Lowering his blade, he said, "Good shot, Murdock. He's dead." The young warrior felt a small sigh of relief, knowing that ending the defenseless being's life would go against his Fighter's Guild code. It would have been a mercy killing, he rationalized to himself.

"That should be the last of them," said the ranger, peering into the surrounding woods. "What were these idiots thinking anyway?"

Over the past week, Harrison's army had swollen to almost two thousand men. The young warrior and his ever-growing army accepted the services of soldiers from the coastal villages of Marqui, Valtalia, Adatic, and Illius. Each town pledged their support for Harrison's cause, signed the Unification Treaty, nominated a member for the Legion of Knighthood, and accepted their portion of the Treasure of the Land. However, on their way to Thrombus, they found themselves in a most unusual set of circumstances.

The Thrombian Peninsula was famous for its beautiful cliffs that, at some points, rose to over 500 feet above the shoreline that touches the Serpent's Sea. A vast lush woodland forest thrived away from the coast, feasting on the moisture that rolled in from the sea.

To Harrison's surprise, the Scynthians had also felt that the area was ripe for a new outpost. To their dismay, the beasts had no idea that a great human army had started to form a little less than a month ago, and that it would be trekking right through their new found land.

With the likes of proven veteran fighters mingled in with Harrison and his men, the Scynthian outpost of fifty warriors stood no match for the human invasion.

"Another stake to our land," said Murdock as he fumbled through the fallen Scynthian's belongings. "As usual, nothing of worth."

Harrison stood motionless, a blank expression on his face. "Why down here, Murdock?"

The ranger scanned the immediate area, taking in the plumes of smoke that rose out of the forest. "They want the land, too. How many of these scattered settlements do you think are still left unfound?"

"More than I care to count." Harrison regained his focus, knowing they needed to regroup with the rest of the men. "Let's head for that outpost."

The two fighters scampered through the underbrush, heading for the center of the compound. Groups of Harrison's men tended to their wounds and weaponry, while others gathered whatever bounty left behind by the fallen Scynthians.

Harrison headed toward a raging inferno in the center of the Scynthian campground. The young warrior recognized several Aegean scouts who stood there conversing about the ambush.

One of the fighters saw Harrison and Murdock approach. "Glad to see you both still alive, sir," he said. "Have you found the rest of your friends?"

The young warrior looked over at Murdock, who shook his head no. "No, and we need to find them."

The sentry nodded in concurrence. "We've stabilized this area. It should be safe enough for you to search for them."

The young warrior made eye contact with Murdock, who took the cue to lead the way around the campground. Harrison recognized the familiar basic design of the Scynthian compound, which resembled all the others that he and his friends had stumbled across in the past.

Murdock made a swift inspection of the semi-circular arrangement of buildings around the inferno. The ranger gazed beyond the bodies, human and Scynthian alike, that littered the area.

"I don't see them anywhere," said Murdock, a hint of concern in his voice.

"They have to be here somewhere," responded Harrison, spinning his head around in bewilderment. "They can't just disappear!"

A crash emanating from inside one of the buildings more than startled the fighters. Murdock used his right hand to grab the hilt of his sword, while raising his left hand to Harrison, signaling for him to be quiet. The young warrior, grasping his battle-axe with both hands, made himself as small as possible and moved silently behind the ranger.

The structure that loomed in front of the two men had a single, closed entranceway. The ranger used caution as he approached the door. Harrison stood on its opposite side. With a nod to the young warrior, Murdock grabbed the door's metal handle and, with a firm tug, opened the portal.

The ranger rushed in first with his sword drawn and ready to strike. Harrison followed, only two steps behind. The young warrior watched Murdock push a Scynthian's back, driving it to the floor. The command that came next startled and confused Harrison at the same time.

"Stop!" said a voice from the other side of the room. Unseen, Swinkle mustered all the courage that he could to separate the Scynthian warrior from the two advancing fighters.

"Stop!" yelled the young cleric again. "Put your weapons away!"

"What's going on in here?" said Harrison, panning the area. Another surprise awaited him; Gelderand and Pondle also stood in the room, looks of apprehension written all over their faces.

Murdock, his brow creased and weapon still in an offensive position, hollered to his friend, "Pondle, why is this beast still alive?" The Scynthian, who had sprawled out on the floor due to the ranger's attack, flipped over, dazed.

The ranger pointed his sword's tip in the face of the creature. "Don't even think about getting up!" The tired, beaten Scynthian leaned on its elbows and signaled its helpless state to the men.

Harrison, witnessing the brute's actions, suddenly understood what had happened in this shack. Bringing his gaze to Swinkle, he caught the young cleric staring at him.

"Swinkle," said Harrison, shaking his head in stunned disbelief.

"We defeated him and he is now our prisoner." The young cleric moved a step closer to the fallen enemy.

"Prisoner?" exclaimed Murdock. "We don't take Scynthian prisoners, just like they don't take human ones!" Jabbing his weapon at the Scynthian, he said, "Isn't that true?" The creature remained motionless, not acknowledging the ranger's question. "What? Don't you understand me?"

"Let him be, Murdock!" said Swinkle, coming to the beast's defense again.

Murdock lowered his weapon, then took his glare from the Scynthian to Swinkle. "You know, I could stomach your self-righteousness ways when it came to arguments over ambushes and the like, but with one of these beasts sitting right in front of us …" The ranger clenched his teeth, unable to continue, his anger rising.

"He's our prisoner. That's that." Swinkle stepped in front of the Scynthian, in an effort to shield the creature from an unprovoked attack.

The young cleric's statement did not sit well with his friend. "That's that?" Murdock took a step in Swinkle's direction and pointed a finger in his face. "Who are you to make a decision like that? Huh?"

Harrison lightly grabbed Murdock's arm from behind. The ranger jerked his arm away and glared at the young warrior. "Don't touch me. Not this time."

Murdock snapped his head toward the cleric, his face the color of the blood pulsing through his veins, nearing a complete rage. "These beasts slaughtered countless innocent people just because they were human or have you forgotten that already?"

Swinkle swallowed hard, but maintained his focus. "Their crimes are hideous as a race, but this single Scynthian cannot be held accountable for all of their atrocious deeds."

Murdock clenched his teeth again, his eyes bulging, but before he tore into a complete tirade, an eerie calmness overtook his body. "All right, Swinkle, have it your way. You can defend this pathetic creature wherever we go and you'll have sole responsibility for its actions. Does anyone object?"

The ranger read his friends' faces. All seemed to understand Swinkle's rationale, but no one wanted this beast anywhere near their new found army.

Harrison, his blade lowered, approached his close friend. "Swinkle, isn't there another way to handle this situation?"

The young cleric shook his head. "Some of the hardest decisions in life come out of circumstances like these." Swinkle peered down at the creature that remained on the floor. "Take a closer look at him."

"What?" said Harrison. "It's a Scynthian. What more is there to see?"

"Does he appear like all the others?" continued the young cleric. "Take a closer look."

The young warrior gazed at the beast. The creature wore the standard leather-like body armor, gauntlets, boots, and its body consisted of the coarse grayish-black hair typical of their race. Harrison stared into the brute's green cat-like eyes, not seeing anything different about this creature.

The young warrior motioned to the Scynthian. "Stand up."

The beast's eyes widened upon hearing the human's command. Being completely outnumbered and unarmed, the Scynthian did as Harrison ordered.

The young warrior watched the creature rise to its feet and instinctively took his gaze upward, expecting the Scynthian to stand a good half-foot taller than him. To his surprise, he directed his eyes downward a few inches.

It did not take Harrison long to figure out why Swinkle was so adamant that this beast should survive. "It's not an adult!"

Swinkle shook his head. "No, he is not."

Harrison's shoulders slumped. He then took his gaze to Murdock. The ranger placed his hands on his hips, looked down, and shook his head, a myriad of emotions coursing through his body.

"We can't kill him," said Harrison in a soft, hushed tone.

Murdock continued to shake his head. "It's always something, isn't it? Nothing's ever cut and dry with anything we do."

"He must be taken as a prisoner," said Swinkle. "He must."

Harrison nodded, not wanting to agree, but he knew that he could not go against his warrior's creed. His enemy was neutralized, defenseless, and most likely a juvenile and not capable of truly understanding the things he had done.

The young warrior called to Pondle, who had remained behind Swinkle and the Scynthian, waiting for the outcome to unfold before doing anything.

"Do you have something that we can use to bind this beast's hands?"

The thief shook his head. "No, but I'm sure that I can find something in this compound. I'll be back." Pondle moved past the Scynthian and headed out of the building in a rush.

Harrison maintained eye contact with the beast, which remained speechless. The young warrior tried to read the Scynthian's face, to get a better idea of what this creature might be thinking. Its eyes stared straight ahead, its breathing deep and shallow; nervous thought the young warrior.

Strong, too, continued Harrison's assessment. The humans had chronicled the Scynthian race, understanding their battle strategies, compound arrangements, utter distaste of humanoid races, but finding a juvenile was something unheard of. Harrison could not recollect ever reading about a young Scynthian;

everything he studied at the Fighter's Guild revolved around defeating creatures in the prime of their lives.

"Can you understand me?" asked the young warrior, wondering if he would get a response.

Harrison saw the beast's pupils dilate ever so subtly. The Scynthian had indeed understood him.

"Answer me," he said in a stern tone.

"I understand," said the Scynthian in a low guttural voice.

"What is your name?"

The creature stood tall. "I Naa'il." Its raspy voice gave the men goose bumps, not expecting their prisoner to speak. "You kill me."

Harrison recoiled in surprise to the Scynthian's statement. "No, you're our prisoner now."

"No!" exclaimed the brute. "You kill me!" The Scynthian started to scan the room in a panic, looking back and forth for something just out of reach. Without warning, a soft green glow enveloped the beast and it dropped to the floor.

Gelderand's hands remained outstretched, his spell complete. "You are playing a dangerous game here. Get that beast's hands bound now."

"What did you do to him?" asked Swinkle in concern.

"I rendered him unconscious, but not for long."

Just then, Pondle returned with a pair of shackles, similar to the ones they all had worn when they were prisoners in a Scynthian holding cell.

The thief saw the creature lying motionless on the ground. "Did you do the smart thing and kill him?" Pondle's words caused all the men to stare at each other.

"What did I say?" said the thief, oblivious to the fact that the Scynthian had requested that very thing.

"Just bind his hands," said Harrison.

Pondle arranged the cuffs around the Scynthian's large wrists, then locked them. The thief gave the shackles a tug and, satisfied with his work, tossed the keys to Swinkle.

"He's all yours."

"What do we do now, Harrison?" asked the young cleric.

"We alert the others to what we have here." Harrison wondered what the army of humans would say about their new prisoner.

"You two are on your own with this one," said Murdock. "Let's get this over with."

"Can you assemble the men?" asked Harrison. "We have to watch over Naa'il."

Murdock took a purposeful step toward the young warrior. "Don't call it that! It's a beast, just like the rest of its race."

"He has a name, just like all of us," chimed Swinkle.

The ranger glared at the young cleric, then pivoted toward the exit. "I'm through here. I'll gather the troops and I'm not coming back." Murdock peered at Pondle. "Are you coming with me?"

The thief, silently siding with his friend, nodded, then left the building with Murdock to perform their task.

Gelderand stepped forward, bending down to take a closer look at the creature that lay on the floor. "He will awaken soon."

"I know." Harrison brought a hand to his forehead, rubbing it slowly.

"Murdock makes a good point, you know," said the mage, peering at his friends, reading their faces. "I'm not saying that we kill the Scynthian, but we have put ourselves in a precarious position."

Harrison, still caressing his temples, nodded while thinking of what to do next. Lifting his eyes, he said, "We take this creature along with us for now and we'll figure out what to do with him later." The young warrior brought his gaze to Swinkle.

"Is that all right with you?"

The young cleric nodded. "That will give us ample time to better understand these beings as well."

Harrison stood tall. "I have to be honest with you, Swinkle, I might not be able to convince the other men to accept this monster. Just look at Murdock's reaction."

Swinkle understood the great undertaking he had assumed in saving this poor creature's life, but something inside told him that he had done the right thing.

"Not everyone will agree with what we have done, but time will tell if our actions were just."

"It's time to leave this place," said the young warrior. Before Harrison and his friends could continue their journey, they first had to wake their new traveling companion.

"How do we snap him out of this trance?" asked Harrison in Gelderand's direction.

"Lightly slap his face. He should respond."

Harrison bent over and stared at the Scynthian, noticing that the creature appeared to be sleeping. With his right hand, he did as the mage instructed. The beast's eyelids fluttered as it tried to gauge its situation. Realizing that it was now bound, the Scynthian swung its arms wildly back and forth, trying in vain to release the shackles.

The young warrior peered into the Scynthian's eyes, seeing the obvious rage, but also understanding another of its raw emotions – fear. Harrison grabbed the Scynthian's binding and tugged it hard, getting the beast to focus on him.

"I realize you're scared," he said, locking his gaze on the creature, "but we won't harm you unless you give us a reason to. Do you understand me?"

The beast stopped his thrashing, listening to Harrison's words. Between heavy breaths, it answered, "Yes."

"The people you see in this room will be the only ones you deal with." Harrison paused. "The others in our army want you dead. Don't be a fool."

The Scynthian stood tall, realizing now that it was a prisoner of a human army that consisted of countless enemy soldiers. Naa'il scanned the room, reading the anxious faces of the beings who stared back at him. A single nod of concurrence followed.

Harrison pursed his lips, then said, "All right. It's time to leave this place and get back to our journey." The young warrior gestured to Swinkle and Gelderand. "You two will escort him on our trip."

The young warrior sighed. "Let's go." After he turned toward the doorway, Harrison made an abrupt stop, spun around, and pointed at the mage.

To Naa'il, he said, "That man is a magician and has the authority to use whatever powers he has to keep you in line; that is if you try to flee in any way." The Scynthian gazed at the robed human, but said nothing.

Harrison waved the group forward and a moment later they all stood in the remains of the Scynthian compound. Soldiers had started to dig graves for the slain creatures, while others set controlled fires to the remaining buildings.

Naa'il looked on in horror. Only a few days earlier, he and his friends had finished erecting the last of their sleeping quarters, followed by the bonfire preparation. Tomorrow, his small tribe of fifty Scynthians had planned to light the sacrificial pyre that signified the completion of their compound. Today, though, the complex lay in ruins, destroyed at the hands of his hated enemy, and worse he had become their prisoner.

CHAPTER 12

¤

Lord Nigel Hammer had arrived in Concur several weeks ago, fresh off his divorce from Troy Harkin and their alliance, and ready to defend his city from The Prophecy. The Concurian leader had already recalled all of his soldiers, save his advance scouts, from all corners of his land in preparation for a battle that he was sure would come; he just did not know when.

Clad in his black, chain-mail armor he toiled in his mansion, analyzing battle plans and pondering strategies that he might employ. Sprawled on a fine oak table lay a large map that detailed his country. Through his dark eyes, Nigel gazed at the possible shortcomings of his walled city. Three large gates led into the municipality, one each from the west, the south, and the east. Though the thirty-foot high walls allowed his sentries to see enemies advancing from long distances, they could be the weak link into storming the metropolis.

Lord Hammer understood the strength of the solid wood doors, but they could be burned or rammed, allowing enemies to pass through in time. A smile graced his face as he ran his finger across the North Gate. This entrance sat at the end of the harbor, which closed the waterway to vessels. There would be no way for anyone to enter from there.

The Concurian leader then took his gaze to another image on his map, this one being a detailed line drawing of his city, showing all of the streets, alleyways, and every interconnecting path within the great metropolitan area. He would fill his streets with guards and armed men. No one will take his city, not without a fight.

Lord Hammer stood tall behind the table, then took his gaze out to the balcony. A beautiful, cloudless day stared back at him, presenting an exquisite view of his harbor. Fishing boats cast their nets into the inland sea, while commercial vessels headed for his city, where they would sell their wares on his streets and be levied a most appropriate tax. Walking to the balcony's edge, he placed his hands on the railing, taking in the sight. A smile came to his lips, for now all was well.

A knock on the door interrupted his quiet time. Agitated, he yelled toward the doorway, "Enter!"

A thin servant made a cautious entry into the room. Percival, Lord Hammer's main personal attendant, had brought welcome news. "Sir, Allard Mourbray is here to see you."

Nigel nodded once. "Send him in."

Percival scurried out of the room and a moment later the great mage of Concur entered. Allard pulled down the hood of his dark blue robe, revealing his bearded face.

Lord Hammer motioned for him to take a seat at the table. "Have you uncovered any more information?"

Allard sat down next to Nigel and shook his head no. "The notes that I compiled about The Prophecy a short time ago have not changed."

"And you found nothing new?" Disgusted, Nigel slammed his hands on the table.

The great mage, used to his leader's outbursts, patiently waited for Nigel to calm down. Sensing that Lord Hammer's anger had dissipated, he continued the discussion by saying, "Everything points to brothers reuniting the land, who we know are Harrison and Troy. They will eventually come here."

"And nothing was said about the battle?"

"No."

Nigel brought a hand to his face, lightly stroking his beard, taking his gaze to a corner of the room and tapping the fingers of his other hand on the table. Locking eyes with Allard, he continued, "Does Concur burn? Do the walls get destroyed?"

The magician again shook his head. "Nothing in the annals documents any of these happenings."

The Concurian leader threw his hands up in the air. "How do I prepare for this war?"

Allard reached a hand out to his superior. In a cool, calm voice, he said, "Nigel, you are an exceptional strategist, fighter, and leader. I know you wish to get even more of an edge on this battle, but the fact is you do know it is going to come. Focus on that and prepare thusly."

Nigel accepted Allard's compliments and deep down he agreed with the advice. "Very well, if you have no more information, then I must go forward with my preparations to protect my city. I want you to remain here in the mansion. Your services will be needed."

Allard had figured on staying with Nigel until after the battle. "I will help Concur in any way." Changing the subject, he asked, "What about Meredith?"

"What about her?"

"Will she remain here as well?"

"That was my plan. Do you disagree?"

Allard shook his head. "No. She can be very valuable in rallying your people to fight the invading army."

"I hadn't thought of that." Lord Hammer smiled. "See, you're earning your keep already."

The Concurian leader was about to relieve the magician for the day when an unexpected knock beckoned at the door again.

"Come in!" barked Nigel.

Again Percival entered the room, averting his eyes. "Sir, there is an unexpected guest from Aegeus here to see you."

Lord Hammer took his gaze to Allard, an eyebrow raised. Shifting his eyes back to his servant, he asked, "Who is this person?"

"Gareth Tyne, sir."

Nigel's body tensed at the utterance of the name. "What is he doing here?" he said through clenched teeth.

Percival swallowed, sensing an outburst. "He says he has valuable information for you."

Nigel took a moment to recall the last time he had encountered Gareth. The Aegean had fought gallantly against the Concurian leader's army, keeping him at bay and not allowing Nigel advancement on their neighboring towns. Because of Gareth's actions, the villages of Argos, Aegeus, and Robus united and formed an alliance against Concur. Now, one of his life's nemeses waited outside his door.

Lord Hammer motioned with his finger for Percival to come close. In a near whisper he said, "After you send him in, I want you to close the door and summon five guards to wait outside." Nigel waved his servant away. "Be gone."

Percival nodded and backpedaled in the opposite direction. "Yes, sir." The nervous servant left the room and a moment later returned with the unexpected guest. "Lord Hammer, I present to you Gareth Tyne of Aegeus."

Both Nigel and Allard rose from their seats as Gareth limped into the room. Unbeknownst to either of them, a small mouse scurried into the chamber, narrowly avoiding the closing door behind it.

"You must be in a dire situation to show your face here," said Nigel, not bothering to hold back his true feelings.

The Aegean fighter pointed to an empty chair. "Might I take a seat? The years of battle have taken their toll on my body and I find it hard to stand for long stretches at a time."

Nigel nodded once and gestured to a chair near the table. Gareth hobbled over to the seat, resting his weary body.

"We fought many battles against each other, Nigel," began the older fighter, "but today we need to prepare for something new – together."

Lord Hammer had no idea what information this man harbored and he said in a sarcastic tone, "I'm all ears."

"The Treasure of the Land has been returned to Aegeus –"

"Yes, I know about that!" interrupted Nigel. "Did you come here to insult me?"

Gareth raised his palms toward Lord Hammer. "In no way did I mean to upset you; I was just stating a fact." Lowering his hands, he continued, "Harrison Cross right now is embarking on a journey to reunite the land, using this bounty as his rallying call."

Nigel noticed a glaring omission from Gareth's statement. "You mean Harrison and his brother Troy, don't you?"

"Troy's dead. I tried to deny Harrison's request to have him buried with Aegeus's heroes, but I believe he did so anyway."

The Concurian leader felt his spirits lift at the news of Troy's passing. The Prophecy spoke of brothers reuniting the land; with Harrison's brother no longer alive, the future became unsettled at best.

Lord Hammer, always careful to keep his emotions in check, said, "That's too bad. I met Troy, even had a brief alliance with him. He was a much more polished leader than Harrison.

"But getting back to Harrison's journey, how is he fairing?" Nigel knew from The Prophecy that the young warrior would end up at Concur.

"I don't know. But I do know that he has already started plans to take down your city."

Nigel's blood began to simmer. He had learned about the ancient predictions from Allard, but to hear that actual strategies were already being employed against him caused his anxiety level to rise.

Shifting in his seat, he squinted and said, "I don't see where you gain anything by telling me this. What's your motive here?"

"Harrison and his friends went against me. They did not respect my position as town elder, and they would not turn over the bounty so that I could decide how it should be used."

Nigel sat back in his chair and smirked. "Poor Gareth doesn't get his way and he runs to his enemy for sympathy? I'm not buying it!"

The elder warrior's eyes squinted and his brow furrowed. "He's giving everything back to their rightful owners! Imagine what one could do with all that loot for themselves."

"The precise reason why I searched for it alone." Nigel leaned forward. "I appreciate your information, but I have no interest in aligning myself with you, if that's your plan."

"We both know that we can't allow all those villages to be on the same footing as us," said Gareth, fixing his gaze on Nigel. "They're not worthy of the bounty. They didn't fight the battles to keep the Scynthians at bay, they didn't help us when we needed them against your army, and they don't produce anything of value from their pathetic villages. You know I'm right."

Lord Hammer seemed unfazed by Gareth's rationale. "I agree with you, they aren't worthy. Nevertheless, you still have not offered me anything that would entice me to align myself with you."

Gareth nodded once, saying, "All right, what if I told you I know how Harrison is preparing his attack on your city?"

Lord Hammer cocked his head. "Now that would be worth something. What do you want in return for this information?"

The Aegean leader paused, wishing to be sure to announce his intentions correctly. "First, you will provide a safe haven for me and another person in Concur until you defeat Harrison's army. Once he is overthrown, we will march back to my hometown, reclaim the Treasure, and set up an alliance between Concur and Aegeus. Together, we will reclaim the land under one flag, using whatever the Treasure has to ensure our coalition comes to fruition."

Nigel took in Gareth's information, then glanced at Allard. The mage gave a slight shrug, telling the Concurian that the decision was his to make. At the same time, the great magician also sensed another presence in the room, a feeling he kept to himself.

"Let's say I do agree to this alliance," started Lord Hammer. "I'm putting up most of the risk for this piece of knowledge."

"The information is worth it."

Lord Hammer pondered the agreement presented before him. If Gareth's information was that valuable, it might lead to Harrison's overthrow, which would bring the Treasure of the Land into the hands of its rightful owner, Nigel Hammer. Furthermore, Harrison's defeat would crush Aegeus's dreams of being the center of the land, allowing for the creation of a Greater Concur. And, he would easily push Gareth along with his pathetic cronies out of power faster than the creation of this fragile alliance.

With those thoughts swirling in his mind, Nigel announced, "I accept your proposal. Now, what do you have to tell me?"

Gareth drew a deep breath. "A small convoy is heading to Concur as we speak. Two people, a man and woman, will enter your city and announce the beginning of a resistance movement designed to implode Concur from the inside. While this happens, Harrison and his army will attack from outside the city walls."

Nigel squinted again. "What resistance? Who's their leader?"

Gareth protected himself with a lie, having learned that their leader was indeed Meredith. "His name is Thoragaard, an illusionist."

Lord Hammer slammed his hand on the table and turned away in disgust. "I knew it! His disappearance was more than a coincidence!"

"I don't know the location of his underground army. He is very adept at keeping himself out of view from what I hear."

Nigel scowled. "Yes, he is a very smart man." Changing directions, he said, "Who are these people who are coming to Concur?"

A gleam shone in Gareth's eyes. "Harrison's woman and an escort."

Gareth's statement took Nigel aback. "Harrison's woman? Why would he send her here?"

"She's virtually anonymous, never has been seen before, and her mission is simple. You would never have suspected her."

Nigel turned his head away again in thought, clasping his hands together and resting them in front of himself. "That boy's smart. What's her mission?"

"All I know is that she is supposed to set the resistance process in motion."

"Do you know what she looks like?"

"Yes."

Nigel paused to think again. "We're going to let her proceed on her mission. I want to know who this Concurian traitor is firsthand. We'll work out the details, but I need you to screen all the young women who enter this city over the next week."

"I can do that," answered Gareth. "So, we have a deal?"

Lord Hammer nodded. "That we do." Nigel shouted toward the doorway. "Guards!"

A second later, five armored soldiers burst through the portal and advanced on the startled Aegean leader.

Two soldiers grabbed Gareth and lifted him out of his chair. "What is the meaning of this? We have a deal!"

"I know. I'm providing you your safe haven." Nigel directed his men. "Take him to the prison."

Allard thrust a hand in the Aegean's direction, then stood. "Wait! There is more to this meeting than meets the eye."

The mage clasped his hands together, mumbled something inaudible, then spread his arms outward. A large web flew from his finger tips and landed in a corner of the room. The magician rushed to the spot where the projectile had settled and found a little rodent squirming, trying in vain to free itself from the stickiness of the trap.

Grasping the netting, Allard lifted it off the floor and brought the mouse to his face. The creature's nervous green eyes stared back at the magician. The mage then placed the webbing back on the floor and began to chant, his words getting louder and louder. As he spoke, the mouse chirped, trying to counteract the mage's spell, but in the end it lost the battle. The rodent transformed into a woman with flowing, radiant red hair and big, beautiful green eyes.

"Hello, Fallyn," said Allard with a smile. "You are a very talented shape shifter, but you really should keep better company." The mage snapped his fingers. "Guards, be sure to keep her bound and in a room with no windows. She's too dangerous otherwise."

The remaining three soldiers led the ensnared woman out of the room behind Gareth and the other sentries.

After Lord Hammer's men had removed the Aegeans from their sight, Allard asked, "Are you really going to honor your word?"

Nigel smiled. "For now; I do need him to identify Harrison's girl. And, more importantly, I need to know who this traitor is. That person is going to wish that they were never born."

CHAPTER 13

¤

Tara shielded her eyes from the high midday sun. From her vantage point, Concur loomed about ten miles away. The young maiden stared at the walled city, recalling the horrifying encounters she had heard from Harrison and his friends about their imprisonment, and how they had needed Thoragaard's help in order to flee the metropolis.

With a sigh, she lowered her hand from her brow, just in time to feel Lance's muzzle rub up against her leg. Tara bent to one knee and gave the dog vigorous rubs behind his ears. Lance wagged his tail at a feverish rate, enjoying his cranial massage.

Tara stopped her scratching and held the pooch's face in her hands. "Everything will be fine, right, Lance?" she asked.

The young girl stared into the canine's brown eyes, then laughed out loud at the funny sight of the animal's scrunched face in her small hands.

"Now I know why Harrison loves you so much — you're so adorable!" Lance yapped with excitement, sensing the sincerity in the girl's voice. A small gathering of fighters interrupted the tender moment.

The tall, blonde-haired warrior spoke first. "This is as far as we go," said Kymbra. "You two will be traveling to Concur alone."

Tara rose and nodded, acknowledging the fighter's remark. "Will we have to worry about running into Concurian soldiers before we get to the city?"

"You might," Kymbra brought her gaze to Justin, "but just tell them that you're going to Concur looking for work."

"I understand our mission," said the Aegean fighter. "We'll be fine."

"Alerting Thoragaard's sentry will be the easy part," added Marissa, moving to the forefront next to Kymbra. "The hard part will be getting access to Meredith."

"Can we really do this?" asked Tara, her blue eyes full of concern.

Marissa came over to the nervous girl and rested a caring hand on her shoulder. "Yes, we can and you'll do just fine. We'll reconvene here after your mission."

"How long do you plan on waiting," said Justin, before catching himself. "Um, I mean, what if we take a long time returning?"

"We're ready to camp here for a week," said Kymbra. "If you don't show up by then, we'll join the army and head your rescue mission."

"It won't get to that," reassured Justin. "It's my job to make sure you're safe, and if things get a bit dicey, we'll leave. You have my word, Tara."

The fair maiden's shoulders slumped a bit, realizing that worrying about what could happen would only zap her strength and compromise their mission.

"I know you'll do your best, Justin." Tara exhaled, relieving herself of nervous energy. "I'm ready. Let's go."

"Very well," said Kymbra. "It's a ten mile trek through the countryside, but as you can see, you have unlimited visibility to the city."

Tara gazed out at the open plains, seeing no obstructions, just like Kymbra said.

"Make contact with the guard, confront Meredith." The female fighter jerked her thumb back for emphasis. "Then get out. Understood?"

"Understood," said Justin, with Tara nodding in concurrence.

"Good. We'll see you in a few days. Good luck."

Justin hoisted his pack onto his back, while Tara secured her things as well. The young girl tugged the straps of her backpack and with everything ready, proceeded to embark on her mission.

"Lance, you lead the way, boy," she said to the little dog. With a yap, the canine put his nose to the ground and led the couple toward the great walled city.

"Stay by my side, Tara," said Justin. "We're supposed to be a married couple and we must be sure to act like one."

Tara gazed at the phony wedding ring on her finger before thoughts of Harrison swirled around in her head. "I will. How long will it take until we reach the city's outer limits?"

"I'm thinking by nightfall. Lord Hammer locks his city down at dusk, so it might be close."

The young girl nodded, although she secretly hoped that they would get inside the unfamiliar walls of Concur in order to start their important mission as quickly as possible. That way she could return to Aegeus and wait for Harrison's successful arrival.

"Let's get there before they bolt the doors," said Tara, quickening her pace. "I don't want to let Harrison down."

The young couple trekked unimpeded through the rolling hills of the Concurian countryside, reaching the great walled city just before dusk. Lance, who had ventured a short distance ahead of the twosome during their journey, stopped in his tracks about three hundred feet from the entrance.

Tara and Justin approached the canine a few minutes later. The young maiden fixed her eyes on the guards who manned their posts a short distance away, then took her gaze to the huge walls.

"This place is so big," she said in amazement, wondering how they will ever find Meredith in such a large metropolis.

"We'll be fine if we stick to the plan," reassured Justin. The young Aegean fighter made a subtle glance around his surroundings, taking in everything in the immediate area, just as he had learned at the Fighter's Guild.

Feeling all was in order, he kept his head down and whispered to Tara, "Don't look now, but the guard on the left is the one we want to speak to. Let me do the talking. All right?"

Tara nodded, before realizing that Justin still had his head down, pretending to find something. "Yes, all right," she answered at last.

"Good. Take my hand." The young man reached in Tara's direction.

The young maiden had an instant of uncertainty, but then realized it would be more than believable for a young married couple to hold hands. Tara, intent on moving the mission forward, accepted Justin's invitation.

At that moment, the fighter gazed into Tara's eyes, realizing how many hearts this girl must have broken before Harrison came along.

With a smile, he said, "Off to Concur, my wife."

Tara smiled back. "Let's go." The young maiden focused on the dog that waited in front of them. "Lead the way, Lance."

The little dog yapped, then turned and marched toward the huge entranceway. Within minutes, the three wanderers reached the guard post. An armored sentry stepped forward, raising his palm to stop the couple. A second guard remained back at the gateway entrance, watching his colleague closely.

"Halt!" he said, looking the people over. "What is your business with Concur?"

Justin pulled Tara closer to him. "My new wife and I are looking for work and we'd be very happy if you'd let us find employment in your fine city."

"That depends," said the sentry. "Where are you from?"

"Aegeus," responded Justin without hesitation.

The guard stared at Tara, admiring her beauty in a not so subtle way. "Lord Hammer always has room in his army for young men like you, and I'm sure the lady can find work." The sentry smirked at his own comment.

Justin attempted to appear offended. "What do you mean by that? She's a hard worker and will be a find for anyone who needs help."

The outburst did not faze the fighter. "What kind of work can she do?"

Tara spoke up upon hearing the question. "I'm hoping that the First Lady needs another handmaiden. I'd like to work for her."

The guard laughed at Tara's enthusiasm. "Like you're the only one looking for a job like that! I hate to tell you, sweetheart, but there's no job opening there."

The second guard took an increased interest in this strange couple's conversation upon hearing that Tara wanted to work as an assistant for Meredith.

The blonde-haired sentry took a couple of steps toward his comrade. "On the contrary, I've heard that Meredith is in need of another helper."

The guard made a subtle glance to Justin, both men staring deep into each other's eyes for a split second. That was enough for the Concurian to know this pair's true motive.

The first fighter wheeled around to face his fellow guardian. "What are you talking about? Lord Hammer has plenty of staff."

"And you don't think he wouldn't want this one walking around his mansion?" The sentry jerked his thumb in Tara's direction, a smirk on his face.

"Ha! You're right!" laughed the first man. "Never thought of that!"

The second sentry waved his friend back. "Go back to your post, I'll handle these two. I know who they need to talk to at the mansion."

"So there really is a position open with Meredith?"

"Yup."

The man looked up in thought, massaging his chin. "Maybe my wife can apply for that position."

"Um, she's not quite mansion material, if you know what I mean," said the blonde man.

The first guardian scowled. "No, I don't know what you mean."

The other man waved his palms in front of his fellow guard. "We'll talk about this later. Let me take care of these folks."

"We *will* talk about this later," said the first fighter, gazing over at Justin and Tara. "Not mansion material…" he mumbled before returning to his post.

The second sentry glanced back at his friend, and when he felt the man was far enough away, he positioned himself before Justin and Tara.

"This will be quick," he started. "Listen well." The young couple nodded, waiting with anticipation to what this person had to say.

"First, hand me ten gold pieces." Justin did not hesitate to remove a small sack from his belt, then emptied the coins into the guardian's awaiting hand. "Good. If anyone's watching they'll be thinking that I'm just doing my job."

The blonde fighter accepted the tribute. "Head up the main street, turn left at the second intersection, go three alleys down, turn right and request a room at the fifth building on the left. Tell the innkeeper that Marshall said that Lord Hanrahan's nephew has arrived and you seek shelter for the night."

Marshall gazed down at the animal that sat by Tara's feet. "Lord Hammer isn't crazy about dogs. Don't let him wander around or you'll lose him."

"He won't leave our sight," said Justin. "How long will it be until we see Meredith?"

"We've spoken for too long," said Marshall. "Do as I said."

The young couple both nodded in understanding. The Concurian turned around to man his post once again.

"Let's get to the inn, Justin," said Tara, a hint of anxiety in her voice.

"Remain calm and all will be fine," he answered, trying to allay her fears. The young Aegean then pointed a finger toward the sitting dog. In a forceful voice, he said, "Lance, stick by our side."

The canine's eyes lit up at the mention of his name, although he could not understand the command. Sensing their imminent departure, Lance stood up and readied himself to leave.

Justin once again took hold of Tara's hand and led her to the checkpoint. Both guards watched the young couple and their dog enter the city.

"Enjoy your stay in Concur," said Marshall. "And good luck with your search."

Justin nodded. "Thank you."

After the twosome entered through the gate, the first guard said to his comrade, "Did you get the extra tariff for the dog?"

"Yes, and with a bonus." Marshall handed his buddy a gold piece.

"It's nice knowing that foreigners have no idea what the actual tax is to enter Concur!"

"Seven for Lord Hammer, two for me, and one for you," said the fair-haired fighter.

The first man smiled wide. "Sometimes I really love this job!" His demeanor changed as he thought back to their previous conversation. "So, what's wrong with my wife?"

Marshall continued to fumble with the coins Justin gave to him. "Did you happen to notice how young and beautiful that girl was?"

"Yes."

"Your wife is the opposite."

"Hey," barked the first soldier, pointing a finger in Marshall's face. "My wife is a good woman! She's just not as young anymore."

"Point taken," said the other man. "Why don't we just drop this subject and start preparing the doors for nighttime?"

The first sentry lowered his digit away from his friend's face. "Yeah, let's." The two Concurians then began their inspection of the area before they sealed the entranceway for the evening.

A bearded man, bound in shackles, sat in dejection near the East Gate. Gareth had put his faith in his alignment with Lord Hammer, but now he contemplated their agreement. Scores of young women came through the eastward facing gateway of the metropolis, but no one fit the profile of the maiden his counterpart had seen. That all changed just minutes before nightfall forced the great doors to close for the evening.

"That's the girl!" he said, pointing in the direction of a young couple who had just entered the city.

The lead soldier jerked his chain in the same manner a cruel master would pull on the leash of his dog. "Are you sure?"

Gareth maneuvered his head to alleviate the tension from his neck. Before answering, he contemplated the benefit of telling this man if he were indeed correct.

His spirit almost broken and Fallyn sealed in a jail cell, Gareth wondered if Nigel would keep his word. This was no safe haven, but he also knew he could not go back to Aegeus and try to save face. He was a warrior at heart and believed that an Aegeus –

Concur alliance would be the most powerful one the land had ever seen.

His bruised faith aside, he answered, "I'm positive."

The leader barked to three of his men. "Follow that couple, find out where they're heading, and report back. Don't do anything else without consulting me."

Three armored fighters acknowledged their orders and carefully followed the unsuspecting duo.

Turning his attention back to Gareth, the Concurian said, "I'll let Lord Hammer know that you cooperated, after we're sure of this so-called plot of yours."

The lost Aegean hung his head, nodding ever so slowly. He then felt the steel handcuffs dig into his skin as another soldier yanked on them, signaling for Gareth to rise.

"Back to your sanctuary," the fighter said with a wry smile.

Gareth hung his head in shame and again wondered if he had done the right thing.

Justin led his imitation bride through the streets of Concur, careful not to draw undo attention to themselves. Lance strutted by their side, taking in all the new sights and smells of the metropolis.

Tara tightly held Justin's hand, her nervous energy evident in her grip. The young couple had already made their turn at the second major intersection and tried to look inconspicuous as they searched for the third alleyway.

The young maiden watched the street vendors pack away their wares for the day, the ensuing nightfall fast approaching. Her thoughts drifted to the man she missed so much, recalling the dangers he faced in this very city. Receiving directions from a stranger, an armored guard no less, sneaking around a foreign land, searching for a building tucked out of the way only made her nerves fray more. A moment later, Justin led her down the third alleyway on the right.

Advancing ever so slowly, the twosome approached the fifth building on the left, The Wanderer's Inn. Appropriate name, thought Justin, considering they had meandered through this foreign town.

"Remember, we're married," said the young fighter. "Ready?"

"Yes," answered the golden-haired girl.

Before entering through the main door, the couple climbed the wide staircase that led to a porch stretching the length of the building.

Tara gazed about the foyer, surprised to see such exquisite furniture and knick-knacks strewn carelessly about the room. Justin approached the middle-aged man who sat behind a desk. The innkeeper was using a finger to follow the words in a scripture he read by candlelight.

The Aegean stood in front of the person, who kept his head down. After a few uncomfortable seconds of waiting, Justin cleared his throat in order to get the man's attention.

"Excuse me, sir, we'd like a room for the night."

Not bothering to look up, the man pointed to a sign off to his right and said, "There's no room in this inn; we're completely booked."

Justin jerked his head in the direction the man pointed. Sure enough, a placard hung to the wall with the phrase "No Vacancy" clearly visible.

The young fighter did his best to curb his anxiety and recalled what the Concurian guard had told him. Leaning closer to the innkeeper, he said in a near whisper, "Sir, Lord Hanrahan's nephew has arrived and seeks shelter for the night."

The man did not look up, but his finger stopped following the book's words. Closing the scripture, the innkeeper's gray eyes met Justin's.

"Lord Hanrahan's nephew, you say?"

"Yes, sir. But we can go elsewhere if there is no room for us here."

The man gazed past Justin, taking in the sight of Tara and Lance just a few feet behind the Aegean fighter.

The salt and pepper-haired man said, "I expected the Lord's nephew to be more ... experienced."

Justin brushed off the man's comment. "Is there a room for us?"

"Of course there is," said the innkeeper with a smirk. He then went to close and lock the front door.

Whisking by the young couple, he motioned with his finger and said, "Follow me."

The three humans and Lance left the foyer to go down the main hallway. Tara anxiously passed door upon door, before arriving in front of a staircase at the end of the corridor. Everyone then climbed the stairs until they reached the third floor. No one spoke.

The innkeeper rushed past four more doors until he stopped at room 333. Attached to his belt rested a ring full of keys; his fingers fumbled through them all until he found the right one. Placing the shaft in the lock, the man turned the key to the right, opened the portal and waved the young couple in.

Tara gazed about the small room. An undersized bureau sat against a wall, and a single bed rested between two windows. The young maiden searched for more amenities, but only a small nightstand and closet remained.

The innkeeper closed the door and locked it. He then turned to face the couple with a frown, revealing his apprehension.

Extending his hand to Justin, he said, "My name is Edward Waluk and we've all been waiting for this day."

The two men exchanged pleasantries. "I'm Justin, and this is Tara." Edward nodded to the young girl.

"What do we do now?" asked Tara, confused at the suddenness of the actions in the past thirty minutes.

"It's up to you to signal the start of the resistance," said the innkeeper. "We must get you to Meredith."

"I'm assuming you have a plan, right?" asked Justin.

"I have a strict protocol to follow," said Edward. "The first thing is to lock you away in this room until your part is set."

Tara's eyes grew wide. "How long will we be locked in here?"

"Not too long, a day or two, hopefully no longer than that."

Justin nodded and gazed at the beautiful woman who stood next to him. Being locked up with her couldn't be that bad, he thought. He then gazed down at Lance.

"Lance will need to go outside from time to time."

"I'll take care of that when I bring you your meals," said Edward, smiling down at the dog. "I had a dog once; I know what to do."

"Thank you," said Tara, before removing her knapsack and placing it on the bed. "Is there anything I should know before my meeting with Meredith?"

Edward shook his head. "No. I'm assuming you have your orders and know what to say."

"I do," answered Tara. "I'm only supposed to tell her."

Edward nodded in agreement. "The fewer people who know, the less of a chance something goes wrong." Changing the subject, he said, "Do you need anything to eat? You must have had a long journey."

Justin realized that he was indeed very hungry and assumed Tara and Lance were, too. "As a matter of fact, I'm starving. Can you also bring us some fresh water?"

"Sure thing," said Edward. "I'll be back in fifteen minutes." The innkeeper was about to open the door when he wheeled around, a finger pointed in the air.

"I almost forgot! Under no circumstance do you open this door unless you hear three knocks followed by 'Lord Hanrahan, are you decent?' Understood?"

Both young people nodded.

"Good. I'll be back soon." With that, Edward left the room, locking the door behind him.

Justin and Tara watched the door close. They were now alone, for who knows how long. Breaking the uncomfortable silence, Justin said, "I'm going to set up my things over there." The young fighter pointed to the opposite side of the room, away from the bed and bureau. "You can sleep in the bed."

Tara gazed at the bedding with its soft mattress and fluffy pillows, then took a gander at the hardwood floors that looked so uninviting.

"Don't be ridiculous, Justin, you can sleep over there." Tara pointed to the left side of the bed. "There's no sense in getting poor rest on account of sleeping arrangements."

The young fighter did not offer much resistance. "As long as you don't mind ..."

"It's all right, really." The young maiden then started to remove the contents of her pack. "We might as well get comfortable. It sounds like we'll be here for awhile."

The young couple then went about settling in, both wondering what lay ahead for them while they stayed in the great city of Concur.

CHAPTER 14

¤

"You say they entered The Wanderer's Inn?" said the Concurian captain upon hearing the report from his sentry. "Have you seen any other movement?"

"No," responded the soldier. "Two fighters from my platoon are watching the building as we speak. They'll report back to me if they witness anything unusual."

The captain nodded slowly upon hearing the news. Lord Hammer had given specific orders to avoid taking the foreigners hostage; he wanted them to guide him to their supposed leader in hiding, Thoragaard.

"Canvass the entire building," said the Concurian leader. "I want all exits monitored, but don't be obvious. We don't want these people to get spooked; we need to follow them to their next destination." A thought came to the fighter's mind.

"Better yet, add more men to the stakeout. I want the perimeter monitored and reinforcements ready at a moment's notice."

"Understood, sir." The sentry stood tall. "I'll report back my findings in four hours, as you have ordered." The young fighter saluted and left his commander in order to continue with his mission.

The Concurian leader smiled. "Lord Hammer will be quite happy, and I'll most certainly get that promotion I deserve."

Tara removed a soft blue blouse from her backpack and placed it in one of the bureau drawers. She had tried to remain calm, but the current situation left her apprehensive. Being a mage in training, she did her best to curb her anxiety and foster a sense of confidence.

"Justin, will we be all right?"

The Aegean stopped his own unpacking to address Tara. "We should be fine as long as we stick to the plan."

"What if things change? I mean, things that are out of our control?"

Justin maneuvered closer to the pretty girl. "Let's not worry about things that might or might not happen. We should focus on completing our mission as best we can. All right?"

Tara flashed an anxious smile. "I suppose." Just then, both of them heard three soft knocks at the door.

"Lord Hanrahan, are you decent?" came a female voice from the other side of the portal.

Justin glanced at Tara, her brow creased. Both of them had expected to hear Edward's voice, but now someone else appeared to be in the fold.

"That's the right code," said Justin in hushed tone to Tara. Taking the initiative, the young man addressed the person in the hallway.

"Yes, I am. You may enter."

A key unlocked the door, followed by a middle-aged woman who entered with a plate full of freshly cooked foods. Once inside she could read the concerned looks on the young faces that stared back at her.

"Don't be alarmed," she said, traversing the room and placing the tray on the bureau. "I'm Edward's wife, Eloise."

She then motioned to Justin. "Please close that door." The young fighter did as instructed, then turned to question the woman.

"What's happening?"

Eloise waved a hand in front of her, shaking out her auburn-haired head. "Nothing you need to worry about. Edward is beginning the process."

Tara, quiet until now, spoke. "Process?"

The older woman turned and approached the young maiden. Reaching her, Eloise extended her hands to clasp the girl's.

Gazing into Tara's lovely blue eyes, she said with pride, "My sweet child, your presence in Concur is to start the Resistance Movement. It has begun."

"But we just arrived," said Tara, shaking her head. "How can we have started anything yet?"

"You don't think that we're leaving this all to chance, do you?" Eloise saw that the girl's head moved no faster. "I didn't think so. History will remember you." She brought her gaze to Justin with a smile. "Both of you."

The young fighter nodded, understanding the monumental significance that this meeting had for the woman before him. "Edward said it might be a couple of days before we leave this room."

"Oh, at the least." Eloise released her grip on Tara's hands. "Edward is just the first link in a series of connections that are about to happen." The elder female smiled again. "Rest assured, your job will be of the utmost importance – when the time is right."

The Concurian woman gestured to the tray of steaming food. "I know you both must be very hungry. I've taken the time to prepare some fresh meat, vegetables, breads, and," Eloise picked up a decanter, filling two pewter goblets, "the finest bottle of wine at the inn."

Justin took his gaze to Tara, raising an eyebrow in surprise. "We're very honored, ma'am."

"I'll take your dog outside tonight," added Eloise, reaching for Lance. Crinkling her brow, she realized that the animal had no leash, let alone a collar to attach it to.

"He won't run off on me, will he?"

"Lance?" exclaimed Tara. "He's a very good dog. He'll listen to everything you say to him."

Eloise bent to one knee and rubbed the canine on his head. "Very well then! Let's go, Lance." The dog barked once at hearing his name, then turned and looked at Tara with an apparent look of concern.

Tara gestured toward the door. "It's all right, Lance. Go with Eloise."

Lance whimpered and lowered his ears, hoping that Tara would accompany him with this stranger.

"He'll be fine," said Tara.

Eloise walked to the doorway, stopping to wait for Lance. Tail drooping, the dog followed a moment later. The woman began to close the door, but held it open a second longer.

"I don't have to bring the dog back right away," she said, raising a mischievous eyebrow. "You've had a long trip and you probably would like some alone time, especially if you're going to be holed up here for a couple of days."

Tara's face turned beet red, while Justin fumbled for words. "No. No, that's all right. You can bring Lance right back. Really."

Eloise shrugged. "If you say so. If it were me, I'd take advantage of my offer, if you know what I mean."

She started to close the door, but left it open a crack. Then her head popped in the room again, and she said, "I'll bring another carafe of wine anyway." Finally the woman shut the door and locked it behind her.

After the portal closed, Justin flashed Tara a sheepish smile. "She doesn't know that we're not a real couple."

"I gathered that much," said Tara, searching for something to break the uncomfortable moment. Gazing at the steaming food, she said, "Let's just eat and try to settle in the best we can."

"Good idea."

The two youngsters relaxed over the meal, the wine helping to calm their anxieties. Eloise returned Lance to their room a half hour later, and after that the couple settled in for a much-needed restful sleep.

Justin was sitting on the window sill, peering down to the street below, when he heard the familiar coded knock at the door. After responding with the correct password, Edward unlocked the door and swung it open, just as he had over and over again for the past two days. This time, though, the young Aegean could sense something amiss.

Justin jumped from the sill. "What is it, Edward?"

"Today's the day," said the innkeeper. Turning to face Tara, who was lying on the bed, he said, "Get yourself ready, Missy. You're going to the Governor's mansion this afternoon."

Tara hopped up from the bed. "It happens today? Am I finally going to meet Meredith?"

"Yes," said Edward with a nod.

Tara noticed that the older man kept looking at the doorway, as if he were expecting someone to come to the room. Someone unwanted.

"Is everything all right, Edward?" asked the young maiden.

The man pointed a finger in the air, then rushed over to the portal, closing and locking it. "There are a lot of Lord Hammer's men on the streets. Something doesn't feel right."

Justin began to take a more interested role in the conversation. "I thought you said everything was in place, that we have nothing to worry about?" The young fighter had promised Harrison that he would keep Tara safe and he intended to do just that.

"There's nothing to worry about," said Edward, raising his palms to the youngsters. "I'll go over the plan now." Tara and Justin huddled next to the innkeeper.

"Tara, you'll be going to the mansion to interview for an opening on Meredith's staff. When you get to the entrance, inform the guards of just that. You'll be allowed to enter, they know you're coming."

Justin intervened. "Are these guards part of the Resistance?"

"No," answered Edward flatly. "They are very loyal to Lord Hammer."

Tara swallowed hard, unable to hide her fear. "Why aren't they involved with our plot?"

"Not everyone wants Nigel overthrown, especially his soldiers," explained the older man. "The fact that there is an opening on Meredith's staff means that she knows the process has started. She knows nothing of you or of the message you hold. My job was to keep you hidden until things were ready."

"And they're ready now?" said Tara aloud, even though she had clearly heard Edward say the very same.

"Yes," said Edward again. "Your interview is set for noon. You will have lunch with Meredith, tell her what you know, and leave the mansion."

Justin interrupted again. "I'm going with her, just in case."

"You will be going there with her, but unarmed. There's no way that you can step foot anywhere near Lord Hammer's residence with a weapon."

"How will I protect her then?"

"You won't," said Edward, staring at the young man. "You are this woman's husband, she needs a job to help your family, and you're there for support. That's all."

Justin shifted his eyes from side to side, then leaned closer to Edward. "What if something goes wrong?" he said in a hushed tone.

The innkeeper shook his head and shrugged. "Others in the Resistance are taking positions in the city, to keep an eye on you." Edward tried to hide his agitation, but failed. "I simply don't know all the guards and soldiers who are on our side. However, they would be the ones to help you if things go awry."

The Aegean recalled Thoragaard relaying him the same vague message. "I wish we had a better escape plan, just in case."

Cocking his head, the older man said, "Are there any other contingency plans?"

Justin thought back to what Kymbra had told him, that if they did not return within a week's time, Thoragaard would commence with a rescue plan.

"That option does not appeal to me," said the Aegean. "What do we say to the guards if they ask where they can reach us with news of employment?"

"Tell them you're staying here; we won't have to lie that you visited us, but you'll be outside of Concur long before they come looking for you."

Justin nodded, agreeing with the plan. He then noticed Lance's subtle maneuver, switching from his seated stance to a restful lying position.

"What about Lance? Can he come with us?"

Edward's eyes grew wide and he shook his head no. "Absolutely not! Lord Hammer would have him run out of town on the next cart leaving the city, or worse, run through with the nearest sword. He hates dogs!"

"So how do we get him back?" asked Tara, concerned.

"Like I said, you'll be watched. We'll point him in your direction after your meeting."

Tara glanced at Justin, both youngsters sharing the same look of apprehension.

The young maiden crossed her arms across her chest. "All these unknown eyes watching us …" she said shaking her head. "I just don't have a good feeling about this."

Edward stared at the girl. "Don't worry; we'll get him reunited with the both of you. I promise."

Tara shook her head, taking her gaze to a random corner of the room, still unsure.

Edward continued. "Your meeting's not for another couple of hours. The two of you get ready. The next time I come knocking, you'll be leaving this room for good."

The innkeeper rested a hand on Justin's shoulder, then extended his other. "Good luck, son," he said, as both men shared farewells. "We're all counting on you."

He then turned his attention to Tara. "You're perfect for this mission. I'm glad to see such bravery in a girl so young."

Edward lingered his gaze on the young couple a second longer, then turned and departed, locking the door behind him.

With the innkeeper gone, Tara turned to the fighter and said, "I'm not sure about this, Justin."

The Aegean tried to suppress his doubts. "These people have planned for this day for years. We have to trust in them." He then took the anxious girl in his arms, hugging her close. "You're going to do just fine. I have faith in you."

Tara hugged Justin back. "Thank you; I know I can do this, too." Moving away from the young man, she said, "It's time for me to get ready."

With that, the young couple prepared for their much-anticipated rendezvous with Concur's First Lady.

CHAPTER 15

¤

Two uncomfortable hours passed while Tara and Justin waited for Edward to return to their room. The young couple had prepared for Tara's meeting by reciting to each other what they intended to say to the people they met along the way.

The young girl frowned, anxious. "So much can still go wrong, Justin."

The fighter nodded, acknowledging Tara's fears. "I know, but let's not think about that. Stay positive." He then took a more serious tone.

"Remember, if you feel at any time that someone has figured out that we are not who we say we are just say nothing. All right?"

Tara, though not completely satisfied with Justin's answer, nodded nevertheless.

Just then, they both heard the familiar rapping of the coded knock at the door. "Lord Hanrahan, are you decent?"

Justin rose from his seated position on the bed. "Yes. You may enter."

The door unlocked and Edward entered the room. "It is time."

The Aegean gazed at Tara, both locking their worrisome eyes. "I'll be with you every step of the way." Justin took hold of the young maiden's hands. "I made a promise to Harrison that I would not allow anyone to harm you. I intend to keep it."

Tara did not say a word. Instead she pulled Justin close and hugged him tightly. "You're a good man, Justin. Let's go."

The two separated and Justin pointed to Lance. "Edward, you'll watch over him for us, right?"

"Yes." The older man nodded and gestured toward the doorway. "Time to get moving."

The three people and Lance walked down the hallway and began to descend the staircase, all the while Edward gave the young couple last minute advice.

"Don't make small talk with Lord Hammer's men – they are trained to ask questions and respond with short answers." The small party reached the foyer.

"Nigel's servants are much more hospitable and accommodating; you can deal with them." Edward extended his hand one final time. "It has been an honor being part of this process. Be sure to go straight to the mansion, conclude your business, and leave Concur."

Justin accepted the man's hand. "Thank you for your help."

"You're very welcome."

"And Lance?" asked Tara.

"Someone is in place to shadow you to the mansion," assured Edward. "That person will make sure that Lance will join you before you depart the city. I promise."

The young couple looked at each other, understanding the heavy burden that they carried. Justin gave the innkeeper one final affirmative nod, then held the door open for his make believe bride. Without saying a word, the young couple left the Wanderer's Inn and headed for the Governor's mansion.

A Concurian sentry watched a young couple exit the building. He squinted to get a better read on the girl – the unmistakable blonde hair, petite frame, and stellar good looks – this was the person they had waited to see for days.

The soldier grabbed his comrade's arm, shaking it vigorously. "That's them! We need to alert the others!"

The second guard gazed at the couple from his rooftop perch as well. "You're right! It's them!"

"Let's go!" The two Concurians jumped to their feet and left their post in haste in order to report their findings to their superiors.

Walking hand-in-hand, Tara and Justin meandered up Concur's main street. The two watched as the townspeople went about their daily activities, oblivious to the young couple's true motive. The girl lifted her head and gazed at the mansion that loomed before them.

"That must be Lord Hammer's residence," she said. The young girl felt a wave of anxiety course through her.

"I agree," said Justin, more worried about the guards who stood outside the building's double doorway than anything else at the moment. "We're going to walk right into that building, Tara."

The young maiden let Justin's comment linger in the air without saying a word.

"It looks like they're heading right for the mansion," said an undercover sentry to his comrade.

"Why would they be going there?"

The first man squinted in thought, then shook his head. "I have no idea."

"You don't think someone on Lord Hammer's staff is associated with those traitors, do you?"

The first soldier had been thinking the same thing. "That person's going to wish they had never been born."

"Get to the mansion and alert Lord Hammer." The first sentry grabbed his comrade's arm for emphasis. "And I mean Lord Hammer directly. We can't trust anyone if there's a mole inside the mansion."

The second soldier took a deep breath, his heart quickening at the thought of talking to his superior one on one. "I'll see you there soon enough. Don't let them out of your sight."

With that, the second sentry left his friend and advanced to the Governor's residency via another route.

Meredith waited pensively in the study off her master bedroom. A moment ago she sent for Catherine, her primary handmaiden, as well as the mansion's head servant, Percival. Lord Hammer's lady had important news to divulge, and time was of the essence.

A soft knock came from the closed door. "Milady, you called for me?" said the anxious female voice from the other side of the portal.

Meredith jumped from her chair and opened the door. "Come in – quickly!" The raven-haired woman grabbed Catherine's forearm and pulled her into the room. She then shut the door tight.

Catherine, squinting, asked, "Milady, what is the matter?"

Ignoring the girl's question, she asked, "Did anyone see you come to this room?"

The young girl of eighteen shook her head, her brown hair waving around her shoulders in the process. "Only Paulo, who sent for me, why?"

Catherine read her superior's face. Meredith's eyes seemed focused on something not in the room, as they darted in every direction. Concur's First Lady then took her left thumb to her mouth and began to chew on her nail as she thought.

"Where's Percival?" asked Meredith.

"I didn't see him on my way here. Did you call for him, too?" The First Lady nodded without speaking.

The young handmaiden was about to ask another question, but a knock interrupted her thought process.

"Milady, it is I, Percival," said the male voice. "You called?"

Meredith reached for the doorknob and opened the portal a crack. Seeing Percival, the head servant, behind the door, the woman gazed past his frail shoulders up and down the hallway. The servant's brow crinkled, noticing his superior's unsteady demeanor.

"Milady, is there a problem?" he asked with genuine concern.

"Come inside and lock the door."

Percival did just that, then turned to face Meredith. A look of surprise graced the thin man's face when he saw Catherine in the room as well. Glancing at the young girl, he said, "I ask again, Milady, what is the matter?"

Meredith paced in front of the two for a moment, took a deep breath, then exhaled her nervous energy. All the while her servants waited with great apprehension, worried that their superior might have grave news to tell them.

The leader turned and faced her people. "Have you heard of the Resistance?"

Percival and Catherine exchanged glances before the head servant spoke. "I have heard rumors of its existence, but I'm sure that they are just that — rumors."

Meredith pursed her lips. "I assure you, they are not."

The main servant tried to put his superior at ease. "Milady, even if an uprising were to occur, Lord Hammer would keep you safe. There would be no way for anyone to harm you."

Meredith raised an eyebrow and cocked her head. The time had come to tell her loyal servants her deep, dark secret. "I am the Resistance."

Percival's mouth fell open, while Catherine covered hers with one hand, the other clutching her chest.

"You?" said Percival, a myriad of thoughts swirling in his head. "How can this be? Why?"

Meredith had waited years, twelve painful years to be exact, to tell someone of her predicament. The time had come.

"Both of you know what Nigel has done to me, my family," began the woman. "He is not my husband! He took me as his trophy when he defeated my father's army." Meredith's eyes began to water, her lips quivered, and her voice cracked.

"Nigel robbed me of my parents, my family, and my way of life." Tears rolled down her alabaster face. "Concur was a great metropolis; people used to enjoy their visits and many loved to live here. Not anymore."

Meredith lifted her azure eyes and locked them on Percival's. "You recall how it was. Remember the joy on the townspeople's faces? Now we have anguish."

Percival nodded, recalling his teenage years as a proud citizen of Concur. "Milady, how did you manage to keep this a secret for so long?"

"It was not easy, but I made a vow to myself that I would avenge my father's demise. I have a person who believes in my cause just as strongly as I do, and he will come to our rescue."

Catherine, quiet until now, asked, "Who?"

"Thoragaard." Both servants nodded, not surprised at hearing the person's name.

"He helped those young boys who came through here a few months ago, didn't he?" asked Catherine.

"Yes, he did," answered Meredith, as a fleeting vision of Harrison entered her mind.

"What is he going to do?" asked Percival.

Meredith took a moment to make sure she had her facts straight. "Thoragaard sent a messenger to the mansion, telling me that someone will come to interview for an open position on my staff. That's the code that we put into place years ago. Now, this person is actually bringing information to me to start the Resistance process."

The male servant could see where the conversation headed. "I will be receiving this person, won't I?"

Meredith walked over to Percival, held his hands and tried to look deep into his eyes. "I need you to be on my side, Percival. You are integral to this whole plan."

Percival took his gaze downward. "I believe in you, Meredith. Nigel is an evil man." The servant lifted his eyes and locked them on his superior's. "However, if I do this for you, who will protect me in the end?"

"I will," said Meredith, unwavering. "Side with me in the Resistance and you will reap the benefits of the new Concur."

Percival pondered his leader's request. Deep down, he loathed Nigel Hammer and blamed him for all of the repression in the city. Aligning with Meredith was not a hard decision; the consequences that would ensue if soldiers found out that he had were another story.

Choosing to follow his heart, he said, "I will side with you. What do you need me to do?"

"Escort this person to me. Do not let Nigel interfere with my interview. I will need this to be done in the utmost secrecy. Can you do this?"

Percival's heart raced. "I can. When will this person be arriving?"

"Noon."

A wave of anxiety raced through the frail man's body. "It's just about noontime now!"

"I know," said Meredith. "Return to your duties at once, then bring this person to this room when she arrives. Understood?"

"Yes, Milady." Percival clutched the doorknob, but before turning it he said, "It will be an honor to die for you."

Meredith rushed to her servant's side. "Don't talk like that! We'll all be better off when Nigel's overthrown."

"That we will." Percival opened the door. "I must go now." The servant quickly exited the room and headed to his post.

Meredith watched the portal shut, then turned to face Catherine. She found the face of a very nervous girl staring back at her.

"Catherine, dear," began the elder female, "I have a job for you, too, if you choose to remain with me."

Tears streamed down the young girl's face. Between sobs, Catherine said, "Milady, I'm so scared for you!"

Meredith rushed to her handmaiden's side and held her close. "Shh, Catherine! Everything will be all right."

The young girl wiped her eyes, shaking her head. "How can you be so sure? Lord Hammer is ruthless!"

Meredith nodded, fully aware of her man's capabilities. "All the more reason to keep our secret." The First Lady of Concur allowed Catherine's sobs to subside. "If you wish to side with me, I have a most important job for you to do."

Catherine, just as Percival before her, understood Meredith's dire situation. "I will do anything for you, Milady."

Meredith understood the danger that her actions placed on her loyal subjects. "I admire your faith in me, Catherine. Percival's, too." The older woman placed a hand under the girl's chin, lifting her head to make direct eye contact with her.

"Listen and listen to me good," started Meredith. "I want you to go to the large temple on the south side of town two hours after sunset. Climb to the top of the steeple and light a lantern. Keep this lamp illuminated for no more than thirty minutes. After that, blow out the light and hide. Do you understand your duties?"

Tears rolled down Catherine's face as she nodded. "How long do I hide for?"

"You will know when the time is right to leave your hiding place."

The young handmaiden sobbed, scared. "Where shall I go now?"

"Continue with your daily chores, but stay close to this room. I will summon you later." Meredith kissed Catherine on the cheek. "You must realize that I love you like a daughter. I'd never let anything happen to you."

The young girl flashed a nervous smile, sniffling. "You're not old enough to be my mother." Her comment lightened the mood.

Meredith smiled back, tears in her eyes. "An older sister then." Catherine nodded. "You must return to your duties now."

Catherine wiped the tears from her face and brushed back her hair in an effort to compose herself. "I'll be awaiting your orders, Milady."

"You're such a good girl, Catherine. Go!" The young girl opened the door and exited the room.

Meredith watched the portal close, then took a seat in a large wooden chair. Thoughts of who might be coming to the mansion swirled about her head, while her stomach churned with worry. All she could do now was wait and hope that her plan would not be uncovered.

Two soldiers stood guard outside Lord Hammer's majestic mansion. Tara and Justin, their hands clutched together, made a cautious approach to the entranceway. Both hoped that their anxiety-riddled appearance would not raise any suspicions.

As the youngsters stood before a twenty-foot wide staircase, Justin felt the guardians' eyes look them over, just as he would do if the roles were reversed. The Aegean took the lead as the young couple ascended the ten steps to the doorway's receiving area. Without hesitation, the guard on the left addressed the twosome.

"What is your business here?" The sentry gripped the hilt of his sword as he awaited an answer.

"My wife," started Justin, motioning in Tara's direction, "is here about the opening on Her Lady's staff."

The guard squinted. "Opening? There are no openings at the mansion."

Justin persisted. "I assure you, my good man, we would not have traveled here for nothing."

Turning to his comrade, the sentry asked, "Is there anything on today's docket?"

The second guard unrolled a parchment, then looked it over. Shaking his head, he said, "Nothing's here."

Tightening the grip on his weapon, the first soldier said, "You best be gone. There's no business for you here."

Justin's stomach felt queasy and he could only imagine what thoughts were running rampant in Tara's head. Edward would not have sent us here in vain, he thought.

Making another effort, he said, "Maybe someone forgot to add our visit to your daily agenda."

The first soldier glanced to his partner, then huffed. "The boy thinks we made a mistake." The guard took two purposeful steps toward Justin, stopping inches from his face. The man fixed his dark eyes on the Aegean. "We don't make mistakes."

The guardian held his ground, trying his best to intimidate the young man who stood before him. Justin wanted nothing more than to put this man in his place, but his fighter training told him otherwise. Recalling his teachings at the Fighter's Guild, he averted his eyes, allowing the Concurian soldier to win this battle.

"My good man," started Justin, making sure to keep his eyes turned away, "we are but a newly married couple with very little money and no place to stay. This position will give us just enough to start our lives together."

Justin peeked at the guard while maintaining his submissive appearance; the sentry's expression remained the same. Lowering his eyes again, he said, "All I ask is for you to see if someone forgot to tell you that we were coming today."

The guard did not move, forcing Justin to stand still in his humble posture. Without removing his stare, the man barked to his comrade, "Fetch Percival and see if he overlooked something."

The second sentry did as commanded and left his post. The soldier then took two steps back and stood in the center of the double doors, watching every move the young couple made.

Justin held Tara's hand tighter. The young girl looked at his face and could see that small beads of perspiration had formed on his brow. The mere sight of the sweat caused her heart to race even faster. Before she could allow her brain to commence pessimistic thoughts, she heard chatter emanating behind the large doors.

"Yes, yes, it's my fault," a nervous voice said from the other side of the entranceway. The portals opened and a thin man appeared before them with the second sentry following right behind him.

The servant waved the young couple forward. "Please, follow me."

Before Justin and Tara could advance, the first soldier thrust his hand in front of them. "Where are they going?"

Percival's shoulders slumped and he appeared out of breath. "Meredith just informed me that they would be arriving for an opening on her staff."

"Why weren't we informed?" asked the guard, his brow creased in a frown, skeptical.

"You know the lady's whims as well as I," said Percival, not missing a beat. "I was on the other side of the mansion when she summoned me and then I had to race all the way over here to greet these people." The frail servant shook his head. "I don't even know their names."

The guardian spun around, stunned. Glaring at the pair, he barked, "Who are you two?"

Tara addressed the question before Justin could speak. "My name is Tara, and this is my husband, Justin. Please, sir, I am so nervous already and all this commotion is making things worse." The girl fluttered her eyelashes, using her sad, blue eyes to her advantage. "Please."

The guard stared at Justin, who was cowered and not daring to look him in the eye. Huffing, the sentry relented, saying, "You may go," he pointed to Tara, "but your husband waits for you in the study."

Tara flashed the guard a wide smile. "Thank you so much, sir. We will never forget this. Thank you."

The guard did not want the adulation, instead he waved the two through the doorway, saying, "Let's go; let's go." Pointing to the room adjoining the foyer, he commanded Justin, "You wait in there."

The young man nodded. "Good luck, sweetheart," he said, before being whisked away.

Tara watched the guard escort Justin to the study, then turned her attention to the smaller person beside her.

"Please follow me, Miss," said the servant. Tara obliged.

The two climbed the main spiral staircase of Lord Hammer's mansion, landing at the top. After taking two steps into the hallway, Percival spun around and addressed Tara in a most concerned tone.

"Meredith awaits you in the room across the hall." Tara noticed the man's apprehension and concluded it could only be from her visit today. "Please, deliver your message as fast as you can."

The young maiden gazed at the door Percival had pointed out. With a nod to the nervous man, she crossed the hallway and lightly tapped the door.

"Hello?"

A female voice answered. "Come in."

Tara turned the knob and entered the room. She found a beautiful woman about ten years her senior pacing nervously with her arms crossed inside a majestic library.

"Close the door!"

Tara did as commanded.

Feeling secure for now, Meredith started. "Who are you and why are you here?"

Tara pulled her head back, confused. Did this woman not understand her mission, wondered the young girl. Keeping to the original plan, she answered, "My name is Tara and I'm here for the job opening."

"Who sent you?"

Tara told the truth. "Thoragaard."

Meredith looked for a seat. The cold reality of the overthrow plot seemed to hit her upon hearing the illusionist's name. "This is really happening," she said, more to herself than to Tara.

"Do you need me to get you something?" Tara noticed a pitcher of water and a pair of goblets on a table nearby. Taking the initiative, she poured the woman a flagon of the cool liquid, then handed it to her.

"Thank you," said Meredith, taking a refreshing sip. Gathering herself, she continued, "What do you have to tell me?"

This was Tara's golden moment and she knew it. "Thoragaard told me that I should tell you everything. This all came about after Harrison Cross and his friends uncovered the Treasure of the Land."

Meredith recognized the young man's name and could picture his handsome looks. Learning that Harrison had discovered the land's ultimate prize made her happy.

Tara continued, oblivious to Meredith's thoughts. "The Treasure instructed his team to search for the Talisman of Unification, which they also found. It's at that time I met him."

The older woman saw the gleam in Tara's eye. Sighing to herself and not letting Tara see her true feelings, she said, "You are his woman, aren't you?"

The young girl blushed, nodding. "It was love at first sight."

Meredith gazed at the girl's angelic face, her beautiful blue eyes, perfect body, and knew no man could resist her, not even Harrison. "I'm sure you two make a very nice couple, but I need to hear your message right now."

"Right," said Tara. "Harrison and his army are in the process of reuniting the land. They have headed south in an effort to garner more men before they attack Concur. Aegeus and Argos have aligned and are making their battle plans as we speak. Their hope is that the Concurians will help overthrow Lord Hammer from the inside even before they arrive. Thoragaard said you would handle the rest."

Meredith took another sip of water as she thought. "He's right. It's up to me now." She replaced the goblet, rose from her seat, and dashed to a door on the other side of the room.

Concur's First Lady opened the portal that led to an adjoining bedroom, finding a young girl stripping a bed. In a hushed tone, Meredith said, "Catherine, come here."

A moment later, the door slowly opened and a nervous girl Tara's age entered the room. "Tara, this is Catherine, my primary handmaiden." The young girls nodded and smiled at one another.

"Catherine, it is time for you to leave the mansion and ready yourself for your task." The girl closed her eyes, sniffled, then nodded. Tara thought she saw a tear roll down her face.

Meredith turned her attention back to Tara. "Is there anything else?"

"No. We were told to leave Concur immediately after this meeting."

The First Lady of Concur nodded in agreement. "When will Harrison arrive?"

"I don't know," answered the young girl. "We'll be returning to Aegeus."

Meredith furrowed her brow, cocking her head as well. "We?"

"I have an escort. Harrison hand picked him to play the part of my husband. He's downstairs."

The Concurian woman's eyes widened. "He's downstairs now?" Meredith's light-skinned face began to flush.

Tara noticed the woman's sudden apprehension. "Meredith, what's wrong?"

"Having a strange man in this house is very bad!" Meredith motioned to the doorway. "Nigel is a very jealous man! You must leave now!"

Tara approached the entranceway. "I hope to see you again in better circumstances."

"I as well," said Meredith. "Give my best to Harrison. We're all praying for him."

"I will. Good luck." Tara departed the room and headed downstairs.

With Tara gone, Meredith turned her attention to Catherine. "Now it's your turn. Leave through one of the back exits. Don't go home. Do exactly what I had told you before. All right?"

Catherine appeared on the verge of tears. "I can't do this!"

Meredith held both of her handmaiden's arms and looked into her eyes. "There's no turning back now, Catherine. You must fulfill your part of the plan. Pull yourself together. I'm counting on you."

The scared girl nodded over and over again in an attempt to calm her nerves.

In a caring tone, Meredith repeated, "You can do this." The woman allowed the younger girl to gather herself. "Now, do as I told you. I will see you soon."

Once again Catherine nodded. Taking a cleansing breath, she clutched the doorknob, opened the door, and left Meredith behind.

Justin fidgeted in his seat. Tara had left with the mansion's servant fifteen minutes ago and he hoped that all was going well.

The young fighter heard the clamor of armor advance toward the room. Justin turned his attention to the open doorway just in time to see a man clad in black, chain-mail armor followed by four similarly dressed henchmen.

"Apprehend him!" commanded Nigel Hammer, pointing at the unsuspecting lad. Two of the soldiers made a swift approach to the defenseless Aegean, lifting him clean out of his chair.

"What's the meaning of this?" said Justin, a tremble evident in his voice.

Lord Hammer thrust a finger in the young man's chest. "Who sent you here?"

Justin stared into the cold, dark eyes of Concur's leader. At that very moment, he understood that their mission had been compromised and his fighter's training took over.

"I don't know what you're talking about," he lied. "I escorted my wife here to inquire about a job."

Nigel's glare remained fixed. "Don't toy with me, boy!" Lord Hammer's demeanor became angrier with every passing second. "Who sent you here?"

His situation hopeless, Justin stood tall and responded, "I have nothing to say."

Nigel clenched his teeth, then smacked the lad with his gauntlet-covered hand, cutting Justin's face and drawing blood. The young fighter wobbled, doing his best to maintain his footing.

Lord Hammer then grabbed the boy by his shirt, pulling his face ever so close to his. "Maybe being locked in a prison cell will jar your memory," Nigel hissed. Tossing the lad aside, he ordered his men, "Take him away!"

The two armored soldiers lifted Justin just enough so that his feet dragged behind him. No sooner had the fighters left the room with the injured Aegean, than a voice shrieked from the staircase.

"Justin!" screamed Tara, shocked to see the young fighter apprehended. The two guards stopped their procession in order to gauge the situation.

Nigel, too, spun on his heels and gazed at the beautiful girl who stood helpless on the steps.

"What are you doing with my husband?" exclaimed Tara, running down the stairs. "Please, let him go!"

Lord Hammer took a moment to look over the young maiden. Always one to enjoy the ladies, the attractive ones in particular, Nigel took great interest in the lovely figure that approached him.

"Your husband is a traitor and shall be punished in accordance to my laws." Nigel snapped his fingers and waved his men onward. The soldiers continued their chore of taking Justin to prison, ignoring the young girl's pleas.

"Please, sir! He has done nothing wrong!"

Nigel appeared unfazed by the girl's blatant lies. What he wanted from this person were the names of the people involved in her plan. "Did you come to see Meredith about a job?"

Tara did not want to answer any questions from this man. At first she opened her mouth to speak, but an inner voice told her to keep quiet. Recalling Justin's plan, she closed her mouth, stood tall, and looked away.

Lord Hammer, as he did with Justin, tried to intimidate the girl by getting very close to her face. Bending down to be level with Tara, he locked his black eyes onto hers, staring a moment longer.

When the young maiden averted her face, Nigel grasped her cheeks and turned her to stare at him. Tara's face flushed.

"You foolish, foolish girl!" Nigel released his grip. "Your pathetic actions give you away!"

Lord Hammer glared at one of the two remaining soldiers. "Fetch me Percival!" The fighter nodded and ran to find the head servant, not wanting to enrage his superior further.

Turning his attention back to Tara, Nigel said, "You can save yourself and your *husband* a lot of pain by answering my questions truthfully." The young girl stood motionless, gazing off to another part of the foyer.

The pretty lass's defiance caused Nigel's blood to simmer. Before he launched into a complete tirade, the soldier returned with a visibly shaken servant.

"Did you allow these people into the mansion?" asked Nigel in a forceful tone.

"That I did, sir." Percival tried his best to be strong, but his voice wavered and cracked.

Nigel noticed the apprehension in his servant's demeanor. He knew that he evoked fear in his house staff, but something seemed amiss with Percival's actions.

"Why are you so nervous, Percival?" Nigel squinted. "You wouldn't be hiding anything, would you?"

"No, sir! Never!" Perspiration began to accumulate on the servant's brow.

Lord Hammer noticed the sweat. Continuing with the grilling, he said, "Who told you that these people would be arriving today?"

Percival did his best not to shake. Aside from Lord Hammer himself, only he and Meredith arranged for meetings at the mansion. Feeling the hopelessness of the situation, the head servant cast his eyes downward and shook his head.

"Meredith told me that they would be arriving today."

Everyone in the room could see the blood pulsing even stronger through the veins in Lord Hammer's neck and sensed the oncoming eruption. The leader of Concur grabbed Percival by the arm and pushed him toward the staircase. In the same manner, he took Tara's small arm and forced her forward.

Lord Hammer glared back at his soldiers. "Follow us upstairs!" The guardians did not hesitate to oblige.

The uncomfortable trio made haste climbing the staircase, then rushed to Meredith's chamber. Without knocking, Nigel flung the door so it crashed into the opposite wall, shoved his two captives inside, then burst in behind them, to the surprise of its occupant.

Meredith looked over the terror-stricken faces of her accomplices and knew at that very moment that she needed to do something to save them.

"Nigel! What's the meaning of this outburst?"

Lord Hammer gestured for the soldiers to remain in the hallway. Closing the door, he pushed his two captives deeper into the room. Tara and Percival now stood next to Meredith.

In an uncharacteristically calm voice, Nigel started, "I've always suspected that people would not adhere to my system of government, that I'd have enemies, and that some day they'd try to topple me. I never thought it would be you."

Meredith did her best to act surprised, something she had become very good at over the years living with Nigel. "What are you talking about? You're being paranoid again!"

"Am I?" Lord Hammer pointed to Tara. "Why is she here?"

Meredith stuck to the storyline. "I wanted an additional handmaiden and sought candidates. Tara learned about the vacancy, needed the job, and inquired about a meeting."

"Is that so?" Nigel turned to Percival. "And he brought her to you?"

The First Lady could feel Nigel's invisible grip around Percival's neck. He was looking for scapegoats, and she did not want her loyal friend to be harmed for something she had done.

"Percival found out only minutes before Tara and her husband arrived at the mansion. He doesn't need to be involved in this discussion."

"Discussion?" Nigel let out a little laugh. "How does this sound to you, Meredith? What if I told you that a visitor from Aegeus turned up a few days ago and informed me that someone would be arriving in Concur to deliver an important message?

"And what if I told you that this person knew who would be coming, pointed that person out to my sentries when they entered the city, and followed her to the mansion today? What would you say to that?"

Meredith did her best to hide her emotions, but it was over. Someone had tipped Nigel off and the best she could do now was try to lessen the damage.

"Percival has nothing to do with this," she said. "Let him go."

Nigel maintained his glare. "You will speak the truth or he goes to prison like the man who came with her."

Meredith sighed. "Just let him go!"

Lord Hammer reached for the doorknob. "As you wish." Opening the door, he motioned with his head for Percival to leave the room. The servant glanced at Meredith before departing.

"Go, Percival. You have nothing to do with this mess." With reluctance, the manor's head servant exited the room.

Nigel commanded one of his men, "No one leaves this mansion until I say otherwise. Lock this place down!"

The soldier nodded and ran for the staircase to fulfill his superior's order, and better yet, to leave the presence of his unstable leader.

To his other sentry he said, "Stand guard outside this room." Lord Hammer then shut the portal once again, locking the door behind him.

Turning to face the ladies, he said, "You can make this easy, or very, very hard."

"Don't be so dramatic, Nigel," said Meredith, crossing her arms. "Let this poor girl go."

"It's not that easy, Meredith, and you know it!" Lord Hammer pointed to Tara. "Who is she with?"

Meredith kept her arms folded and turned away, not answering.

Nigel stood tall and announced, "I'll tell you who she's with – Harrison Cross!" Lord Hammer took two purposeful steps in Tara's direction. "You are his woman, are you not?"

Tara did not know what to do. Quivering and completely intimidated, she said, "I don't know."

Lord Hammer scowled. "You don't *know*?" His tactics working, he allowed his slow, lustful gaze to rake the pretty girl from head to toe, then continued, "You *are* his girl. Any man worth his salt could figure that out."

Nigel glanced at Meredith, smirking. Returning his stare to Tara, he said, "How does this sound? If he finds out that I'm holding you prisoner, he'll come and try to rescue his poor little maiden in distress." Motioning with his head to Meredith, he said, "Her, too."

Tara closed her eyes, holding back her emotions. She knew Harrison would stop at nothing to save her, even risk his own life for the benefit of hers. Making matters worse, she also knew that Nigel understood the same thing.

Another voice in the room broke her train of thought. "Nigel," started Meredith, "this is all my doing, not Tara's. She is merely a girl caught in a very dangerous game. Let her go."

Lord Hammer did not waver. "I know how Harrison thinks. He's a warrior, just like me. The fool over thought his battle plan and placed someone he cares about in a precarious position."

Nigel paused, allowing his comment to linger. "Harrison's actions have made Tara nothing more than another soldier in this new battle."

"She is not a soldier!" shouted Meredith.

Lord Hammer thrust a finger at his woman. "She is now!"

Meredith knew Nigel had made up his mind and nothing she could say would change that fact. Accepting defeat for the time being, she said, "What do you intend to do with us?"

The Concurian leader interlocked his hands behind his back and began to pace. "You will both be held captive here. Harrison, the noble boy that he is, will try to rescue both of you, and I'll be waiting for him.

"Furthermore, my army will be awaiting his. Your resistance has ended before it even began. Concur will NOT fall!"

Lord Hammer then advanced to the doorway. In Tara's direction, he said in a mocking tone, "Enjoy your stay in Concur."

Nigel entered the hallway, locking the door behind him. "Go and tell the sentries that Nigel Hammer has ordered the gates closed until further notice!" he barked at his guard standing watch. "No one enters or leaves from this point forward!"

"Yes, sir!" said the soldier, who then ran to fulfill his duties.

Nigel gazed at the closed door behind him, scowling again. The news uncovered today disturbed him more than he had let on. How could a great leader allow someone so close to him plan a resistance movement right under his nose? Promising to avenge his shortsightedness, he left the area to prepare for Harrison's return.

CHAPTER 16

¤

Justin felt nothing but shame and humility as the two guards dragged him out of the governor's mansion and to the nearby prison. Along the way, several more Concurian soldiers joined their comrades to escort the newfound traitor to his prison cell.

The poor Aegean fighter withstood the punches and shoves down the stone corridors of the jail, culminating in front of a large wooden portal. One of the prison sentries took a key from the ring on his belt and unlocked the door, which swung open with a loud creak, revealing another shorter corridor.

Justin lifted his heavy head just long enough to read the single digits designating the cell numbers that would soon become his holding chamber.

The soldier supporting him on his right made an abrupt stop. "Where do we dump him?" he snarled to the guard in front.

"He gets locked up with the other traitor," said the lead fighter. Looking at the number '7' chiseled in the stone above a solid metal portal, he said, "This is the one."

After unlocking the door, the guard flung it open, then gestured to his comrades, indicating that he wanted Justin secured to the wall to the left.

While the soldiers attended to their task, the young Aegean could not help but notice the broken man chained across from him. At first Justin thought his eyes had deceived him; but getting a better look at the middle-aged man, he definitely recognized him. It was Gareth Tyne.

Oblivious to Justin's discovery, the Concurians finished locking their prisoner to the wall. The lead guardian hovered over the young man, examining his bonds. He gave each one a firm tug, the cuffs scraping deeper into Justin's wrists and ankles with every yank.

Satisfied with their handiwork, he said to his cronies, "He's not going anywhere. Our work here is done."

The first two soldiers exited the cell. Before the last guard left the chamber, he turned and addressed the men chained to the walls, "Enjoy your stay in Concur!" He then slammed the metal door shut, culminating with a resounding thud. Next, the Aegeans heard the unmistakable sound of a bolt sliding home. Justin and Gareth were officially prisoners of Concur.

Justin, now that the guards had disappeared, took a moment to inspect his bonds. The lad hung in a precarious position, suspended from the wall by two-foot long chains whose cuffs dug into his skin the more he squirmed.

"Don't fight it," said the tired-looking man from across the room. "You'll only end up hurting yourself more."

The young man studied the former decorated warrior. "Gareth, is that you?"

Gareth did not bother to lift his head. The Aegean felt Justin's eyes upon him, as the lad tried to figure out why one of his mentors hung from the walls like him, and why the fighter was even there in the first place.

Justin called out again. "Gareth?"

"Stop calling my name, Justin," said the broken man. "It is I."

The young fighter's brow furrowed. "What are you doing here?"

Gareth dreaded the question already, the one he knew he would have to answer for the rest of his life. The one of his own doing; his own, foolish, doing.

Lifting his bloodshot eyes, he said, "I made some very big mistakes, Justin."

The younger man gazed at one of his former mentors, waiting for enlightenment. He had looked up to Gareth Tyne as one of the most decorated warriors ever to come from Aegeus, along with Marcus Braxton and Brendan Brigade before him. Now, Justin needed answers.

Sensing something gravely amiss, the young man squinted and asked, "What did you do, Gareth?"

The older fighter gave his head a slow defeated shake. "I only did what I thought would be right for Aegeus." The man fixed his eyes on his younger counterpart. "Harrison's discovery can aid everyone in ways unfathomable. But he is too inexperienced to handle what he has found."

Justin disagreed. "Harrison has a sound plan, one agreed upon by all the elders other than you. Why didn't you offer to help him instead of going against everything they mentioned?"

"Because I'm the one with experience!" said Gareth in the loudest voice he could muster. "I helped train that boy, got him ready for his journey. When he walked into town with the Treasure of the Land, he should have handed it over to me. I earned that respect!"

Justin could not believe his ears. The lure of great wealth and power had corrupted the man chained before him, even without Gareth having the actual treasure in his possession.

Defending his new leader, the young fighter said, "You would have had your respect if you had taken a different attitude toward Harrison. He probably would have asked you to join him on his mission to reunite the land."

Gareth had contemplated those same thoughts over the past few days in his dark, dank prison cell. Still, he felt his intentions were just.

"This treasure is not something to be taken lightly," he started in his defense, "and simply dispersing it to everyone is the wrong thing to do."

"Didn't the Ancient Kings instruct the finders of the treasure to do just that?"

Gareth shook his head. "The kings died over a thousand years ago. Times were different. They controlled the whole land and governed all people."

"This is what they told Harrison to do, reunite the land under a single rulership!"

"No!" barked Gareth. "Not Harrison! He's too young! No one will take him seriously!"

Justin let the older man's words linger in the dank air. "Does the age of one person make him a better choice to rule than another? Just because Harrison is young doesn't mean he won't be a righteous ruler."

Gareth huffed. "I suppose so, but a more experienced leader will be able to handle many more situations, simply because he has more life experience to draw upon."

"Sometimes you must learn along the way," said Justin, shaking his head in disgust. "You just wanted the Treasure of the Land for yourself, plain and simple."

"Yes, but I know what to do with it."

Justin stopped believing in what the older man had to say on that topic. Taking a new course of conversation, he asked, "What have you done to land yourself in a prison cell in Concur?"

Gareth stirred in his shackles. What *did* I do to get myself locked in here? Hadn't I bargained with Nigel in good faith, and this was his way of thanking me? A safe haven indeed, thought the battered warrior.

As the older man gazed at the young, innocent soul across from him, he could not help but see a visage of his former self staring back at him. Gareth recalled the joy he had felt serving in the Aegean army, rising to be one of its highest decorated ranking officers. However, an unfortunate battle injury prevented him from becoming Aegeus's ultimate warrior. During a conflict, which his platoon handily won, a rogue Scynthian fighter had hurled a javelin in his direction, which hit its mark and ripped through Gareth's thigh. The Aegean felt his flesh tear as the jagged, metal tip shredded both muscle and bone. The old warrior squirmed at the thought.

His field clerics and mages stopped the blood from spilling, but they could not prevent the constant pain and eternal limp the wound had made. The Scynthian had no more skill at throwing the projectile than a dwarf had of growing to be six feet tall, yet the beast hit his target like a marksman. Gareth would never be the same again, in body or mind.

Justin appeared to him now as the new face of Aegeus, just like Harrison. Gareth's time was over, and the fact that he shared a prison cell with this strapping young man only drove home the point more forcefully.

"I made a covenant with Nigel Hammer," stated Gareth, "and he betrayed me."

Justin shook his head. "You partnered with Concur? What deal did you make?"

"I just needed to point out the young woman that you escorted to Concur." The elder warrior gritted his teeth, agitated that Nigel double-crossed him.

"I just wanted to help bring Aegeus the power it deserved! The Treasure of the Land would have accomplished the task, but I needed to possess it in order to make that happen."

"Gareth, one man cannot accomplish everything." Justin rattled his shackles in disgust. "You're a traitor! Once we return to Aegeus, you'll be brought up on charges of treason!"

Pushing the young man's exclamation out of his mind, he asked, "What has Harrison planned?"

Justin thought before he spoke. He took a closer look at the older man before him – the dry, caked blood on his clothing, the battered appearance, and the broken spirit; he needed to tread lightly going forward.

"How can I trust you now that you've partnered with Concur?"

The older warrior drew a heavy sigh. At this very moment, he understood that Harrison, Justin, and a younger army would lead Aegeus to prominence now, not him. Beginning to realize the sad reality, he knew that his time for repentance had come.

"I had hoped that Nigel would honor our agreement, but it appears that he will not. All I wanted was to help bring Aegeus to a state of prominence, but I've failed."

The young fighter did not relent. "Nothing that you say can make me change my mind. You're a traitor, and your foolish acts have gotten us both in this position." Justin rattled his shackles in anger. "You pointed out me and Tara to the enemy! How could you?"

Gareth allowed the verbal assault, knowing deep in his soul that his actions had been wrong. The older man cast his eyes to the stone wall, then the ceiling. "They also have imprisoned Fallyn."

Justin recognized the shape shifter's name. "Fallyn Tierany?" Gareth nodded slowly.

"You brought another innocent life into your tangled web?" said the fighter with attitude. "Good job, Gareth."

"We need to set her free. She can help us."

Justin lifted the chains that secured his wrists. "And how do you suppose we do that? Neither of us can perform magic, can we?"

Gareth averted his eyes. "No. We'll just have to think about this a little more."

Justin huffed in disgust, knowing that escaping from a locked prison cell built of solid stone slabs would be nearly an impossible task.

"I suppose we have no choice."

Dangling from their shackles, the two prisoners ended their discussion, pondering how they could ever escape from such a fortified complex.

Meredith's heart sank as soon as Nigel locked her and Tara into the study, effectively making them his personal prisoners. The dark-haired woman knew just how ruthless Lord Hammer could be and also sensed the anxiety Tara exuded. Turning to the younger girl, she took the maiden in her arms to deliver a firm hug. The young maiden began to sob.

"Don't worry, Tara," comforted Meredith. "We'll figure something out."

"This was supposed to be a simple mission," said Tara, sniffling. "We should be leaving Concur right now!"

"I know, dear, but things have changed. It's time to be strong."

Tara stepped away from Meredith, nodding and taking a hand to cover her mouth. "Harrison would want me to be strong."

"Yes, he would."

Tara, as well as Meredith, knew that once Harrison learned of their predicament, he would stop at nothing to save them both.

"What will Nigel do now?" asked Tara with concern.

"He knows something's happening," answered the older woman. "He just doesn't know what."

"Will he think Harrison's coming to Concur?"

"I'm sure he does."

Tara began to tremble, realizing that the man she loved might be heading into a trap. "We need to warn him! He needs to know that our mission failed!"

Meredith motioned for the girl to take a seat. "We still have another chance."

Tara's normally smooth brow crinkled. "I don't understand."

The raven-haired woman sat down and moved her chair closer to Tara. In a near whisper, she began, "A servant of mine will signal the Resistance tonight."

Tara's eyes grew wide. "Isn't that a dangerous thing considering what has happened to us?"

Meredith nodded. "Very dangerous, and if I could stop it, I would."

"Why do you want to stop the Resistance?" asked Tara in a soft tone.

"Because my servant's a very good friend of mine and I don't want her to get hurt."

Tara understood just how Meredith felt, since Harrison had struggled with his conscience before sending her on a similar mission. "What is she supposed to do?"

Meredith wrestled with her thoughts, wondering if she should tell this young maiden what was about to happen. "I guess you're going to be with me for a while." The woman pointed a finger in Tara's direction. "You cannot reveal to anyone what I'm about to say to you. Understood?"

Tara nodded and leaned forward with wide eyed anticipation.

Meredith put her hands on her knees and sighed. "All right. About two hours after sunset, my handmaiden Catherine will head to the large temple on the south side of Concur. This building has a high steeple that houses a very large bell. It rings once a week to summon the townspeople to pray.

"Catherine will arrive at the temple, climb the twisted staircase to the top, and light a lantern. The lamp will remain illuminated for no more than thirty minutes. After the allotted time has passed, Catherine will extinguish the light and hide. Hopefully, the right people will see the signal and start the Resistance."

"A single light in a tall building is going to start such a major movement?" The young girl shook her head. "It sounds all too simple to me."

"Many battles have begun under similar circumstances. I pray we'll be successful as well."

"Will we be able to see the light from here?" asked Tara.

Meredith's eyes widened at the question. "As a matter of fact, yes!" The woman rose from her seat and drifted to the open window with Tara close behind.

The Concurian woman shielded her eyes from the daytime glare and stared into the distance. Pointing to a high-rising building, she exclaimed, "That's the temple!"

Tara maneuvered herself beside Meredith and gazed in the same direction. Just as Meredith had described, a tall steeple climbed high into the sky with a visible opening at its apex.

"The bell you speak of must be in there," said Tara, pointing to the square cavity exposed in the structure.

"That it is," said Meredith. The raven-haired woman panned the area, then spoke again. "The right people should see Catherine's lantern from almost every corner of the city."

"And if all goes well, we'll be saved."

Meredith drew a heavy sigh. "If all goes well."

Eloise heard the soldiers coming. Her husband had already briefed her on what to do, and the woman prayed that she would not be visiting a dank prison cell that afternoon. The lady did her best to appear to be tidying up the foyer area, but even the animal that stood near her feet could feel her anxieties.

Lance sensed something was amiss and whimpered, trying to get the woman's attention. Eloise ignored him. A second later, everything changed.

Without warning, the inn's main doorway flew open and three Concurian soldiers bolted inside the building. Eloise jumped, not so much at the sight of the advancing fighters, but from the burden of knowing that the information stored in her brain had planted the seeds of revolution. And, these men had more than an inkling of her involvement.

"Woman, do you own this building?" asked the lead warrior.

Eloise put a nervous hand to her chest. "Yes, along with my husband."

"Where is he?" snarled the soldier.

The woman appeared perplexed. "He's attending to a problem in one of our rooms." In a trembling voice she added, "Is there something wrong?"

The warrior took a step in her direction. "For your sake, there better not be." After an uncomfortable moment, he said, "What room is he in?"

Eloise's brain scrambled for the answer. Putting a hand to her forehead, she shook her head and mumbled, "He's on the second floor; one of those rooms."

The lead Concurian made eye contact with his comrades, and with a nod, the two others headed for the next floor. Turning to face the woman, he said, "You stay right here and don't move."

Eloise nodded, her nerves beginning to get the better of her. "May I sit?"

The soldier did not see any harm in letting the woman gather herself and nodded yes. Eloise found a chair and waited for the other soldiers to return.

Lance, who had stood by the woman's side, followed her to the chair. Unsure of the situation, the little dog began to yap at the fighter.

"What does he want?" snapped the Concurian.

The innkeeper looked down at the dog. He knows he should leave this place, she thought. "I'm afraid he needs to be let out. He's been cooped up all day. Can I bring him outside for a moment?"

"No!" said the fighter. "You stay put. I'll open the door for him."

"But he might run away!" The woman feigned a protest.

"I'm sure he knows his way back home." Eloise could only hope that the dog knew just that. The fighter waved the dog over as he walked to the front door. "Come on! Outside!"

Lance gazed at Eloise, who nodded her approval. The canine saw the portal open and ran to it. A second later the bright sunshine warmed his body and he raced down the street, never stopping to look back.

The soldier started to object, but thought better of sending additional men to chase a rogue dog. "He'll be back again, I'm sure."

Eloise nodded and turned away. "He'll be fine."

The mood turned sullen as the two soldiers returned to the foyer with Edward Waluk in tow. With a shove, the fighters pushed the innkeeper to the forefront.

"What do you people want with us?" asked the disheveled man.

The lead soldier leaned closer to Edward. "I think you know."

The man looked over to his wife, his brow furrowed. She shook her head, unsure as well. "Know what?" he asked.

The fighter grabbed Edward's shirt and pulled him to his face. "Don't toy with me!" he said, then pushed the older man back. Edward fell and landed in a chair beside Eloise.

The innkeeper took a moment to gather himself. When he was ready, he looked at the menacing character who loomed over him. "I'm telling you, sir, I don't know what you want!"

The Concurian soldier stood tall. "Did a young couple stay here for a few days?"

The owners glanced at each other before Edward said, "Yes, they did."

"When did they arrive?"

Edward shrugged. "I'm not sure; a few days ago."

"When did they leave?"

"This morning," said Edward, raising a finger. "That I'm sure of."

The soldier leaned nearer and squinted as he asked, "Why didn't they leave this building for three days?"

"Did you see those kids?" interrupted Eloise. "They're a young married couple, newly wedded. I'm surprised they didn't stay in that room together for a week."

The warrior took his gaze to the woman. "Even so, I find it odd that they stayed put for so long. To me, they were waiting for something."

Edward spread his arms, shaking his head. "I couldn't tell you if they were or if they weren't."

"Don't play games with me!" yelled the soldier. "Those 'kids' are being detained at the Governor's mansion! Why in the world would that happen?"

Edward shrugged. "I don't know."

The lead soldier stepped back, standing tall. "I see," he said. "Maybe some time in jail will jar your memory — for both of you." The Concurian waved his henchmen forward. "Shackle their hands and feet, then escort them to the prison!"

"What?" exclaimed Edward, while tears welled in Eloise's eyes. "We've done nothing wrong! You don't have the authority to do this!"

"I do have the authority," snarled the soldier. "Lord Hammer put forth a decree to imprison all suspected traitors of Concur."

"We're not traitors!" said Eloise, scared at the thought of spending an unknown amount of time in a cell. "This is a big misunderstanding!"

"You'll have to tell that to Lord Hammer himself." The fighter watched his men bind the two poor souls and usher them out of their building. Closing the door behind him, the warrior muttered to himself, "This is just the beginning."

Lance bolted from The Wanderer's Inn and scurried along Concur's side streets. In the distance, the little dog heard a loud grinding and he ran as fast as his legs would take him.

Being a little after noon on a bright sunny day, Lance found his journey hindered by throngs of people in the streets. Furthermore, most of the townsfolk were oblivious to what had transpired at the Governor's mansion, and now stood in their places wondering why the city's leadership had decided to close the gates so early.

Lance wove through the huddled masses, trying his best to remember his way back to the forgiving countryside. In his little mind, he sensed that Tara and Justin would not be coming back for him, and he longed to find his true master.

The East Gate's gears ground ever so slowly as the soldiers began to close the massive gateway. Lance, about two hundred yards from the exit, raced down the main street that led out of town. Dashing past dozens upon dozens of townspeople, the little dog could see the exit shrinking with every passing second.

With fifty yards to spare, a guard noticed the canine running right for him. The sentry sheathed his sword and put up his hands before him. "Stop, boy!"

Lance ignored the guardian's command and continued on his mission to leave the metropolis. To his dismay, as he approached the entranceway, the sentry jumped in his path and scooped up the canine.

"Where do you think you're going?" asked the young fighter with genuine concern. "You almost ran clear out of town!"

The little dog sensed that the sentry meant him no harm, but his escape route was rapidly disappearing.

"Let's get you back to your master," said the guardian. But before he could take another step, Lance nipped at the lad's hand, causing him to recoil and drop the dog.

"Hey! Why did you go and bite me?" The fighter lunged for Lance, but before he could snatch the pup again, the little dog disappeared into thin air, reappearing fifteen feet ahead of the startled guard.

"What the ..." mumbled the Concurian soldier as he tried to regain his senses.

Lance, knowing he had no time left, scurried through the closing doorway, escaping the city seconds before the portals closed with a resounding thud. The little dog kept running, not bothering to look back until he stood a good quarter mile from the city's shut gate.

The canine climbed a small hill, then found a soft place to lie where he could overlook the city. Panting heavily and exhausted, Lance let out a final whimper of defeat and rested the remainder of the day.

The brilliant radiance of the sun's beams faded to a softer shade, bringing a purplish hue to the approaching evening sky. Catherine clutched a small lantern in her right hand, while she used her other to carry a sack containing a most important item.

The young girl, nervous almost to the point of shaking, wandered away from the center of the town toward a temple that sat in the southeast corner of the city. Being careful to follow Meredith's orders to precision, she at long last saw the spiraling steeple in the distance.

Shifting her eyes from side to side, the maiden watched the townspeople bring in their wares from the streets, while others began their nightly congregation in the town's taverns. Catherine tried her best to look inconspicuous, and after several minutes of uninterrupted trekking, she began to feel calmer about her mission. A sudden call of her name changed everything.

"Catherine!"

The handmaiden recognized the voice right away. Turning in its direction, she caught the lad's unwanted stare.

Catherine's shoulders slumped. "Christopher! You nearly scared the wits out of me!"

Christopher, a boy of fifteen, also worked in the Governor's mansion and fancied the young maiden. "What brings you out to this part of town?"

The young girl knew that she did not need this interruption, especially in such a time critical operation. "Nothing really," she lied, "my aunt hasn't seen me in a long time and she asked me to visit for supper." Catherine began to walk toward the temple again.

The young boy did not relent. "You mean your Aunt Elizabeth?"

The handmaiden nodded, keeping her head down, continuing her trek. "Yes, and I'm late, so if you don't mind I need to get going."

Christopher sensed the girl's fib. Walking at her pace, he said, "That's funny. Your aunt lives on the west side of town, right?"

Catherine glared at the boy. "Yes, you're right. I'm just taking my time getting there." The young lass cringed after hearing her own horrible-sounding lie.

"I see," said the boy with one eyebrow arched. "What do you have in the bag?" The lad reached for the pack.

Meredith's servant jerked it away from the curious boy. "There's nothing for you to see!" Huffing, she added, "Christopher, please leave me alone."

"Fine," said the boy.

Catherine restarted her trek, but after taking two steps she found Christopher following her again.

"Don't you have someplace to go?" she asked with a huff. The lass put her head down and did not look at the lad.

"Nope," he said with a boyish grin.

"Well, I don't like being followed."

Christopher took a quick step ahead of the young maiden, leaned over, and gazed into Catherine's eyes. "Where are you really going?"

The young girl started to get upset. Huffing again, she said, "I can't tell you! Now leave me alone!"

"Meredith has sent you out again, hasn't she?" The boy's eyebrows raised almost to his hair line, sensing he was right. Christopher had watched Catherine more times than she knew, and many times Concur's First Lady would send her loyal subject to fetch her things.

Catherine, realizing that her white lies were not working, decided to try stretching the truth. "Yes, she's sent me on a secret mission, if you must know."

"I knew it!" shouted the boy. "So where are we going?"

"*We* are going nowhere!" said Catherine. "If you don't stop following me, I'm going to make sure that Meredith terminates your job at the mansion."

Christopher stopped in his tracks, defeated. His family needed his income, albeit small, in order to make ends meet. "Fine. Don't tell me where you're going." The boy spun on his heel and began to walk in the other direction. "I'll see you tomorrow."

Catherine kept walking straight ahead, the temple in her sights. Christopher, on the other hand, took advantage of the girl's mistake, peeling out of sight and into the shadows. After about a minute, he resumed his menacing stalk, lurking in the ensuing darkness, following the girl of his dreams.

Meredith's handmaiden reached the temple at last. The young girl sighed; the building was huge. Ten twenty-foot long stone stairs led to two large wooden doors that acted as the structure's entranceway.

Catherine frowned. I just can't walk through the front door, she thought. The young maiden took her gaze upward, noticing the ever-brightening moon. It was getting late and her two hour window was almost up. Quickening her pace, she went to the left side of the building where she knew another door existed.

A moment later, she stood in front of a smaller wooden door that the monks used to enter the temple. The doorway also led to a spiral staircase, which finally led to the steeple.

The young maiden gripped the door's handle, and just as she turned it to open the portal, a voice more than startled her.

"Boo!"

"What are you doing here?" yelled Catherine, her heart racing.

"I should be asking you the same question," said the boy, placing his hands on his hips.

Catherine knew time was against her and dealing with Christopher just complicated things. Having no room for further delays, she grabbed the boy's arm and said, "Come on!"

The young maiden flung the door open and pulled Christopher inside with her. The girl's lantern provided a soft glow in the otherwise darkening temple. Both intruders gazed about the vast inner sanctum of the holy place. Wooden pews encircled a central altar that rested in the middle of the structure; to the right of their position stood a closed doorway, which she knew led to the steeple access.

"Follow me," said Catherine, yanking Christopher in the direction of the portal.

"Why are you here?" asked the boy with a hint of worry, unsure if he wanted anyone to see him inside a holy shrine with the young girl.

"I don't have time to explain," said the maiden, determined to succeed with her mission. A moment later, both adolescents stood by the entranceway.

"This leads to the steeple," said Catherine as she turned the door's handle. The portal was unlocked and when opened yielded the spiral staircase. "And we're going to the top of the spire."

The young girl did not wait for Christopher's response; instead she made haste in ascending the stairs. Both youngsters climbed higher and higher, their breath straining due to their exertion. A couple of minutes later, Catherine and Christopher stood at the top of the staircase with another entryway staring back at them.

Catherine again did not hesitate to open the door. The young girl swung the portal open to find two large bells resting harmlessly in front of the backdrop of the nighttime city, as well as an ominous sight.

"Be careful," said Catherine, looking down the shaft of the steeple. "That's a long way down."

Christopher gazed downward as well, the sight of the spiral staircase winding into a dark chasm giving him a sense of dizziness.

"I didn't realize we climbed so high." The boy then backed away from the shaft, bumping into the ledge. Jerking his head, he had an unobstructed view of the area, which caused his knees to turn to jelly.

Catherine noticed the boy's antics. "Christopher, try to find a place to sit down!"

The lad felt his head spinning with the onset of an anxiety attack. Before he could black out, Christopher felt a hand grab his arm and force him down.

"Sit here and don't move!" commanded Catherine. The maiden knew she had to place her lantern on the steeple's ledge, but she also needed to be sure that Christopher would be safe as well. The boy curled up in the corner, hugging his knees to his chest, sweating.

The young girl gave the lad one last look and, satisfied that he was no longer in imminent danger, she went back to the task at hand. Catherine rested her small lantern on the ledge, then reached into her backpack and removed a much larger lamp. She lifted her head to gaze at the city that bustled before her. Picking the most strategic position on the ledge, she placed the lantern, lit it, then backed away, allowing the beacon's bright flame to illuminate the bell tower.

Catherine then sat down, curling up in the corner opposite Christopher. She too hugged her knees to her chest, then peered over at the young boy who sat in a similar position.

"Are you all right?" she asked, the flickering light giving the boy's face an orangey glow.

"I don't know what got into me," he said with embarrassment. "I guess I didn't realize how high up we were."

Catherine shook her head, unimpressed. "We kept climbing higher and higher. Of course we'd be way above the ground."

Christopher cast his eyes downward, mumbling, "Well, I guess I didn't know." Changing the subject, he said, "Why are we even here?"

"*We* weren't supposed to be here together," answered the maiden. "You're a part of this now, like it or not."

"A part of what?" Christopher had always had a sense of adventure, but many times his youthful exuberance had clouded his judgment. This time was no different.

Catherine knew she needed to choose her words carefully. Meredith had entrusted her with this task, and she did not want to fail her. "Someone of importance asked me to carry this lantern to the top of this steeple, light it, and wait for thirty minutes. That's all I can say."

Christopher did not see any harm in this mission, other than being in a place where they should not be, which he enjoyed. "Looks like you succeeded."

"We're not done yet. Only a few minutes have gone by."

The boy's curiosity continued. "Who's this important person?"

Catherine rolled her eyes. Another question? Will he just be quiet? "I can't tell you. You'll compromise the mission."

"Mission? I do things like this all the time!" The boy began to feel better about his situation. "Come on! Tell me!"

The young girl glared at the boy. "No! And stop asking so many questions!"

Christopher smirked. He was going to get the answer, even if it drove the pretty girl in front of him crazy. The lad then rose from his position, careful to place both hands on the ledge and bracing himself before gazing about his surroundings.

Catherine watched the boy's actions with concern. Furrowing her brow, she said, "What are you doing?"

The boy scanned the area, taking in the great city. "You can see *everything* up here." He then turned his focus to the beacon. Taking two steps, he was upon it. "Why would someone want you to light this lantern?"

The young maiden sprung to her feet. "Get away from that flame!"

Christopher placed his hands on either side of the lamp, feeling the blaze's heat warm his hands. "Come on, tell me who sent you."

Catherine's eyes grew wide. "I'm warning you, get away from that lantern."

The boy arched an eyebrow. "Or what? Are you going to slap my hand?"

The young girl could not believe this boy's stubbornness. She decided to try another tactic. Channeling sad memories, she managed to well her eyes with tears.

"Christopher," she began with a sniffle. "The people who commanded me to bring this lamp up here told me that they would harm my family if I didn't do what they said. Please, I'm begging you, leave the beacon alone." A tear, rolling from her left eye, completed the lie.

The lad, who always fancied the young maiden, removed his hands from the lamp. "Who would want to harm you?"

Another sniffle. "Who do you think?"

Christopher looked away in thought before a name came to mind. "Lord Hammer?" Catherine nodded repeatedly, then started to cry.

"Why would he threaten your family if you didn't do this?"

The girl gazed at the boy with tearful eyes. "Does he really need a reason?" Catherine read the look of genuine concern on the boy's face; the lie had worked.

Christopher stepped closer to Catherine, wrapping his arms around her. "I'll protect you. I'm not sure how, but I will."

The girl rested her head on the boy's chest, and unbeknownst to him, rolled her eyes. Sniffling, she said, "That's sweet of you, but all we need to do is finish this task and everything will be over."

Before the boy could respond, both young people heard the clambering of footsteps ascending the stairs.

Catherine stepped back, wiping her eyes free of the feigned tears. "Someone's coming!"

"What are we going to do?" said Christopher, nervous. Looking in all directions of their platform, he found no escape route, save confronting the oncoming intruder or jumping to their death.

Catherine leaned over the railing, gazing downward at the spiral staircase. A bobbing torch made a rapid advancement. The young girl turned away, deep in thought; a myriad of scenarios swirled about her head. The faint glow of the torchlight illuminated the bell tower. Catherine stared at Christopher, who maintained a frozen gaze on her. With no time to spare, the maiden lunged for the lad and planted a long kiss upon his lips.

A torch-bearing older man appeared in the steeple's tower, his cold glare fixated on the kissing couple. "What in the god's name are you two doing up here?"

The youthful pair separated, their eyes wide with surprise. "Oh my," said Catherine, covering her mouth with a hand.

The gentleman oscillated his gaze from person to person. A second later, his eyes stopped on Christopher. Shaking his head, he said, "Of all the places to take a young woman." The man then found what had originally caught his eye.

Taking two strides, the unwanted fellow positioned himself next to the lantern. Again panning the young couple, he said, "This lamp can be seen from everywhere! Do you want Lord Hammer to throw me in jail himself?"

The angry man then moved the lantern from its resting spot to place it on the wooden floorboards. Next, he turned down the wick, extinguishing the flame.

Catherine watched the scene with anxiety. Had the beacon remained lit for thirty minutes? She did not think so. All she could hope for now was that someone in the know saw her signal. Her mission, though cut short, was done. Now she needed to get away from this man, and Christopher, too.

Taking the lad's hand, she pleaded to the man, "Please, sir, don't tell our parents. We didn't mean any harm coming up here."

The man, still fiddling with the lantern, lifted his eyes and said, "You could have burned this tower down. You're lucky I stopped you before a disaster happened."

"We only wanted to be alone," continued Catherine's lie.

The young girl's story did not impress the townsman. "You trespassed on hallowed ground. You must repent."

The youngsters exchanged a glance. "Repent how?" asked Christopher.

Rising from his position, the older person wagged a finger at the couple and said, "You will tell no one that you managed to climb this steeple undetected." He motioned toward the staircase.

Catherine and Christopher nodded, but before they could leave the area, their punishment followed. "I expect both of you to be present at the morning service. Agreed?"

The youngsters answered in unison. "Agreed."

Pointing to the exit, the man said, "Leave."

The couple descended the staircase as fast as their feet would take them. A moment later they found themselves outside the temple, panting. Catherine clutched her sides, trying to catch her breath, while Christopher hunched over, his breathing heavy.

"That was close!" said the boy, rising from his position.

Catherine nodded, then poked the lad in the chest. "We never were here! Understood?"

Christopher took a step back, shrugging his shoulders, frowning. "Sure, whatever you say."

The young girl looked the boy over, knowing very well that he could not be trusted, but hoped that this one time he would keep his word. "I'll see you at the service tomorrow."

"You're really going to go?"

"Yes!" said Catherine, a look of surprise overtaking her face at the boy's remark. "And you will, too!"

Raising his palms to calm her, Christopher answered, "Fine. If it'll make you happy, I'll be here, too."

Catherine nodded once. "Thank you. I'm going home now and I don't want you to follow me." The girl then turned and headed away from the lad.

Christopher watched Catherine leave, then a moment later blurted, "Thanks for the kiss!"

Catherine momentarily stopped in her tracks, thought better of speaking, and continued on her way.

The young boy smiled as he watched his new girlfriend head homeward. "That was almost better than seeing her disrobe before her bath," he said to himself before leaving for his own home.

CHAPTER 17

¤

Harrison shielded his eyes from the setting sun. Over the past few weeks, the young warrior and his ever-growing army had recruited soldiers from Thrombus, Nordic, and Lars, and now the righteous legion camped for the night, a day's travel from hopefully their biggest prize, Arcadia.

The young warrior, his friends, and the army's leaders had discussed the importance of gaining Arcadia's loyalty. The city was the land's cultural center with a large population, a ship-friendly harbor, and the focal point of trade and commerce in the southern part of the land. Harrison understood that an Aegeus-Arcadia allegiance would be formidable indeed; one that could overthrow Nigel Hammer and tear down the walls that encircled Concur.

With that thought in mind, the young warrior traversed the makeshift campsite. Harrison looked about the area, taking in the small fires, the varying ages of the soldiers, all hoping that their world would be reunited at last, ensuring prosperity for everyone. The young warrior acknowledged the nods and waves from his troops as he headed for his friends who congregated on the other side of the encampment. Everything was going well.

There must be three thousand men here, thought Harrison, and for the first time in a long while, he felt comfortable about his mission. Up ahead he saw Murdock and Pondle attending to a fire, preparing food for the group.

"What are we eating tonight?" asked the young warrior.

Murdock continued to skin the animal, not bothering to look up, as he said, "I hope you like rabbit. We couldn't find anything else in the woods this time."

Harrison cringed. "Rabbit?"

After hearing the word he just uttered, the young warrior thought of his faithful companion Lance and how he used to chase the fleet-footed rodents whenever he saw one. Tara's face came into focus as well, and he hoped that his canine friend was doing his job of protecting her.

The ranger broke Harrison's train of thought. "We have plenty of dried meat to go around, but I like something fresh from time to time."

"It's not as bad as it sounds," added Pondle, sprinkling herbs into a pot of boiling water. "These will add more flavor to the meat."

Harrison nodded. "I'm sure it will." Taking his gaze beyond the two makeshift cooks, he found Swinkle and Gelderand with their prisoner. "I'll be back in a little while."

Murdock glanced at the robed members of the group, shaking his head and saying, "I still can't believe that beast's alive today."

The young warrior heard the ranger's comment, but chose to ignore it. Just as Murdock had said, the juvenile Scynthian sat on a log next to Swinkle and Gelderand. The beast was eating something foul, as far as Harrison was concerned.

"How's everything over here?" asked the young warrior.

Harrison took a subtle glance at the Scynthian's unbound hands. Over the course of their journey, the beast had behaved so well that his captors had given him more liberties. The young warrior did not completely approve of having a brute capable of fighting them at a moment's notice permitted free, but allowing the creature to eat without bindings seemed the most humane course of action. Still, the young warrior had his concerns.

"We're settling in," said Swinkle.

"Take a seat," added Gelderand, pointing with his staff to a vacant spot on the ground.

Harrison obliged. "Arcadia is only a short trek away," started the young warrior, who placed his pack down in order to retrieve a package of dried meat. "We'll be there before you know it."

The young warrior peered at the Scynthian. Naa'il continued to eat his food out of a hand-carved wooden bowl, not paying much attention to the humans.

Out of curiosity, Harrison pointed to the cup in Naa'il's hands. "Did you make that yourself?" The Scynthian, not thinking that the young warrior had addressed him, kept his head down and continued to use his fingers to scrape food from the side of the bowl.

"I'm talking to you," said Harrison in a terser tone.

Naa'il looked up, locking his gaze on the young warrior. With his fingers still in his mouth, the juvenile nodded yes. He swallowed his food, then said, "I make this with my hands."

Harrison took a closer look at the wooden cup. The darkness of the wood highlighted its crude construction. The young warrior thought back to his studies at the Fighter's Guild and recognized the timber.

"That bowl is made from trees of the Empire Mountains region, isn't it?"

Naa'il nodded. "We chop down trees and make our things."

"Is that where you're from?"

The Scynthian hesitated, an uncomfortable feeling coursing throughout his body. "Yes, why you ask?"

Harrison fiddled with his dried meat. "I'm just trying to learn a little bit about you and your race." The young warrior tore at a piece of his food. "Aren't you curious about us?"

Naa'il's expression did not change; it remained stoic. "No."

The beast's answer surprised the young warrior. "Why is that?"

The juvenile Scynthian shuffled his feet, apprehensive. "My people no like you people. You hate us like we hate you."

Harrison glanced at Swinkle and Gelderand before returning his stare to the Scynthian. "What have we done to cause you to hate us so much?"

A moment passed before he answered. "You exist."

The young warrior's blood began to simmer and his bicep tingled, but taking a deep breath helped calm his nerves. "Who taught you these lies?"

"Lies?" The Scynthian looked away.

Harrison did not relent; he wanted to know the answers. "I ask you again, who taught you this?"

"No one teach us anything. When we old enough, we go with leaders to fight humans and expand empire."

"So you don't even know why you're fighting us?"

Naa'il shrugged. "If that what you want to believe."

Harrison again looked at Swinkle and Gelderand. Both men were listening intently to the conversation. "Where in the Empire Mountains do you hail from?" Naa'il fidgeted, not wanting to answer the question.

The young warrior noticed the brute's actions. "You can tell me. We're not going to march our troops into your highly defended land. To be honest, we want nothing to do with your country."

The Scynthian took in what Harrison said. "Mahalanobis. I from Mahalanobis."

Harrison wrinkled his brow, then glanced at his friends who sported the same confused look. "Mahalanobis? I've never heard of the place."

Naa'il sat as tall as he could from his position, pushing his chest forward. "Mahalanobis a great Scynthian achievement. It my home."

Naa'il's answer fascinated the young warrior. For the first time in his recollection, Harrison heard the name of a Scynthian metropolis. The young warrior needed to learn more.

"Is this city constructed like your compounds?" Harrison was all too familiar with the rag-tag wooden buildings that encircled a bonfire area. Visions of Scynthian barracks surrounding a massive sacrificial pyre swirled about his head.

Naa'il shook his head. "No. Outposts look same, but home different."

"How so?"

The juvenile did not like answering so many questions, feeling as if he were betraying his race. "Why you want to know so much about us?"

"Can't you see?" said Harrison. "Dialogue like this can help ease the tensions between our people."

"Not happen." Naa'il placed his food bowl down. "No Scynthian talk to you."

"You are."

The beast shifted in his seat. "No choice."

"I'm not forcing you to say anything."

The creature leaned forward, his green cat-like eyes locking on the human. "Then let me go."

The young warrior equaled the brute's frozen gaze. "No. You will remain our prisoner until we feel the time is right to set you free."

Disgusted, Naa'il turned away and refused to say another word. Harrison pointed to the bowl on the ground near the monster's feet.

"Are you finished eating?"

The Scynthian peered at the dish, then looked at Harrison. Again, he said nothing.

The young warrior took the prisoner's act of defiance as a yes. Harrison motioned to Swinkle, saying, "Have Pondle bind our prisoner again until he's ready to cooperate." The young cleric scurried from the campfire to search for the thief.

Harrison tried to converse with the Scynthian again. "All we want is to make things better between our people. You have to believe that." The beast looked away, speechless.

Pondle and Swinkle reentered the area, where the thief approached Naa'il and cuffed his large hands. "He's secure," said Pondle.

"Good," said Harrison. "We need to discuss our plan for Arcadia."

Pondle peered behind the young warrior. "Murdock's eating over there. I'll join you in a moment. I want to make sure this creature doesn't entertain any plans of escaping."

The young warrior allowed the thief to attend to his task while he meandered over to where the ranger worked on his meal. Murdock sat next to a campfire, skewing the rodent. Upon seeing the young warrior, he motioned with his finger for him to take a seat.

"I bet you want to discuss our next course of business," said the ranger.

"Are my actions that obvious?" asked Harrison. Murdock tilted his head toward the young warrior, saying yes without uttering a word.

Harrison sat down, along with Gelderand, Swinkle, and Pondle. "I figure that the time has come to talk about Arcadia's leader," said the young warrior.

Murdock nodded. "Bracken Drake."

Harrison acknowledged the Arcadian's name. "He's a decorated warrior and popular leader."

"And a free thinker, from what I hear." Murdock pulled the rabbit out of the boiling pot and away from the fire.

Harrison had heard the tales of the fearless Arcadian, how he always put his city and its citizens ahead of his own needs. Brendan, Marcus, and the other elders at the Fighter's Guild would reference many of Bracken Drake's battle strategies in their daily teachings. The young warrior had contained his excitement about meeting the famous fighter until now.

"My studies suggest that he's a fine and decent man," said Harrison. "I would think that he'd embrace our cause."

Murdock cocked his head, scraping the cooked meat into a bowl. "He is a good man," said the ranger, licking his utensil. "It'll be good to meet with him, to put forth our plan for the countryside."

Harrison raised an eyebrow, not used to having Murdock sound like a diplomat. "I suggest that we meet with him alone. From what I've studied, he'll command that respect."

Pondle added to the conversation. "I think we need to station our army a good five miles away from Arcadia and send an envoy to the city. If the Arcadians see all of our men marching toward them, they might get the wrong idea."

"Good point," said Murdock. "We should send a small platoon and inform Bracken of our intentions."

"I'm fine with that," said Harrison, "but who do we send?"

Murdock studied the five men situated around him. "Us. We're the core group, the ones who found the Treasure and Talisman. It must be us."

The young warrior gazed at his friends with pride. "Look at what we've done so far." Harrison took his line of sight to the throngs of soldiers that settled around the encampment.

"We've accumulated three thousand soldiers, signatures of leaders from villages across the land, and an ever-growing confidence that the reunification process will work."

The young warrior took a moment to smile. "Murdock's right; we'll be the ones visiting Arcadia."

Swinkle agreed. "We have accomplished so much with very little resistance. I feel that Pious is looking down upon us and smiling."

The young cleric's inspiration did not motivate the ranger. "I don't care what god is looking down upon us; we're riding a wave of momentum that we should take right into Arcadia."

"Agreed," said Harrison, but he had further news for his friends. "I have a plan for you two," the young warrior pointed to Murdock and Pondle, "once our scouts have brought us to the five-mile limit."

"What's that, giving that beast a bath?" Murdock glanced over at the Scynthian, who fumbled with a bowl, his shackles limiting his dexterity.

Harrison watched the creature as well. Naa'il dropped the dish, then looked up, sensing eyes upon him.

"No, that's not your task," said the young warrior, taking his stare away from the Scynthian. Instead, he reflected on his teachings.

"You never send all of your leaders into a potentially hostile situation. Therefore, I'd like for you two to head an initial envoy to Arcadia. You'll meet with their leadership and explain our intentions before we enter their city."

Murdock raised an eyebrow in Pondle's direction. "Sure," said the ranger, "we can do that. What are the specifics?"

"Try to arrange a meeting with Bracken Drake. Tell him that we need to speak with him."

"That's all? Shouldn't we mention that three thousand or so men waiting on his doorstep are coming in peace?"

Harrison bobbed his head from side to side. "Of course, I figured that you'd fill in the gaps."

Murdock pointed a finger at the young warrior. "This is a big prize for us. We can't fail in securing Arcadia's allegiance." The ranger shifted his gaze to Pondle, who nodded in concurrence.

"We won't," said Harrison. "We can't."

"This will be easy enough," said the ranger. "We'll be ready in the morning like everyone else."

"Thanks. This is a most important mission."

Murdock nodded in understanding. Pointing beyond the young warrior, the ranger said, "Keep an eye on Lord Fumblehands." Everyone turned to look at the Scynthian, who began fiddling with his bowl again.

The young warrior shook his head, saying to no one in particular, "What are we going to do with him?"

"You know how I feel," added the ranger.

"That's not an option. I'll see you tomorrow." Harrison motioned to Gelderand and Swinkle, who followed the young warrior away from his other friends and closer to their prisoner.

The two robed members of the group, although they remained an ample distance away from Naa'il, still considered themselves the beast's guardians.

Noticing their leader's close approach to the Scynthian, Gelderand asked, "Are you satisfied with our plans?"

"With a little luck, we'll be meeting Arcadia's leadership sometime tomorrow."

"That's good news," said Swinkle, before taking a subtle glance at Naa'il.

Harrison witnessed the action. "Have you put any more thought into what we're going to do with him?"

Swinkle sighed. "I have been thinking and praying, but I still cannot give you a definitive answer."

Gelderand wagged a finger in the beast's direction. "I'm surprised he has not tried to run off yet."

The young warrior had similar thoughts. "If he were older, he would have fought us to the death."

"That is why we cannot harm him," said Swinkle. "I believe there is inherent good in him and I intend to bring it out."

"I hope that you do," said Harrison. "In the meantime, don't let him out of your sight."

The young cleric, determined to make things right, said, "As a matter of fact, I'm going to speak with him now."

"Do you want us to go with you?" asked Harrison, concerned about letting his friend be alone with the unpredictable beast.

"No. Let me talk to him myself." At that, Swinkle made a cautious approach to his captive.

The Scynthian had tossed his dish to the ground and was staring off into the empty forest. Swinkle studied the prisoner and felt a sense of pity for him. The young cleric knew firsthand how it felt to be a captive – the apprehension, anxiety, fears – and wanted to try to put the creature at ease.

Naa'il jerked his head in Swinkle's direction, stopping the young cleric in his tracks. Swinkle looked into the brute's eyes and thought he saw a positive response.

The young cleric pointed to a spot on the ground. "Do you mind if I sit here and talk with you?" Naa'il shrugged and turned away.

Swinkle thought back to his teachings at the monastery in Robus, how he believed in compromise and diplomacy, and how he knew the creature in front of him deserved a better fate than death.

"I really have no intention to harm you."

"Why not let me go?" said the Scynthian. "You only prolong my death."

"I'm not going to let anyone harm you." Swinkle used a soft voice, trying to put the beast at ease.

"You might not," Naa'il motioned with his head to the legions of soldiers who nestled around the campfires, "but they will."

"Not if I can help it." Swinkle gestured to the ground. "May I?"

Naa'il nodded.

The young cleric sat cross-legged on the forest's floor and faced the Scynthian. "I would like to talk with you about our peoples." Naa'il kept the same sullen expression.

Swinkle decided to take a different approach when talking to the creature. "Are you scared of us?"

Naa'il stared into the human's eyes. "No."

"Even with all of these soldiers brandishing weapons?"

The Scynthian scanned all the other men milling about the makeshift campground. "I fight to death. That what I taught."

Swinkle's eyes lit up. "Why would you fight to the death?" The beast's answer confused the young cleric since Naa'il's culture conflicted with Swinkle's teachings. "Would you not consider conceding a battle for the benefit of all?"

Naa'il paused, as if pondering the question. "No."

The young cleric pushed the issue. "Why do your leaders teach you to fight first and negotiate second?"

"No negotiate!" barked the Scynthian, rattling his shackles. "We fight! We strong!"

Swinkle raised his palms to the beast. "All right, don't get excited. I'm only trying to understand your people better." The young cleric had hoped to see remorse in the Scynthian's eyes for his outburst, but he did not observe any.

"What makes you hate humanity so?"

Naa'il did not hesitate to answer this question. "You destroy all we build! You burn buildings, dismantle compounds, and kill us with you sorcery."

"I could say the same about your people," said Swinkle. "You sever the arms of our women and children, torture us, and burn us while we're still alive. Why?"

"To intimidate you! Make you share this part of the land. We need new place to live."

Swinkle suspected that Naa'il had just divulged an important piece of information. "Why do you need a new place to live?"

The Scynthian shuffled his feet, looking at the ground; he had said too much. "Forget it."

"I know you are trained not to believe us, but we can help you." Swinkle locked his gaze on the creature. "What's wrong in your part of the world?"

"It cold," said Naa'il, pain evident in his voice. "Our young die early, before fighting age. Our food disappear."

Swinkle felt a pang of sorrow in his heart for the juvenile. "Is that why we have found so many Scynthian outposts throughout the land?"

The beast nodded, still keeping his head down, fumbling with his fingers. "You keep pushing us around."

"Maybe it is because we do not know of your predicament. Why have you not tried diplomacy?"

"You not listen to me?" barked the Scynthian. "We not do that! We not trained for that!"

The young cleric felt a unique possibility existed between their races right now. "We can help each other. Me and you can bring our races together, just the two of us."

Naa'il smirked. "You joking. Never happen."

"It must start somewhere and I am willing to work for peace. Others have mocked me before for my beliefs, yet I still persevere for the benefit of all mankind. I hope you will do the same for your race."

"It not that easy as you sound," said Naa'il, shaking his head. "I not even pass warrior's tests. The elders not recognize my existence until I do."

"They do not listen to you because you are young?"

Swinkle found it hard to believe that a race would not nurture their children; rather they would put them down and make them feel insignificant until they passed certain tests.

"Must prove worth to elders or risk banished." Naa'il could not look Swinkle in the eye with his last statement.

"Banishment?" The young cleric's heart sank. "Where do you fall in all of this? Did you ever feel that you would be banished?"

Naa'il stared off into the woods for a moment. "I banished now."

"Why?"

"I let you capture me and not kill myself."

"That is because we did not allow you to commit suicide."

"All the more reason for banish. No way I go back to my people now."

"What circumstances will they accept you back?"

The Scynthian peered past the young cleric. "I kill everyone, then take elders back to your burning camp and tell them I destroy all of you."

Swinkle slumped. There was no way that Naa'il could slaughter all of them, not that he would even be given a chance to commit such a heinous deed. The young cleric chose a nobler route.

"I suggest that we learn as much from each other, that way when the right circumstances arise we can bridge the gap between both our peoples."

Naa'il shrugged. "I suppose."

Swinkle smiled. "Good. It will take some time to get used to one another, but in the end we will both benefit. All right?" The Scynthian nodded, obliging.

From that point onward until late into the night the unusual couple discussed everything from the foods that the two races shared to honest Scynthian virtues and beliefs. Swinkle also introduced the idea of religion and his god Pious to the atheist being. The young cleric could not fathom the thought that creatures such as Naa'il did not pray to a singular god, rather they worshipped pagan symbols and nebulous higher spirits.

Swinkle glanced back at the shrinking campfires, then yawned. "I think we have talked long enough tonight. It's time to get some rest."

Naa'il nodded. "Yes, tired." The Scynthian yawned as well.

The young cleric peered over his shoulder again, taking in the three guardsmen who watched over the camp. Swinkle knew that they were watching him converse with their prisoner, and if he did not secure Naa'il for the night, they would do so for him.

"I need to lock your shackles to the chain," said the young cleric with remorse. "I do not want to do this, but if I don't, the soldiers will and they won't be as forgiving as me."

Naa'il's gaze caught the stare of one of the sentries. "I understand."

Swinkle uncoiled the long chain that Pondle had secured to a rather large tree and taking the Scynthian's bound hands, clipped the shackles to one of the links. He then fastened a lock to the chain and through the clip. The Scynthian could not escape now and would be safe from the guards, at least for tonight.

Swinkle pointed to the nearest glowing embers. "I'll be right over there."

The creature, still with its hands outstretched to the young cleric, nodded in understanding. Even though the two had shared several productive hours, Swinkle could see the sadness in Naa'il's eyes.

"I cold," said the beast.

Swinkle pointed a finger in the air, then went for his backpack. The young cleric removed a blanket from his sack and approached the Scynthian.

Unfolding the covering, Swinkle wrapped it around Naa'il's upper body. The breadth of the beast's shoulders made the hand-sewn cover look more like a handkerchief than a blanket.

"This will keep you a little bit warmer," said Swinkle.

"Thank you," responded Naa'il. The Scynthian then lay on the ground, curling up in an effort to maximize the warmth of his body.

Swinkle returned to his own campsite and found a soft spot on the forest's floor. The dying flames provided enough heat to warm him. The young cleric gazed over at the prisoner, who did his best to tug on his small blanket with bound hands.

Even Lance and Rufus are allowed to roam freely among us, thought Swinkle. The young cleric shook his head in disgust. Deep down the religious man knew that the Scynthians as a collective were evil, but this individual certainly was not. His upbringing screamed at him to help this creature, and if everything went well, maybe, just maybe, he could be the driving force in getting their races to live in harmony. A daunting task lay ahead of him, but his encounter with Naa'il gave him hope. Without a covering to warm his body, the young cleric curled up in a ball next to the heat source, and in a few minutes, he fell fast asleep and would not awaken until morning.

CHAPTER 18

¤

A light morning drizzle woke the men from a night of restful sleep. Harrison, accustomed to the follies of the weather on his journey through the land, took the inclement conditions in stride.

Many of the soldiers had readied themselves for the trek to Arcadia, and Murdock and Pondle were no different. The young warrior found his friends inspecting their weapons and armor when he joined them.

"Just say the word and we'll lead us out of the woods," said Murdock, counting the arrows that stared back at him from his quiver, waiting for action.

"How long until we're close to Arcadia?" asked Harrison.

"Half a day, give or take," said the ranger. "We'll see Arcadia from a distance; it's not nestled in the middle of a forest, you know."

The young warrior knew full well that the southern metropolis rested at the end of a large bay without any forestation to hide it. What really concerned him, though, was the fact that they would be meeting with the town's dignitaries, people he had never met.

He had heard the tales of Bracken Drake, the warrior who possessed a sword that could act as a boomerang. No one else in the land owned a weapon of this caliber, and his battle skills rivaled no others. Even Brendan and the Forge brothers, accomplished fighters indeed, held Bracken in high regard.

"I understand," said Harrison, "I just want to be very sure that we make a good impression on these people. Having Arcadia in the fold will solidify our plan of getting this land united."

"They'll join," said Murdock. "Especially when they hear about our plans for Concur. I'm sure there's no love lost for Nigel Hammer."

"Murdock, I just want you to know that this is very important to me." The young warrior shook his head. "I can't put my finger on it, but I have a feeling that this meeting is bigger than we think."

Murdock stopped counting his arrows and placed a hand on the young warrior's shoulder. "You can count on me, Harrison. We'll be fine." The ranger cocked his head. "All right?"

"I'm sure you'll be successful."

"Good. Let's round up the army and head out."

Harrison nodded in concurrence before going off to consult with Gelderand and Swinkle. The young warrior found them next to their steeds, preparing their animals for their journey.

"Murdock and Pondle are ready to lead us to Arcadia," said the young warrior. "They're about to alert the soldiers."

The men watched as the ranger removed a horn from his horse's saddle, then gave it a mighty blow. The sound reverberated throughout the encampment, alerting all three thousand men that the time to travel again had come. The soldiers had become accustomed to stopping what they were doing, gather their belongings, and fall into ranks at the sound of the instrument. Today was no different.

After several minutes of preparation, Harrison and his friends followed Murdock, Pondle, and their elite scouts. The procession to Arcadia had finally begun.

The ever-growing army marched across the leveling countryside, escaping the covering of the forest and arriving about five miles from the southern metropolis. Just as Murdock had said, the trip took only half a day.

Harrison saw the small convoy hold its position a hundred yards ahead of the trailing army. As they gazed into the distance, the Arcadian buildings revealed themselves to the men, sitting harmlessly on the horizon.

Murdock and Pondle waited for their leaders to accompany them. Harrison maneuvered his animal next to the ranger's.

"What do you want us to do?" asked Murdock to his friend.

The young warrior looked into the sky. The position of the sun told him it was mid-afternoon, and a five mile trek to the city would take a little more than an hour.

"Proceed to Arcadia like we planned," said Harrison. "I'd like to have this meeting tonight."

Murdock nodded. "Pondle and I will take the other scouts with us; we'll be back soon."

"Be sure to speak to Bracken," said Harrison before the ranger could depart. "I'm sure that the Arcadians can see our soldiers from here. He needs to know our intentions immediately."

"Where do we find Bracken?"

From his studies Harrison recalled the great building that sat in the heart of the city. "The Great Hall of Arcadia," said the young warrior with a sly smile. "You can't miss the place."

"Understood," responded Murdock. Turning to his small platoon, he said, "Pondle, lead us to Arcadia!" The thief kicked his steed's sides, causing his animal to bolt from its position, with the rest of the convoy following his lead.

I hope Bracken is in a good mood today, thought Harrison while he watched his friends disappear into the backdrop of the looming city. In a little while Murdock and Pondle would return with good news and all would be well. At least that was what he hoped.

The small convoy of two leaders and five scouts made an uneventful trek to Arcadia. The men traversed the bridge over the Arcadian River that separated the Thrombian Peninsula from the Arcadian countryside without incidence.

Murdock did not expect any resistance, although he kept a watchful eye out for anything unusual. The Arcadians were a peaceful people, not known as fighters, but he took no chances.

"Pondle," called the ranger, "I don't see any soldiers patrolling the streets."

The thief scoured the upcoming landscape, taking in the buildings, side streets, and bustling crowds of people. "Me either," he answered, "which concerns me."

Being a former thief, Pondle knew that trouble lurked everywhere, even when it did not appear evident. Trying to be as inconspicuous as possible, the halfling led the small platoon to the outskirts of the town before signaling for the others to stop. Pondle then dismounted his animal.

Murdock got off his horse as well. Holding the animal's reins, he guided the steed to Pondle. "Why did you get off your horse?"

"I think we'd look less out of place if we walked into town, don't you?"

The ranger gazed about the area. No one else rode a horse; everyone was walking to where they needed to go. "You're perceptive, I'll give you that."

"Someone has to be." Pondle flashed his friend a smile. "Now we need to find this Great Hall."

The platoon entered the metropolis known for its cultural markings. Murdock took in the sights – dining establishments, shops, street performers – and wondered why rogue armies had not overrun this city before. The ranger enjoyed the solitude of the wilderness, not the bustling streets filled with families and their screaming children, vendors shouting at them to sample their wares, or the closeness to strangers for that matter.

Pondle pointed to a large, majestic building that loomed ahead of them. "Looks like a place where dignitaries would gather, don't you think?"

Murdock squinted. The two-story structure had a row of steps, some fifty feet long that led to an entrance adorned with magnificent columns. The ranger then panned his head from side to side, taking in the nearby buildings. No others compared to this one in terms of importance. If any place existed in this town to house city leadership, this would be it, thought the ranger.

"Let's give it a try," he answered.

As the group approached the building, they noticed armed guards strategically placed before two sets of large, ornate wooden double doors. Murdock took the time to marvel at the fine chain-mail armor, boots, and gauntlets the men wore, but the battle helmets adorned with red plumes caught his eye the most. Regal, he thought, but a bit much.

The ranger pointed to five posts left of the building's staircase. "Let's tie our steeds over here, and we probably should remove our weapons as well."

Pondle approved of his friend's suggestion. "I think we need to leave one of the soldiers behind to watch over our things, too."

Murdock nodded. "Agreed." The ranger then addressed the other fighters. "Everyone, remove your weapons and leave them on your horses. We don't want to alarm these people in any way."

The ranger pointed to one of the sentries. "You stay here with our belongings." The soldier nodded in concurrence.

With the weapons and animals handled, the men followed Pondle and Murdock up the steps. Arcadian guardsmen stood tall, watching their ascent.

Murdock took the initiative to proceed to the guarded portal closest to him. He took two steps before the decorated sentries crossed their long-handled battle axes in front of the ranger, stopping him in his tracks.

"What is your purpose here, warrior?" asked the guard on the left.

Murdock stood tall. "We have come to speak with Bracken Drake."

The guard frowned, perplexed by the ranger's request. "Is he expecting you?"

The ranger fumbled for words. "Um, well, no, but ..."

"Then how do you expect me to let you enter our sacred Hall?" Both sentries waited for an answer, their weapons still blocking the doorway.

"We bring an urgent message from Harrison Cross," said the ranger after some thought.

"Who?" said the man on the right. "We've never heard that name before."

Murdock knew he was getting nowhere with these men. Changing tactics, he said, "Harrison is teamed with Brendan Brigade of Aegeus, and Octavius and Caidan Forge of Argos." The ranger observed the two guards exchange glances, both of them recognizing the new names. "I assure you, what I have to tell Bracken is of the utmost importance."

The guards stared at each other for another second, then removed their weapons from the entrance. The guard on the left said, "Follow me, ranger, and do as I say."

The soldier opened the portal and led the men inside the Great Hall. Murdock and Pondle entered the foyer first, then stopped in their tracks in order to take in the sights of the grand entranceway. The ranger had figured to see ornate decorations, but what he witnessed even took his breath away.

The doors he and the men passed through led to an open, rectangular indoor courtyard. Twenty feet apart from one another stood thick, spiral columns chiseled from fine marble, which supported the second floor. Murdock's eyes focused on the upper level, where military people patrolled the corridor that followed the perimeter of the area. A series of red buntings, similar to the military garb worn by the soldiers before him, adorned the wooden façade. Even the tapestries that hung on the walls contained red drapes that tied into the overall Arcadian decor.

The sentry motioned for the men to follow him. "Bracken's residence is on the other side of the building."

The men traversed the fine stone flooring, several times crossing over red area rugs meant to protect the floor from unwanted wear. Pondle gazed down to marvel at the fine craftsmanship of the tiles. Each three-foot by three-foot slab fit perfectly into the next, and although he was not well trained in the area of tile cutting, he knew expert designers had laid the flooring.

The guard led the small party across the two hundred-foot long open area to one of several doorways that stood on the far wall. Swinging open the portal, the men again followed the guardian into a smaller area.

"Wait here," he said.

Pondle took the time to whisper to his friend. "Murdock, what do you think?"

The ranger shrugged. "We'll find out soon enough."

The sentry returned a few moments later. "Bracken will see you now. Follow me."

The ranger and his friends heeded the guardian's command, though all the following had begun to wear on Murdock's patience. Passing through yet another doorway, the group finally reached their destination. The sentry then left the men behind with his leader.

Murdock took his gaze about the room. Now, this place seems more like a warrior's residence, he thought. Battle-worn armor and weapons littered the walls; a full backpack rested in a dark corner; used plates and mugs sat alone on an indiscreet wooden table. He did not see any fancy tapestries or sculptures, no vibrant reds, only lit candles and lanterns that shed just enough light for all to see without squinting into darkness.

The Arcadian leader sat behind a large oak table. Murdock tried not to stare at the patch that covered the warrior's left eye; instead he averted his line of sight to that of a regal map, which the man rolled up before the ranger could interpret any symbols.

"You come to me unarmed while an army sits across the river of my great city," said the mustached man. "I expect an explanation. Now."

Murdock matched the cold stare of the Arcadian hero. "Harrison Cross has sent me to arrange a meeting between our peoples."

Bracken assessed the men before him, considering them no threat at this time. "What is his urgency and why does he come with so many men?"

The ranger, not one for diplomacy, chose his words as carefully as he knew how. "I think you should ask him that question yourself."

"Oh, really? This man, who I don't even know, brings an invading army on my doorstep and expects to meet with me?"

Bracken rose from his seat, exposing three daggers on either side of his belt and jabbed a finger at the ranger. "You better give me a reason to meet with him! I'm assembling my army as we speak and your exit has been compromised."

At that moment, a platoon of soldiers appeared in the doorway behind the men, brandishing long swords and battle axes.

Murdock raised his palms to the Arcadian. "Look, I'm just bringing you the message from my people. We're not here to overrun you, if that's what you're thinking." The ranger cringed after hearing those words come out of his mouth.

"Overrun us?" snarled Bracken. "Arcadia will never fall to your hands! Every man, woman, and child will fight you to the death!"

Murdock closed his eyes and clenched his fists, but only for a second. "I'm not the diplomatic type, as you can tell, and I'm sorry if I offended you," started the ranger, "but all we want is for you to meet with our leadership. Please."

Bracken smirked. "You *are* very bad at this."

Murdock felt the tension ease a bit. "I'm a warrior like you, and I assure you, we're on a noble quest that you need to hear about."

The Arcadian paused again, reading the signals from the men before him. "I'll tell you what. Go back to your people and I'll send an envoy to escort them to me."

"We'd like the meeting to be tonight," said the ranger.

Bracken placed his fists on his hips and shook his head. "And now you want to dictate the time of the engagement. In the future, have your leaders designate another ambassador."

Murdock nodded. "I suppose I should have asked if we could have the meeting tonight."

"I'm sure you're a good fighter," said Bracken, doing his best to remain calm and not get upset at the inexperienced diplomat before him. "My men will bring your people to me within two hours. Go, before I change my mind."

The ranger nodded, then half bowed, backpedaling. "Thank you. See you soon."

Bracken stared at Murdock, waving him away. "Just go."

The Arcadian soldiers led Murdock, Pondle, and the rest out of the room, closing the door behind them. Bracken stood staring at the closed portal, wondering just what these people wanted with Arcadia.

CHAPTER 19

¤

Bracken's sentries escorted Harrison and his men out of their campsite and through the streets of the southern metropolis. Darkness began to creep over the city and Harrison observed more and more people illuminating their homes and businesses with the soft glow of candlelight. Even though evening began to fall, the townsfolk continued to bustle throughout the streets. Many times Harrison and his friends had to maneuver their steeds through throngs of people.

The young warrior admired the cityscape with its many fine architectural details, but nothing readied him for the structure that stood before the group. The Great Hall of Arcadia loomed a hundred yards ahead, its large spiral columns holding up the massive façade.

Swinkle noticed his friend's look of astonishment. "Impressive, isn't it?"

Harrison nodded. "We don't have anything that resembles this in Aegeus."

"Maybe we will someday."

The Arcadian escorts told the men to dismount and follow them up the large stone staircase that led to the building's main entrance. The same two guards who had stopped the previous group flanked either side of the large wooden double-doors. When the escorts approached the entrance, the sentries simultaneously swung open the portals.

Harrison entered the Great Hall, along with Murdock, Pondle, Swinkle, Gelderand, and a handful of soldiers. To his surprise a fully decorated warrior sporting a patch over his left eye stood tall in the middle of the room with three armored fighters. The young warrior noticed the regal red undergarments that peeked out from beneath the gold chain-mail armor. However, the gauntlets that the Arcadian leader wore caught Harrison's eye the most. Instead of metal, the arm coverings were made of a tough leather hide. Encrusted in the right gauntlet rested a single brilliant, red ruby.

The young warrior had heard countless stories about the Arcadian with the magical sword, capable of being flung toward an opponent and recalled by its owner. Harrison tried to take a subtle glimpse at the warrior's weapon, but he could not see a similar jewel.

While Harrison investigated the Arcadians, Bracken Drake also took a moment to look over the men who stood before him. Stepping ahead of his guardians, the Arcadian leader extended his hand.

"Gentlemen, welcome to Arcadia." Bracken approached Harrison first, figuring that the armor-clad warrior was the group's leader. Accepting the young warrior's hand, he said, "You must be Harrison Cross."

Harrison nodded, trying to emulate the leader in front of him. "That I am," he said, giving the Arcadian's hand a firm shake.

Bracken glanced at the other men, offering his hand to each one as well. Without saying a word, the Arcadian examined each person in Harrison's platoon, silently wondering what this inferior group of fighters harbored for his great city.

The Arcadian leader brought his full attention to the young man before him. "Harrison, what news do you have that brings you to my fine city?"

The young warrior knew this was the beginning of the most important dialogue of his life. "We bring to you an offer greater than this land has ever seen."

Bracken cocked his head, intrigued. "I'm very interested in what you have to say." Before escorting the group further inside the Hall, the Arcadian pointed to Swinkle, who held a bulky, tarp-covered object. "What does he have there?"

Harrison smiled. "An additional gift for Arcadia."

"Very well," said the leader with a nod. "Let's convene where we can all sit down and discuss everything in further detail."

The Arcadian gestured to his sentries, who then led the men through the wide open courtyard. As they began to move, Harrison gazed about the Great Hall, taking in all of its history. Bronze statues of Arcadia's past leaders stood in various fighting positions throughout the area. The young warrior noticed the one of Bracken; the warrior wielding his broad sword, gallantly fighting over a fallen enemy.

The men followed Bracken and his soldiers out of the courtyard and down a torch-lit corridor. The passage ended with access to a large room that featured walls decorated with tapestries, weapons, and armor.

The Arcadian motioned to a sturdy wooden table set with goblets, plates, and utensils. "Make yourselves comfortable. Food and drink are on the way."

The men did as instructed and took advantage of the Arcadian's hospitality. Servants, dressed in the same garb as the soldiers, served the men ale, bread, and an assortment of meats, fish, and vegetables. Harrison and his friends tried their best to not gorge themselves on the delicious food.

When everyone had settled in, Bracken asked, "What offer do you have for me?"

Harrison had waited his whole life for this very moment. Trying to contain his excitement, he started, "After several months of adventuring, my friends and I returned to Aegeus with the Treasure of the Land and the Talisman of Unification. The latter prize has instructed us to reunite humanity as in the days of the Four Kings.

"We have been doing just that, visiting village upon village in the hope of bringing this master plan to fruition. At each stop, we've given a piece of the Treasure to that town in return for soldiers and a representative to the Legion of Knighthood. Our journey now has taken us to your doorstep and we wish for Arcadia to join our cause."

Bracken's face sported an unaccustomed look of astonishment. "You mean to tell me that you," the Arcadian pointed while panning to Harrison's friends, "and your men accomplished all of that?"

Harrison nodded with a sense of pride. "Yes, we did, but we had a lot of help along the way."

"I would think so," said Bracken. Wagging a finger at the group before him, he continued, "And all the other peoples of the land are on board with this unification of humanity?"

The young warrior gestured to his friend. "Swinkle, can you please hand me the treaty."

Swinkle took a moment to rummage through his backpack in order to find the elusive parchment, then handed it to Harrison.

The young warrior continued to take the lead, unrolling the scroll and presenting it to Bracken. "Aegeus, Argos, and Robus have pledged their allegiance, as have all the coastal villages." Harrison leaned across the table, pointing to the various signatures. "And as you can see, each town's leadership has signed the treaty."

The Arcadian took a moment to scan the document. "I notice that Concur is not on board with your master plan."

Harrison shook his head no.

"That's the other reason why we've come to Arcadia," said the young warrior. "We also hope that you'll support our effort to take down Lord Hammer and liberate Concur."

"That's another whole situation in itself!"

"We understand that, but if we had help from Arcadia, we could defeat him."

"Possibly, at best!" The Arcadian shook his head. "Nigel will not go down without a fight. He'll never concede defeat. Never."

Harrison pressed the issue. "We already have a plan in place." The young warrior knew he needed to make a perfect pitch to Bracken, at this very moment.

"Brendan Brigade and the Forge Brothers are waiting for our return. They've already planned an attack from the north. We'll converge on Concur from the south."

"And we have twenty clerics from Robus to aid our troops," added Swinkle. Bracken took his blank stare from Swinkle back to Harrison.

"You cannot believe that Arcadia will join in this fight simply because you have a strategy in place!" exclaimed the decorated warrior, his face reddening. "I don't appreciate being put in this position!"

Harrison raised a finger, allowing the Arcadian to finish his exclamation. "I understand your apprehension, but we did what we did because we felt that we could overthrow Nigel with the troops from the coastal towns, even if you didn't offer men to help."

Bracken squinted, focusing on Harrison. "You think those fighters are on par with seasoned Arcadian warriors?" The decorated leader finished his question. "They're not even close!"

The young warrior tried to step back from his comment. "I didn't intend to demean your army, sir. We have three thousand men, and we feel that is a good number to have against Concur. Having Arcadia's support would put us over the top."

Bracken performed a quick mental calculation, figuring he could add a thousand men to the cause if he so desired.

"Do your three thousand men include those from Aegeus and Argos?"

"No."

The Arcadian let his strategist's mind wander. "I know Brendan and the Forge Brothers would not go into this battle without sufficient forces." Bracken took a hand to his face, rubbing his mustache as he thought.

"They probably have a thousand men between them, correct?"

Harrison did not know for sure, but figured this man's calculations were right. "Give or take a hundred."

"My men would give us a five thousand strong army."

Harrison's eyes lit up. "Does that mean you'll help us?"

Bracken turned his head away in thought. The Arcadian leader knew his city was strong and did not need the support of this new alliance. However, he understood the cause that these men had undertaken and admired their efforts to date.

"I'll tell you what I can do," started the Arcadian warrior. "I'll offer troops and supplies to your cause, and I'll even accompany my battalions in the skirmish, but Arcadia will not join your overall alliance."

Harrison and the others stared straight ahead, stunned. "Why don't you want to be a part of the greater good?" asked the young warrior.

Bracken offered his rationale. "Arcadia is a thriving metropolis. Our people are free, business is doing very well, and our army is strong. There's no sense in joining other villages just for the sake of saying that we're all somehow united."

The young warrior could understand Bracken's situation, but he had promised the ancient kings that he would succeed on his mission.

"Sir, if I may, having Arcadia part of the new kingdom will show the smaller towns the legitimacy of our cause. All we ask is that you have a representative at the Legion of Knighthood, a symbol that we're all in this together."

"And then what? Poor Nordic has a famine and we have to offer food to them? Robus is engulfed by a tidal wave and we come to their rescue? It has taken a long time for Arcadia to be the place that it is, and I'm sorry if this sounds heartless, but we're going to enjoy this while we can."

Harrison clenched his teeth, trying to hold back his disappointment. Making a bold statement, he said, "If you won't join our unification effort, then we cannot give Arcadia her share of the Treasure. The ancient kings have decreed this."

Bracken dismissed the young man's outburst with a wave of his hand. "So be it. We have enough here that anything you could offer would just be surplus."

The young warrior did not care for the decorated leader's arrogance, but he still tried to persuade him. "I still would like for you to accept one gift," he said. The young cleric carried over the container shrouded with a tarp.

Harrison accepted the object from his friend, then removed the covering. Inside a makeshift birdcage sat a falcon. The young warrior opened the door to the cage, allowing the bird of prey to climb onto his gauntlet-covered forearm.

"The Treasure of the Land contained magical birds like this falcon. We'd like Arcadia to have one."

Harrison leaned toward Bracken, encouraging the bird to hop to the Arcadian. The warrior, ever watchful of the bird that dug its talons into his fine leather arm covering, tried his best to remain cordial.

"I thank you for this most unusual gift, but if you say it is magical, what does it do?"

"The Treasure instructed us to disperse a falcon to every town and village, which will then be used as a way to send messages between them. All the birds inherently know how to get to and from the cities in the land."

"And how do they know that?" asked Bracken, but he no sooner waved off his comment. "Never mind, you said they were magical birds, right?"

"Yes."

The Arcadian glanced at one of his soldiers. "Take this gift and keep it in the Great Hall. I'm sure it will be of use some day."

The soldier grabbed the birdcage and gently urged the creature back inside. When the falcon finally nestled on its perch, the young man closed the cage's door and took Harrison's gift away.

Bracken waited until the soldier left the room before turning his full attention to the men before him. "Now, let's talk about this battle with Concur."

The men argued for hours about the best way to attack the great walled city, neither side willing to concede much ground. Servants brought a continuous line of ale, which began to flow a bit too easily.

Harrison pointed a finger at Bracken, his speech impeded with a slight slur. "For the last time, Nigel must be taken prisoner! Case closed!"

The Arcadian ran his fingers through his thick, black hair, frustrated. "Lord Hammer will never succumb to imprisonment. Our best course of action would be to kill him honorably in battle."

Murdock, fully feeling the effects from the alcohol, added, "And what if it doesn't come to that? Then what?"

Harrison did his best to clear his cloudy head. Through the course of the evening, numerous arguments had surfaced about what to do with Nigel once Concur had fallen. Swinkle, on every occasion, had voiced his disapproval of killing the ruthless leader, albeit under his breath to Harrison.

The young warrior took advantage of a brief pause to say, "What if we allow him to flee? He'll have nowhere to go after we liberate Concur."

"Keep him alive?" Bracken shook his head, looking at Harrison's partners for approval. "That would be the worst thing that could happen."

Murdock nodded repeatedly to Bracken's statement. "I agree with him," he began before serving a hearty belch. "He'd be too dangerous kept alive. He's crafty, he's a survivor. He'd wreak havoc on Concur until he reclaimed his prize."

Harrison understood there would be opposition to his plan. "If we force him into a pact, then he'd be bound to its conditions."

"He'd never go for that!" exclaimed Bracken. "You're giving him a free pass to regroup and come back again in the future!"

The young warrior stood his ground. "I'm fine with him dying in battle, but if the opportunity arises to allow him to flee, we must consider that, too." Harrison paused. "What if it were your city under attack? Wouldn't you listen to the incoming leadership if they offered you safe passage out of your city?"

The Arcadian grimaced. Bracken understood the horrors of battle, but never figured on losing. Harrison's army had grown to three thousand men, and if Arcadia sent brigades as well, they might be looking at five thousand soldiers, enough to topple Concur. Nevertheless, given Harrison's argument, if that many troops attacked his own stronghold, he knew that it would be prudent to listen to offers of exile.

The Arcadian broke the silence. "Harrison, what you say sounds fine now, but there is a good possibility that Lord Hammer would think otherwise. Plus, I'm sure that there are a lot of people inside Concur who would want to see their leader dead."

The young warrior sensed the tide was turning. "When the time comes, let me talk to him. He'll listen to me."

The decorated leader grabbed Harrison's forearm. "Your heart is very large for such a young man." Bracken then addressed the rest. "The chances are slim, but if the situation arises, I suggest we go along with his plan."

"Just to be clear," said Gelderand, "if we corner Nigel and he somehow surrenders, we keep him alive until Harrison has a chance to speak with him?"

Swinkle nodded, looking for assurances from everyone else. Murdock huffed, sat back, crossed his arms, and nodded once. Pondle, taking the cue from his good friend, also gave the mage a reluctant nod.

Bracken stared straight ahead. Shaking his head slowly, he said, "Then it's settled. I can't believe this is what the verdict is, but we'll abide by Harrison's request."

Harrison felt a great burden lift from his shoulders. Though Nigel was his sworn enemy, every warrior had a right to survival. It wasn't like Lord Hammer was a Scynthian, he rationalized to himself. Furthermore, he figured Meredith would not want Nigel's blood on her hands as well.

The young warrior tried not to appear too overjoyed. "I'm glad we came to an agreement. Now the next question is when do we leave for Concur?"

Bracken paused a moment before answering. "Give me a week and I'll have a thousand men prepared for battle. You can keep your army where it is for now. Nigel won't know what we're up to since we're well enough away from his land."

Harrison observed that his friend's expressions agreed with the Arcadian leader. "A week it is."

"Oh," said Bracken. "I also have a surprise for Nigel; something he hasn't anticipated."

"What's the surprise?"

The Arcadian leader smiled. "You'll see. In the meantime, I suggest your leadership remain behind so that we can continue with our battle plans."

"We can return tomorrow," said Harrison. "With a week to spare, we should have more than enough time to set forth a strong attack strategy and we'll need to inform our army of our intentions."

Bracken rose from his seat. "Agreed. Why don't you stay the night? There's no need trekking back to your camp in darkness."

"As long as you supply us with more ale," said Murdock with a grin. The rest of the men sported smiles as well.

Bracken smirked; he had started to take a liking to these young men with large dreams. "But of course, I wouldn't have it any other way." The Arcadian then summoned a soldier.

"Prepare adequate lodging for our most distinguished guests; be sure to make them very comfortable." The sentry nodded and left the conference room in haste.

Servants brought Harrison and his friends more flagons full of ale, and the carousing continued for several more hours. The young warrior pondered the events planned for Concur and could not help but think of Tara and her mission.

He had consumed most of his time visiting with new towns and villages, convincing their leaders and elders to join his cause. The young warrior took it as a good sign that he had not heard any news regarding Tara; had things gone wrong, someone would have sent a scout to inform him of the unfortunate event.

Lost in thought, Harrison did not see Swinkle approach until he took a seat next to him. "I'm getting very tired," said the young cleric.

"So am I." Harrison, fresh with visions of the fair-haired beauty in his head, asked, "Do you think Tara succeeded with her task?"

The young cleric shrugged. "I have prayed for that, but I could not tell you in all honesty. I have to believe that someone would have alerted us by now if she had not."

Harrison nodded, having convinced himself of that very thought a moment ago. "I can't wait to see her again."

Swinkle knew how much his friend cared for the young lady, but he had further concerns. "Unfortunately, you won't see her for a long time. Attacking Concur will be more than a challenge."

The young warrior stared straight ahead, taking in Swinkle's comment while watching the others continuing to eat and drink. "Nigel Hammer will never relinquish control of his city."

"It is noble of you to want to take the diplomatic approach with Nigel, but do you really believe that you can sway him to step down?"

Harrison looked down, drawing a heavy sigh. "You always preach compromise and diplomacy over fighting. The least I can do is try to give him a way to leave gracefully." The young warrior pivoted in his seat to face his friend. "But if he doesn't accept my offer …"

Swinkle nodded, understanding what Harrison meant. "At least you are going to try to negotiate. That in itself is what makes it right."

The young warrior took a final sip of the bittersweet ale. "I'll worry about that when the time comes. I think we need to get some sleep." Harrison called to his friends. "Time to call it a night."

Murdock pointed a finger in the air, then gulped the last of his ale. Slamming the flagon on the table, he stated, "Now it's time!"

The young warrior motioned to one of Bracken's men. "Can you please show us to our quarters?"

The men followed the Arcadian guard to their sleeping place. Harrison bid his friends good night and closed the door to his room. The young warrior took a few moments to prepare for bed, then lay his head on his pillow.

Once again, Harrison's mind raced with thoughts of Tara. *She must have succeeded*, he tried to convince himself, but a nagging feeling kept telling him otherwise. *If something went wrong, he would know, right?*

No one from Thoragaard's contingent has contacted us, his thoughts continued. Surely that meant she was fine and Justin had returned her to Aegeus safe and sound. Trying to hold onto that last thought of the evening, the young warrior rolled over, closed his eyes, and drifted off into a deep sleep.

CHAPTER 20

¤

Harrison stood at the forefront of his new army. A week ago, he and his friends had left Arcadia having gained the allegiance of a powerful ally, albeit without their commitment to join the new order. Despite that setback, the seasoned Arcadian warriors should be enough to topple Lord Hammer and his soldiers, reasoned the young warrior.

A four-thousand strong army began their trek to Concur on a cloudy day, confident in their mission. The Arcadians marched a mile or so to their right, along with their ultimate weapon – a massive battering ram aimed specifically at crumbling Concur's massive walls – and taking a route that would eventually position them on the southern side of Concur. Bracken had explained to Harrison that a simultaneous attack from the west, south, and east would compel Nigel to divide his forces, thinning them considerably.

Pondle and Murdock, along with five other scouts, had set out several hundred yards in front of the platoons of men, surveying the immediate landscape. The thief had noticed nothing out of the ordinary for most of the journey, but something suddenly grabbed his attention.

Not taking any chances, Pondle shouted to his friend, "Murdock, up ahead!" The thief pointed to the right of Murdock's position and at the oncoming horses.

"I see them!" responded the ranger. Murdock maneuvered his own horse out of the intruders' direct line of sight and into the underbrush. Squinting, the ranger counted four horsemen with no noticeable markings.

Using hand signals, Murdock directed the five scouts to set up a perimeter to intercept the unknown foreigners. Both he and

Pondle carefully watched the riders, who rode straight into their trap.

With a yell, Murdock signaled to the other men to stop the advancing steeds. The sudden actions of the trained soldiers startled the four riders, forcing them to stop in their tracks and scramble to gauge their situation.

Murdock jerked his horse's reins, pulling the animal into a tight circle, and slid to a stop before the surprised men. The ranger, initially thrilled at the prospect of battle, grimaced instead, for before him sat four nervous boys, barely over the age of seventeen.

Approaching the small group, the ranger barked, "I'm only telling you this once – divert your course." Murdock pointed to the west, redirecting the boys away from the advancing armies. "If you do, then your lives will be spared and no one will ask you questions that you don't know the answers to."

One of the young men spoke for the group. "Sir, I need to ask you an urgent question."

"What?"

"Is there an army heading this way?"

The lad's question took the ranger aback. "What makes you think that there's an advancing army?"

The boy, anxious about his predicament, blurted, "I must give a message to the commander."

"I can speak for the leader," said Murdock. "What's your message?"

The young rider glanced back at his nervous friends, hoping for reassurance. "Thoragaard has news from Concur."

Motioning to the four lads with a wave toward the army, Murdock said, "Follow us!"

The mixed group of scouts and horsemen made haste in returning to the scores of men. Murdock searched for Harrison, finding the young warrior at the head of the first convoy.

The sight of his friend caused Harrison to crinkle his brow. "What's the matter, Murdock?"

Using his thumb to point at the boys, he said, "They have an urgent message from Concur."

The young warrior's mind immediately turned to Tara. "What news do you bring?" he said, his voice full of anxiety.

"Thoragaard's scouts have reported that Justin and Tara did not return to the rendezvous point at the appropriate time."

"Have they returned at all?"

The young lad took his eyes to the ground, shaking his head no.

Harrison's stomach churned, beginning to realize that his love might be in dire trouble. "Has anyone heard from them?"

"No one has made contact with them since they left for their journey to Concur." The boy's shoulders slumped. "And to make matters worse, Lord Hammer has secured the city. No one is allowed in or out."

Harrison could not believe the news he had just received. Tara's mission was a simple one; how could things have gone so wrong, he wondered. The young warrior felt the pit in his belly sour even more. *And I allowed her to go!*

"We must go after her! This is my fault!"

"Just hold on, now," the ranger started, knowing full well how Harrison's righteous ways tended to cloud his decision making. "We have two armies already on their way to Concur. If Lord Hammer has indeed locked down his city, he already knows we're coming."

Pondle added to the conversation. "And I'm sure that Tara and Justin are alive."

The young warrior looked over at the thief. "I hope you're right."

"Think about it," said Pondle. "If he eliminated them, what bargaining chips would he have left?"

Harrison let his friend's words sink in. Surely, Nigel would not kill Tara and Justin, knowing that he would do anything to save his woman. Right?

"Let's assume they are alive," said the young warrior. "How do we rescue them?"

While the men thought of answers to Harrison's question, another voice entered the discussion. "Thoragaard has the solution," said Swinkle, accompanied by Gelderand. "He knows that city just as well as Nigel."

"Rufus will be able to find Tara," said the mage, stroking the cat in his hands.

Harrison's eyes widened, remembering how the feline had successfully scaled the rocks leading into the dragon's cave. "You'll be able to see the whole landscape through the cat's eyes!" The magician nodded in concurrence.

"The best strategy would be for us to continue to Concur, find Thoragaard, then figure out a new plan of attack." Murdock shook his head. "Harrison, we can't simply stop these armies from advancing on Lord Hammer!"

"I agree a hundred percent," he said with a heavy heart. "Thoragaard will be able to get us into that city somehow."

"Do not underestimate Nigel Hammer," said Gelderand. "He has managed to rebuff every attempt at bringing down his demise. He will be more than ready for us."

The rest of the group allowed the elder man's message to sink deep into their souls, all of them remembering just how arduous their task was.

After a moment of reflection, Harrison said, "We have a job to do, and we're getting behind schedule. Let's meet with Thoragaard as soon as possible. The faster we do, the sooner Tara will be with us again."

Harrison brought his attention to the four young horsemen. "Go back to Thoragaard and tell him that you met with us. We'll advance the army into the Concurian countryside and stop five miles from the city. Tell him to advise us from there."

The lead rider nodded and turned to face his friends, but before they could depart, the young warrior added, "If Concurian soldiers intercept you before you reach Thoragaard, you must not tell them of our plan, no matter what the consequences."

Again, the lad nodded, understanding the serious nature of their mission. A minute later, the messengers departed just as fast as they had arrived.

Harrison stood watching the horses gallop away; all the while his thoughts were transfixed on Tara and her predicament. The young warrior imagined the poor maiden cuffed and shackled to the wall in a dingy prison cell. A firm hand on his back broke his trance.

"Come on, Harrison," said Murdock, striding past the young warrior and toward his steed. The ranger understood the inner turmoil that his friend was enduring and knew that getting him focused on their new task would be the best thing for him now.

With a look back, Murdock added, "We have work to do."

Harrison shook the morbid thoughts out of his head for the time being and joined his army as they continued their procession to the Concurian countryside.

Harrison's army spent the next ten days trudging across the Thrombian Peninsula, working their way through the Great Forest and to the outskirts of Nigel's land. The men chose this route over the one that would have led them around the Ridge of Dracus and close to Death's Desert. No longer having to worry about an attack from an evil dragon, the men had hoped to avoid a conflict with an even more formidable beast, the sphinx Silas.

Nightfall had come and the mass of men set up camp for the night. Harrison rested from the day's long journey with his core group of friends.

Swinkle positioned Naa'il close to them and provided him with his dinner, before gathering food for himself and taking a seat next to the young warrior.

Settling in, the young cleric said, "We're almost there."

Harrison used bread to scrape the remains of his food off his plate. "It's been so long since we started this journey." After swallowing the morsel, he continued. "I didn't think we'd ever make it this far."

"I am sure that Pious has watched over us." The young cleric tore a piece of bread, said a prayer, and tossed the food over his shoulder. The portion remained on the ground, undisturbed.

Harrison witnessed his friend's action and a pang of sadness overtook him. Every time Swinkle had performed his sacrifice in the past, Lance had been there to gobble it up, sometimes even before it touched the ground. The young warrior could only wonder where his faithful companion rested tonight.

"Where do you think Bracken and his army are right now?" asked Murdock, taking a seat next to the young warrior, breaking his inner turmoil as well.

Maintaining his stare on the discarded food, Harrison answered, "I would imagine that he's keeping his distance to the south. He said that he'd maneuver his troops across Nigel's land and set up camp a few miles from the South Gate."

Murdock took a mouthful of food, nodding in the process. "Thoragaard'll be looking for us, you know." The ranger glanced over at the Scynthian that ate all too close to their group, suppressing his desire to reprimand Swinkle for trying to include the beast in their meal.

Harrison did not hide his apprehension. "The sooner the better. Nigel has held Tara captive for far too long." The young warrior made eye contact with Gelderand, who was holding back the anxiety he also felt in regard to his niece.

Pondle, the last of the men to join them for dinner, took a seat next to Murdock. "I'm going to take a few scouts and make a complete sweep of the area after we eat." A soft breeze blew through the trees above them, the leaves rippling ever so slightly.

The thief gazed upward at the low-hanging branches, then glanced in all directions. "Something's not right."

Murdock knew his friend's idiosyncrasies and Pondle's last statement brought a wave of concern through his body. "What's the matter?"

"I don't know," said the thief, shaking his head. "I can't put my finger on it."

"Well, I'm going with you when you perform your reconnaissance."

"I expected you to say that," said Pondle with a smile.

"Finish up," said the ranger with a huff. "I don't like it when you get these *feelings*."

"I'll be finished in a few minutes. Go gather your things."

Murdock rose from his seat, intent on putting his friend's unsettling sensation to rest. "Don't you dare leave without me."

Pondle waved his friend away. "Have I ever embarked on a mission without you?"

"As a matter of fact, you have!"

The thief brushed off the ranger's comment. "Get your things!"

Murdock left the small camp to retrieve his gear while Pondle finished his meal. Putting the last of his food in his mouth, the thief stood and collected his belongings.

"If I don't hurry, he'll be back here pestering me until I'm done anyway," muttered Pondle, knowing all too well what he said was true.

"Be sure you report back after you return," said Harrison. "I don't want us to take any chances so close to our big battle."

"I will," said Pondle.

Before he left the camp, he looked back and said, "I'm sure it's nothing. Don't worry." The thief then headed off to gather Murdock and the sentries he needed to make a sweep of the general vicinity.

Harrison watched his friends embark on their new mission, but Gelderand's voice broke his concentration.

"What do you think he has done with her?"

The young warrior had pondered that very question over and over, ever since the young horsemen had arrived in their camp. "I don't think he's harmed her; that would be foolish."

"Tara is not a warrior," added Swinkle. "Lord Hammer would treat her much differently than a soldier."

The mage listened to his friends' comments, but his anxiety did not wane. "Nevertheless, I do not like our predicament."

"Neither do I," said Harrison. "But I promise you that we'll save her. We must."

"Rufus will be ready for his task, as will I," said the mage with confidence.

"And I will do anything in my power to bring her back safe," said the young cleric.

Harrison flashed a weak smile. "It's time to find Thoragaard."

Pondle and Murdock escorted six advance scouts along the perimeter of their army's compound. The thief gazed about the landscape – light forestation, minimal lunar luminosity, and not many places for someone to hide.

The ranger made a cautious approach to his tracker friend. In a whisper, he said, "I feel it, too."

Pondle nodded, not uttering a word. The thief then raised two fingers and motioned to the right. Murdock nodded, then gathered two scouts and proceeded to flank the right side of the camp.

The thief gestured for the other four sword-wielding fighters. "What shall we do, sir?" whispered one of the young men.

"Space yourselves twenty feet apart and follow me."

Pondle sensed the intruders, but he could not get a clear sense of their position, which was unusual. Utilizing his infravision, the thief led the small platoon deeper into the woods.

The trees and underbrush began to thicken. Pondle's keen sense of hearing alerted him to the men flanked around him, and at the same time, he realized the absence of the soft patter of Lance's feet, which had accompanied him on so many other missions.

The thief squinted and found a small rock formation huddled next to two average-sized trees. With complete certainty, he knew someone or something hid in the vicinity. Pondle waved his comrades over, then pointed in Murdock's direction.

One by one, the scouts began to move toward the ranger. Before the final sentry had a chance to depart, Pondle caught up with him and grabbed the fighter's arm.

In a hushed tone, the thief said, "Tell Murdock to go back to the compound, as well as all of you."

The young man wrinkled his brow, confused. "What about you, sir?"

"I'll meet you there, too. Go!"

The scout hesitated a moment, then left to fulfill his task. Pondle, on the other hand, followed his men for fifty yards, not daring to turn around and give his enemy any inkling of his true plan.

Shifting his eyes left and right, Pondle found heavy thickets on one side, but lighter underbrush on the other. Taking the easier route, the thief made an elaborate arc back to the suspicious rock formation.

Patience was one of Pondle's greatest strengths and it proved to be a virtue again. The thief estimated that it had taken him about fifteen minutes to double-back to the strange place. Staying low in the underbrush, the thief panned the immediate area, searching for anything out of the ordinary.

A few minutes later, his patience paid off. A human figure grasping a sword appeared behind the stones. The person sheathed his weapon and, when he did, disappeared from view.

I really hate magic, vented the thief to himself. Pondle made some mental calculations. There must be more than one person here, he contemplated. But where?

Pondle relied on his night vision to guide him ever so slowly around the formation. About fifty feet ahead of him, the thief found the subtle markings of a hidden campsite – flattened underbrush, broken twigs, rustled leaves, and charred logs. Then, finally the break he sought.

Three female soldiers removed their weapons, making themselves visible. Pondle watched as the tallest of the women gave orders before they sheathed their swords again. Though he could no longer see them, Pondle witnessed the underbrush bend and sway in the army's direction. They were heading toward Harrison.

The thief had almost risen from his position when he felt another unmistakable sensation. Someone else was still here. Pondle gripped the hilt of his short sword tighter. His eyes darted from side to side, his concentration sharp, his senses acute. With amazing quickness, the thief spun from his position, flailing his weapon in front of him.

"Your skills are honed, my friend," said a robed figure.

Pondle stared at the shadowy character, his heart racing and his sword still raised. "Thoragaard?"

"Pondle, is it not?"

"Yes, it is."

Thoragaard waved his hand at Pondle's sword. "Please, I'm not going to harm you," he said in his familiar monotone voice.

"Who are these people and why are they using magic?" asked the thief as he sheathed his weapon.

The mage smirked. "You have seen my work in the past. Why wouldn't I employ it to my advantage?" Thoragaard knew he had to put Pondle at ease. "They are my personal entourage. They are loyal to me and very talented."

"Are you seeking Harrison?"

"Yes. It is imperative that we speak as soon as possible."

"I can escort you to him. What about your soldiers?"

"They will follow us."

Pondle scanned the area. "Where are they?"

Thoragaard gave a little shrug. "Probably twenty yards or so from Harrison."

"Impossible. I wouldn't let anyone get that close to our camp."

"How can you stop them if you are conversing with me?"

Pondle squinted, realizing the truth in this man's assessment. "Let's get back to our site."

"Please, lead the way."

Pondle escorted the mage through the light forest and to the outskirts of their camp. Fifty feet in front of him, both men found a man flanked by six sentries.

Sporting a thunderous frown Murdock said, "You know how I feel about you going it alone!"

Pondle brushed off the ranger's comment. "I didn't have time to elaborate on my course of action. If I had, they would have known what I was up to."

"Your friend made the right decision," said Thoragaard. "My soldiers did not notice nor sense him."

"Your soldiers?" The ranger panned from side to side. "What soldiers?"

As if on cue, three female warriors unsheathed their swords, revealing themselves. Murdock and the six sentries stood wide-eyed at the fighters who flanked the mage.

"I'd like you to meet Kymbra, Marissa, and Adrith," said Thoragaard, gesturing toward each leather-armor clad woman as he mentioned their name. "My personal entourage."

The magically appearing women did not faze Murdock. "I know how you perform that trick," he said, recalling the time that Gelderand had given him a magic ring that allowed him to disappear whenever he sheathed his weapon.

"It doesn't matter if you know how the trick works," said the tall, blonde soldier. "It matters if you can detect us."

"We would've found you eventually," said Murdock in a defensive tone.

"When, after we're on top of your leader, ready to kill him?"

Before the ranger could continue his argument, another warrior appeared out of nowhere. "I would not have allowed that," said the recognizable fighter.

"Brendan!" exclaimed Murdock, surprised to see the Aegean leader appear before his eyes.

"I usually don't care for magic," said the decorated leader, walking over to Thoragaard while removing a ring. "But under the circumstances, it was the best course of action." Brendan handed the item to the mage. "It's best not to be seen in Nigel Hammer's land unannounced."

Thoragaard accepted the ring, then turned in the ranger's direction. "We must speak with Harrison. Can you escort us to him?"

Pondle, shocked to see Brendan as well, took the lead. "Sure, follow me," said the thief, keeping his gaze locked on the Aegean.

The small entourage walked past Murdock and the six scouts. As they did, the ranger and Kymbra challenged each other without speaking, communicating that their discussion would continue later.

Harrison sat talking with Gelderand and Swinkle when he noticed the posse approaching him. The young warrior jumped to his feet upon seeing the new group of people.

"Brendan! Thoragaard!" exclaimed Harrison. The Aegean nodded in acknowledgment, as did the mage.

Staring at his leader in disbelief, Harrison asked, "Brendan, what are you doing here?"

"Thoragaard informed me of the situation in Concur," started the Aegean, "and when I heard what had happened, I knew that I would need to lead your new army."

Harrison wanted nothing more than to march his battalions to Concur, but he, as well as Brendan, knew that his heart would be intent on rescuing Tara. Because of that, he had no issue in relinquishing control to the elder Aegean.

"Are all your men in place?" asked the young warrior, though he had a more pressing question to ask.

"Octavius and Caidan are leading the combined Aegean and Argosian contingent, and they are waiting for you to position your men," said Brendan. Pausing, he continued. "And from what Thoragaard has heard, Nigel is most upset."

Harrison's gaze shifted to the mage. "Has he hurt Tara?" blurted the young warrior.

Thoragaard raised his palms to the sky. "That, I do not know." The young warrior hung his head, not happy with the answer.

"Harming defenseless girls is not something he does," added the illusionist, hoping to put Harrison more at ease. "Imprisoning men who go against him is more his style."

The young warrior thought back to his only time in Concur, and how Nigel's men beat and jailed him for simply having dinner with Meredith.

"But she is being held captive," said Harrison

"I have to believe so, along with Meredith."

The young warrior frowned. "Meredith, too?"

"Again, since Tara did not return, Nigel must have figured out her intentions, which would mean he would learn about Meredith's involvement in our plot."

"They're both in trouble," said the young warrior, his voice trailing off. "We must save them." Harrison's eyes widened. "What do you think Nigel has done to poor Justin?"

Thoragaard took a step toward Harrison. "Son, I know you have a vested interest in saving them all. But I tell you now; we must proceed with extreme caution."

"We can make this situation right, Harrison," added Brendan.

The young warrior nodded, agreeing with the more experienced leaders. "Do we storm the city from all fronts?"

Thoragaard shook his head. "No. We're going into the city as part of a rescue mission."

"All of us?"

"No, just a small platoon – my three soldiers and a small group from your army."

"Like I said before," started Brendan as he swept his arm in the direction of the massive group of warriors, "I'll lead this army into position."

Harrison glanced at his close friends, reading their faces, looking for signs of concurrence. Murdock, standing by the young warrior, slapped a hand on his shoulder.

"Count me in," he said.

Pondle stepped forward. "Me, too."

"I would not let you do this alone," said Swinkle, standing tall next to his friend. "We will succeed."

"Tara needs us," said Gelderand, "and far be it from me to allow a ruthless dictator to hold her another day."

The young warrior smiled, ready yet again to embark on the most critical of missions. "Let's bring Tara home."

"First, we must go over how we will enter the city," said Thoragaard. Gesturing toward the campfire, he said, "Let's all have a seat. We have a long night of planning ahead of us."

The rescue party sat on the outskirts of the Concurian countryside, plotting how they would rescue Harrison's love and Concur's First Lady, all the while knowing that Nigel Hammer would be more than ready for their arrival.

CHAPTER 21

¤

Tensions had risen on the streets of Concur for the past few weeks. Lord Hammer had announced to his people that an imminent threat against Concur had commenced and that everyone must be vigilant to locate the unwanted intruders. Simple townspeople and shop owners sensed something gravely amiss after Nigel ordered his soldiers to shut Concur's massive gates for an undisclosed amount of time. Now, they all waited in fear.

Marshall Braun, hand picked by Thoragaard to be part of the Resistance, gazed into the distance atop Concur's great wall. The young, fair-haired sentry shielded his eyes with his hand as he gazed to the west.

"There they are, Richard!" exclaimed the excited boy, pointing into the countryside.

"Where?" said Richard Waluk. The young man followed his comrade's line of sight and found a large mass on the horizon. Richard swallowed hard. "Is that what I think it is?"

"There must be 5000 men out there!" Marshall started to say something else when he heard a deep voice bellow.

"You two!" shouted a Concurian captain. "It's time to rotate out. Your next assignment is kitchen duty at the prison." Two new young soldiers advanced to take their comrades' place atop the wall.

Marshall and Richard gathered their weaponry and heeded their commander's order. The two lads traversed the top of the barrier for a few more minutes until they came to a ladder that would lead them down thirty feet to the ground.

Marshall descended first with Richard close behind. "I hate prison duty," said Richard, trying his best not to step on his friend's hand.

"It could be worse," said Marshall.

"How so?" said the dark-haired guard. "That place stinks, it's cold, and it's filled with traitors."

Marshall had held his secret placement in the Resistance from everyone, even his close friend, but circumstances had arisen that made him challenge his oath. The young man detested Nigel Hammer, the way he handled his army, belittled those beneath him, but worst of all, his imprisonment of the fair Meredith Bilodeau.

Marshall's father had told him of the battle that Nigel had waged against Meredith's father, how he mercilessly defeated the original Concurians, assumed control of the city, erected the sterile walls, and murdered their gallant leader, William Henry Bilodeau. The final straw came when Nigel announced his "marriage" to Meredith, stealing the city's most sacred prize. Many people died in the beautiful woman's honor, and those who did not perish, remained repressed for fear of persecution if they announced their true beliefs.

A fire burned inside the young lad just thinking of the history that was related to him, as well as the new information he had received. Concurian soldiers remained on duty for weeks at a time, even though their families lived in the city. It was not uncommon to stand guard on the great walls for extended periods, never leaving their posts; another way Nigel stunted information flow throughout his city, even in the ranks of his own military.

The Resistance, though small, penetrated Nigel's system, providing pockets of information gatherers. The key to their success was never verbalizing their intentions to anyone outside the Resistance and to patiently bide their time.

The two sentries started their trek to the prison. Marshall noticed that fewer townspeople than normal inhabited the streets, even though it was early afternoon. The young man recalled the army he had seen on the horizon and that image gave him the courage to speak.

"Richard, what do you know about this Resistance?"

His friend jerked his head in Marshall's direction. "They're a bunch of traitors! That much I can tell you! Why do you ask?"

"Do you ever think that they might be right?"

Richard halted in his tracks. "What kind of talk is that?" The young man took a step toward his friend, thrusting his face closer to Marshall's. In a whisper, he said, "If Lord Hammer ever heard you talking like this, he'd throw you in prison with all the others!"

Marshall did not back down. "That's just the point. I don't believe all the people in prison are traitors."

Richard motioned with his head, suggesting that they should keep walking. "Lord Hammer wouldn't jail innocent people."

"But what if he did," pressed Marshall.

Richard did not answer, instead he searched for an answer. "Then maybe he made a mistake! People do make mistakes, you know!"

"All right, let's say he made a mistake. How do we get them out of prison?"

Richard huffed. "I suppose you'd have to petition the courts for their release."

"And how long would that take?"

The dark-haired sentry shrugged. "How should I know? Weeks? Months?" Richard glanced at Marshall. "Whoever's in prison unjustly probably did something to have Nigel think otherwise." The boy squinted. "Why do you ask?"

Marshall looked up ahead; the prison yard loomed a hundred yards away. "I need to show you something, but you can't be alarmed."

"What do you mean?"

"Promise me you won't do anything rash once you see what I have to show you."

Richard shook his head. "Sure, whatever you say."

"Good," said Marshall. "Just remember your promise."

The two sentries entered the prison grounds and proceeded to head for their next work assignment. The stone walls and pathways gave the detention center a cold, sterile disposition with no signs of warmth anywhere. The guards continued on their way, passing armed men like themselves, as well as prisoners in chains and shackles.

The men were heading down another corridor when Marshall made an abrupt left turn, which led away from the main passage. Richard followed his friend.

"Hey! The kitchen slop is down that way," he said, pointing from whence they came. "Only prison cells are down there."

"Precisely," said Marshall. "Follow me and be quiet."

Individual cells stood on either side of the stone passageway with small barred windows the only means of seeing the poor souls who rotted inside. This particular area of the jail faced away from the courtyard, thus no prisoners on this wing had seen a ray of sunlight for as long as their incarceration.

Marshall stopped a few feet before a set of locked doors. "Get a good look at the traitors in these cells."

Richard gave his friend a quizzical look. For some reason that he did not quite understand, his heart begin to race. Taking a step toward the doorway, he gazed through the small bars that sat at eye level in the portal. Inside, he found a distraught older woman sitting on a hard cot.

Why is *she* in here, wondered the young man. A glimpse of the lady's auburn hair took his breath away. The person, sensing someone outside the doorway, looked over, her sad eyes locking on Richard's. A wave of anger coursed through the young guard's body.

"Richard?" called the woman, as she rose from her seat and rushed to the doorway.

The guard's eyes widened, his body frozen in shock. "Mother!"

"Oh, Richard," said Eloise as tears started to stream down her face. "Get me out of this desolate place!"

Tears welled in the boy's eyes. "Mom," he muttered, grabbing the bars that separated him from his mother.

Eloise averted her gaze, not wanting her son to see her in such filthy conditions.

"I'm going to get you out of here," said Richard, on the verge of crying.

From further down the hall, both sentries heard yet another plea. "Son? Is that you?"

Richard's eyes widened yet again as he spun his head in the direction of the new voice. "Father?" The lad gazed at his mother, then ran two stalls down.

A bruised face met the boy's frantic stare. Upon seeing his father's black eye, Richard began to cry. "What have they done to you? Both of you!"

Edward gave his son stern instructions. "Son, you must get both of us out of here, and you must do this now. Things will be happening. Big things."

Thoughts of all kinds swirled about the young lad's head. "What are you talking about?" A thought sprung into Richard's mind – this was the traitor's wing!

"Why does Lord Hammer think that you two are traitors?" exclaimed the sentry.

"Look in the other cells, son," said Edward. "He's imprisoning anyone who he thinks might be a threat to his city."

Richard gazed down the dank corridor. By this time, other prisoners had heard the commotion and were standing at the doors to their cells as well. The bewildered sentry panned the hallway; everyone resembled his parents – downtrodden, middle-aged, ordinary townsfolk.

The young guard felt his stomach churn and his head swoon. Turning to face his father, he said with an anxious voice, "What things are going to happen?"

Edward's face went blank, not sure if he wanted to divulge his long-harbored secret. Before he could answer, Marshall interrupted the conversation.

"We're all part of the Resistance, Richard."

Richard spun on his heels, staring at his comrade. "Part of the Resistance!" The boy began to sweat, knowing full well what Nigel would do to him now that he understood the gravity of the situation.

Marshall did his best to use a soothing tone in talking to his friend. "Lord Hammer's going to do whatever he wants with his people, using them as pawns in his evil game."

Richard's heart raced. "This can't be happening," he muttered to himself, recalling that less than an hour ago he had innocently worked his shift on the great wall, not knowing that his life would soon be changing.

"We're all dead now, Marshall! Dead!"

The blonde-haired sentry stood tall. "Then we have no choice but to fight."

"Against our own people?"

Richard's friend grasped his forearm. "Listen to me, Richard! Nigel's going to be in for the fight of his life! The time has come to choose sides." Marshall took his gaze to the occupied cells, full of Concurian commoners; Richard's eyes mimicked his friends.

"We need to free these people and join with our new comrades," continued Marshall, desperate to gain his friend's allegiance.

"Son, listen to your friend," added Edward. "Time's running out!"

Richard shook his head, dazed. "Where do we go?" he said, his voice barely a whisper. "What do we do?"

"There are others who are aligned with us. Many are in Nigel's army," said Marshall. "Are you with us?"

A single tear flowed from the lad's eye. Richard knew his life was going to change from this moment onward. Sniffing, he asked, "And who do we follow now?"

Marshall stood tall, full of pride. "Meredith."

Richard shook his head, shocked at the name that had come from his friend's mouth. "The First Lady?"

"She has planned this movement since the day her father lost his city to Nigel's hands. She's willing to die for her cause, and so am I."

Die? The poor sentry knew the rigors of battle could end his life some day, but today, this way? With a sigh, he said, "I ask again, what do we do now?"

"Free these prisoners, get out of this complex, and join the rest of the Resistance fighters." Marshall cocked his head. "So does this mean you're joining our cause?"

Richard bobbed his head, indicating neither yes nor no.

"That's not good enough," said Marshall, subtly gripping the hilt of his sword. "I need to hear the words come out of your mouth."

"I … I … suppose," Richard said in a feeble voice.

The fair-haired fighter whipped his sword from its sheath. "This is your last chance, Richard. Don't make me do something I don't want to do!"

"What are you doing?" exclaimed Eloise from her cell, barely able to see the two young men in the corridor. "Please don't hurt him!"

"Richard, listen to the voice of reason!" shouted Edward, frantic at the course of events.

The scared lad did not know what he should do. All his life he had trained in Nigel's army, stood guard on Concur's walls, and protected his city. He was not ready for the commitments thrust upon him today. Marshall's blade entered Richard's midsection, piercing his body, causing his blood to spill.

Richard buckled and he dropped to his knees. The young man jerked his head upward in Marshall's direction, his eyes bulging. His parent's wails of horror and despair swirled in the background. He coughed and blood flowed from his mouth. Next, his friend's cold blade entered his back again, causing the poor lad to gasp and fall to the floor. Seconds later, Richard Waluk was dead.

Marshall pulled his sword from the fresh corpse, tears streaming down his cheeks. The young man brought his gaze to Edward's bloodshot eyes, while Eloise's cries of misery echoed throughout the chamber.

"I had to do it," said Marshall through sobs. "I had to."

Edward did not respond; he just kept nodding his head. "You did what you must," was all he could muster.

Marshall searched the passageway, knowing that each prison wing had a supply closet. The young sentry found blankets inside the cabinet, which he used to cover the dead body. Next he went about unlocking the cells, releasing the prisoners who resided inside.

Edward pushed through his door and approached his son's lifeless body. Bending to one knee, he placed a hand on the still warm corpse and sobbed.

Eloise also left her cell and grieved with her husband as the rest of the prisoners looked on in despair.

Marshall allowed the Waluks to mourn for their son, but he knew that they had spent much too long in this desolate compound.

"We must go now," said the fair-haired soldier.

Eloise rose from her position, crying, and punched the young boy repeatedly in the chest. Marshall grabbed the frail woman's hands, forcing her to stop her attack. The poor woman began to sob uncontrollably and Marshall held her close to his chest.

"Please, Eloise, we need to leave."

Edward also rose from his position and took his wife into his arms. To the distraught soldier, he said, "Lead us away from here. Don't let Richard's death be in vain."

Marshall nodded, then led the small group of fifteen people away from the young man's dead body and out of the compound through secret channels. The Resistance, already in full force, had claimed its first victim.

CHAPTER 22

¤

Nigel stared at the harbor from his lofty perch atop the terrace of his mansion. As he awaited the arrival of his generals, he wrestled with battle plans that he longed to put into place. A loud knock at the door interrupted his train of thought.

"Enter!" barked the governor of Concur as he strode into his meeting room.

Percival swung the double-doors open and announced four decorated soldiers from Nigel's grand army to his boss.

Lord Hammer glanced in his servant's direction. "Leave us!" More than happy to oblige, Percival quickly departed, closing the doors on his way out of the room.

Nigel gestured toward the chairs around a fine wooden table, each of his soldiers taking the cue to sit. Lord Hammer took his customary seat at the forefront, then said, "Last report stated that the enemy had taken up positions on each side of my city."

The man seated closest to him took the initiative and spoke. "Yes, sir, it's true that there are armies amassed on all sides of Concur, save the open waterway."

Nigel looked away and grimaced. He had taken control of Concur over ten years ago and no one had since hinted of threatening his sovereignty. Now, he knew the person behind this invasion – Harrison Cross. Far be it from him to allow an inexperienced warrior to defeat him at his own game.

"What are the specifics of these battalions?"

"From what our scouts have gathered," started the general, "it appears that the Arcadians have taken position to the south, the platoons from Aegeus and Argos are to the east, and a unified army has marched into our territory from the west."

Nigel remained expressionless. "How many men are we talking about?"

All the soldiers cast nervous glances at one another before the lead man spoke again. "From our best estimates I'd say about 5,000 soldiers."

"Five thousand," muttered Nigel under his breath. "What's the current total of our army?"

The general sighed. "Fifteen hundred, two thousand at the most." The soldier allowed his figures to sink in, then added, "And that includes young men and boys without formal military training."

Nigel stared at his men, hissing, "Every man, woman, and child shall become a soldier of this fine city! Concur will never fall as long as I'm alive!"

Nigel's men nodded in concurrence, even if they harbored doubts. "How shall we proceed?" asked the lead general.

"Now that the gates are secured, I want you to proceed with Operation Overhaul."

The generals seated around their leader tried not to gasp. Each man understood the ramifications of Operation Overhaul, a mission designed to incur catastrophic damage to all factions alike.

"Sir, if I may," started the general, "in enacting this tactic we could conceivably destroy us all. Shouldn't we execute this as a last resort?"

"My decision is final," said Nigel, dismissing his commander's concern. "Concur will fight to the end, if that's what it takes." The ruthless governor let his comments linger for a moment before continuing.

"What are the foreign armies doing now?"

"They appear to be waiting for a signal before commencing their attack."

"Have we determined what this indicator is?"

All four men fidgeted in their seats, seemingly afraid to speak to the man at the head of the table. Nigel witnessed their reactions, his blood simmering.

"What are you not telling me?" he barked.

"Sir, we believe that this sign might be coming from inside Concur itself."

Lord Hammer could not believe what he had just heard. With Meredith and Tara sequestered in this very building, had he not diffused the internal struggle before it had even begun? Nigel had expected a rescue mission from Harrison, which he gladly awaited, but surely Concurians would realize how foolish they would be to partake in any action against Lord Hammer and his authority.

"How many traitors have we arrested?"

"We have rounded up and jailed about one hundred people, and they're awaiting sentencing."

"And all charges are justified?" asked Nigel in a matter-of-fact fashion.

"I suppose," started the general. "We followed your doctrine to the word."

Nigel looked away in thought. Meredith's defection forced him to gaze inward, to his own citizens. His doctrine stated that anyone suspected of traitorous activity would be imprisoned indefinitely, no exceptions.

Lord Hammer brought his glare to the men seated next to him once again. "Erect a staging in the center of town today, enough to hang each and every conspirator at the same time. Send word out to the townsfolk and have them gather for the event. No one will think of defecting after what they are going to witness this afternoon."

The lead general, knowing that his superior's word was usually final, added his thoughts anyway. "Sir, I understand your rationale, but the people jailed are ordinary townspeople, not military personnel. Most of their crimes are circumstantial at best."

"Do you have a problem executing a direct order?" said Nigel with a snarl. "Because if you do, I'll replace you with someone who will follow my commands and you'll find yourself joining your traitorous friends on the staging today."

"No, sir! I just wanted to state my thoughts for the record!"

"Your statements have been noted." Nigel rose from his seat. "Get started! I want a report of your progress in three hours. And, you know how I hate being disappointed."

Nigel's men followed their superior's lead and stood from their chairs. Nervous nods followed as they accepted their leader's order, then all hastily departed the room. After his men had left, Lord Hammer called for his servant.

A moment later, Percival scurried to his master's side. "What do you need, sir?"

"Have my guards prepare Meredith and Tara for an event this afternoon," he said. "Be sure that they are bound and have a clear view of the staging." The frail man nodded and left as fast as he could.

Nigel then strode out to his terrace once again, taking in the beautiful view. "After today, there will be no more traitors within Concur!" he said aloud to himself. He then went off to prepare for the day's festivities.

Harrison and his friends followed Thoragaard and his female escorts to within a mile of the great walled city. Finding a place that remained out of sight from the sentries who patrolled Concur's high wall, the small platoon halted their procession.

The young warrior had a very important mission ahead of him, but before he could commence with that, he needed to resolve another lingering situation first. Swinkle had marched with Naa'il through the Concurian countryside, furthering their fragile bond, but with the impending invasion set, the Scynthian's presence only complicated matters.

Taking a step toward his friend, Harrison asked, "Have you made a decision regarding Naa'il?"

The young cleric nodded once, saying, "That I have."

The small platoon had had a heated debate about what they should do with Naa'il before embarking on the first leg of their rescue mission, with Brendan, Murdock, and Thoragaard strongly objecting about taking the beast along with them. Harrison tried to persuade Swinkle to abandon the Scynthian at that time, but the young cleric relented saying it would be inhumane to leave Naa'il so close to thousands of his hated enemies. The elder men of the group acquiesced to Swinkle's overtures on one condition – that the young cleric must decide how to release the beast before their final trek to Concur. If he could not, then the others would make the decision for him.

Swinkle turned and faced their prisoner. He then gestured for the Scynthian to raise his bound hands. Taking his key, the young cleric unlocked the beast's bonds, relieving him of his shackles for good. Naa'il stood wide-eyed before the group, unsure of their intentions.

"We have learned a lot about each other, but it is now time to go our separate ways," started Swinkle. "I hope that you will try to do all that you can to gain your people's acceptance, then you can relay your experience to your elders and let them understand that our peoples can have a dialogue of peace."

Naa'il's eyes darted in every direction, wondering if this human's latest act of kindness was genuine or just a cruel hoax. Would they imprison me for weeks only to kill me now, he wondered.

Hoping that they would spare his life, he said, "I try. No promises."

Swinkle smiled, then opened his backpack to retrieve a tankard of water and a sack of food, which he handed to the Scynthian.

"Take these and be gone," said the young cleric. "However, I warn you now that the whole countryside surrounding this city is teaming with human armies that will not be as merciful as we have."

Naa'il nodded, accepting the precious gifts. "Thank you."

The creature, not knowing how he should act at this awkward moment, backed away from the small group, then turned and scampered off in another direction.

Harrison approached Swinkle. "They would have killed all of us, yet you found good in him."

"He is not an adult and still has time to change his ways," said Swinkle, watching the creature disappear in the tall grass. "I pray his people understand that we can all live together in harmony."

The young warrior hoped for the very same thing, but that would have to wait for another day. "We have more important business to handle today."

Regrouping with his friends, the young warrior turned his attention to Thoragaard. "Explain again what you plan on doing?"

Thoragaard fumbled with his pack while answering Harrison's question. "After we enter the city, there needs to be a way to distinguish those who are part of the Resistance from those who are not." The mage removed a leather water skin from his pack. "And this is how it will be done."

"Do we need to drink what's in there?"

"No," said Thoragaard, approaching the young warrior. "I need to place a drop of this solution in each of your eyes."

"In my eyes?" said Harrison, frowning. "What's it going to do?"

"When the time comes, your eyes will transform, and you will be recognized as part of the Resistance." Thoragaard motioned toward the ground. "Please kneel so that I don't spill too much of this precious liquid."

Harrison noticed that his friends all sported anxious stares, waiting to see what might happen. The young warrior obliged, and dropped to one knee.

Thoragaard positioned the tip of the skin on Harrison's right brow. "When I squeeze the tankard, a single drop will enter your eye. Do not wipe it away."

Harrison nodded in understanding, then the mage compressed the water skin. Just as Thoragaard had said, a single drop dripped out of the tankard and plopped into the young warrior's eye. Harrison accepted the liquid, then closed his eye gently in an effort to retain the solution. To his surprise, his eyeball stung. Next, he raised his eyelid and all went black.

"I can't see!" he exclaimed, panicked.

"That's only temporary; it will pass in a few minutes. I need to perform the same to your other eye."

Harrison again obliged, and a moment later he submitted to total blindness. While he waited for his sight to return, he heard the wizard instruct his friends to do the same and, after several minutes, better than half of the party had lost their vision.

"Are you going to administer this solution to all of the soldiers?" asked the young warrior.

"Yes," said the mage. "Not me personally, but I have instructed members within your army to handle the task."

Changing the subject, he continued, "Obviously, we will wait here for some time until all of you are ready to journey again."

The young warrior recalled his fighter training and allowed his other senses to take over for his loss of eyesight. Harrison heard the three females conversing as they watched over the immediate area, but he sensed a bit of anxiety in their voices. A moment later, he felt another presence; a very welcome presence.

As best as he could hear, something seemed to be bounding in his direction. He heard Kymbra, Marissa, and Adrith talking, but was not able to fully understand what they were seeing.

The sound of rustling, high grass intensified, followed by a yap and the feeling of soft fur rubbing against the young warrior's body. Harrison reached down and felt the familiar canine that could only be one animal.

"Lance!" exclaimed Harrison, a smile beaming across his face. The young warrior dropped to his knees, allowing the little dog to jump on his chest, licking his face.

Harrison could not contain his happiness, laughing as his little friend continued his canine greeting.

"I've missed you, boy! You must have had some kind of journey!" With the greeting over, the little dog yapped repeatedly.

"Slow down, boy," said Harrison. The young warrior tried to understand Lance's barks, interpreting the words 'Tara' and 'trouble'.

Harrison hung his head. "We're going to save her now, Lance." The little dog whimpered, seeming to understand. "We'll be leaving in a little while."

The young warrior called out for Thoragaard. "How does this make us look different to others?"

"I will perform a spell once we safely enter Concur, which will act as a signal to commence fighting within the city. At that time, the transformation will take place and you will easily identify those with a similar agenda."

Harrison looked before him and could see a dark silhouette, which he took as Thoragaard. My vision's returning, he said to himself.

"How do we get into Concur unnoticed?"

Thoragaard hesitated. "That is a bit trickier."

Harrison's friends huddled around the two men as best they could. Lance, seeing the familiar faces, greeted each member, rubbing against them and yapping with delight.

Murdock homed in on the voices and said, "I'd like to hear this plan, too."

"Without going into the specifics, we'll be entering via the waterway," said the wizard.

"By boat?" asked the ranger. "They'll see us coming!"

"No, not by boat," said the mage. "With the help of your friend," Thoragaard gestured to Gelderand, though no one could see his motion, "I will put forth a spell that will allow us to enter under the water."

Gelderand assumed that Thoragaard meant him in his statement. "Just how am I going to help?"

"I'm sure that you can create a diversion of some sort. We can discuss that later."

"How are we going to breathe under water?" asked Harrison, confused.

Thoragaard did his best to paint a mental picture to the group. "Imagine, if you will, large bubbles with each of us inside."

"And we just float into the city?" said Murdock, his tone sarcastic.

"So to speak, yes."

The ranger shook his head. "This ought to be interesting."

Harrison still seemed unsure of the plan. "Won't the sentries see us swimming in the water?"

Pondle, one who never cared for entering the vile liquid, nodded repeatedly, agreeing with Harrison's observation.

"No, we'll be submerged for the whole trip," said the illusionist.

"Submerged?" The young warrior furrowed his brow. "We can't hold our breath for that long!"

"You won't have to, trust me." Thoragaard changed the course of the conversation. "Rest now. We will be venturing to the waterway close to dusk."

The men sat in the rolling hills of the Concurian countryside, waiting for their sight to return and their journey to the metropolis to commence.

"How much longer until that staging is ready?" barked Nigel to one of his generals.

"Lord Hammer, our men are working as hard as they can, but erecting a structure that large takes time," said the armored man. "We will be done in a few hours."

"Then be sure to have enough torches lit to illuminate the area," said Nigel. "I want to make certain that everyone has a good view for this event."

"It will be done, sir," said the general. "And I'll make a point to send a sentry to inform you of our progress." The military man then nodded and left his leader to ensure that their project would indeed be completed this evening.

Lord Hammer gazed out at the harbor, its waterways reflecting the bright rays of the hot sun. *Soon, any inkling of an uprising will be quelled before it even has a chance to begin,* he thought as he not so patiently waited for the evening's festivities to commence.

Harrison's eyesight had returned without incidence less than a half hour after Thoragaard had placed the drops in his eyes. The young warrior now listened to Kymbra, who had led the platoon to the outskirts of the massive city.

Crouching in their position among the reeds of the wetlands that surrounded the area, the female warrior motioned toward the great barrier.

"The wall ends over there," pointed Kymbra to where the water met the base of the wall. "That's where we'll enter the harbor."

"What's the plan from here, Thoragaard?" asked Harrison.

The illusionist did not answer right away; instead he analyzed his surroundings, making sure everything appeared to be in place. Something, though, seemed amiss.

"I feel a sense of great anxiety and apprehension."

Harrison did not understand. "What did you mean?"

Thoragaard shook his head. "I'm not sure, but something does not feel right."

"We must continue," said Harrison. "Tara's waited long enough."

"I do not intend to wait a moment longer, either," said the mage. "But be prepared for anything."

Gelderand had listened to the conversation and waited for his turn to speak. "What do you need from me tonight?"

Thoragaard brought his gaze to the top of the wall, then down to the waterline. "There seems to be fewer sentries patrolling this evening. We won't need that diversion after all."

"I'll be ready if you need me."

Thoragaard nodded once, then gestured for all to come closer. With everyone listening intently, he began, "I am going to perform the spell now. When it is in place, we must enter the water and swim across the harbor. Be sure to follow me; I will be heading toward the docks. After we get there, we will regroup in the shadows away from the main roads."

Thoragaard fumbled with his pack, searching for ingredients for his spell. "Remember, follow me."

Pondle, more than apprehensive about entering the water, asked, "Is there no other way? Won't we be soaked to the bone?"

Thoragaard flashed a sly smile. "I assure you, you will be impressed with this spell."

The bearded mage then began to chant. A dark, purplish haze began to form around his hands, and when he achieved the proper state, Thoragaard approached his entourage, running his hands over them. He then did the same to each party member including Lance and Rufus; the fog clung to all.

Harrison reached out and felt the substance covering his body, its texture similar to a thin coat of slime.

Thoragaard waved everyone over and pointed to the water. "Hurry, follow me and do not lag too far behind."

Before they could leave, Harrison had one more question. "What about Lance? How can he join us?"

The mage glared at the young warrior. "You will have to carry him in your pack. Let's go."

The small party scampered from their position, leaving the protection of the tall reeds to reach the great wall. From Harrison's vantage point, the rocky coastal wetlands, lush with tall, green, marsh plants that poked their heads above the surface, gave way to the deeper waters of the Concurian harbor. The high barrier protruded into the waterway, leaving no fertile ground to walk on.

Thoragaard took his gaze upward and, noticing no guards, signaled to his warriors before plunging into the water. Kymbra, Marissa, and Adrith positioned themselves behind Harrison and his friends.

"All of you go before us," ordered Kymbra. "We'll bring up the rear."

Harrison motioned to Murdock and Pondle. "You two are first. Wait for us on the shore." The thief frowned, accepting the fact that he would indeed be entering the waterway.

"Don't do anything stupid, Harrison," said Murdock. "Do just as Thoragaard said."

"I will, now go!" The young warrior watched his two friends enter the water, and after they disappeared, turned his attention to Swinkle and Gelderand, noticing Rufus' head poking out of the mage's pack in the process.

"Are you ready?" he asked.

"As ready as we will ever be," answered Swinkle.

Harrison smiled. "We'll be saving Tara tonight."

"Don't get ahead of yourself," said Gelderand. "We need to survive this test first."

The young warrior nodded. "Go!"

Gelderand and Swinkle waded into the water and disappeared. Harrison knew it was time for him to enter the harbor, too. The young warrior scooped up Lance, arranged him in his backpack, and headed to the outskirts of the cool harbor.

"Here we go again, boy." The little dog did his best to look over Harrison's shoulder, giving him a lick on the ear for good luck.

"You need to go now!" commanded Kymbra, anxious to get everyone out of view.

The young warrior walked to the water's edge, stepping in ever so cautiously. To his surprise, his foot did not get wet; rather, it seemed to repel the water. Harrison waded deeper into the cool liquid, remaining dry.

With the water nearing chest-level, the young warrior twisted his neck in Lance's direction, saying, "Take a deep breath, boy." A moment later, man and animal plunged under the water.

Harrison opened his eyes, trying his best to see in front of him. Ahead of his position he saw the outline of a giant, vaguely man-shaped, bubble-like substance, and figuring it was either Swinkle or Gelderand, did his best to follow. The young warrior used the same swimming technique his father had taught him as a child, regardless of whether he felt the water or not.

Each stroke caused his lungs to burn before he realized that he had held his breath since diving into the harbor's waters. Cautiously, Harrison exhaled, relieving his lungs and inhaling fresh oxygen. The young warrior marveled at the spell to himself, watching the dark blue walls of water sweep past him with every stroke.

The docks that Thoragaard had alluded to sat a good four hundred yards ahead of him, well away from the great wall and deep enough into the harbor to allow large ships to anchor. From the docks, one could follow the pylons to the shore, as long as the pounding waves did not heave you into the heavy wooden poles, crushing you with every swell. Tonight the water was calm.

Figuring that they had reached the midway point, Harrison gazed about from his watery position, trying to determine his exact location. Being no more than five feet under the water, blurry dots of light shined from his right, leaving his left side to view total darkness. The dock is over there, he thought, looking away from the blackness. Squinting and peering in front of him, he saw a cloaked figure struggling to maintain his speed about fifteen feet ahead.

Moments later, the young warrior reached Gelderand. The older man's body cowered at the sight of a shape appearing next to him. Harrison read the mage's body language – round eyes, heavy breathing, flailing arms – and knew Gelderand was in trouble.

Harrison reached out to grab the older man's arm, but instead an invisible force moved Gelderand forward. That's odd, thought the young warrior. I can't grab him, but I can *push* him.

The young warrior positioned himself behind Gelderand and using the spell's hidden boundaries to his advantage, propelled the mage forward. Gelderand zoomed ahead, the same way someone would jettison forward if they had been shoved on a sheet of ice. The mage quickened his pace with Harrison's help and reached the pylons just before the young warrior.

Both men traced the wooden structure with their hands and rose to the surface, popping their heads out of the water. Gelderand gripped the dock's wooden poles, gasping for air, trying to regain his senses. Harrison, noticing the man's antics, positioned himself next to him.

Through ragged breaths of his own, the young warrior said, "Look over there!" Harrison pointed toward to shoreline. In the distance he could see figures wading away from the deeper water and advancing toward the coast.

"We need to follow them!"

"I must ... catch my breath ..." said Gelderand, bobbing in the surf. A wave caught the mage by surprise, ramming him into the post.

"You need to go now," said Harrison, grabbing the old man's arm. "We need to catch up to them." Before they could start their new trek, both men heard the sound of three people breaching the water.

"Move faster," barked Kymbra through ragged breaths. Marissa and Adrith swam toward Harrison and Gelderand.

"Let us help you," said Marissa, maneuvering toward the mage while Adrith positioned herself near Harrison.

"He needs help with that cat," said Marissa, noticing that water kept splashing Rufus' head while he tried to lick the water from his coat. The warrior positioned herself next to the mage and in between waves carefully extracted the feline from Gelderand's backpack.

"I'll take Lance with me," said Adrith, fishing for the dog in Harrison's pack. Kymbra, treading water, motioned with her head toward the shoreline.

The young warrior took his cue and forced Gelderand forward. As he did, he realized something strange had happened to the five people present. They were wet. The rising waves only compounded the situation, making it harder to grip the slick wood, as well as to push them into the unforgiving pylons.

Gelderand waited for the next wave to pass, then began his trek toward the shoreline. The mage searched for footing, but it appeared that the water's depth remained above his head. The older man allowed another modest wave to push him into the next post.

"You're doing fine!" said Marissa, trying to reassure the magician while keeping Rufus safe.

With Gelderand in good hands, the young warrior swiveled his head to search for Lance, finding him with Adrith. "How are you, boy?"

"Wet," yapped the canine, bringing a smile to Harrison's face.

"We all are!"

Marissa guided Gelderand to the next pylon. "I feel the bottom!" exclaimed the mage, sensing that a heavy burden had lifted from his shoulders as he fumbled to secure his footing.

"Keep moving forward, don't stop now," said the woman, who also felt the rocky bottom under her feet. Glancing ahead, Gelderand could see his friends beckoning them forward, trying their best to keep out of view.

"Look," said Marissa, pointing ahead. "They're waving us on!"

Feeling more confident with every step, Gelderand began to wade toward the others, allowing the waves to push him away from the harbor's depths. Two minutes later, Murdock and Swinkle grabbed the older man's arms and pulled him to safety.

"I didn't think you were going to make it," said the ranger, guiding Gelderand into the dock's shadows while Swinkle led Marissa out of the water, too. Kymbra trailed close behind.

"I had my doubts myself," said the mage before smirking. "But only for a moment."

Harrison followed Adrith and Lance out of the water and into the relative darkness of the dock's underside. The female warrior carefully placed Lance on the ground and Marissa did likewise with Rufus. Both animals shook the excess water from their coats, happy to feel dry earth under their paws. A dark figure witnessed their actions and awaited them.

"It is imperative to stay out of sight," said Thoragaard. "This city is on high alert and will be in chaos before the sun rises tomorrow."

"When do we get out of these clothes," said Pondle, arms outstretched and dripping, a look of shear annoyance on his face. "I need to take these off now!"

Thoragaard crinkled his brow. "In due time."

"Halflings don't like the water," said Murdock in his friend's defense. "We're lucky he made the trek at all."

"Be that as it may," started Thoragaard, "we must go to our next destination now." The illusionist turned and scanned the city of Concur. Meredith needed him tonight.

"Three blocks to our left sits a building that will suit our immediate needs," said Thoragaard. "We must depart for that now."

The illusionist gestured to the dripping women. "You know where the sanctuary resides." Thoragaard motioned to several building that bordered the harbor. "Between those structures lies an alleyway; lead us there."

Before the females could commence with their task, Thoragaard gestured to Pondle. "We will utilize your night vision to guide us as well."

The thief advanced to the forefront, still annoyed at his state of affairs. "If it gets me to drier clothes ..." he mumbled before turning to Harrison. "I could use Lance with me."

Harrison called for his canine companion. "Lance, go with Pondle." The dog heeded his master's request and trotted to the thief's position.

"Looks like we're ready," said Pondle. Without another moment to spare, the thief, along with Thoragaard's entourage, began to lead his friends into the awaiting Concurian neighborhood.

CHAPTER 23

¤

A soft knock beckoned from Meredith's door. The raven-haired beauty glanced at Tara, who sported the same look of surprise. Rising from her seat on the bed, the First Lady of Concur answered, "Come in."

Percival entered with his usual expression of anxiety. "Milady, I am sorry to inform you of this, but Lord Hammer has ordered his men to gather you two."

Tara rose from her chair and met Meredith's gaze. The First Lady gestured for the nervous girl to stand next to her, taking hold of her hand.

"What does he want with us?" asked the Concurian with a slight quiver in her voice.

"He's planning something for this evening," said her servant. "Something awful."

"Oh, Percival, what is he thinking now?" asked Meredith, turning away in thought.

"I overhead him speaking to his generals about ending the Resistance tonight. I don't know how, though."

Meredith again looked to Tara. "Nigel won't hurt us," she said with confidence. "He might be a ruthless man, but we are too important to him. He'll want us alive, and for a long while."

The young girl squeezed Meredith's hand tighter. "Are you sure he won't harm us?"

Meredith nodded. "Yes, but I can't speak for anyone else in his path."

Harried footsteps ended their conversation. At the doorway entered three soldiers, their eyes fixed on the women.

"Please don't make this more difficult than it has to be, Milady," said the first soldier.

Meredith brought her gaze to the iron cuffs the fighter held in his hands. The First Lady stood tall. "Are you going to bind us? Seriously?"

"Lord Hammer's orders. I'm sorry."

The lead soldier waved his two comrades forward, handed them the hand cuffs, and said, "If it makes you feel any better, I disagree with Lord Hammer's course of action, Milady."

Meredith remained stoic, giving the man a slight nod before presenting her wrists to one of the fighters. Turning to Tara, she said, "Do as they say. These men know better than I do that the consequences would be far worse for them if something happened to us."

The young maiden, like her counterpart, offered her hands with reluctance to the other soldier. Tara, mimicking Meredith, stood tall, not looking the fighter in the eye. Seconds later, both women were bound.

"Where are you taking us?" asked Meredith to the lead soldier.

"Lord Hammer has arranged an event that you must witness. That's all I know."

"Then do your duty and lead us onward," commanded the defiant woman.

The two other soldiers gently led the ladies toward the entranceway. Before departing, Meredith gazed deep into her servant's eyes, then said, "Be careful tonight, Percival." The two women then left the room, the armored men following close behind.

Percival watched the sad procession, fearing for his leader's life and that of the beautiful young girl. "May the gods have mercy tonight," he muttered, then left to attend to his mansion duties.

A large staging constructed in the town's center loomed ahead of Lord Hammer. Along with it, Nigel's men had erected enough scaffolding to hang a hundred men. The townsfolk began to filter into the heavily torch-lit area, unsure what the night's events had in store for them, only knowing they had been ordered to attend. As people moved closer to the platform, gasps of shock and looks of horror graced their faces.

Nigel smiled. A good night for justice, he thought.

Armored soldiers ushered more and more townsfolk toward the structure, making sure everyone had a good view. Lord Hammer panned the area, taking in the sight. Making a mental calculation, the ruthless leader figured that a good five hundred people had congregated for the festivities. More would come, and for those who did not make the event, they would surely hear what transpired tonight.

Lord Hammer turned to face one of his lead generals who stood several feet away from him. Gesturing with his head, he indicated he wanted a word with his soldier. The general quickly obliged, rushing to his superior's side.

"Is there something you need, sir?" asked the soldier.

"Where are my two distinguished guests?"

"I sent for them ten minutes ago," answered the general. "They should be arriving soon."

Nigel nodded once, then turned to speak to another soldier on his left. "When are the traitors due to arrive?"

"My men are corralling them now, sir. It won't be long."

Again, Nigel nodded and smiled. All was going according to plan.

The cell door's sudden slam into the stone wall caused the inmates to jump in their shackles. A guard pointed to Justin and Gareth.

"Take them, too," he shouted, and a moment later two fighters entered the cellblock and began to unshackle the men.

"Where are we going?" asked Justin, his heart racing.

"Lord Hammer has something special planned for you," said the guard, who then peered over at Gareth. "Both of you."

The fighter removed the shackles that secured the young man to the wall and fastened new cuffs to his wrists and ankles. Likewise, the other guard locked Gareth's bonds. Satisfied that they had both prisoners under their control, the three fighters proceeded to escort the two men from their cell.

The first guard then approached the adjacent holding room. He unlocked the door and swung it open, revealing a disheveled, auburn-haired woman. Like her counterparts, Lord Hammer's men had shackled her to the wall.

The soldier looked over his shoulder and, noticing that his cronies were occupied with the other prisoners, decided to handle Fallyn himself.

Fallyn tried her best to appear apprehensive, knowing that she would only have one chance to escape. The man advanced, fondling the key that he had secured to his belt.

"It's a shame Lord Hammer wants to put you to death like the others," he said shoving his face close to the woman's. Fallyn turned away in disgust.

"Just say the word and I can make sure you're spared," he said with a leer. The guard took his gaze up and down Fallyn's body, admiring her feminine curves and haunting green eyes. "If only I had more time to be alone with you ..."

The soldier bent to one knee and unlocked the shackles around the woman's ankles. Almost there, thought Fallyn, closing her eyes and hoping this disgusting man would release her hands.

From the hallway shouted a voice, "Hurry up in there! We're already behind schedule and we don't want to keep Lord Hammer waiting any longer!"

Heeding his comrade's outburst, the guard stood and grabbed Fallyn's wrists to unlock the manacles. He then reached for the set of handcuffs on his belt.

"Now just stand there and don't do anything foolish."

Fallyn nodded once, playing the role of a scared woman. Taking a deep breath, she closed her eyes.

"Don't worry, wench, I won't hurt a pretty woman like you," said the guard.

With a new pair of cuffs in one hand, the soldier reached for Fallyn's wrists. At that moment, the woman transformed into a rat, scurried across the stone flooring and headed toward the exit.

"What in the god's name?" exclaimed the dumbfounded fighter. The small rodent ran as fast as its little legs would take it, exiting the cell.

His eyes round in shock, the fighter yelled to his comrades as he ran for the doorway. "Stop that rat!"

The soldier bolted from the cell and looked down the passage, where he saw confused faces staring back at him.

"What are you talking about?" said one of the other guards. "Where's your prisoner?"

The first man pointed to the rodent heading down the hallway. "That's her! Catch it!"

The other soldiers frowned, unsure what their crony meant. Before any of the fighters could comprehend the actions transpiring, the small rat morphed into a cat and ran into an open cell.

All three armored men witnessed the strange metamorphosis and dashed to the holding room that the feline had entered. The guards reached the cellblock at the same time, and peering in, they found the small animal sitting at the end of the room, staring at them with big green eyes.

Removing his sword, the lead soldier pointed at the cat. "Apprehend her!"

The guardians entered the room with weapons drawn, but before they could reach the animal, the feline sprung from its position and jumped toward a barred window. In one smooth motion, the cat's muscular frame transformed into that of a bat; then it flew through the small opening and away to safety.

Outside the prison block, the animal batted its wings at a feverish clip, flying through the open-air courtyard and climbing higher into the clear nighttime sky. Seconds later, Fallyn was free.

"Did you see that?" exclaimed one of the guards, rushing to the window, gazing upward.

"What just happened?" said the other guard.

Thinking quickly, the lead soldier said, "No one reports this! There's no documentation on these prisoners yet and, for all we're concerned, she never existed here. Got it?"

The two soldiers both nodded in agreement, knowing full well that an incident such as this would only mean unwanted hardship for those involved.

"Good," said the main man. "We need to get these other prisoners out of here, now!"

The three soldiers then went back into the corridor and began to escort the detainees away from the prison block.

Justin, who witnessed the strange scene as well, took an anxious eye to Gareth, who returned a similar look. A firm hand landed on the young lad's shoulder, forcing him forward.

Whatever had happened to Fallyn no longer had any bearing on his predicament, and the Aegean began to wonder just what his fate tonight would be.

"How long do we stay in these wet clothes?" lamented Pondle, his disdain for the foul liquid reaching disproportionate levels.

The hopeful rescue team had trekked through the dark Concurian streets, arriving at a safe house three blocks away from the main road. Thoragaard unlocked the front door to the mysterious building, allowing everyone to enter. In relative safety for now, the small group planned their next moves for the night.

"In a moment you will all be dry," said Thoragaard, addressing the thief's most pressing concern. The illusionist gathered ingredients for his spell, then motioned for the group to huddle together.

"Hold each other's hands," said Thoragaard. With everyone in the room doing as commanded, the mage then began to mumble aloud.

Harrison felt a warm sensation course through his body, before a dry heat enveloped his clothing and armor. The young warrior could feel the wetness evaporate into the dank, dark air. In less than a minute he and his friends were totally dry.

"I can't thank you enough," exclaimed Pondle in Thoragaard's direction.

"It is time to tackle more important issues," said the mage. "I still sense a feeling of uneasiness throughout this city. Something is going on."

"I have felt it, too," said Gelderand. "I want to find Tara as soon as possible."

"What's our next course of action?" asked Murdock, folding his arms across his chest.

"Kymbra, Adrith, and Marissa will secure our movements," started Thoragaard. "They will lead us to our contacts, who will then inform us of Tara and Meredith's location."

"It can't be that simple," said Murdock. "This place is going to be crawling with military men, especially with three large armies surrounding the city!"

"You are right, I am simplifying the plan, but I assure you we will find the women."

Murdock recalled the frustrations that Marcus encountered when he dealt with Thoragaard, and the mage's short answers only solidified that belief in him.

"When do we begin this rescue mission?" asked the ranger, knowing he would not get the whole story.

"Right now," said Thoragaard. The mage turned in the female soldiers' direction. "Locate Marshall, retrieve the information, and report back. Go!"

The women started to leave the room before Murdock stopped them. "Wait! I think we should go with them," said the ranger, using his thumb to point to Pondle. "That way we can get a better lay of the surroundings."

"And what would you need that for?" responded Kymbra in a snide tone. "You'll just slow us down."

"Oh, really," said Murdock. "The more we know about this place, the better we can navigate our way around. Who knows, we may need to save you at some point and it would be a good idea if we knew our way back."

Kymbra folded her arms, shook her head, and looked away. "You won't need to save us."

"On the contrary," interjected Thoragaard. "I think it would be a good idea for them to go with you. While the women secure the information, you two can analyze Lord Hammer's military strategy."

"Whatever you wish," said Kymbra with noticeable reluctance. "Stay close to us and try not to get lost."

Murdock clenched his teeth, not liking this woman getting the better of him, but before he could respond, Kymbra had already opened the portal and began leading the small group outside.

The ranger gave Harrison a confident nod and proceeded out the doorway with Pondle in tow. Thoragaard closed the door behind the platoon, locking it in the process.

"They should be back in thirty minutes," said the mage.

"What are you hoping to learn from their excursion?" asked Harrison.

"Marshall is the guard who allowed Tara and Justin to pass through the West Gate," said the mage. "He should have given your friends the proper directions."

"Well, they're captured now," said the young warrior.

"This might be true, but the real question is how far into their mission did they get?" Thoragaard let his comment linger for a moment before adding, "That is what I wish to learn."

"So what do we do in the meantime?"

"We wait."

The three women did their best to lead Murdock and Pondle through the dark alleyways, but their companions had other thoughts.

Kymbra, sensing the ranger on her heels, stopped short and glared at Murdock. "For the last time, back off!" she said in a stern, yet hushed tone. "I'm leading this platoon!"

"And I want to know where we're going!" said the ranger.

"Didn't you listen to Thoragaard? I need to locate Marshall!"

"I've asked you three times where this Marshall is, and you've said nothing!"

"I'm not telling you, and it's been four times."

Murdock felt his blood boil. Jerking his head to the left, he said to his friend, "What do you make of this city so far?"

Pondle gazed about the area from their location in a dark alley. Kymbra had led them through a maze of passageways, purposely keeping them out of sight from the soldiers who patrolled the streets. However, the thief sensed a problem.

"I expected to see many more guards," said Pondle. "We've only seen a handful."

"He's right," said Marissa, biting her bottom lip. "I figured to run into a lot more resistance."

"Where is everybody?" added Adrith.

Kymbra nodded, understanding her cohorts' concerns, since she too was uneasy about the lack of security in the area. "Marshall's not far away. Let's continue to tread lightly."

The small platoon remained in the shadows for several more minutes, passing vacated buildings and shops, ones that usually had townspeople inhabiting them. Tonight they stood empty.

Pondle took a moment to gaze inside one of the windows, noticing a table set with half-eaten meals. People were here not too long ago, thought the thief. Where are they now?

Not wanting to stray too far from the group, Pondle quickly followed the others to the back of an older, stone finished building. The thief made a cursory check of the general area and found the edifice to be a bit out of place.

Builders had constructed most structures throughout the city out of wood, not stone. Furthermore, this one had tall columns on each side of the doorway with menacing gargoyles perched at the top, staring down at them.

Kymbra's voice broke Pondle's trance. "Help me push the top of this column in."

The rest of the group came to Kymbra's aid. On a count of three, everyone reached as far up as they could on the column and pushed with all their might. The solid stone pillar slowly tilted inward.

Pondle watched in amazement as the column started to move downward and fall into the building. The thief heard what sounded like springs and hinges creaking as the pillar came to rest at a forty-five degree angle, extending into the darkness of the building.

Kymbra called the thief over. "You first," she said, pointing into the void.

Pondle peered at Murdock, who gave him a cautious stare in return, then proceeded to gaze into the newly created dark corridor. Using his infravision, Pondle could see that the column led to a narrow passage.

"It looks like we slide down this incline to the corridor below," said the thief.

"Do it," said Kymbra.

Pondle unsheathed his sword, then advanced to the top of the slope. With cautious steps, the thief positioned himself on the slant, then slid down into the awaiting darkness. Within seconds, he had navigated the incline, taken a few steps forward, and stood in a cramped passageway. Making a quick examination of the area, Pondle determined that the corridor he stood in separated two adjacent rooms.

Kymbra, Murdock, Adrith, and Marissa followed the thief's lead and entered the tight passage.

Pondle caught Kymbra's eye. "Now what?"

"You can see, right?"

"If you mean in the dark, yes, but only for a short distance."

"Good." The female warrior used her fingers to scour the right wall for something just out of reach. Finding the elusive switch, she pulled down on the lever causing the column to revert to its original position, leaving the group in total darkness.

Kymbra's voice permeated the void. "Pondle, this hallway goes forward another twenty feet. At that point there is a handle that will open a hatch in the floor. Find it."

The thief nodded in understanding, though no one saw his actions. "Stay close to me; I'm beginning my trek now."

Pondle took cautious steps forward. Years of adventuring had taught him that acting as the front man had its perils, and being in a small, enclosed space – the corridor's width was no more than three feet – more than convinced him to stay alert.

One more step forward revealed another of the passageway's secrets to the thief. "Stop!" said Pondle in a hushed tone.

"What's the matter?" whispered Kymbra.

Pondle squinted, allowing his eyes to focus better on the object in the flooring, but the tinge of light that emanated from just beyond the handle drew his concern.

"Someone's down there," he whispered back. "I can see a little bit of light. Couple that with the fact that we didn't run into any cobwebs, and this leads me to believe that people came this way not too long ago."

"That makes sense," said Kymbra. "Marshall must be here."

Again Pondle nodded in the darkness. "I'm going to reach for the handle and slowly open the hatch."

"Pondle," said an anxious male voice from behind the tall female. "Have your weapon ready. If something pops up from that opening, we can't help you from back here."

The thief knew Murdock always had his well being in mind, and his friend was right. Pondle gripped the hilt of his sword tighter, then reached for the handle. As soon as the thief grasped the knob, the mechanism caused the covering to spring open and a discernable light shone from the hatch. Everyone squinted and instinctively recoiled at the new sight.

Pondle peeked into the new opening and found a ladder leading down to a dirt floor. The thief looked back to the others.

"Go down," said Kymbra.

Pondle nodded once before making his descent. The thief's heart raced, knowing full well that someone had created the light source ahead and awaited their confrontation. Using both hands to grip the wooden sides, the halfling proceeded to descend the rungs of the ladder. Being a thief, he was accustomed to unsavory conditions, and what happened next did not totally surprise him.

The thief felt two hands grab the armor on his back, pulling him off the ladder, spinning him around and forcing him into the dirt wall. Next, Pondle felt a cold, metal blade against his throat.

"How many are with you?" barked the young, blonde-haired soldier.

Pondle's eyes grew wide as he tried to come to grips with his new predicament.

The man's eyes shifted to the hatch's opening, then back to Pondle. "How many?"

Just then a female voice came from above. "Pondle, are you all right?"

The soldier stared into Pondle's eyes and shook his head, signaling for the thief not to answer. The young man, keeping the knife pressed against Pondle's neck, then gripped the halfling's face with his other hand and gazed deeply into his eyes, pulling the thief's face closer to his own.

"Pondle!" said the voice from above again.

The thief took the initiative and mumbled, "Thoragaard."

The soldier released his grip on Pondle's face. "Thoragaard sent you here?"

"Yes," said the halfling, the dagger still too close to his neck for comfort. "We have a message."

The young soldier's eyes widened as another figure began to descend the ladder. Kymbra took one step, then jumped to the floor; Murdock followed right behind her.

"Take that knife away from his neck!" said Murdock, clenching his sword tighter.

The fair-haired fighter ignored the ranger's plea; instead he focused on the woman.

"Kymbra?"

The female raised an eyebrow after hearing her name. "Marshall?"

Marshall removed the blade from Pondle's neck. "You came at the right time!"

Pondle wiggled away from the young man, rubbing his throat in the process.

The young fighter turned to the thief. "I'm sorry, but I had to be sure you weren't one of Lord Hammer's men."

"Do I look like a Concurian soldier?" said Pondle, still flustered.

"Thoragaard has sent us to gather information from you," said Kymbra. As the two conversed, Adrith and Marissa joined the rest of the party in the dirt passageway.

Marshall gazed at the women, and when no one else descended the ladder, he asked, "Is that all of you?"

"Yes," said Kymbra.

The young fighter closed the hatch, then motioned for the group to follow him. "Let's gather somewhere else." He proceeded down the corridor with the rest trailing.

Pondle examined every aspect of the twisting, musty passageway, figuring that it traveled under the building and quite possibly away from the land owner's property line. Lit torches spaced every ten yards or so, provided enough light along the way to allow the humans to see, though Pondle found their luminosity a hindrance to his infravision.

A few minutes later, a brighter illumination emanated from around a corner. Marshall entered the room first, with his new companions close behind.

Being a thief, Pondle made a quick survey and found that the thirty-by-thirty foot dirt room penetrated deeper under the city's streets. He also noticed the countless number of eyes staring back at him.

"Marshall, what is this all about?" asked Kymbra with surprise, shocked to find so many people crammed into such a small place.

"Nigel's Death Row," deadpanned the young fighter.

The female warrior wrinkled her brow. The desperate faces that peered back at her with shallow eyes and long frowns could not possibly be a threat to Lord Hammer, she reasoned. Her stare lingered on an older couple, the man placing his hands gently over his auburn-haired wife's shoulders, both in obvious despair and sporting looks of anguish on their faces.

"Why does Nigel wish them dead?" asked the blonde warrior.

"He considers them traitors and they must all pay the ultimate price."

Kymbra maintained an incredulous stare. "What have they done?"

"Most of them, nothing," said Marshall. "Only a handful were involved with our Resistance operation."

"And the others?"

"Victims of circumstance," said the fair-haired soldier with a shrug. "Some happened to be with our helpers at the time Nigel's soldiers apprehended them, while others are just relatives of our friends."

"We need to get them out of here," said Kymbra with conviction. "Thoragaard will help us."

"I have more to tell you," said Marshall. "Lord Hammer has planned a mass hanging in the town's square for all so-called traitors."

Kymbra's eyes widened in shock. "For when?"

"Tonight."

"Thoragaard needs to know this!" exclaimed the blonde woman, glaring back at Murdock, Pondle, and her sister warriors.

Murdock cleared his throat and said, "We need to get some information first, remember?"

"Of course I do," snapped the woman, who then turned to face Marshall again. "Thoragaard needs to know where Tara, Justin, and Meredith are being held."

"We all saw the beacon glowing from the top of the temple's spire a few weeks ago," started Marshall. "That, coupled with Tara's encrypted message, told us to start the Resistance, but we needed to wait for Thoragaard's signal.

"However, something went wrong. I'm assuming the women are at the governor's mansion. He's locked that building down; it would only make sense, and I haven't seen them on the prison docket."

"And Justin?"

Marshall cast his eyes downward and drew a heavy sigh. "He's part of the mass hanging."

"What?" exclaimed Murdock and Pondle in unison.

"We need to go now!" said the ranger, knowing that every second wasted could cost the young boy his life.

Kymbra locked her eyes on Marshall. "Is there anything else that you know?"

"The mansion will be heavily guarded following this event, more than usual with the two prisoners." Marshall paused. "Nigel knows you're going to try and rescue Tara."

"I'm sure he does," said Kymbra. "Anything else?"

"That's everything," said the young soldier. He then took his gaze over his shoulder. "We need to get them out of here and to a safe place."

"Marshall, they're going to have to wait for the signal," said Kymbra.

"When will that be?" asked the fighter, a look of exasperation on his face. "We can't stay here too much longer."

"I know, but we can't risk having Nigel's soldiers see all these people." Kymbra gazed past the young man, taking an inventory of the townsfolk who huddled together. "Serve as their lookout, station yourself at the entrance of the building, and when the Resistance starts, have them all flee."

"How will I know what the signal is?"

"Easy, wait for the ensuing chaos." Kymbra turned to the others. "Time to go."

Adrith and Marissa took the lead and began to leave the small room, followed by Murdock and Pondle. Kymbra instructed Marshall one last time.

"Remember, wait for the signal," she began. "If it's taking too long, you'll have to come up with your own escape plan."

With that, she left the expressionless young man standing in the enclosure with his fellow anxious townspeople.

CHAPTER 24

¤

Nigel Hammer stood near the staging, his hands on his hips, and a grimace on his face. An anxious general stood beside his superior, waiting for the onslaught he knew would happen.

"What is this I hear about a soldier defecting and freeing almost a hundred prisoners!" barked the furious leader.

"Sir, it appears that we had a breach in our security forces," said the general, knowing that he could say nothing that would appease his leader's rage.

"It *appears*?" hissed Nigel, eyes squinted, his face inches away from his soldier's. "It *appears* that *you* have a problem!"

"I have my men scouring the city for this traitor and hope to have him and his cohorts on this staging tonight."

Nigel allowed his glare to linger a moment longer, before growling, "For your sake, I hope so." Before the governor could continue his tirade, a cloaked figure approached the two.

Lord Hammer glanced over, a smile almost gracing his face. "Allard, I had hoped that you wouldn't miss this event."

"I don't take pride in these kinds of rituals, Nigel," said the magician dryly.

Lord Hammer brushed off his mage's remark. "Nevertheless, what happens tonight will stop those pathetic rebellious souls in their tracks."

Allard cocked his head and said, "It should get the point across."

Nigel's demeanor turned dour as he glared at his general once again. "Commence with this event immediately! Parade the traitors into the square!"

The soldier nodded, stepped back, and said, "I will see to it that the prisoners are brought to the staging." A second later the armored man scurried off to heed his superior's command.

With his general gone, Nigel said to Allard, "After tonight, only a fool would attempt to fight me."

"There seems to be five thousand or so fools surrounding this city."

Nigel scowled. "Let them try to bring these walls down! I'm going to relish in our victory soon enough!"

Allard closed his eyes and arched his brows, as one would react when he does not believe what he has heard. "My powers are limited, Nigel. You must understand this."

Lord Hammer glared at his mage. "Then I expect you to perform at your best." The dark fighter took his gaze back to the staging. "But first, we must stop this uprising before it even gets a chance to start."

Thoragaard paced anxiously, the news Kymbra had delivered to him being most unexpected.

"How many soldiers did Marshall say there were?" asked the illusionist.

"He didn't specify," said the female warrior, "but I have to believe that most of them are at this event. That would explain why we entered the town so easily." The mage nodded, continuing his pacing.

Harrison took the moment of silence to interject his main concern. "Do you think Tara and Meredith are part of this tragic occasion?"

"I doubt it, but I cannot say for sure," said the mage.

The young warrior made up his mind. "Then we have no choice but to witness what's happening! If they're there, we must save them!"

Harrison's friends concurred. "I don't like waiting around for something to happen either," added Murdock. "I'm with Harrison – we should go now."

"And I am not fond of sitting idly by while my niece has a death sentence on her," said Gelderand.

The cloaked magician knew he had no decisions to make. "I agree with all of you," said Thoragaard. "However, we must proceed with caution."

"Always the cautious approach!" said Murdock, agitated with the slow course of events. "Let's get going already!"

Harrison brushed off his friend's remark. "What do you propose?" he asked, his apprehension on the rise with every passing second.

Thoragaard addressed the female warriors. "You say that most of Lord Hammer's men are congregated in the town square, along with the rest of the townsfolk?"

"That's what Marshall said," responded Kymbra as Adrith and Marissa nodded in agreement.

The illusionist looked up in thought, then said, "I need to get close to the crowd before I commence with the Resistance."

Harrison cocked his head. "I thought we were going to save Tara and Meredith!"

"Trust me," said Thoragaard with a sly smile. "What happens after I begin the uprising will be written in history books."

The metal bindings that secured Tara's thin wrists began to dig into her soft skin. The young maiden, along with Meredith, followed two lead soldiers toward the anxious mob.

The young girl whispered to her companion. "Where are we going?"

Meredith leaned closer to Tara and said in a soft voice, "Knowing Nigel, someplace where he can make a statement."

Tara took in the information, her heart racing with every step. As the young girl drew closer to the crowd of people, she noticed a large structure looming before them. Further examining the platform, the maiden stared at the ominous sight of a hundred dangling nooses. Her heart beat even faster, wondering if one of the cables of death were meant for her. The two evil men standing next to the staging only compounded her anxiety even more.

Lord Hammer's eye caught a glimpse of the small procession approaching his location, and without bidding his counterpart good-bye, he maneuvered to their position.

"I'm glad you two could attend," mocked the Concurian leader.

Meredith's blue eyes stared down Nigel. "It's not like we had a choice, now did we?"

"No, you didn't." Nigel waved five more soldiers over. "Surround our guests and make sure they have a clear view of the staging. But most important of all, don't let anyone close to them."

Tara took solace in Lord Hammer's words, figuring that he had spared her life - for now.

The soldiers formed a semi-circle around the prisoners and, just as their superior had commanded, provided the ladies with an unobstructed view of the stage.

After Lord Hammer's men had positioned themselves, Meredith said, "Nigel, just what do you want with us?"

Lord Hammer took a step in his woman's direction, standing directly in front of her. Craning his neck down over the First Lady, he hissed, "Tonight ends everything you have tried so hard to begin, and I want you here to witness it."

Meredith's eyes grew wide. "I don't know what you're talking about! What ends? What are you going to do?"

"You take me for a fool!" barked Nigel. "Your pathetic resistance will fail, and as for you," Lord Hammer's head snapped in Tara's direction, "your precious little Harrison will die before he ever has a chance to save you!"

Tara tried to take a step back, but one of Lord Hammer's men prevented her. Nigel continued.

"I know he's planning to rescue you. That's his nature and his downfall!" Nigel sneered. "You're going to like living in Concur."

Tara held her breath after Nigel's last comment. Harrison was coming, raced her thoughts. And this wicked man knows it. How is he going to save me?

Sounds of wailing and sobbing broke the young maiden's train of thought. All heads turned to the procession that had formed behind the mob.

"Finally," said Nigel, who left the women and ventured closer to Allard.

Tara felt a little more at ease with Nigel away from her, yet her nerves remained frayed. The moans and shouts intensified as the line of prisoners drew closer.

The young maiden stood on her tiptoes to get a better view. From her vantage point, it appeared that the prison guards had chained the detainees' wrists together, forming one large procession line. Furthermore, all wore black hoods over their heads, completing the haunting sight.

"This is not good," whispered the blonde girl to Meredith.

"Be strong, child," said Concur's First Lady.

Tara took a moment and glanced at Meredith. The young maiden could see the look of pain on the older woman's face, but even more she could feel anguish emanating from the First Lady's very soul. Something awful is going to happen here tonight, she thought, before feeling her own heart sink.

"I need you to fan out and find Meredith and Tara," said Thoragaard to his entourage. The illusionist had led the small group through Concur's shadowy streets, eerily empty save for the throng of people gathered in the city's center.

"I'll take Adrith and Marissa with me," said Kymbra, before addressing Murdock and Pondle. "You two should come as well."

"What if we encounter Lord Hammer?" asked the ranger in Thoragaard's direction.

"Leave him be. We need the townspeople to witness his response to our plan."

Murdock gave the mage a reluctant nod, understanding his rationale. Turning his attention to Harrison, Swinkle, and Gelderand, the ranger creased his brow, pointed at his friends, and asked, "What about them?"

"His face is too recognizable," said Kymbra, gesturing with her head in Harrison's direction. "You of all people must remain in the shadows."

"I'm not staying here!" retorted the young warrior as Lance came by his side.

"You will be fighting tonight," said Thoragaard. "Keep your other friends close to you; their powers will be tested as well." The mage drew a deep breath, then stared at the immense crowd only a mere fifty yards away.

"It is time," he said. "The Resistance starts now."

Thoragaard removed a sack from his pack and unloaded its contents after placing it on the ground.

Harrison watched the bearded man pour out a small mound of what looked like black sand. Upon closer inspection, the young warrior could see bright orange flakes mixed in with the darker particles. The mage's mumbling interrupted his investigation.

Thoragaard squatted in front of the pile, closed his eyes, and began reciting his spell. Seconds later, the orange flakes grew brighter. The mage placed his hands about six inches away from either side of the mound, then slowly raised to a standing position. As he did, the particles followed him and became circular in nature. Everyone glued their eyes on the dark sphere with bright flecks, which upon another key word began a slow rotation.

Harrison, like the others around him, had no idea what to expect next. With the black globe spinning between his hands, the mage opened his eyes and issued a command.

"Let the Resistance begin!" exclaimed Thoragaard, who then threw the orb toward the crowd.

The sphere began to levitate away from the group, its orangey flecks sparking. A moment later, the globe morphed into a smoky fog, its sparks flashing like lightning in a gathering thundercloud. The strange mist started to spread in all directions, all the while tiny, orange flashes lit up the fog.

Harrison watched as the cloud began to permeate his small gathering. The substance enveloped the young warrior, its coarseness irritating his skin the way sand would feel during a sandstorm. Flashes lit the area ever so subtly, revealing expressions of anxiety and curiosity amongst the group members.

The dark cloud swirled about the young warrior's head before reaching his eyes, causing them to start burning. Harrison instinctively brought his hand to his face.

"Try not to rub your eyes," said Thoragaard to his startled friends. "You will only irritate them further."

Harrison did his best to heed the mage's command, but the uncomfortable feeling of what felt like sand crystals annoyed him.

The unpleasant sensation began to dissipate as the mysterious cloud hovered away.

The young warrior blinked in rapid succession, hoping to alleviate the burning. Taking his gaze to his friends, he found that everyone's appearance had changed.

"Swinkle," he said to his friend who stood closest to him, "your eyes!"

The holy man stood frozen, unsure of what to say. Pointing at the young warrior, he said, "Yours have changed, too."

A look of utter surprise flashed across Harrison's face. Taking the time to give Swinkle a closer examination, he found that his friend's eyes had become darker, and his irises resembled the pattern of a tiger's coat.

"Do mine look like tiger stripes?" asked the young warrior.

Swinkle nodded.

Scanning the area, Harrison found that all eyes resembled the great feline's markings. The young warrior swiveled his head back and forth, searching for Thoragaard and he found the cloaked figure staring toward the town square, motionless.

Approaching the illusionist, the young warrior asked, "Why has our appearance changed?"

Thoragaard continued facing away from Harrison. "Now we can know with certainty who is part of the Resistance and who remains sided with Lord Hammer."

Harrison did as Thoragaard and brought his gaze toward the large crowd gathered in the town square. The flashing dark cloud continued its trek toward the unsuspecting mob. The young warrior's eyes widened as the mage's comment sunk in.

"Not everyone is part of the Resistance, are they?" asked Harrison.

"No."

Harrison's heart began to race, the importance of the moment beginning to overwhelm him. "You know what's going to happen next, don't you?"

"Yes," said Thoragaard, turning to face the young warrior with tiger-like eyes. "Chaos."

The young warrior returned his gaze to the horde of people and anxiously awaited the fog's unexpected arrival.

"Get them all on the staging!" barked Nigel to his henchmen.

The pitiful procession of Concurian townspeople tripped and stumbled as the soldiers led them up the rickety stairs of the makeshift platform and to their respective places on the staging. The receding twilight, coupled with the dim light of the hand-held torches, prevented anyone from seeing the oncoming dark cloud.

Lord Hammer, along with Allard, watched as his men placed a noose around the neck of each poor soul. Nigel watched with anticipation as one of his generals inspected the handiwork of the other soldiers. Satisfied that his men had properly secured all of the prisoners, he glanced at Nigel and raised his thumb, signaling for proceedings to continue.

"We're ready to go," said Nigel to no one in particular. Swiveling his head over his right shoulder, he spotted another of his soldiers. "Sound the bell!" The armored man nodded once and raced away to begin his task.

Nigel smiled, then gestured to the soldiers on the platform to remove the prisoners' hoods.

Justin heard heavy steps approach his position, then his head jerked back as the soldier removed his head covering. The young lad's heart raced as he tried to gather his bearings.

The Aegean, a noose firmly placed around his neck, gazed out at a large crowd of anxious people. Alongside him stood countless Concurian townspeople, all in a similar predicament and scared just the same. Justin panned to the left and found a familiar face.

The boy's blood simmered as he stared into Gareth's soulless eyes. "This is all your doing, Gareth," said the angry Aegean through clenched teeth. "How are we going to escape from this?"

The elder fighter slumped, a defeated man. His ankles and wrists remained bound, and his own noose's thick twine dug into his neck. The gravity of his erroneous decision making throughout the course of his ill-fated alliance with Lord Hammer gnawed at his insides.

Summoning whatever strength he had left, Gareth said, "Can you find it in your heart to forgive me, son?"

Before the young man could answer, a deafening bong resonated throughout the area. The death bell had been sounded.

"There's no forgiving you, Gareth," said Justin.

Bong.

"You have sealed our fate and possibly that of Aegeus," continued the younger man.

Gareth turned his head away and slumped further.

Bong.

Tears welled in Tara's eyes and her mood turned from bad to worse after the soldiers removed the hoods from the poor souls' heads. Seeing the terrified faces on the townspeople paraded to the staging drove home the gravity of the situation.

They're all going to die, she thought, her eyes wide and glued to the platform.

Bong.

Tara tugged on the sleeve of the woman standing next to her, and both sets of blue eyes locked on each other.

"He's going to kill them, isn't he?" asked Tara, her voice trembling.

Meredith said nothing, nodding once and looking away.

Bong.

Tara took her nervous stare back to the staging, then felt her heart sink further and her stomach churn. The young maiden covered her mouth.

Staring at a lad her age, she said in a wavering voice, "That's Justin up there!"

Meredith followed the young girl's line of sight, stopping at the same handsome man. The Concurian woman's heart sank as well.

Bong.

The cloud continued its advance on the anxious mob. The fog reached the outer fringes of the crowd and its spell began to take effect.

A woman, clutching her two children, instinctively brought a hand to her eyes, trying to rub away the contaminant. Blinking, she heard her children complain about debris hindering their vision, too. She then bent to one knee to be at their level. Her son gazed back at his mother with wide eyes and a frown.

"Mother!" exclaimed the eight year-old boy. "Your eyes look funny!"

Bong.

The townswoman's heart skipped a beat and she peered at the people around her. Many continued to rub their eyes, but she did her best to focus on their faces. People she considered friends now stood around her, some with markings like hers, and others that remained unchanged.

"Mommy," said the woman's little daughter, tugging on her mother's arm. "Why do you look different now?"

The Concurian woman said nothing; she stood tall and frantically gazed about. A mysterious fog started to cover the crowd with strange, orange flashes that looked like excited fireflies glittering throughout the dark mass.

Bong.

The woman took a hand and placed it over her open mouth. "It's really happening," she said aloud in a shocked voice.

The ever-thickening cloud permeated the throng of people, transforming eyes for some, not for others. Confused townspeople shouted and yelled, pointing to their fellow Concurian, unsure what to do next.

Lord Hammer and his men squinted into the distance, trying to get a better fix on the odd circumstances. Getting an unsettling feeling, Nigel glared at his men on the staging, yelling, "Summon the executioners! Get them ready for their task!"

Bong.

Nigel swiveled to Allard. "I know who's behind this!"

The great mage nodded. "Thoragaard."

"He's here, isn't he?"

Allard waved his arm toward the oncoming fog. "Need you more proof?"

Lord Hammer clenched his teeth, seething. "He will not stop us tonight! Can you diffuse his magic?"

Bong.

The magician pushed back his robe, then clasped his hands. Mumbling to himself, Allard began to rub them together as fast as he could, creating a friction that started to turn his hands red. He then stopped, leaving them glowing like fire embers. Again speaking something inaudible, he threw his hands toward the dark cloud. An orange-red flash flew from them and bolted toward the haze.

Bong.

By now, people within the crowd witnessed both Allard's actions and the menacing oncoming fog. Seconds later, above the defenseless townsfolk, the reddish blur intersected the black, flashing mass.

Lord Hammer watched the scene unfold with wide eyes, smiling all the while. Allard had never let him down, and this trick from a two-bit illusionist would surely fail at the hands of a well-experienced mage.

To everyone's surprise, the black void engulfed the new energy source, intensifying its own strength. Nigel watched in horror as the massive cloud coursed through the crowd, then blew across the staging, morphing eyes, revealing more traitors.

Bong.

Nigel glared at his magician. "You failed!"

"Sometimes there is no stopping fate," said Allard, unfazed at his spell's failure.

Lord Hammer pointed a finger in Allard's face. "Wrong answer!" The Concurian leader then spun around and barked at the soldiers on the platform. "Are we ready?"

Bong.

The first soldier peered at his comrade some ten feet away and noticed something amiss. His friend's eyes now had a strange orange and black striping pattern associated with them. Investigating further, the fighter found that not all of the prisoners sported transformed features.

Already feeling the intense burning sensation coming from his leader's glare, the man turned and faced his superior from above. "We have a problem, sir!"

Every muscle tensed underneath Nigel's black armor. The Governor gripped his sword's hilt and unsheathed his weapon. The soldier, sensing an impending eruption, pointed to his comrade.

Nigel followed the man's extended finger that came to rest on a Concurian soldier. *Traitors in my ranks,* fumed Lord Hammer. He had to think, and think fast.

Bong.

Glaring at the fighter he said, "Commence with the operation! Hang these traitors!"

The soldier turned and faced his transformed comrade. To his surprise a second, and then a third soldier, all with striped eye markings, advanced on his position. The first man drew his weapon, only to be overtaken by the three other fighters. Fortunately for the first fighter, his three comrades only subdued him, removed his weapon, and rendered him unable to fight.

Nigel witnessed the scene, his anger reaching unparalleled levels.

Bong.

Harrison watched from afar, Lance by his side, Swinkle and Gelderand close behind. The young warrior had already witnessed the females escort Murdock and Pondle around the crowd and into the ensuing darkness. They would be ready, he knew.

"What do we do?" asked Harrison in Thoragaard's direction.

"I am sure that Meredith and Tara are part of this event," said the monotone mage. "We find them, follow their every move, then rescue them from this hell."

Bong.

Harrison accepted the older man's assessment, but he wanted to find his mate now. "Where do you suspect they are at this moment?"

Thoragaard motioned his head toward the staging. "I am sure Nigel is giving them a front row view of his atrocities."

The young warrior gazed toward the platform. An orange flash had just appeared, and no sooner had it arrived, it disappeared, making the dark haze larger.

Harrison noticed that the townspeople had begun to yell and shout, and some were shoving their fellow man. Just as Thoragaard had said, the chaos was just beginning.

Bong.

"Release him!" ordered Nigel, thrusting his sword toward the traitorous fighters who stood on the platform. Not one of the armored men heeded their superior's command.

Lord Hammer's blood simmered. Panning, he took a keen interest in those whose eyes had morphed into a disloyal state and sought his honorable men. He found more soldiers on his side than the Resistance.

"All of you," barked Nigel to five of his men who stood at the base of the staging. Motioning with his sword, he commanded, "Apprehend those traitors!"

Bong.

The five soldiers did not flinch and ran onto the staging, confronting the three resistance fighters. After a short and failed negotiation, the five men drew their weapons and engaged their fellow comrades in hand to hand combat.

Nigel tried to hide his pleasure at seeing his men take the initiative, but something did not seem right. The three unfaithful men had not put up a fight; instead they allowed Nigel's men to apprehend them.

The Governor leered at the platform, noticing that not all the nooses had bodies assigned to them. Pointing to three empty stations, the dark leader commanded, "String them up as well!"

The five men, holding their comrades still for the time being, hesitated. Each person gazed at the fighter next to him, unsure what action to take.

Bong.

Nigel clenched his teeth, his soldiers' inactivity infuriating him. "What are you waiting for?"

On the platform, one of the captured fighters peered into the dark eyes of his friend. "Don't do this," he said loud enough for all to hear. "Look at the people on the staging," he continued, motioning with his head for the others to look behind him.

Nigel's men peeked over their shoulders ever so subtly, knowing the menacing eyes of their superior were on them. The

Concurian soldiers saw the torment and despair on the faces of the poor souls with nooses around their necks.

Bong.

Waiting a moment longer to speak, the fighter said, "This is all wrong and you know it."

"It's not your choice to make!" barked a fighter loyal to Nigel. "You took an oath to serve Concur, as did I!"

"That was before Lord Hammer imprisoned my family, these families," said the soldier. "What did they do wrong in their lives to be put up here on this stage?"

While the five loyalists pondered their allegiance, one of the captured comrades, in one smooth motion, unsheathed his sword and thrust it into the man in front of him.

"I'm sorry, but this is how it must be," he said, removing the blade from the fallen body. A sword then pierced his side before he even had a chance to defend himself. The other soldiers joined the skirmish and the internal battle for Concur had finally begun.

Bong.

Meredith gripped Tara's arm and pulled her close. With her eyes fixed on the melee upon the platform, she said in a forceful voice, "Stay with me and do as I say at all times."

The young maiden nodded and watched with anxious eyes as blood began to spill. Groans erupted from the crowd as people became aware of the battle taking place on the stage.

Concur's First Lady continued. "People will be forced to choose sides – for better or for worse."

Tara took Meredith's hand, squeezing it tight. Panning, she searched for her love, knowing that he must be around someplace, but where?

Bong.

Nigel rushed the staging. The mysterious haze had engulfed the immediate area, infected all who had stood there, then lifted away toward the great walls and toward the awaiting legions of soldiers in the countryside, seemingly unaware of the chaos it had created. Now, Lord Hammer's raw energy fed off the ensuing madness.

Brandishing his long sword, the Concurian leader came to his soldiers' aide, slashing at the traitors. Blood squirted from fresh wounds as the disloyal men resisted fighting, sacrificing themselves in hope of inciting the Resistance fighters who stood and watched from the crowd.

Lord Hammer thrashed at the defenseless men, his fighters backing away to avoid their superior's blade. When the three men lay dead, he turned in a rage toward his soldiers and barked, "Hang the prisoners now!"

Bong.

Again, Nigel's men hesitated, not sure if they wanted to heed their leader's command. Each man gazed at the crowd in their own way, taking in the shock on their faces, the erupting hostilities, the sobs from the women, the screams of children. Eyes scarred with tiger markings glared in all directions, each person waiting for something more to happen.

Nigel squinted, clenched his teeth, and hissed at the man closest to him, "I said hang these people!"

Bong.

The soldier took a second to peer at the bodies closest to him. "But sir, not all these people have the Resistance markings!"

Nigel took a purposeful step in the soldier's direction. "I will not say this again. Hang them all!"

The soldier peeked at his comrades; no one would look him in the eye, he was on his own. "I can't do it. I'm sorry, sir."

"Me, too." In one swift motion, Nigel drove his sword through the fighter's armor, stabbing him and dropping the soldier to the staging's floor.

Bong.

Nigel swiveled his head in all directions, searching for the lever that would spell the traitors their doom.

"Flank over there," yelled Kymbra to Murdock. The ranger heeded the woman's command with Pondle in tow.

The two men had maneuvered between two buildings directly across from the platform where the throng of Concurians stood. Kymbra, Adrith, and Marissa had fanned out and began to enter the crowd, searching for fellow Resistance fighters.

Pondle gazed near the staging to a mass of armored men. "I can't see Tara or Meredith, but that group of soldiers looks like they're protecting something."

The thief's friend heard his comment, but a more important target presented itself. Murdock readied his bow. The people on the stage thrashed about, but now one figure stood alone.

"He's in my sights, Pondle. Do I shoot him?"

Bong.

Harrison, Lance, and his close friends now stood to the left of the assembly, waiting. The young warrior wanted nothing more than to rush through the crowd and save those people on the staging. His warrior training started to beckon him when a voice interrupted his thought process.

"Remember," said Swinkle, "you made a vow to yourself and the others." The young cleric made sure he drove home his point before the entire scene erupted into chaos. "If you can take Lord Hammer unharmed, you must do so."

Harrison, his battle-axe more than ready for melee, nodded. "I will engage him only if I must."

"Our objective is to save the women," said Thoragaard, watching with a careful eye.

"Let me know what I can do as well," said Gelderand, holding Rufus in his arms, stroking his fur, and waiting patiently for his orders.

"In due time," said Thoragaard.

Bong.

Justin knew he had precious little time, but his hands were bound and no one appeared to be coming to his aide. To his left, Nigel Hammer had just slaughtered his own soldier, and the ones who revealed themselves as being part of the Resistance had died for their cause.

To his near left, Gareth watched the scene unfold with solemn eyes, seemingly ready to accept his fate. The older man felt eyes upon him, catching the younger Aegean staring.

Sighing, he said to Justin, "You were right and I was wrong." Gareth cast his eyes downward. "You should not die because of my foolish mistake."

The younger man tried to take solace in the warrior's remark, but the point seemed moot now. Justin took his gaze away from the older man and began to pray.

Bong.

The elder warrior peered out at the crowd again and saw something strange. A winged creature flew above the chaos and headed straight toward him. Hovering a few feet above him now, Gareth gazed into the bat's large green eyes.

"Undo what I have done," he said to his transformed mate, then lowered his head. "Save that poor girl."

Fallyn, unable to rescue her love, heeded Gareth's advice and flew away from the madness.

Bong.

Five yards away from Nigel rested the elusive lever of death. Lord Hammer located the harmless device and advanced in its direction. The Governor's actions did not go unnoticed. Several townsmen, their eyes both marked and plain, yelled from their position.

"You can't kill them all!" shouted one man, his eyes similar to the great beast.

"Where's the justice?" yelled a second with normal features.

"Have you no shame?" exclaimed yet a third with plain eyes.

Another man took offense at the first man's comment. "What do you mean don't kill them all?" The Concurian with plain eyes, continued. "Kill only the traitors, like you!"

Bong.

The man then attacked his fellow townsman with orange and black markings. The other two non-marked men rained punches on the supposed traitor, striking the poor man over and over again.

Other Resistance fighters, witnessing the new melee, came to their comrade's aid, this time brandishing weapons. As more and more people entered the clash, smaller skirmishes began to erupt throughout the crowd. Chaos had begun.

Bong.

"He's moving!" said Murdock.

"Thoragaard said not to fire on him!" shouted Pondle, surprised at the words that came out of his mouth.

The ranger followed Nigel's every move with his bow, its arrow ready to fire. Murdock had used all the resolve he could muster not to let the projectile fly. He understood Thoragaard's rationale that they needed the townspeople to witness firsthand their leader's atrocities, but to have his hated enemy in his sights and ignore the opportunity to eliminate him gnawed at his insides.

Murdock pulled the string on his weapon back a bit further. "To hell with him," he said, but before he could release the tension from his bow, he felt someone shove him from behind.

Bong.

The ranger stumbled forward, then spun around to find two men staring at him with similar eye markings.

One of the people, a simple townsman, gazed at Murdock and Pondle with wide eyes. "We didn't know you were one of us!"

Pondle came to his friend's side, his short sword drawn and ready to strike. The two men raised their hands in the air, surrendering.

"What were you thinking?" exclaimed Murdock, more embarrassed that he allowed a simple Concurian to sneak up on him. "I had my arrow locked on Lord Hammer!"

All eyes then focused on the platform.

Bong.

Justin finished his prayer, then opened his eyes. Before him, a massive mob of people, soldiers and townsfolk alike, battled amongst each other. Sobs and horrified sighs permeated the air on the platform, as the prisoners awaited their deaths. Pleas for their lives to be spared fell on deaf ears.

Nigel Hammer took purposeful steps to the lever that connected all of the traitors. Facing the conspirators, he exclaimed, "Your cause ends here!"

The Governor of Concur grasped the wooden shaft with two hands, then forced it down. All at once, wooden slabs released from under the feet of the prisoners.

Bong.

Justin had a split second to look down at the void that awaited him. His body whooshed downward, then he heard an awful snap followed by an intense pain at the base of his skull. To his left, Gareth's lifeless body swung from side to side. A few seconds later his pain disappeared, his body went limp, and all around him went black.

Tara screamed, as did hundreds of others, when she saw Justin's body drop through the trap door beneath him. The dreadful sound of snapping necks caused her to gasp, and at that very moment she knew Justin was gone. The young maiden brought a trembling hand to her face, as she covered her mouth and began to cry. Her stomach wrenched, and she buckled to the ground to heave on the bare dirt. She then started crying uncontrollably.

Meredith, also in shock, dropped to her knee and propped the crying girl up. Squeezing the lass with all her might, she said, "Stay with me, Tara! You must remain strong!"

"Justin's dead!" cried the young girl. "He's dead!"

"And there's no bringing him back now," said Meredith, her eyes swollen with tears. "Get a grip of yourself!"

"It's my fault," she said, pulling away to look into Meredith's eyes. "I shouldn't have come!" Tears rolled unfettered down her face.

"Justin took on a noble assignment and died a hero," said the First Lady of Concur. "Many will die for this cause, Tara, and they all will be heroes."

Tara tried to take solace in Meredith's words, but the heaviness she felt in her heart would not go away any time soon. The menacing figure that approached the girl brought her to her feet.

"You monster!" yelled the young maiden as she ran at Nigel. Upon reaching him, she began to pound his chest with her small fists.

Lord Hammer allowed the girl to strike him, then motioned for his soldiers to remove her from the scene.

"You're a beast!" she yelled as Nigel's henchmen dragged her away. Several other fighters surrounded Meredith as well, apprehending her.

"Take them both back to the mansion and lock them away," ordered Nigel. "I have business to handle here."

Surrounded by platoons of soldiers, Nigel, along with Allard, strode back to the platform. Only handfuls of horrified people noticed their leader on the staging, most others pointing to the lifeless bodies as they swung ever so slowly on their thick ropes.

The dark leader glanced at his magician and nodded once. Allard took the cue and grasped his wooden staff. He waved it once and three purple missiles hurtled through the air, only ten feet above the crowd. After the projectiles passed the fighting people, they exploded, gaining everyone's attention.

Nigel, having achieved his people's reluctant awareness, raised his palms toward the crowd. As the mob simmered down, he lowered his hands and grasped his sword.

Lord Hammer then removed the weapon from its sheath and raised it in the air. "Let tonight's events be a message to everyone who is part of this pathetic resistance. You will be destroyed! No justice, no prisoners, only death!"

Nigel's people stood still, waiting for more. "I call on all Concurians who believe in our way of life to fight the armies that have amassed around our great city. Soon they will begin their attack, but we will beat them back. Fight the foreigners with all of your might, but first, I call on you to round up those traitors who no longer will call Concur their home!"

A smattering of cheers and boos emanated from the crowd. Concurian soldiers then rushed the masses, in search of those with tiger-marked eyes. One by one, armored men began to gather townsfolk who were part of the Resistance, forcing them together, separating them from those without markings. However, instead of people laying down their arms, the Resistance fighters fought back. Within minutes, swords clashed, objects were thrown, and people scattered. Chaos erupted yet again.

Nigel watched in disbelief. Allard's voice snapped him from his trance. "Nigel, might I suggest we leave this place and return to our safe haven?"

Lord Hammer's mind churned and the thought of Harrison riding into Concur on his white horse brought him to a new level of anger.

"Yes, we must prepare for Harrison's arrival."

The two men, along with scores of security forces, left the staging and returned to the Governor's mansion.

CHAPTER 25

¤

Harrison stood in disbelief. Only seconds ago almost a hundred innocent souls lost their lives at the hands of a ruthless dictator. The young warrior watched with swollen eyes while Nigel Hammer barked at the crowd, limp bodies swaying during his rant. Then his warrior instincts took over.

His jaw clenched and eyes focused, Harrison glared at the man on the platform. The time had come to confront the evil that lurked inside Concur. The young warrior turned to face the men alongside him.

"Swinkle, Gelderand, we're going after Nigel," said the young warrior with conviction in his eyes.

"Harrison, I know what you just saw has upset you," started Swinkle, "but try and keep a level head."

The young warrior thrust a finger toward his friend. "I understand what you're saying, but this has to stop! We have Concurians on our side and we're all going to defeat him!"

Another voice of reason chimed in. "Harrison, don't forget about Tara," said Gelderand, trying to regain the young man's focus. "She is our top priority at this time."

Harrison's thoughts immediately shifted to his love. Where is she, he wondered, disturbed at the notion. Is she safe? Probably not.

Thoragaard's monotone voice broke his concentration. "There is one last order of business before we rescue the women." The illusionist pointed to the dark mass that engulfed the high Concurian walls. "Men atop the structure have a final chore to perform."

All eyes focused on Concur's most recognizable feature. Torches bobbed in erratic movements, skirmishes seemingly underway. Harrison gazed at the sight, wondering if soldiers who had stood together during battle for years were now choosing sides against their dark lord.

Suddenly, flashes erupted and projectiles hurtled into the air. Explosions akin to a fireworks display illuminated the surrounding area, shedding light on the faces of everyone below.

Melees and skirmishes between Concurian soldiers and Resistance fighters halted for a moment as heads gazed upward at the exploding sky, most not understanding its true meaning.

"Why is this happening?" shouted Harrison, his eyes fixed on the red and orange explosions.

Thoragaard faced the young warrior and his friends, smiling. "Now, everyone is alerted to our plans. The final battle has truly begun."

Brendan Brigade knew that the Forge Brothers and the Arcadians were witnessing the same aerial display over Concur. The Aegean gazed upwards into the dark sky. The field generals had agreed that a night offensive would be difficult to coordinate. Knowing that, the Aegean leader summoned the head cleric from Robus.

"Sister Martel," he said to the cloaked, middle-aged woman, "assemble your people and have your mission ready by first light." The Robusite monk nodded and commenced with her task.

Brendan then began to bark orders to his soldiers, preparing them to storm the walled city. The warrior gazed up in thought, keeping his eyes fixed on the impressive explosions.

"Coordinate your attack fifteen minutes after you see the signal," he said aloud, shaking his head, then added, "that is, if you see the sign during the day," reiterating the battle plans that he, Thoragaard, and the other leaders had agreed to.

With the indication coming at night, he knew that the advancing armies would need to wait until daybreak to begin their advancement on Concur.

"May the gods have mercy on us all."

Murdock and Pondle had remained hidden in the shadows for much of the evening, witnessing the night's happenings from a safe distance. After watching Lord Hammer fulfill his traitors' death sentence, the duo regrouped with their fellow warriors and hurried back to Harrison's position with some much-needed news.

"Thoragaard, Lord Hammer's security forces are rushing Tara and Meredith back toward the Governor's mansion," said Kymbra while everyone listened with intent. "Nigel's heading in that direction as well."

Harrison gripped his battle-axe tighter. "It's time to save Tara, and if we're lucky, confront Lord Hammer, too."

"Not so fast," replied the illusionist. "We cannot take on so many soldiers alone. Furthermore, our Resistance fighters will not know our plan."

The young warrior stared at the magician, a dumbfounded expression on his face. He wanted to save his love, and at this very moment. "We finally locate the women and now we're not going to rescue them!"

Thoragaard approached the young man, resting his hands on his shoulders. "Concur is on the brink of attack and it is our responsibility to get those gates open. However, the surrounding armies will not rush the city at night, giving us a bit more time to meet our objective of gaining the allegiance of as many Concurians as possible, soldiers included. You must help with this." The illusionist paused for effect.

"Harrison, many who patrol the great walls are confused and are not sure if they want to remain loyal to Lord Hammer. We must turn them – *you* must turn them."

The young warrior understood the importance of what Thoragaard had just said, but he wanted to save Tara more than anything in the world. Kymbra's voice interrupted his thoughts.

"What if we," the female gestured to her fellow warriors, as well as Murdock and Pondle, "provided reconnaissance around the mansion? That way we can determine the exact whereabouts of the women."

Gelderand took a step forward. "I might be able to help with that, too."

The illusionist locked his gaze on the cat that the magician stroked in his hands. "Is Rufus your apprentice?"

The older mage cocked his head, looking upwards. "Oh, I wouldn't call him that, but he knows his tasks."

The young warrior listened to the two men converse, knowing exactly what Gelderand had in mind.

"You're going to have Rufus do the same thing he did at Dracus's lair, aren't you?" asked Harrison. The elder man nodded.

Harrison recalled the cat had performed his chore to perfection, the only problem being that the ruthless dragon had outsmarted them.

"How close to the mansion do you need to be?" asked Thoragaard, understanding the limitations involved for Rufus to handle his task.

"I cannot be much further than a hundred yards away from him," said Gelderand. "The closer the better."

"That might be a difficult task," said Thoragaard, grimacing.

Swinkle added to the conversation. "I can help as well." All eyes turned to the young cleric.

"I can create diversions if need be," said Swinkle, fixing his eyes on Thoragaard. "Gelderand will be incapacitated with his spell, which will leave us to make sure Rufus completes his mission."

"I will be counting on you then," said the illusionist.

"Many of the soldiers will have problems with their allegiance and I can help sway them to our cause," added Swinkle.

"You are optimistic, young man," said Thoragaard. "I hope you are right with your assessment."

"Furthermore," said Gelderand, "I have a ring that will help us on our mission."

Thoragaard nodded at the firm plan coming together. "Good. Take advantage of the darkness. The armies surrounding Concur will be storming the city at dawn, which should divert Nigel's forces quite nicely."

"And they," Harrison pointed to the rescue team, "can use that diversion to monitor the movements around Lord Hammer's mansion." The young warrior felt better about the strategy. Gazing at the illusionist, he asked, "What do we do from here?"

"We head for the West Gate and help get the entranceway opened." Thoragaard turned his attention to his reconnaissance team.

"Remember, find out as much as you can about the building's layout, locate the women, then hold your positions." Thoragaard stared at each individual in the group. "The ultimate plan is to converge on Nigel, trapping him inside his mansion. We will reconvene after the armies storm the city. Try to get some rest before that time as well."

"Let's get moving then," said Kymbra. "We should be able to use all the commotion going on tonight to our benefit."

"Wait!" said Harrison, before dropping to one knee to address his canine friend. "Lance, go with Swinkle and Gelderand. Find Tara!" The little dog yapped once in affirmation, his tail wagging with vigor.

"Now you can go," said the young warrior.

With the plan finalized, the small posse left Thoragaard and Harrison, then ventured deeper into Concur's shadows, away from the turmoil in the Town's Square.

Harrison watched his friends leave for their mission, and after they had trekked out of sight, he turned to address the magician. "Let's open that gate."

Thoragaard approached Harrison and rested his hands upon the young warrior's broad shoulders once again. "We will need your strength, your conviction, and your determination to succeed.

"Harrison, finding the treasures throughout this land, bringing armies together, convincing leaders to join your cause, all of this must come to fruition with the fall of Concur." Thoragaard paused to let the young man digest the gravity of the situation. "If we fail now, everything is for naught."

The young warrior brought a firm and purposeful gaze to the magician. "Then we won't fail."

Thoragaard smiled. "Time to convert some souls." The illusionist then led Harrison away from their current position and headed toward the West Gate.

Nigel and his entourage entered the governor's mansion. Only moments before, the Concurian leader's men had escorted

Meredith and Tara to the First Lady's bedroom, where he had ordered that they remain imprisoned.

The dark leader motioned for his generals to enter the study off the main foyer. Allard and Nigel followed.

Lord Hammer took a moment to look into the eyes of his soldiers, searching for any signs of dissention. He found none. Satisfied, he began to bark orders.

"This citadel will be fortified with your most elite men," started the governor, taking turns focusing on the generals. "I want the high walls readied with boiling water and oil. When the foreigners began their ascent, have your men scorch them."

Next, Nigel turned to Allard. "How many mages do you have at your command?"

The cloaked man responded, "At least ten, if no one has defected."

Lord Hammer scowled, but managed to control himself, understanding that an outburst would be fruitless at this time. "Do what you must to gain their allegiance. I will spare no cost to retain their services." Allard nodded once in concurrence.

Taking his gaze back to his henchmen, he continued, "As for your foot soldiers, have them round up all traitors and lock them away in prison. Double, triple them in cells if you must."

One of the dark leader's generals spoke. "Do we imprison any foreigners that we might apprehend?"

"No," said Lord Hammer and with emphasis added, "kill them." The general nodded, as did the other soldiers.

"As for our townspeople, we do owe them protection, but I expect them to fight alongside us," said Nigel. He then pointed at his men, "But if they choose not to fight, treat them as a defector and lock them away."

Lord Hammer stood tall. "I know you have your doubts about our chances," said Nigel, reading the uneasiness in his men's eyes, "but I will not die without a fight. Harrison Cross is on his way, and," Nigel pointed to the floor, "I'm positive Thoragaard is leading him here."

"What do we do if we find Harrison, Thoragaard, or any of his men?" asked another decorated fighter.

"Apprehend Harrison if you can," said Nigel. "Otherwise kill him and his men."

"What shall we do with his body?"

"Bring it to me and I will display his corpse for all to see," said Lord Hammer. "No one gets the best of Nigel Hammer!" The dark leader's men again nodded, not daring to go against their superior.

"This is going to be a long and difficult battle," continued Nigel. "Go off, ready your men, and perform your tasks. I'll give you further orders at the appropriate time."

Nigel's men all nodded once, then filed out of the study to heed their superior's commands. Allard stood by Concur's governor.

Lord Hammer waited an additional moment until his soldiers left the building. "Allard," said Nigel, his gaze still fixed on the doorway. "What do you think our chances are, realistically?"

The mage pondered the question, then said, "Five thousand men surrounding our city, turmoil in the ranks, disloyalty among the populace," started Allard. "Sounds like a typical day for you."

An uncharacteristic smile graced Nigel's face. "I suppose so," he said. "But I'll tell you one thing; I won't go down without a hell of a fight."

"Now, that I believe," said the mage, smiling. Changing his demeanor, Allard continued, "I think we should go over our end game strategy."

Lord Hammer knew exactly what Allard meant. "Yes, let's, but I hope it doesn't have to come to that."

"I hope not either."

CHAPTER 26

Kymbra guided the small posse through the city's alleyways, steering clear of the brawling that had overtaken the streets. The female warrior knew the terrain well, almost better than most of Lord Hammer's men, but she did not know how many soldiers would defect to Meredith's side.

Taking her gaze to the fighters on top of the walls, she knew that Thoragaard and Harrison needed to open the massive gates to allow the invaders access to the city, which was the only way they could possibly win this war. If the gates remained closed, the foreigners could not enter, simple as that. She knew that Thoragaard had his infiltrated men in place and could only hope that they now had the upper hand in the battle.

Kymbra thrust a hand in the air behind her, halting the procession. The posse had positioned themselves in a dark alleyway between two establishments that rested to the right of the government compound. She then peered across the square at the mansion looming a hundred yards away.

Murdock maneuvered next to her and watched patrol after patrol mill about the complex's grounds.

"How do we get in there?" he asked, exasperated. "We can't just walk right in!"

The female warrior pursed her lips, shaking her head. "Our goal is to find out where Nigel's holding Meredith and Tara, right?"

The ranger nodded.

Raising a condescending eyebrow, she asked, "Don't you think that an invading army would provide a sufficient diversion for us?"

Murdock felt stupid. "Of course it would," he said, rolling his eyes. The rest of the group then huddled next to their leaders.

Kymbra brought her stare back to the governor's building. "Lord Hammer and his men must have escorted the women back inside by now."

The ranger nodded. "That only makes sense. What's our next move?"

"We need Gelderand to get that cat in place, perform his spell, and locate the women," said Kymbra.

Gelderand and Swinkle had listened with intent to the conversation. "I am not sure how Rufus is going to slip by those guards," said the mage, a hint of concern in his voice. "You do realize what will happen to me if a soldier slays the cat?"

Kymbra swiveled to face Gelderand. "Actually, no I don't."

The magician's eyes widened with surprise at this woman's lack of knowledge. "I could be killed!"

Kymbra nodded once, trying to put the older man at ease. "All the reason to take the appropriate precautions." She then maneuvered to better face the two anxious men.

"I'm willing to bet that no one is expecting an animal to waltz into the mansion, correct?" Gelderand and Swinkle nodded in concurrence.

"So," continued Kymbra, looking up in thought as she said, "if we can create enough of a distraction, Rufus should have no problem getting inside the compound."

Murdock's eyes widened with delight. "To be honest, this is going to be easy!"

Gelderand did not feel quite the same. "How so?" he deadpanned.

The ranger peered around the building's corner and made a thorough inspection of the governor's mansion. "Look," he said, pointing to the structure. The rest of the group looked around Murdock for a better view.

"If Rufus can sneak through the landscaped bushes, he'll just slip by the guards without them seeing him."

Gelderand did not feel quite as enthusiastic as the ranger. Using a sarcastic tone, the mage added, "And he will simply open those large double doors himself and walk right in."

Murdock wrinkled his brow, now adding into the equation how the feline would open such heavy portals. "I guess he'll need more of our help."

Gelderand stood tall, folding his arms. "To say the least, but I think I know what will work." All eyes focused on the mage, waiting to hear his plan.

"If I could get close enough to the mansion, I could use my invisibility ring to our advantage."

Murdock's eyes widened, remembering how effective the magic trick worked when he used it to disappear from advancing Scynthians.

"I like the sounds of that," said the ranger. "The ring worked wonders against those stupid barbarians."

Gelderand's mind continued to churn, formulating a strategy. "Murdock, what is the activity around the complex from our position?"

The ranger stepped forward and peeked around the corner again, searching for a place to take cover, but found nothing.

With a huff, he said, "Guards are milling about the compound and aside from where we're standing, there's no place to hide."

The mage threw his hands up in the air, exasperated. "There must be another way into that mansion!"

Kymbra thought hard, recalling the intricacies of the compound. "The stables sit around back," started the woman. "They don't connect directly to the main building, but they're not too far away from the living quarters."

Gelderand's eyes sparkled, thoughts churning in his mind. "I am sure that a cat or two has been seen wandering around the barns that house the horses," he said. "And, I am willing to bet the riders would pay them little attention."

Kymbra smiled. "Having Rufus enter the mansion via the stables is brilliant, Gelderand." The elder man accepted the unexpected complement with a sheepish smile.

"All right, how do we get to the stables unseen?" asked Murdock.

Gelderand took his gaze to Kymbra. "How much activity have you witnessed from Lord Hammer's riders?"

"Not much, to be honest," said the female warrior. "Nigel's positioning his men around the city and his mansion, but not many are on horseback."

"That makes perfect sense," said Murdock, drawing on his fighting background. "Nigel's expecting armies to attack his city; fighting them on horseback in such a congested area would prove difficult."

"I agree," said Kymbra. "He's gearing his men for massive hand-to-hand combat."

Gelderand brought his gaze to the main entrance of Lord Hammer's compound, taking a moment to digest the information before looking at Kymbra.

"We have too many of us to travel together," started the mage. "Might I suggest that Swinkle and I handle this mission alone?"

"You two? Alone?" chimed in Murdock before Kymbra could speak. "You'll just get yourself captured or worse."

Kymbra shook her head. "I have to agree with him," she said, jerking her thumb at the ranger. "It's too dangerous. Furthermore, Thoragaard said to hold our positions after we got you in place."

"Very well then," said the mage, "why don't you provide us cover to the stables and we will proceed from there."

Murdock brought his gaze to the blonde warrior, who gave him a single nod of acceptance. Satisfied with their new course of action, Gelderand asked, "Now that that is settled, who is going to lead the way to the stables?"

"That's us," said Murdock, motioning in Pondle's direction. "We'll get you there safely."

"We're all going," said Kymbra through squinted eyes, alluding to her female counterparts as well. "This is what we're going to do," she said to the group, recalling the intricacies of Lord Hammer's compound.

"First, we double-back behind these buildings." Kymbra pointed to the structures behind and to the right of their position. "From there, we should be able to loop around the compound to the stables."

The blonde warrior thought for a second. "If I remember correctly, there are high bushes that act as a natural boundary separating the stables and riding area. That's the best place to sneak into the complex."

Gelderand appeared satisfied. "I am sure that it will be a bit more difficult than you have explained, but I agree with your strategy."

"And as soon as you're safe, we'll take up positions around Lord Hammer's complex and await Thoragaard and Harrison," added Kymbra. The mage nodded in understanding.

Continuing with her plan, Kymbra summoned her fellow fighters. "Marissa, Adrith, take the lead with Pondle." She then said to Murdock, "You'll stay with me and protect the magicians."

The ranger pursed his lips. "Wonderful."

Harrison's battle-axe clashed with Lord Hammer's men high atop the Concurian wall near the West Gate. The young warrior had followed Thoragaard through the dark alleyways until they reached their destination, the gate that needed to be open. The illusionist explained to Harrison that each gate worked via a massive pulley system. Atop the wall near each massive portal rested a mechanism that resembled a ship captain's wheel that, when operated, would churn gears and either slide an individual door open or closed. With ten men needed to operate the massive device, Harrison understood that gaining the allegiance of Concurians was of the utmost importance.

Along the way, the men intercepted a small platoon of Resistance fighters and together they had scaled the zigzagging staircase that led to the pinnacle of their journey. While four soldiers ventured with the illusionist to help solidify defenses to the left of Harrison, the young warrior raced with three fighters in the opposite direction.

Harrison took a brief moment to gather his surroundings. Using the teachings from the Fighter's Guild, he gazed about the immediate area, creating a complete mental image of the landscape. The crisp night air cooled his face as he tried to take in Concur's panoramic view. To the east, the purple evening sky became the drop back for the soft orange glow of torches placed in strategic positions along the wall top.

Bringing his eyes downward, he found a twenty-foot wide pathway that encircled the city. "More than enough room for fighting," he said to himself, but his concerns heightened at what lay in front of him.

Five Concurian soldiers advanced on him and his newfound fighting partners. Swiveling his head to relay his commands, the young warrior said, "Hold your ground and don't attack unless I order you to do so!" The three Resistance fighters heeded Harrison's command and planted themselves in a defensive stance.

The young warrior then turned his attention to the oncoming soldiers. Harrison watched as the first two armor-clad men in black raised their swords, while the others waited for something to happen.

One of the Concurians stopped in his tracks upon seeing Harrison's morphed eyes. Pointing his sword at him, he shouted, "Lower your weapon! You're under arrest as stated by Concurian law!"

"What have I done to warrant your actions?" asked Harrison, his weapon in a defensive posture with his battle-axe held across his torso.

"Your eyes tell me that you're part of this pathetic attempt to overthrow Lord Hammer," snarled the second fighter, maneuvering closer to Harrison. "I for one don't think we should take him alive!"

After his last remark, the Concurian lunged at the young warrior, only to have his sword deflected. Harrison stood tall, not wanting to hurt these men. All during their journey to Concur, Harrison waged an internal struggle with himself, unsure of the righteousness in killing misguided soldiers.

"Your allegiance to Nigel is wrong," the young warrior said, holding his ground. "He's the enemy, not me."

The first man did not agree with the foreigner standing before him. "That's for us to decide, not you!" The Concurian attacked Harrison a second time, only to have the young warrior rebuff him again.

Harrison knew he had to plant a seed of doubt in their minds. "For the last time," shouted Harrison, "lay down your arms!"

The fighter to his left brandished his weapon. Snarling, he yelled, "You're a traitor and part of the Resistance! We'll never listen to you!"

Harrison remained in his defensive posture, not engaging the men before him. "Do you know who the leader of the Resistance is?" The men before him momentarily stopped their attack, unsure of the answer. "It's Meredith."

The Concurian on his right frowned, his weapon poised and ready to strike. "Impossible! She'd never betray Lord Hammer!"

Making a quick glance to his left, Harrison found the second soldier contemplating the young warrior's remark. He didn't know about Meredith, thought Harrison, and began in earnest to garner this man's support.

"You," said the young warrior to the anxious Concurian, "do you wish to remain held hostage in your own city?"

"Foreigners like you don't understand life in Concur," said the soldier, trying to come to grips with Harrison's statement.

"Tell me then," said the young warrior with conviction, "were any of your friends or relatives left swinging in the gallows at the hands of Lord Hammer?"

Both Concurians made eye contact with each other, neither man knowing for sure what Harrison spoke about. Their fellow fighters lowered their weapons and maneuvered closer in order to better their hearing.

"What do you mean, swinging from the gallows?" asked the man on the right, his weapon remaining poised.

"Did you not witness the atrocity at Town's Square?" asked Harrison with genuine concern, realizing that these sentries might have been patrolling the wall and did not know what had transpired this evening.

"Why don't you fill us in," said the second soldier, eager to hear the young warrior's tale.

"Nigel executed a hundred people that he said were traitors, people he had arrested and imprisoned," said Harrison. "They're all dead."

"Who were these traitors? Foreigners?" asked the same fighter.

"I doubt it," said Harrison. "Not many of us have entered your city and surely not a hundred."

The shocked fighter turned to his comrade. "I know the names of some the people Lord Hammer imprisoned! Good people!"

The first man's face went blank. "Two of my cousins were arrested just yesterday," he said, his voice trailing. The three other Concurians muttered amongst themselves as well, shocked at the news.

Harrison knew the time was ripe to gain the allegiance of these men. "Nigel won't stop with just these souls. He'll continue to kill anyone who he thinks stands in his way, regardless of who they are.

"If you believe in Meredith and feel that she'll bring honor back to the city of Concur, then I ask you now to join us and help her rise to power."

Both men looked at each other, unsure what to do. The soldier on the left asked, "What do you need us to do?"

Harrison beamed. "Open these gates! Allow our armies into the city and we'll liberate you from your wicked lord!"

"How will Meredith rise to power?" asked the man on the right.

"She's being held by Nigel as we speak," said Harrison, uttering the truth. "And we must rescue her before he does something rash."

The sentry lowered his sword. "I will join your cause," he started, "but I warn you, if Meredith does not become our new leader, we will never stop hunting you down."

"You have my word," said Harrison. "But we must hurry; the armies will be storming the city soon."

"Follow us," said the fighter on the left.

The small group of sentries then led Harrison and his fighters toward a larger gathering of Concurian soldiers. With cautious optimism, the young warrior continued his quest to open the West Gate, which lasted into the wee hours of the night.

Racing ten paces behind Pondle, Marissa, and Adrith, Murdock and Kymbra escorted the two cloak-wearing men on their mission, trekking through the dark alleyways and taking an elongated route away from the city's main compound. Lance kept pace with Pondle, helping to avert danger every step of the way.

Up ahead, the thief made an abrupt stop, pressing his body against the closest building. Adrith and Marissa did likewise.

Murdock and Kymbra took their cue from their friends ahead of them, pinning themselves against the closest wall as well and signaling to Gelderand and Swinkle to do the same.

"What do you think?" asked Murdock to the blonde warrior.

"Concurian soldiers, I'm sure. Be ready to fight."

The ranger heard the sound of running footsteps heading in their direction. Murdock moved his hand to his sword, unsheathing it slowly, trying not to make a sound.

Seconds later, Pondle, Adrith, and Marissa pounced on five unsuspecting soldiers, the sound of clashing weapons filling the air.

Murdock took no time in deciding his next course of action. With his weapon firmly in hand, the ranger headed for the melee. He was about to use his sword for the first time in a long while when he felt a hand grab the back of his armor and yank him away.

The sudden jerk caused the ranger to stumble. Murdock tried in vain to regain his footing, but instead he tripped and fell to the ground, landing on all fours, his weapon spinning away. Instinctively, the ranger huddled to the ground, waiting to feel the pummeling that never came.

Instead, Murdock felt a hand under his armpit, lifting him to his feet. "Get up," said Kymbra. "We're all right."

The ranger gazed at the woman in bewilderment, then surveyed the area. The five Concurian soldiers stood amongst his friends, their breathing heavy. The ranger was about to protest, but realized why the fighting had stopped almost as soon as it had began; the men who stood before him had the same eye markings as he.

"What's going on here?" asked Murdock, trying to rid himself of the embarrassment that he felt from tripping into the middle of a battle.

"These men are on our side," said Adrith.

"The foreign armies will be coming!" said one of the men. "We need to get into position!"

"What are your orders?" asked Kymbra, stepping to the forefront.

"To open the gates."

"Which gates?" pressed the tall blonde.

"It doesn't matter," said the soldier. "Whatever one has the least resistance."

Kymbra knew that these men had little time to speak with their group. "Before you continue on your mission, can you tell us anything about the security at the mansion?"

"Lord Hammer has two high-level prisoners that he's guarding," said the young fighter. "The place is on the highest security."

"Thank you," said Kymbra. "Go!" The five sentries took a moment to gather themselves, then trotted away, leaving Kymbra and the rest behind.

The lead female caught the attention of her fellow soldiers and ordered, "Lead us on again." Adrith and Marissa, along with Pondle, started toward the stable grounds.

Murdock, concealing his anger until now, allowed Gelderand and Swinkle to move past him before saying to Kymbra, "Why did you grab me back there?"

The female warrior maintained her forward stare, following her friends in the darkness. "I had to stop you; you hadn't noticed their eyes."

"You made a fool of me!" The ranger's rage simmered with every step he took.

Kymbra brushed off Murdock's exclamation. "If I hadn't reacted like I did, you would have made a huge mistake."

Murdock grabbed Kymbra's arm, spinning her to face him. Having the woman's full attention, the ranger started his tirade.

"I don't appreciate your condescending tone, and I certainly don't like to be made a fool of in front of fellow warriors!"

Kymbra did not back down. "It's my job to make sure you and your friends succeed on this mission. I can't help it if I hurt your feelings along the way!"

Murdock thrust a finger in the woman's face. "We're going to succeed regardless if you're here or not!"

"Take that finger out of my face!" Kymbra's cold stare locked on the ranger's dark eyes. Murdock's digit remained in place.

"I'll take it away when I'm ready," said Murdock with conviction. "If you haven't noticed, I don't like taking orders from you." The ranger then lowered his hand.

"I only take orders from Thoragaard," said Kymbra. "The sooner you realize that, the better you'll understand my actions."

"I still don't like you," said Murdock.

"And I don't like you," responded Kymbra, placing her hands on her hips. Gesturing with her head in the direction of their friends, she said, "We need to keep moving."

The female warrior then went to rejoin the others, with Murdock following a moment later. Neither person spoke again until they reached their destination.

Remaining in the dark alleyway, Murdock and Kymbra watched from their position in the shadows as Pondle and the other women secured the immediate area. The ranger observed his friend's moves, figuring that he was determining the best way into the mansion's stables.

Murdock then glanced back at Gelderand and Swinkle, several feet behind him and Kymbra, and who awaited their next task. Satisfied with their safety for now, he peeked at the female warrior, who watched her people's movements.

"Have you ever been inside this compound before?" asked Murdock in a low voice, not wanting to alarm his friends with the uncertainty of the situation.

"No."

"So you don't know the intricacies of the stables?"

Kymbra kept her focus forward. "No."

Murdock tried to keep his unhappiness in check, but that proved fruitless. "What's your problem? You've been nothing more than cold to all of us since we met."

"Don't take it personally," said Kymbra, again not bothering to make eye contact. "I'm just doing my job."

The ranger, upset at this woman's lack of emotion, moved to stand in front of her, blocking her view of the complex.

"I do take it personally," started Murdock. "If I'm going to risk my life at your hands at some point, I want to know that you don't have a personality conflict with any of us!"

"Fine, I'll act like I care!"

Kymbra's answer only enraged the ranger further. "No, that's not good enough! Either you change your attitude toward us or leave! How does that sound?"

The blonde warrior rolled her eyes, with them finally locking on the ranger's. "I promised Thoragaard that I'd help you and that's what I intend to do. I'm sorry if you got the wrong message." Kymbra turned again and searched for the others on patrol.

Murdock was not through. Realizing that he would never get the answer he wanted with this tactic, the ranger decided on another approach. Perhaps I could find out why she is doing this for Thoragaard, since she dislikes us so, he thought.

Using caution, he grabbed the woman's armored arm and pressed her carefully against the building's wall, startling her in the process.

"What do you think you're doing?" asked Kymbra, her brow wrinkled and eyes narrow.

"You're going to tell me right now. Why are you so loyal to Thoragaard?"

Kymbra cocked her head before answering. "He recognizes my superior fighting skills and has chosen me to help overthrow Lord Hammer."

Murdock shook his head. "No, that's not it." The ranger fixed his stare on the warrior with no intention of removing it until he heard what he wanted.

The tall blonde wilted under the ranger's glare. "He tried to save my family from the evil clutches of this ruthless leader. I owe him as much as I hate Lord Hammer."

"Tried?" said Murdock, raising an eyebrow. "Kymbra, where's your family?"

The woman's strong exterior started to wane. Taking her gaze away from Murdock, she said, "Lord Hammer imprisoned them. Thoragaard took the initiative to save them." The woman bit her lower lip and refused to look at the ranger.

"Kymbra," said Murdock, giving her a slight shake and regaining her focus. "Where is your family?"

A single tear rolled down the woman's high cheekbone. "They were executed." Kymbra sniffed and turned away.

Murdock's usually ambivalent heart dropped, beginning to comprehend fully how this beautiful woman's rough exterior came to be.

"I'm sorry," said the ranger, searching for words. "How long ago did this tragic event happen?"

The blonde warrior's teary eyes met Murdock's. "Less than two years ago."

The ranger released his grip on the woman. "I'm glad I understand now."

"No one knows that story except Thoragaard," said Kymbra, regaining her composure, standing tall again. "And I want to keep it that way."

"Sure thing," said Murdock. The ranger then let his eyes wander to their task at hand. Pondle, Adrith, and Marissa had finished their examination of the area and were waiting for him and Kymbra.

"We better join the others," said the ranger.

"Thank you," said Kymbra.

Murdock nodded once. "We'll get that bastard; I'll make sure of it." The female warrior smiled, then led the way to their friends. The ranger called for Gelderand and Swinkle as well, who heeded Murdock's request and joined the rest of the party.

Pondle waved the approaching group to his position next to an adjacent building. From their vantage point, Lord Hammer's compound loomed a hundred yards away.

Murdock gazed about the place, then asked, "What's the activity level like?"

"Heavy," answered the thief. "Nigel's men are all over the place."

"Can we get to the stables?" asked Kymbra.

"Yes, but we need to loop around that way." Pondle gestured with his hand to the left of the complex. "From there, we can gain access to the rider's area, then the stables themselves."

The female warrior followed Pondle's hand movements, but did not agree with his assessment. "Look at how many soldiers stand between us and our destination! We can't go that way!"

The thief understood the ramifications of his suggestion. "I've thought this out and have taken into account the soldiers before us. Do you have a better idea?" asked Pondle with attitude.

"Give Kymbra a moment to figure this out," said Murdock. Pondle gave him a strange look for that support.

Kymbra examined the area again and realized that Pondle was right. "We'll do what he said."

Pondle crinkled his brow, surprised that the temperamental woman had just agreed with his strategy.

"There are all kinds of activity over there, but once we get to the cover of the barns, we should be in a better position for our next task," said the thief, continuing with his analysis. "The only problem I see is that we need to get across that street and enter the rider's yard. And with all the commotion going on, we'll be easily seen."

Gelderand surveyed the area, panning from the street to the mansion, then over to the area shielded by the bushes.

"How did you figure on entering the complex unseen?"

Pondle flashed a sheepish smile. "We were hoping that you could answer that."

The mage nodded, anticipating as much. While Gelderand thought of another course of action, Swinkle joined the conversation. "Don't you have a spell that could cloak our appearance?"

The young cleric continued. "Remember the time when you created a sanctuary for us," added Swinkle, recalling that the magician had done just that in the Concurian countryside.

Gelderand nodded once, saying, "I can, but I am not sure how that will help us now."

Swinkle made a quick calculation. "That spell needs to encompass about a hundred yards. Can you do that?"

"A hundred yards!" exclaimed the mage. "My spell would cover only a fraction of that distance, and furthermore people will be able to walk into and out of the sanctuary with no resistance." The mage shook his head. "I am afraid that plan will not work."

Gelderand then cocked his head and looked up in thought. After a moment of reflection, he said, "What if we wait until the morning to start our task? I would be willing to bet that as the night goes on, less and less people will inhabit the streets, including soldiers."

Kymbra nodded in concurrence, understanding Gelderand's line of reasoning. "We'll be able to sneak over to the stables almost undetected." The woman peered over to the thief. "Pondle?"

The thief shrugged. "That sounds reasonable, but how do we stay unnoticed until then?"

Gelderand raised a finger in the air. "I can certainly create a safe area right here, encompassing the group, provided that you all feel that this is a secure place to remain."

"We'll make it safe," said Kymbra, bringing her gaze to her female cohorts, as well as Murdock and Pondle. All nodded in assurance.

"Then it's settled," said the mage. "I'll prepare my spell. As long as we wait in this alleyway, I can create a sanctuary that covers ten square feet."

"And no one will see us, right?" asked Kymbra.

"Correct, as long as we stay in this zone."

"It's settled then," said the female warrior. "We rest here until the break of day. We'll set up a watch rotation while you go about your business."

Gelderand nodded, then went about readying his spell, while the rest of the group determined who would keep lookout first. A few minutes later, the magician created a refuge and instructed everyone to remain inside its parameters throughout the course of the evening. After a long and stressful day, the small posse took advantage of their invisibility from the world and enjoyed a much-needed rest.

CHAPTER 27

¤

While Nigel's men prepared for the impending invasion, Brendan Brigade shouted his last orders to his troops. The decorated Aegean leader knew that the other armies would be launching their coordinated attack very soon.

Brendan looked over the two thousand or so soldiers, feeling his adrenalin flow. Many years had passed since he had engaged in an attack of this scale. At that time, he had aligned with the Forge Brothers and their elders to keep back a familiar emerging threat – Lord Nigel Hammer.

Nigel, a brash young warrior, had stormed the coastal town of Concur with a renegade army of loyal followers. Lord Hammer crushed the incumbent rulership led by William Henry Bilodeau, slaying him and taking his daughter, Meredith, as his woman.

The Aegean leader scowled, recalling the heated debates amongst the dignitaries of the local villages in reference to aiding Concur, and instead their allowing Nigel to turn the metropolis into the walled city that it was today. Now that Harrison had gained the allegiance of the coastal towns, the time had come to take down the man who hid behind the high walls.

Sister Martel approached the warrior, interrupting his thoughts. "My brethren are ready to begin our chant."

Brendan nodded. "Do what you must, and rest assured we will protect you."

The cloaked cleric nodded once in agreement. "Remember, we will be completely vulnerable to an attack and rendered defenseless."

The Aegean leader had discussed the Holy Shield strategy with Sister Martel and her counterparts at length the night before. The clerics would pray over the battlefield, forming a strength defense over the invading forces, and if they were fortunate enough, their timed maneuvers would spread the shield over the fighters from Argos and Arcadia.

"I'll have my men guard you as we advance on Concur," said Brendan. "You have my word."

The Robusite departed the meeting and took her place with the other clerics. The holy people then held hands and began to chant in unison, at first in a low murmur that turned into a loud prayer.

"Dear Pious, bless our cause," they prayed together. "Come to our aid and defend your children." The monks then repeated the phrase, "Defend your children."

As they did, a soft white glow began to envelope the area. All who stood in the proximity of the religious people felt a surge of energy course through their bodies. The soldiers were ready for battle; the prayer enhancing their defenses.

Brendan watched as the twenty clerics continued their chant of "Defend your children" before they released hands, and one by one pressed their palms together before dispersing to their assigned positions in the battlefield. The Aegean knew the time for combat had come.

Unsheathing his sword and thrusting it toward the heavens, he yelled to his troops in the predawn air, "Let the battle begin! The fall of Concur starts now!"

A mighty roar erupted from the soldiers and they hastened their trek to the walled city that loomed a few miles away.

Finished with their war strategy session, Nigel and Allard sat in a room that overlooked Concur's harbor. The governor opened the double-doors that led to the terrace, giving him the best view of his city. Lord Hammer gazed about the chaotic streets where townspeople and soldiers clashed while fires erupted, giving much-needed light to the predawn darkness. His reign was being tested, he knew, but the ruthless leader also relished times like these in order to show all how powerful he had truly become. And, if Harrison failed, he might sway others to give him the Treasure of the Land, to have it in the hands of a true leader.

The dark warrior brought his focus to the walls that surrounded the city. In the distance he saw torches bob and fall – his soldiers fought with traitors in an attempt to keep them from overtaking his city's most valuable asset.

Deep down, Nigel knew he lived on borrowed time. The armies surrounding his metropolis would attack soon, and if they succeeded in entering Concur, there would be little resistance to stop them. Staring at the melees, he knew he needed to protect his only bargaining chip.

"What are you thinking, Nigel?" asked Allard with concern.

"Our time grows short," said the dark warrior. "The foreigners are coming."

The magician raised an eyebrow. "Are you insinuating something more?"

Allard had known Nigel for a long time, understood his ruthless behavior and quest to rule, but he sensed an uncharacteristic pang of doubt in his leader.

"When the fighting is over, I want to be certain that we'll escape unscathed."

"Leave that to me," said Allard with confidence. "No one will be taken prisoner."

Nigel brought his gaze back to the high walls and the continued fighting. "That was never an option anyway."

The magician nodded. "I know." Taking a risky turn, Allard asked, "How do you plan on handling Harrison?"

The sound of the young warrior's name brought a scowl to Nigel's face. "Facing him is inevitable, but I know what to do."

"Enlighten me."

"I know how that boy thinks, his righteousness, how he's always doing the noble thing," said Lord Hammer, his anger rising. "I'll play his strengths against himself. That will spell his doom."

"A sound plan if what you say is true," said Allard. "Are you sure you know him as well as you *think* you know him?"

Lord Hammer spun on his heel to face his trusted mage, thrusting a finger in his direction.

"Don't challenge my intelligence!" barked the ruthless leader. "I've battled that boy, made him question his beliefs, and tapped into his brain. He's a weak-minded fool and can be dealt with. Furthermore, I won't let him or those pathetic foreigners walk into my city and knock on my front door! This mansion will not fall without an epic battle!"

Allard allowed his superior's outburst to pass before asking, "What about your captives?"

"The women?" Nigel let out a laugh. "This, my friend, will be Harrison's classic downfall because I know he's coming to try and rescue them. I'll double the security around their room anyway. They're not going anywhere."

Lord Hammer headed for the doorway again. "I suggest you bring your bag of tricks and that staff of yours."

The cloaked man nodded. "That I will. And, I'll summon my apprentices."

Nigel stopped at the entrance. "Very soon, this mansion will be the cornerstone of one of the greatest battles in Concur's history, and I plan to be the victor. Harrison's quest will end here!" The two men then departed the room and prepared for their unwanted guests.

Harrison stopped his trek atop the Concurian wall after hearing a faint roar emanate from the west. Bringing his gaze to the countryside, he could have sworn that he saw a white mist filter through the ranks of advancing soldiers in the distance.

The young warrior felt his heart race. *The gate's still closed,* he lamented, knowing full well that the Unified Army could not enter Concur if the massive portals remained shut.

During the course of the evening, the young warrior encountered more frustrations than victories, finding that many Concurians had not heard of their attempt to liberate Meredith. Much to his dismay, a majority of the Concurians he encountered had decided to fight for their city rather than to free their First Lady. The young warrior believed in all his heart that Nigel Hammer had misguided these people and they simply did not understand the ramifications of their actions. In the end, Harrison needed to keep pushing forward in order to save Meredith, and of utmost importance on a personal level, to rescue Tara. With very little rest over the nighttime hours, Harrison continued to persevere.

Ahead of him battled more Concurians and Resistance fighters, neither side gaining any meaningful ground. Harrison gazed at the melee, sensing the uncertainty flowing through the fighters' veins. It was time for a bold statement.

The young warrior called to the ten men behind him. "Follow me!" he shouted and, after a series of purposeful steps, Harrison joined the melee.

Using his weapon of choice, the young warrior pushed aside an ally of his and engaged three Concurian soldiers. Harrison wasted no time in establishing his battle plan, hacking one of the fighters to his left with his battle-axe, while deflecting a blow from a sentry on the right.

"The time to declare your allegiance is over!" barked the young warrior, attacking again and slicing a deep gouge in the man in front of him. The Concurian fell to the ground, never to rise again.

Harrison took his fury to the man on the right, engaging him with a parry of blows that rendered the fighter unconscious. The last soldier leaned his back against the wall, holding his long sword in a defensive posture.

"Decide now!" barked Harrison, his battle-axe raised.

"Or die?" asked the fighter, his breathing heavy. "Your rulership will be no better than Lord Hammer's!"

The young warrior let the man's comment linger for a moment. "I'm not here to overrun your city," said Harrison, his brow furrowed and glazed with sweat. "Have you not heard that we're liberating Meredith? So that she can take control of Concur?"

The sentry continued to hold his weapon in front of him. "That was never relayed to us!" The guardian's face turned red with anger. "If we had known that, we would have laid down our arms!"

Harrison lowered his blade. In a diplomatic tone he said, "Then go spread the word and help us open these gates. The time has come for your liberation."

"How do I know this isn't a trick?"

The young warrior extended his hand. "You'll have to trust me."

The Concurian gazed into Harrison's eyes, looking for any sign of deceit, but he found none. He then glanced past the young warrior and to the men who used to be part of his patrols; they all sported the same appearance of hope.

The fighter lowered his weapon and took a step toward Harrison. Taking firm hold of his hand and shaking it with vigor, he said, "If what you say is true, then I'll do whatever I can to help you free Meredith."

Harrison released his grip. "I need you to open this gate and at this very moment."

"Consider it done." The sentry then gestured to the men around him. "Open the gate!" he yelled at the top of his lungs. Shouting again, he said, "And spread the word about freeing Meredith! Long live the First Lady!"

The men, Concurians and Resistance fighters alike, raised their weapons and cheered in unison as they ran to begin their task. Harrison followed close behind, smiling. News about Meredith's liberation started to spread, and more importantly, the West Gate was about to be opened.

Brendan Brigade led the charge against Concur's West Gate. The rag tag army of two thousand or so men raced toward the massive outer wall. Midway, the Aegean felt a strange surge of adrenalin, which he attributed to the prayers conveyed from the twenty Robusite clerics.

Platoon upon platoon advanced to within a hundred yards of the metropolis before stopping, per Brendan's command. The Aegean warrior guided his steed in front of the men, glaring at the wall ahead of him.

Brendan bided his time, remembering what Thoragaard had told him. "You cannot enter the city until my men open the gates," he recalled the illusionist saying. "Approaching too close to the structure will only lead to unnecessary peril."

The Aegean brought his gaze to the wall tops. Arms flailed, weapons clashed, and an internal battle brewed. The gate, however, remained sealed. Brendan took the time to rally his troops.

Atop his war horse, the elder warrior called to his men. "The gate remains secure, but rest assured, it will open soon and when it does I want everyone to burst through the entryway." The decorated leader traversed in front of his army, continuing with his speech as the troops erupted in cheer.

"The Concurians will stop at nothing to deny us entry," Brendan barked, "but we must persevere. Do all that you can to enter the city and hasten the fall of Lord Hammer!"

"Sir!" interrupted a soldier, shouting and pointing at the massive doors. "The gates! They're moving!"

Brendan wheeled his horse around to face Concur. Sure enough, the large double-doors had moved. Not wasting another second, the Aegean leader barked, "Everyone! Charge the stronghold!"

All of the men yelled in unison as they began their stampede toward the walled city. To their surprise, sporadic arrows began to rain down on them as they reached the halfway point.

"Use your shields!" ordered Brendan, hoping that his men would be smart enough to realize that they could thwart the aerial attack. To his dismay, many fell to the ground howling in pain with arrows protruding from their bodies.

A second wave of projectiles followed the first volley. Still, the Aegean-led army raced toward the entranceway. Brendan reached the huge gate first, along with a platoon of his men. The doorway stood motionless, only open enough to fit one or two men at a time.

The Aegean leader knew it would be suicide to enter the heavily-guarded city one man at a time, but his options were limited.

Brendan dismounted his horse and waved over the men nearest to him. Again, arrows pelted them, dropping soldier after soldier. The Aegean grabbed the man closest to him.

"Squeeze everyone through this opening!" he said, glaring at the soldier. "And when they get inside, make sure they scale the walls! We need this gate wide open!"

"Where will you be, sir?" asked the worried fighter.

"I'll be leading the way," said Brendan, pointing with his sword. "Follow me!"

The Aegean advanced to the slim opening. Peering through, he saw blurs of running men clad in black armor, doing whatever they could to protect their city.

Brendan understood his mission and he was not about to back down now. He also knew that Bracken Drake would be commencing his run to the South Gate, and the Forge Brothers would be attacking from their position as well. Concur was ripe for a fall.

The Aegean led with his weapon through the opening; a second later, he stood inside Concur. To gauge his surroundings, Brendan made a quick survey of his current predicament. A wide, dirt roadway led from his position and ran deeper into the city. Buildings and neighborhoods rested on either side of Concur's main artery, while people of all sorts congregated in the chaotic streets. Fighting abounded everywhere, and the Aegean did not have to wait very long to join the fracas.

Brendan took two steps before meeting his first resistance. The decorated warrior blocked the attack of the first fighter, using his sword to deflect the younger man's weapon. A second Concurian soldier came to the aid of his comrade, using a long sword to attack the intruder as well.

Brendan took on a defensive posture, using extreme caution as he pushed his way further from the gate, and more importantly, allowed his men access to the metropolis. The Aegean used his experience to deflect blow after blow, as well as to glance into the eyes of his adversaries; they were normal and not marked, unlike his.

Without a second to waste, Brendan went on the attack. Using his sword, the elder warrior pushed the first soldier back, then slashed across the second fighter's midsection. The young man buckled and backed away. Next, the Aegean advanced on the first fighter, deflecting another blow, then piercing the Concurian in the side. Copious amounts of blood flowed from the fresh wound.

Brendan, his initial battle won, wasted no time in directing his men before scores of Concurians raced to their position. Then, a most unusual turn of events occurred.

In the midst of positioning his soldiers within enemy lines, the decorated Aegean noticed a small band of fighters heading his way. Squinting, he recognized the man rushing toward him, bringing a wide smile to his haggard face.

"Brendan!" shouted Harrison, brandishing his battle-axe. A small posse followed the young warrior.

"It's about time!" yelled the elder fighter, lowering his weapon.

Harrison's group surrounded the Aegean leader. "We're about to open the gates!" said the young warrior.

Brendan nodded, then took his gaze beyond Harrison, finding soldiers in uniforms of the enemy. Pointing his weapon at a man clad in black armor, he said, "You've persuaded the Concurians, I see."

"Not all of them," admitted Harrison. "We still must be cautious." The young warrior gestured to the fighters beside him. "Unlock that gate!"

Turning back to his old mentor, Harrison said, "Tell your men to keep fighting. This battle is far from over!"

Brendan called to his soldiers. "Climb the walls! Get these doors open!" shouted the Aegean leader. "Remember, the eyes!" Bringing his focus to the man before him, he asked, "Where's Thoragaard?"

"I left him atop the wall," said Harrison. "I'm sure he's rallying his people."

The two men watched as one by one, Brendan's soldiers entered the city and battled Concurian loyalists. The Aegeans panned the area; Concurian soldiers raced to try and stop the breech to their city's security, simple townsfolk sought cover, and fighters clashed everywhere.

"Let's get battling," said Brendan, as both men raised their blades.

The elder warrior had only another moment to reflect on his current position. Thoragaard had promised support from men loyal to him and his cause, and these fighters would target their attacks against those protecting the gates. Brendan's job was to force his army into Concur, securing access to the West Gate. That process was underway.

Harrison pointed down the main roadway that led from the massive gate to the town. "Look, more of Lord Hammer's men are coming!"

The Aegeans found more Concurians advancing in their direction, none seemingly sympathetic to their cause. The men clad in black armor quickly advanced to their position and engaged Brendan's men in battle. Both Aegeans took their cue and began to fight back in earnest. The battle for the West Gate had begun.

"Caidan," yelled Octavius Forge to his younger brother, "flank more platoons to the right!"

The Forge Brothers had marched from Aegeus with a smaller, yet just as potent, army with their task being to breech the East Gate. Octavius, the official leader, had directed his battalions to maneuver several miles away from Concur before taking a direct route to the bolted entrance. Now the brothers prepared for their attack run.

Octavius and his band of soldiers held their ground to the left of the closed doors, while Caidan positioned his men on the right. While he waited for his brother's men to complete their maneuver, the elder Forge gauged his predicament.

Atop the East Gate, Concurian and Resistance fighters clashed, while other sentries prepared for an imminent attack. Octavius grimaced, knowing that the surrounding area contained rockier terrain than the land in front of the other gates, which made positioning his troops more difficult. That and the lack of cover left his men in a precarious position.

The elder Forge panned to his left, catching the eye of his lead marksman and motioning for him to come over.

"What is your assessment?" asked the Argosian leader.

"We can hit any target from here, sir," said the main archer with confidence, "but we don't know who is part of the Resistance and who are Concurian loyalists."

"Fire your arrows," said Octavius, dismissing the marksman's concern. "And be sure you ignite them before shooting."

The archer nodded once, his eyebrows arched. "As you wish, sir."

"Wait for my mark," added the elder Forge as the bowman returned to his fellow archers and prepared for their attack.

Octavius then glanced at Caidan's platoons, seeing everyone in position and waiting. Confident that they were ready to commence with their attack, the elder Forge signaled to his lead sentry. The fighter brought a horn to his lips and gave it a mighty blow.

Hearing the attack signal, the fifty or so marksmen ignited their arrows, drew back their bows, aimed at their targets, and awaited their leader's order.

Octavius raised his sword in the air for all to see. A second later, he slashed the blade to the ground and shouted, "Fire!"

Fifty-plus glowing projectiles hurtled through the early morning air, heading toward their unsuspecting targets. Men atop the great wall toppled, their screams audible to the soldiers down below.

The Argosian archers readied their bows again and, on their leader's mark, sent another volley of flaming arrows toward the wall. More sentries disappeared, and plumes of smoke and flames began to rise from behind the structure.

Octavius took his cool stare to his brother, whose men stood waiting to attack the city as soon as the gate opened. Confident that his battalions were prepared for battle, the Argosian leader signaled for his marksmen to launch another round of arrows toward the great wall, while everyone else bided their time.

Bracken Drake and his army were not fairing as well as his allies. The Arcadian leader sat atop his war horse and paraded in front of his troops. Soldiers in full battle gear that included large, oversized shields with ornate designs, war helmets with red plumes, sharpened blades for fighting, and gold-colored body armor highlighted by red markings under their chain-mail, awaited their first taste of battle.

The Arcadians had positioned their men in battalions of a hundred soldiers apiece. Each division contained a sentry who carried a long pole adorned with a red flag that uniquely identified each cadre of fighters. Archers and slingers positioned themselves within each division to provide aerial cover for the soldiers, and tucked safely behind the front lines sat the Arcadian's greatest weapon – their battering ram.

Positioned a few hundred yards away from the South Gate, the Arcadian battalions were now under heavy attack from Lord Hammer's loyal men. Concurian archers pelted the Arcadians with arrow upon arrow, many doused with oil and flaming toward their awaiting targets. Bracken's men used their oversized shields to buffer the projectiles, which slowed their march to the great doors.

Knowing that Resistance fighters clashed with Lord Hammer's men, Bracken had hoped that their new allies would have opened the doorways by now. To his disdain, the entranceway remained secured.

The Arcadian, with a two thousand strong army, deemed it time to employ his ultimate weapon. Lagging behind the platoons, two hundred men rolled a massive battering ram into position. Bracken paraded his war horse before his troops as the weapon sat ready for use.

The decorated warrior gauged his position while arrows whizzed through the air, hitting the ground all around him. Keeping his battle shield raised, he figured that they loomed a hundred yards from the massive double-door.

Bringing his gaze to his prized possession, he found a hundred loyal soldiers manning each side of the battering ram, waiting and ready for action. Each man placed his hands on a four-foot long piece of wood that protruded from the base of the weapon. The cylindrical, wooden device, two hundred feet long and ten feet wide, sat atop a rolling platform that awaited war.

Bracken barked to his troops. "Ready yourselves! You will begin your attack run on my mark!" All the men assumed their positions.

Arcadian archers gazed at their leader for their orders. "Shoot your arrows when the weapon nears its mark!" said Bracken. "Your comrades will need your cover. Rain fire from the sky!"

With all of his men ready for battle, Bracken lifted his shield high. "Today will go down in history as another epic day for the great city of Arcadia!" yelled the leader. Keeping a frozen gaze on the huge doorway, Bracken ordered, "Charge!"

The Arcadians started their daunting task of moving the battering ram. Legs churned, muscles burned, and the device's wheels began their slow roll forward. Within a minute's time, the weapon's pace quickened and began a rapid advance towards Concur, its lacquered head racing in the direction of the massive, secured gate.

The Concurians did not allow the maneuver to go unnoticed. Those loyal to Lord Hammer volleyed more arrows at the oncoming weapon in hopes of deterring its momentum.

Bracken Drake's steed kept pace with the lumbering device. Reaching the midway point to the closed city, the Arcadian leader witnessed hundreds of glowing projectiles flying overhead from behind his position. The battering ram's cover had commenced.

The wooden unit barreled without mercy toward the awaiting entranceway, a collision of monumental proportions all but certain. Arrows continued to rain down on the Arcadians, many hitting their mark, eliminating soldiers from their task. Yet, enough men survived to keep the weapon rolling toward its target. Ten feet from impact, all remaining armored fighters dove away from the weapon's path, allowing the battering ram to perform its intended task.

The massive projectile collided violently into the defiant wooden doorway, buckling it at points, but not rendering it useless. Concur's South Gate had withstood the first attack.

Bracken, aware that the odds of destroying the massive doorway on the first try were very low, nevertheless scowled at not seeing the structure come crashing down.

"Retract the battering ram!" he ordered. "Get ready for another run!"

As his men regrouped and tried to push the weapon away from the massive wall, another unfortunate obstacle presented itself. Lord Hammer's men, realizing that they had an opportunity to stop the Arcadian's weapon from being used again, began to dump heaping amounts of black liquid over the walls.

The boiling oil covered many of Bracken Drake's men, sending the horrified soldiers running from the scene, their scorched and mangled skin destroyed beyond repair.

The Arcadian leader fixed his stare at the wall tops. Where were the Resistance fighters, he lamented. Concurian archers pointed their bows down at his men and began firing. Soldiers on the ground did their best to protect themselves with their large shields, but many men dropped to the ground, never to rise again. Another round of scorching liquid followed the aerial attack.

Bracken barked more orders. "Destroy those archers!" he said to his marksmen, while commanding his foot soldiers, "Get away from that wall!"

Heeding their leader's command, hundreds of arrows flew toward the men atop the high walls, while the battering ram moved away at a painstakingly slow pace. The battle for the South Gate had commenced, but its preliminary results were not what the Arcadian leader had expected.

CHAPTER 28

Tara rose from her seat and walked to the open window. Outside, the soft orange glow of the morning sun began to give way to a blue sky. A beautiful day weather-wise started to take shape in Concur, although an awful period of fighting and bloodshed had already commenced.

The young maiden watched flaming projectiles fly to and from the city, sparking fires along the walls, and the clash of weaponry permeated the area. A thunderous crash more than startled the girl, causing her to step back from the windowsill.

"What was that?" she asked, eyes wide.

Meredith rushed to the window as well, taking a moment to respond. The First Lady of Concur looked down at the city streets, where people ran to hide, as well as fight. A pensive smile graced her face.

"Harrison and his friends are here," said Meredith, bringing her gaze to Tara. Placing her hands on the young maiden's arms, she said, "This will be a long day of fighting; we must pray that Harrison's army defeats Nigel."

Rustling in the hallway stopped the women's conversation. Meredith knew what was happening.

"Nigel is adding more security around our room," said the dark-haired beauty.

"Why are we so important?"

Meredith drew a heavy sigh. "I'm afraid we are the game pieces to the chess match between Nigel and Harrison."

Tara crinkled her brow. "How so?"

"Nigel knows that if he starts losing his city, he can always use us as bargaining chips." Meredith paused. "Harrison will not let Nigel harm us, and Nigel knows that."

Tara reflected on the older woman's statement. Her man was noble and righteous, qualities that she loved, but disadvantageous traits in times like these. The young maiden went back to the window and gazed about the immediate area.

"What if we tried to escape?" she suggested, maintaining her outward stare. "If we were gone, Nigel would have nothing to bargain with!"

Meredith thought for a moment, almost agreeing with the younger woman's rationale, but in the end decided to stick with her plan.

"That would only enrage Nigel more, forcing him to do something even more terrible than what he has already done today."

Tara continued looking down. "But it's not that far to the street! We could scale down from here, somehow."

"Tara, no."

"So we just sit here and wait," said the young maiden, spinning around to face Meredith, her arms spread wide in exasperation, the thought of Justin's death still fresh in her mind.

"I know it's not an ideal plan," said Meredith in her most convincing voice, "but it's the best course of action. Remember, there are so many more lives at stake besides ours. My fellow Concurians need me alive to lead them and I can only do that once we rid this city of Nigel. I hope you truly understand."

Tara sighed. "I don't like playing the maiden in distress."

"You think I do?" said Meredith, placing her hands on her hips. "It's a very humbling position, no?"

The young maiden shook her head in concurrence, not answering the older woman. Realizing the inevitable, she said, "Then we wait."

Meredith huffed. "Yes, we wait."

Murdock fiddled with his food while he stood guard over the small group. Lance huddled next to the ranger, who offered the grateful dog a morsel. The morning sky lightened, bringing an end to the long night. The ranger cast his eyes to his friends, peaceful for the time being. His sight then wandered over to Kymbra, lingering on her beautiful face. He took another bite of food before he heard the crash. The slumbering party members all jumped in unison, the ranger almost choking on his food.

"What's happening?" said Gelderand to no one in particular, his heart thumping.

Kymbra knew the sound could only mean one thing. "The armies are attacking the city! We need to act now!" She cursed under her breath, upset at herself for sleeping so long.

Pondle scurried over from his position and took his gaze from the alleyway to the city's streets. Suddenly, soldiers and townspeople alike flooded the area, with many of the armored men racing to and from the mansion.

"Everyone follow me," said the thief. "Let's use this diversion to our advantage."

Kymbra began to wave the group forward. "I agree," she said, then looking to Pondle, "lead us toward the stables."

The thief nodded once, then motioned to the group. Pondle knew that they needed to cross the main road in order to make their advancement to the complex. The apprehensive company heard battles raging around them in every direction. All the commotion and the absence of bright sunshine had allowed the small band of fighters to scurry in plain view over to the outskirts of the Governor's compound, where they hid behind the stables. To passersby, they appeared to be nothing more than nervous freedom fighters searching for a place to hide, with nobody paying them much heed.

Pondle, along with Murdock and the female warriors, tried to gauge their current situation. The thief took a reading of his surroundings – large trees provided shade and cover behind the horse shelter, ideal for launching a covert mission.

"This is a good place to hide," said Gelderand, holding Rufus and stroking his fur.

The mage took a step to where Pondle peeked around the stable's corner, gazing at the mansion that loomed a short distance away.

"What do you make of this, Pondle?" asked Gelderand with concern.

"This will be easy," said the thief. Pondle drew a line with his eyes from their position, across a courtyard, to a staircase that led into the mansion.

"All we need is for Rufus to cross the yard and scale those stairs, then he's inside."

"How does he open the door?" asked Gelderand.

Murdock had been listening to their conversation. "Give me that ring of yours and I'll make sure he gets inside."

The mage smiled and placed Rufus on the ground in order to give the ranger the gold ring of invisibility. Murdock accepted the magical item with a grin.

"I kind of like this ring," said the ranger, placing it on his left hand, disappearing from the group in the process. A second later, Murdock reappeared, having removed the item from his hand.

"Let's get this done," finished the ranger.

Kymbra agreed with the makeshift plan. "Once the cat's inside, can you direct him at all?"

Gelderand shook his head. "Not really; he is pretty much on his own." The magician bent down to the cat's level.

"Rufus, we need you to go inside that building and find Tara," said the mage, pointing to the governor's mansion. "Can you do that for us?" Rufus gave his master a vacuous stare, then meowed in affirmation.

"He can do it," said Gelderand, nodding with confidence.

Murdock rolled his eyes. "I hate leaving so much up to these stupid animals."

"I believe in them," said the mage.

"That scares me even more," said the ranger shaking his head. "Are we ready?"

"I must begin my spell," said Gelderand. The mage retrieved the ingredients from his pack, then went over to Rufus.

The magician petted the cat, then began to mumble while sprinkling a dusty substance over the feline. Moments later, Gelderand's eyes began to morph into that of a cat.

The mage blinked a couple of times, then said, "The spell is working." Gelderand picked Rufus up and gazed into his eyes, seeing himself in the process.

"Go find Tara," he said, then gently placed Rufus down and pointed him in the structure's direction.

"I'll escort him," said Murdock, who placed the magical ring on his finger, disappearing in the process.

"Be back in two minutes," said the invisible man.

Rufus meowed once, then began his trek from the stables. Gelderand dropped to his knees and squinted, getting a better fix on the cat's progress.

"He's crossing the courtyard," said the mage.

"I see him," said Pondle, peering around the corner of the shed, along with Lance. "All he has to do is climb that staircase."

Gelderand could see the stairs looming before the cat. "He's traversing a stone patio," said the mage, as he watched Rufus pass elegant palm trees and exquisite flowering plants.

"He's at the stairs!" exclaimed Gelderand, his heart beating a bit faster with all the excitement.

The mage watched stair after stair go by until Rufus finally stood at the entrance and waited for Murdock to open the door. Several uncomfortable seconds went by, but the portal remained closed.

"Why hasn't Murdock opened the door?" asked Gelderand in Pondle's direction. All eyes swiveled from the mage to the thief.

"He's invisible," said Pondle, "I don't know why." Suddenly, a very audible pop came from the entranceway and the door swung ajar.

"That's going to attract attention," said the thief, never removing his stare from the entry. He then witnessed the portal closing and the cat disappearing from view.

"Rufus is inside!" exclaimed Gelderand. The mage watched the cat trek down a long hallway, then felt the animal scurry in another direction. Next, black boots entered his view.

"Soldiers!" said the mage, beginning to sweat.

"That means trouble," said Pondle, scurrying from his position. The thief knew that if Lord Hammer's men rushed out of the building they would be spotted right away. With that thought in mind, he continued, "We need to find a better hiding place just in case. Everyone, take cover."

Kymbra and Swinkle came to Gelderand's aid, lifting the older person and getting him on his feet.

"Pondle, lead us somewhere safe," said the female warrior, as she and Swinkle guided the magician.

"Follow me," said the thief.

Knowing that they had little time, Pondle led the group deeper behind the stable and away from the mansion. Fifty feet away from their original position stood a doorway that led into the barn. The thief used caution in opening the door, then waved everyone inside. Seconds later, the small party found an empty stall, which they used for the time being.

Kymbra and Swinkle led Gelderand to a comfortable spot, then allowed the older man to kneel on the soft hay.

"What do you see?" asked the female warrior with anticipation.

"Rufus is scared," said the mage, droplets of sweat lining his brow. "People heard Murdock."

As if on cue, the ranger reappeared in front of them. "The door was locked," he said, holding the ring up for all to see. "I had to force it open."

"You couldn't have picked the lock?" said Kymbra in exasperation.

"Maybe you should have sent Pondle," said the ranger, not amused. "The cat's in the mansion, isn't he?"

Kymbra stood up and flailed her arms toward Murdock. "And now soldiers are investigating the noise!"

"It's all right," said Gelderand. "The men have run by Rufus." The mage moved his body to the left, then the right, mimicking the cat's movements. "They have left him alone."

Kymbra made eye contact with Pondle. "Make sure those fighters don't come this way." The thief nodded, then motioned for Murdock to follow him as the two men left the stall.

Bringing her attention back to Gelderand, she said, "Where's Rufus now?"

Gelderand squinted. "He's in the kitchen," said the mage. The cat looked upwards, giving the magician a clear view of hanging utensils, pots, pans, cutting boards, butcher blocks, and various pieces of fruits, vegetables, and assorted meats.

"Lord Hammer eats well," said Gelderand, maintaining his trance-like state. Rufus then continued his trek.

Kymbra tapped Swinkle on the shoulder, then whispered, "The cat's on the right path. The kitchen's at the end of the mansion and I'm assuming that the women are being held somewhere upstairs."

"I see people!" said Gelderand.

"More soldiers?" asked Swinkle with concern in his voice.

The mage crinkled his brow. "No. They are dressed like servants."

"Good," said Kymbra. "Lord Hammer hasn't imprisoned his staff."

Rufus continued on his trek through the governor's mansion, when he stopped in his tracks. A rather frail, thin man noticed the feline and took purposeful steps toward the animal.

"One of Lord Hammer's staffers is shooing Rufus away!" exclaimed Gelderand. The mage felt the cat dart around, trying to elude the servant.

"He's trying to grab Rufus!" Gelderand bobbed and weaved as the cat scurried in vain. The animal found an opening that led to another hallway and ran away from the man.

Gelderand kept his stare fixed straight ahead, concentrating on the information being fed to him via the feline's eyes. The corridor that Rufus ran down was quite long and ended with two large double doors. Sentries stood posted at the entranceway and they too saw the animal coming.

"Guards!" moaned Gelderand.

The feline also saw the guardians, who lowered their weapons and attempted to catch the cat as well. The two sentries teamed up to block Rufus's path, forcing the feline to stop. The animal swiveled his head back to whence he came, only to find the servant obstructing that path.

Gelderand suddenly jerked himself upward, fumbling to a standing position. "One of the sentries has grabbed Rufus by the scruff of his neck!"

Everyone held their breath, their eyes fixed on the mage and his continuing story. Two men appeared from around the stall's opening, breaking the tension.

"We didn't see any activity from Lord Hammer's men," said Murdock. With their chore over, the ranger asked with anticipation, "What's going on? Has that cat found Tara and Meredith yet?"

"One of Nigel's men captured Rufus! We need to rescue him!" said Swinkle.

Gelderand began to regain his bearings. "Not so fast," said the mage. "I see the servant and he is talking to the guard." The mage squinted, staring straight ahead again. "He's handing Rufus to the man!"

The mage felt a little better about the situation since the servant cradled Rufus and stroked his fur as he spoke with the guards. One of the sentries leaned closer to the cat, still saying something to the thin man and pointing at Rufus in the process. The guardian then pointed upwards.

"The servant is moving with Rufus," said Gelderand.

"What do you see now?" asked Kymbra with anticipation.

Gelderand took a moment to respond. "I see elaborate artwork, a large foyer, and ..." The mage hesitated. "He is taking Rufus up an elegant spiral staircase."

Kymbra and Murdock's eyes met. "I think they're in the main foyer and heading upstairs," said the woman.

"Meredith's master bedroom's probably up there," added the ranger.

Swinkle then directed a question to Gelderand. "Can you describe the servant to me?"

Gelderand tried to gather his thoughts as images of fine tapestries, paintings, and statues passed through his mind. "Rufus is not looking at him anymore, but he is thin, a bit frail."

"Young or old?" pressed the young cleric.

"Definitely not old," said Gelderand. "I would say mid-to-late thirties."

Swinkle recognized the man. "Percival."

Murdock frowned, shaking his head. "Who?"

"I met Percival when Harrison and I visited the mansion a little while back," started the young cleric. "He is a decent man and has probably sided with Meredith."

Murdock's eyes widened, taking his stare to Kymbra. "This is a good thing, no?"

"A very good thing," said the woman with a smile.

Gelderand's eyes widened, his face going pale. "Oh, no."

Everyone turned to the mage. "What is it?" asked Kymbra with concern.

"It's Lord Hammer!" All party members gasped.

The female warrior maneuvered closer to Gelderand and in a soothing voice said, "What do you see?"

The elder mage swallowed nervously. "He's calling the servant over." Gelderand swallowed again. "He's staring at Rufus and he's not happy."

Kymbra glanced at Murdock, but the ranger maintained his attention on Gelderand.

"Lord Hammer's yelling, pointing at the cat," said the mage, visibly shaken. "Rufus is very scared."

The blonde warrior knew she needed to temper the current situation and encourage Gelderand to focus on the feline's surroundings.

"Gelderand, tell me everything you see right now."

The mage made several quick nods, regaining his focus. "The servant has ascended the staircase and turned to his right." Gelderand rubbed his sweaty hands together. "Lord Hammer and three armored men are to the right as well."

Kymbra allowed the older man to continue, placing a caring hand on his arm. "What else?"

"He's so angry," reiterated Gelderand. Gathering himself, the mage continued, "The hallways are long with many doorways."

Without warning, the older man seemed to perk up. "He's letting the servant go on his way!"

Smiling, Gelderand continued, "The man has turned away from Nigel and is walking the other way down another corridor. There are ..." the mage counted to himself, "ten soldiers this way, all manning their posts."

"The women must be up there," said Kymbra to Murdock. "Why else would there be so many men loitering around?"

"I agree," said the ranger. "Lord Hammer needs security as well."

Gelderand had more to say. "The servant is still walking." Again, the mage counted to himself. "Three doors down and to the right. The servant is speaking to the sentries guarding the doorway."

The mage watched as one of the guardians removed a key from his belt and unlocked the portal. The door swung open and two very surprised women sprung to their feet.

"Tara!" exclaimed Gelderand, tears forming in his eyes. "I see Meredith, too!"

Kymbra flashed a wide smile. "They're still alive and we know where they are now!"

Gelderand raised a hand, signaling to the woman to wait. "The servant has entered the room. Rufus is moving closer to Tara! She's reaching for him!"

Tara used all her restraint to remain calm at seeing the familiar tabby cat. The young maiden accepted the feline from Percival and pulled him close to her chest, the cat meowing all the while.

"I found the animal wandering the mansion," said the thin servant. "I was on my way to see if you needed anything, Milady, and I scooped him up. I thought you might like a companion while you are here."

"Percival, what are we going to do with a cat?" said Meredith, gazing at the animal in Tara's arms.

"I'll take care of him, Meredith," said Tara, her eyes trying to convey a subtle message.

A male voice interrupted the trio. "Are you finished?" said the sentry to Percival. "We have strict orders to allow you in this room only to attend to the Lady's needs."

Percival turned to face Meredith again. "Do you need anything, Milady? Food? Water?"

"Yes, as a matter of fact we do," said Meredith, sensing something more to the odd situation. "We would like some water and small foods, nothing heavy. And I suppose something for the cat."

The servant nodded once. "Consider it done, Milady."

Percival turned and headed for the doorway, followed by the guard, who locked the portal after both men departed.

After she heard the bolt secured, Meredith gazed over at Tara, her brow wrinkled in confusion. "Why do you want this animal so much?"

Tara lifted the cat in front of her and looked into its eyes. "It's no ordinary cat, Meredith!" said the young girl, excited. "It's Rufus!"

The First Lady of Concur did not recognize the name. Shaking her head, she said, "Rufus?"

"My uncle is a mage and Rufus is his vehicle," said Tara. "He's looking through his eyes as we speak!"

Meredith's eyes widened in surprise. "He is?"

"I'm sure of it."

The older woman turned and paced, her mind racing. "That means they're trying to find us." Meredith stopped and looked at Tara. "Are they close by?"

"No more than a hundred yards," said Tara with a wide smile.

Meredith stared at nothing in particular; instead she focused her mind on this newfound information. "They need to know exactly where we are."

"You can write something down and place it in front of Rufus," said Tara. "He'll look at the paper and my uncle will be able to read it."

The dark-haired woman darted to a bureau. "That just might work." Meredith opened the top drawer and rummaged through its belongings before she found a scroll, ink, and pen. She then placed the items on top of the furniture and began to scribble her note.

As she did, Tara said aloud in a pronounced voice, "Hi, Uncle! Tell Harrison I miss him!"

The First Lady of Concur stopped what she was doing and raced over to the young maiden. In a hushed tone, she said, "Shhh! Don't mention any names! Someone may be listening!"

Tara nodded, caught off guard by the woman's actions. "I'm sorry."

Meredith went back to her note. "It's all right. We just need to be extra careful." The woman then made haste in finishing her message, and when she completed that task, she walked over to Tara.

"Keep Rufus still," she said, before unraveling the scroll in front of the cat's face. Rufus's eyes wandered all over the interesting parchment.

"Meredith has written us a note!" exclaimed Gelderand.

"Smart girl," said Murdock with a smirk.

"What does it say?" asked Kymbra with anticipation.

The mage squinted, focusing hard on the message. "It says, '*Second floor, hallway to the left, third door on the right. We are safe. Heavy security.*'"

"I say we go and rescue them," said Murdock, knowing that the alternative was to sit and wait.

"Not so fast," said Gelderand. "I need to get Rufus back in order to break this spell."

The ranger pursed his lips, forgetting for the time being the operation's delicacy. "How do we get him back?"

The mage sighed. "I'm hoping that Tara is smart enough to realize this as well."

Meredith lowered the scroll. "I hope they saw my note."

Tara pulled Rufus close to her chest again. "I'm sure that they have." The young maiden had an additional concern. "We need Rufus to return to my uncle now."

"What?" asked the older woman in bewilderment. "Why do we need to do that?"

"So my uncle can break his spell."

Meredith averted her gaze, nodding once. "I see," she answered, thinking about their next move. The First Lady of Concur raised a finger in the air. "I know what do next!"

"What?"

"I'll have Percival remove the cat from the room. I'll say that we don't want the animal locked in here with us."

"The guards will enter the room with him," said Tara with concern.

"Leave them to me."

The two women then found a seat and anxiously awaited Percival's return.

"Have they done anything more?" asked Murdock.

"It appears that Rufus is in Tara's arms and she is sitting down somewhere," answered Gelderand.

The ranger scowled. "Why aren't they doing anything?"

"They're locked in that room," said Kymbra, agitated. "Meredith can't just open that door and simply let the cat scoot out."

Murdock was about to say something else when the sound of voices interrupted his thought process. Everyone crouched lower, not wanting to be seen.

"Who's that?" whispered the ranger, concern in his voice.

Pondle took the initiative and peeked around the corner. He quickly jerked his body back into the stall, planting his back against the wooden wall.

"Lord Hammer's men!" said the thief.

Before anyone could utter another word, a very recognizable voice resonated throughout the barn.

"Prepare my steed," barked Lord Hammer. "We ride to the South Gate!"

"As you wish," answered one of Nigel's henchmen.

Pondle remained motionless, as did everyone else. The sound of hoof beats, the jingling of reins, and the thump of saddles being thrown on horses filled the dank air.

Everyone strained to breathe, no one wanting to make a sound with so much commotion happening very close to their hiding place. Pondle gazed upwards, then across the corridor from his position; horses occupied both stalls. Lord Hammer's riders will surely see them, he worried.

Without warning, Swinkle dropped to his knees, closed his eyes, and pressed his hands together in front of his chest. The young cleric then began to pray. A moment later, he opened his eyes and brought a finger to his lips, signaling for all to remain quiet. He then rose to a standing position.

The sound of heavy boots came dangerously close to the group's position. From their vantage point, everyone in the group could see the rider's shadow approach their stall. To their dismay, the rescue team watched a second man advance towards their position.

"Can we really beat these armies back?" asked one of Lord Hammer's men. The soldier prepared the steed in the animal's holding cell adjacent to the small group.

"I sure hope so," said the second fighter, walking over to the stall across from the nervous party.

Pondle gazed at the men with wide eyes, unsure how neither rider had seen them yet. The soldier attending to the horse across from the thief glanced into the group's stall, yet appeared to see no one.

"We better hurry," said the first man. "Lord Hammer's waiting."

Both men guided their respective horses out of their confines and led them away from the stable. The anxious group waited another minute, no one daring to say a word.

Just then, Gelderand perked up. In a whisper, he said, "Someone has entered the women's room again."

"Thank you, Percival," said Meredith, accepting a tray containing a pitcher of water, two glasses, a bowl of fresh breads and small cakes, and a saucer of milk for Rufus. "This will do for now."

The servant took a subtle glance to the sentry who remained in the room before asking, "Is there anything else you need, Milady?"

"Yes, Percival," said Meredith. "Can you send Catherine to my room when she arrives?"

"No, not allowed." The guard wagged a finger back and forth. "Lord Hammer's orders."

"You mean to tell me that only Percival is allowed to attend to my needs?"

The guard nodded. "I'm afraid so."

Meredith huffed and turned her attention to her servant once again. "Percival, please take this cat and be sure to let it loose outside the mansion. I think it'll be happier outside instead of being cooped up in one room." The dark-haired woman took Rufus from Tara's arms and handed him to the servant.

"Send him out the back, near the stables," continued Concur's First Lady. "I'm sure there are plenty of mice and rats that he can hunt out there."

"Of course, Milady. I will be back with your formal breakfast in an hour." Percival then turned and departed. The sentry left the room next, bolting the door behind him.

"Does Rufus know where to go?" asked Meredith.

"He better or my uncle's in big trouble."

"How did they not see us?" Murdock asked Swinkle.

"The power of prayer and an invisible sanctuary," said the young cleric with a smile. "I knew Pious would not let us down."

Suddenly, Gelderand perked up. "Rufus is on the move again!"

"And so are Lord Hammer and his men, or did you just forget about them?" Murdock jerked his thumb to the now empty stalls.

"Keep an eye out for any more activity," said Kymbra. "We're not moving until that cat's back safe and sound."

"What do you see?" asked Murdock to the mage.

"The servant is carrying him again," started Gelderand, "but this time he's taking Rufus out of the room."

"That's a good thing," said the ranger. "Hopefully he'll send him back outside."

"That's just what he's doing!" Gelderand started to rise. "The servant is bringing him down the corridor Rufus traversed before."

Kymbra made eye contact with Murdock. "That leads to the door right outside these stables," said the female warrior. Kymbra was about to order Murdock and Pondle to investigate, but they were already one step ahead of her.

"We'll check that door," said Pondle. The two men then cautiously left the stall and exited the building.

"The door is opening," said Gelderand, focusing hard, beads of sweat forming on his brow. "He's running down the steps and traversing the courtyard." The mage's eyes then opened wide with surprise.

"I see Murdock and Pondle! They're waving Rufus over!" Seconds later, the two men returned to the stall with Pondle holding the orange tabby in his hands.

"I believe this belongs to you." The thief handed Rufus to Gelderand.

The elder man stroked the cat's fur. "Enough adventures for you," he said, positioning the feline in front of him. Gelderand then mumbled something barely audible, breaking the spell in the process.

Kymbra waited until she saw the familiar shape of Gelderand's eyes, albeit with the Resistance markings. "The spell's broken!"

"That it is," said the mage, relieved.

"You need rest now," said Swinkle, understanding that concentrating at that high an intensity level for such a long period of time would drain Gelderand of his precious energy.

"How long do we need to wait?" asked Murdock. The ranger had kept his desire for battle in check, but now they stood too close to rescuing Tara and Meredith to wait any longer.

"As long as it takes," responded Kymbra. "Gelderand has given us valuable information, something that he should be rewarded for."

"I will wait here with him." Swinkle knew full well that his talents would be better served protecting Gelderand than to battle Concurian soldiers.

"Are you sure?" asked Kymbra. "What if something happens to you two?"

"I will make sure that nothing does," said Swinkle. "I do have some prayers that will be useful and Pious will look over us as well." The young cleric gazed at their canine friend.

"I have Lance here to protect us, too." Lance wagged his tail at the sound of his name.

"So that means we can leave this place, right?" asked Murdock, sensing that his duty as a guardian was all but over.

Kymbra raised a finger in the ranger's direction, signaling for him to wait. "Adrith, Marissa," called the lead female. "Keep lookout for Gelderand and Swinkle."

"Where are you going?" asked Marissa, her brow crinkled.

"I'm going with them to find Thoragaard," said Kymbra, pointing to Murdock and Pondle.

"Thoragaard?" said Murdock, the sound of surprise in his voice. "I thought we were going to rescue Tara and Meredith?"

"We don't have enough force to liberate them," said Kymbra. "Plus, now that we know where they're being held, we can better direct Thoragaard and Harrison to their position."

Murdock looked to Pondle, who gave him a single nod of affirmation. "They should be storming the West Gate right about now."

"I agree," said the female, "and we need to find them."

"Let me guide us out of here," said Pondle, taking a firm hold on his weapon's hilt. "This city's crawling with activity."

"Fine," said Kymbra, who then turned to speak to her counterparts. "The next time I see you we'll have Thoragaard and Harrison with us. Stay safe." Adrith and Marissa nodded in confirmation.

Kymbra then gestured to Pondle. "Let's go."

The thief peered out of their stall and finding the area clear of soldiers, waved Murdock and Kymbra forward. A moment later, the trio disappeared into the Concurian backdrop.

Adrith watched the posse leave the confines of the stables. "We're on our own now."

"I suggest that we stay in this sanctuary," said Swinkle. "My prayer will last a little while longer."

"We'll keep watch," said Adrith, as Marissa joined her.

The small group took advantage of the relative safety of the stables, while Concur waged war.

CHAPTER 29

¤

Lord Hammer and ten of his loyal soldiers galloped their horses toward the South Gate. The Concurian leader had heard the deafening crash that the Arcadian battering ram had made a short time ago. Knowing that a breach would be devastating to his city, the ruthless leader decided to defend this part of his metropolis first.

The men raced on their steeds through the town's streets, townsfolk and army members dodging their rapid advance. Nigel, a sly smirk on his face, could not wait to meet his unsuspecting adversary, for the dark fighter had something special in store for his enemy.

Minutes later, the convoy reached the South Gate. Nigel brought his horse to an abrupt stop, signaling for his men to do the same, some fifty yards away from the locked portal.

Lord Hammer canvassed the structure, making a quick and thorough inspection of the entranceway. The Arcadian's weapon had smashed the gears that were part of the huge pulley system beyond repair and they would not withstand a second attack. Furthermore, the portals themselves were badly damaged and Nigel knew another thrust would cause them to collapse inward on his city — something that he hoped would happen.

During his leader's inspection, a sentry dashed over to give his superior a report.

"Sir," started the nervous soldier, "we've battled valiantly, but we can't stop the Arcadians from making another attack." The guard swallowed hard, his nerves getting the better of him. "They will enter the city on their next run."

"Unsecure the doorway!" barked Nigel. "Let their battering ram destroy the portals."

The sentry's eyes grew wide and his brow furrowed. "Sir?"

"Go to your post and do as I say!" commanded Lord Hammer. "Make sure that the sentries atop the wall continue to douse our enemy with boiling oil and water!"

The soldier saluted, then said, "Yes, sir!"

Nigel watched as his sentry raced to the great wall to fulfill his order. The Concurian leader turned to one of his henchmen. "Fetch Allard and his men. It's time to put them to the test."

The general nodded, summoned three of his men, and galloped away to retrieve the great mage.

Lord Hammer wasted no time in barking his next command. Pointing to another of his generals, he said, "I want you to give me a report from atop the wall. Tell me how many Arcadians are in the countryside, their attack formations, their weapon – everything! Report back to me in five minutes, no later!"

The loyal soldier nodded and went off to perform his task. As he did, Nigel surveyed the immediate battlefield. The South Gate stood a couple hundred yards away from any buildings that resided inside Concur. Lord Hammer brought his gaze from the massive entranceway to the small buildings that rested away from the wall. Many of the structures in this part of his city were residential, meaning that they could be sacrificed for the greater good of Concur. Satisfied with the thoughts of minimal meaningful casualties to his city, Nigel raised his head and watched as scores of sentries maneuvered the mechanism into the unlocked position. The South Gate was now unsecured.

Moments later, three horses, each with a rider and cloaked figure, galloped to Lord Hammer's position. Allard and three of his mages dismounted and approached their superior.

"You said you had ten magicians," said the Concurian leader, perturbed.

"It has been a trying day, Nigel," said Allard, his concern and displeasure over defections in his ranks evident. "Are we still on track with your plan?"

"Yes," said Nigel. "One of my generals is on his way back now with the information we need."

An armored figure ran from the great wall over to Nigel, Allard and the rest of the men. Speaking between ragged breaths, the general delivered his report.

"About two thousand men," he started, gasping for air. "All of their soldiers have large shields, which they're using to deflect our aerial attacks. Their platoons have a hundred or so soldiers and appear to be arranged in strike squads with fighters and archers.

"The Arcadians are preparing their battering ram for another run. I'd say they'll attack us within the next ten minutes."

Nigel nodded, then turned to Allard. "Prepare your counterattack."

The mage returned a single affirmative nod, then motioned for his apprentices to follow him to their predetermined positions.

With Allard taken care of, Lord Hammer barked his next order in his general's direction. "Command your men to slaughter each and every Arcadian who enters the city. Be merciless!"

"Yes, sir!" exclaimed the soldier, who then ran off to perform his task.

Nigel, his plan ready for execution, waited for the Arcadians to destroy the South Gate.

Bracken Drake monitored his situation with a careful eye. Many of his men howled in pain, their bodies scorched from boiling oil and water that Nigel's men had poured on them from high atop the great wall. Nevertheless, the Arcadians pressed on with their attack plans.

From his steed, the Arcadian leader bellowed to one of his lead soldiers, "Are you ready for another attack?"

The fighter took a moment to gauge his situation, and when satisfied, he turned and said with pride, "Yes, sir! Say the word and we'll start our next run!"

Bracken nodded, then raised his sword in the air. At the top of his lungs, he yelled, "Destroy that gate!"

Upon hearing their leader's exclamation, the two hundred Arcadian soldiers assigned to push the massive weapon commenced with their attack run.

Bracken then barked another command. "Everyone, follow your brethren and be ready to defeat the Concurians when that door comes crashing down!"

The Arcadians cheered with delight. Scores of men followed behind the battering ram as it rattled toward the awaiting doorway. Bracken allowed half his men to pass him by before summoning his closest advisors to follow and join the attack.

Your reign is almost over, Nigel, Bracken thought as his horse galloped toward the battered South Gate.

Allard and his three apprentices positioned themselves a hundred yards away from the wounded entryway. The great mage surveyed the area, staring at the damaged entrance, determining the exact spot to place himself. The Concurian stood directly in line with the relative center of the massive doorways and, without saying a word, gestured to each magician and pointed to where he wanted them to stand, creating a triangle of equidistant points ten feet away from him.

He then closed his eyes and began intense concentration, summoning the dreadful spell from deep within his soul. The mage's eyeballs shifted rapidly, as he slowly lifted his hands; the three magicians surrounding him did likewise. A moment later, a small black sphere appeared above Allard's head.

The great mage started to chant aloud, along with his apprentices. The globe grew larger with each passing second and, as it did, the object started to rotate with dust and small debris hurtling toward the black sphere.

Bracken's men disregarded the arrows and steaming liquids that seemed to fall from the heavens; instead they remained steadfast on their mission. Just as in their previous attack run, when the soldiers advanced ten yards from the massive gateway, they dove out of the way to allow the battering ram to slam into the blocked entranceway.

The massive weapon struck the portal, but this time instead of being repelled, it crushed the doors, splintering them inward. The force of the blow tore the great stone walls, parts of the structure crumbling down. Scores of Concurian fighters who had perched themselves on top of the wall fell to their death.

The Arcadian's ultimate weapon, finished with its primary mission, continued to steamroll through the South Gate and penetrated further into the city of Concur.

Bracken Drake smiled as he watched Concur's unmistakable symbol of strength buckle under the force of his weapon of destruction. The South Gate now breached, the Arcadian leader waved his men forward, as they all began to enter Lord Hammer's sacred city.

The black void that hovered precariously over Allard's head rotated at an incredible speed. Aside from the mage and his apprentices, objects and debris began to fly toward the sphere. Upon making contact with the darkness, the object disappeared, ceasing to exist.

The sudden crash, followed by massive wooden doors flying into the city, tempered the mage's intense concentration. Maintaining his composure, Allard summoned all of the strength that he possessed to keep the sphere in place.

The great mage had to open his eyes to gauge the distance of the incoming object, but struggled to avoid losing his focus. Peering at the vacant doorway, Allard found a huge projectile rolling in his direction.

Seconds ago, the battering ram had burst through the South Gate with hundreds of Arcadian soldiers in tow. Saving the city at this moment rested solely on Allard's shoulders.

Barreling toward the foursome at an incredible rate, the Arcadian's weapon showed no signs of slowing. It was time for Allard to act.

"Forward!" shouted the magician to his fellow mages. Each man maneuvered to face the oncoming object.

Allard channeled his inner strength and took sole responsibility of the black globe. With a deep bellow that would startle a slumbering dragon, the great mage pushed the sphere in the direction of the oncoming projectile.

The ten-foot wide ball of darkness and the massive battering ram collided seconds later with a deafening sound. The dark void erupted in a violent explosion, knocking everyone and everything in a hundred yard radius flat.

Allard and his apprentices fell to the ground, covering their ears. The great mage stared at the collision point and watched his evil spell annihilate the Arcadian's battering ram. The black void did not stop there; after obliterating the gigantic weapon, it then absorbed the crippled doorways, chunks of the stone wall, and finally anything in the area that remained unsecured.

Soldiers, Concurian and Arcadian alike, screamed as they hurtled toward the dark sphere, unable to stop themselves from certain death.

Allard felt an intense pull, the spell's final act trying to drag its creator to his demise as well. The great mage's legs started to slide in the direction of the newly created void. The magician reached for something to grab, but his hands found nothing but earth.

The mage, his heart racing, stared at the super-rotating globe. His apprentice closest to the void lifted off the ground and sped toward the sphere. A second later, he was gone.

Allard knew that the duration of his spell would be short, but incredibly intense. He had taken great precautions to perform the spell a sufficient distance far away from the intercept point. At this moment, he questioned his calculations.

His second apprentice rose from his position, flew into the globe of death, and died. The sphere dragged Allard to one hundred feet of its epicenter. The mage witnessed all kinds of matter flying into the darkness and knew that nothing could prevent him from doing the same. His legs began to rise from the ground, the sucking becoming even more intense.

Just as Allard lifted off the earth, another deafening explosion erupted and the dark sphere imploded. The mage fell to the ground and immediately covered his head.

Shielded, Allard waited for another catastrophe to occur; nothing came. The great mage raised his head ever so slowly and took in the surrounding area. To his delight, the battering ram no longer existed, nor did the massive doors of the South Gate. Holes riddled the great wall, the void having consumed huge portions of the stone structure.

Allard squinted and scoured the immediate area for Lord Hammer. The Governor of Concur was nowhere to be seen. The mage then canvassed his surroundings and found his final apprentice lying on the ground, still alive. The individual sported an expression of horror, shocked at the turn of events, but happy to still be living.

The great mage then began to laugh. "It worked! It worked!"

Before regaining his composure, Allard found his apprentice pointing at the dilapidated gateway with wide eyes.

Taking his gaze back to the broken landmark, Allard understood the gravity of his apprentice's appearance, for wave upon wave of Arcadian soldiers came unabated through the gaping wound. Men on foot, as well as horseback, stormed into Concur from the countryside with no resistance.

Allard rose from his position and raced to the other man's side. Grabbing his arm, the magician said, "Tyrus, we have to run! There's more to do!"

The younger mage stared into nothingness, still in shock from the scene he had just witnessed. The elder magician knew there was no time to waste.

Shaking the man, he yelled, "We must go now!" Allard used all the strength he had left to jerk the man off the ground.

Pointing to Concur's interior, he commanded, "We must get to the harbor!" The apprentice appeared to understand, and while foreigners invaded their city, the two men began their trek to continue with their mission.

CHAPTER 30

¤

"More battles are coming our way," said Brendan with a scowl as he pointed deeper in town.

Harrison glanced in the direction the elder warrior indicated and, sure enough, more squadrons of Concurian soldiers advanced. The young warrior took a moment to assess their situation.

Brendan and the Unified Army had breached the West Gate, where they met Harrison and a small contingent of freedom fighters. At first, the young warrior had convinced scores of Concurians to join their cause, which helped in opening the massive gates. However, these same soldiers had trouble conveying Harrison's true message deeper into the Concurian ranks.

Harrison raised his blade as more men advanced on their position. Gesturing to the Unified soldiers on either side of him, the young warrior commanded, "Flank to both sides and allow the Concurians to come forward! We'll surround them!"

Just as commanded, platoons of men dispersed away from their leaders, allowing the men clad in black armor to attack.

Brendan, his long sword brandished and ready to strike, kept an eye on the advancing men. Facing the young warrior, he said, "I hope you've thought out your next maneuver!"

"Just be ready to fight!" Harrison, abandoning all hope of turning these men to their side, gritted his teeth and began to battle in earnest.

The young warrior went on the offensive, along with Brendan and the thirty fighters around him. Fifty Concurians entered their space, yelling and flailing their weapons.

Harrison took turns fending off Concurians eager to rid their city of the invaders. The young warrior channeled his teachings at the Fighter's Guild to ward off his fatigue, but the men clad in black continued to come in droves.

The young warrior surveyed his surroundings again, while slashing a host soldier in front of him. Men allied with him continued to pour into the city, but they were meeting heavy resistance. Furthermore, the charging Concurians cramped their fighting quarters, stalling their advancement to the Governor's mansion.

Suddenly a deafening crash emanated from the south, stopping all fighting on both sides. Harrison, with eyes wide open, shouted in Brendan's direction, "What was that?"

The elder Aegean in reply said, "Reinforcements, I hope." He then started his melees again.

Before Harrison could continue his own battles, he heard another crash coming from the east. This time, plumes of purple and black smoke rose into the sky from the area near the East Gate.

"Thoragaard," said Harrison with a smile, knowing that the Forge Brothers would be following close behind.

Gelderand's eyes widened and he knew right away that the sound he had just heard was no ordinary explosion. Mustering all the strength he could gather, he pushed himself off the ground and rose to his feet.

"We must leave and at this very moment," said the mage in a most serious tone.

Swinkle gazed at the magician, never seeing such conviction in the elder man's eyes before.

"What is the matter, Gelderand?" asked the young cleric. "That blast is just another indication that our friends are entering the city."

Marissa and Adrith witnessed the conversation of the two men with great concern.

"I fear something greater is upon us," started Gelderand. "A force only a wizard could summon."

"The others told us to wait here," said Marissa, wishing to stick with the plan.

"If we leave, no one will know where we have gone," added Adrith, both females displaying wide, anxious eyes.

"Nevertheless," said Gelderand, "I believe it is our time to join the action. If what I believe is true, then I might be the only person to stop whatever may happen next."

Swinkle took a step toward the older man, lightly grabbing his forearm to stop his forward progress. Again, the young cleric looked deep into Gelderand's eyes and with a nervous tone asked, "What is it?"

The mage drew a heavy sigh. "You will see." Gelderand gestured to the women, as well as Lance. "Please escort us out of the stables and away from the mansion. Use Lance as your guide."

"Aren't you weak from your spell?" asked Marissa, concerned for Gelderand's well being.

"That I am, but we must persevere." The magician waved the females onward, encouraging them to perform their task.

"Lord Hammer's men will see us," lamented Swinkle, trying to change Gelderand's mind.

"Trust me, it makes no difference who sees us now."

Marissa and Adrith called for Lance to join them, and a moment later the small posse left the stables behind and ventured into the chaotic streets.

Murdock grabbed Kymbra's arm from behind. The tall blonde-haired woman stopped in her tracks.

"That didn't sound right at all," said the ranger, panning the area in search of what caused the deafening noise.

Pondle, who was leading the trio through the dangerous streets, took a few steps back to his friends. "What in the world could have caused that?"

"Thoragaard?" asked Murdock in Kymbra's direction.

The female warrior bit her lower lip, unsure. Thoragaard had performed many spells and illusions, but nothing this dramatic.

"I don't think so."

"Then what do you suppose we do?" The ranger was not one for standing idle in such a volatile place. Moments later, a second blast startled the group again.

Kymbra swiveled her head to the east, sensing that this new explosion occurred there. The sound of the outburst told the female warrior that this blast lacked the intensity of the first one.

Murdock and Pondle craned their necks to look in the same direction as Kymbra. The thief pointed to the eastern sky.

"Black and purple smoke!" yelled Pondle.

"That doesn't appear natural to me," added Murdock.

Kymbra smirked. "Not natural at all. It's Thoragaard's handiwork."

Murdock took his gaze to the south, his brow furrowed with confusion. "If Thoragaard is over there," the ranger gestured to the east, "who caused that other explosion?"

"The Arcadians are marching from the south," said Kymbra. "They must have done it."

Pondle stared toward the south, but the building before him blocked his field of vision. "What have they brought along with them to cause such a ruckus?"

"I have no idea," said Kymbra. "All I know is that we need to meet up with Thoragaard." The female took a step in the direction of the hazy, purplish hue.

"Wait a second," said Murdock. "I thought we were meeting Harrison at the West Gate?"

"It's obvious that Thoragaard isn't there," said Kymbra, defending her position. "Thoragaard will direct us when we find him."

Pondle added his thoughts. "She has a point," started the thief. "If Thoragaard is helping the Forge Brothers at the East Gate, it only means that Harrison has things well in hand at the other entrance."

Murdock pondered his friend's rationale. Shaking his head, he gestured toward the East Gate and said, "You two better be right. Let's go!"

Without a second to spare, the trio abandoned their plans to reunite with Harrison and ventured off to meet Thoragaard.

Before Harrison could complete his final thought, the area filled with the sounds of men yelling and trampling of feet coming from the South Gate – the Arcadians had finally arrived.

Soldiers, adorned in crimson and gold, stormed through the Concurian streets, beating back their adversaries and forcing them into a contentiously restricted area between themselves and the invaders storming through the West Gate.

Harrison and Brendan, along with their Unified Army pressed forward against the Concurians, while Bracken Drake squeezed the black-clad men from the south.

Weapons clashed, blood spilled, and battles raged for the better part of an hour. Though the Concurians knew the terrain better and fought valiantly, in the end the two experienced invaders who had stormed their city outmanned and overmatched them.

Harrison, sweat and blood staining his chain-mail armor, sensed that the battle had turned in their favor. Noticing the intense apprehension and anxiety on the faces of the men clad in black before him, the young warrior knew he needed to make things right at this very moment.

Taking a defensive posture, Harrison held his ground, his weapon brandished before him. With a mighty yell, he commanded, "Concurians! Stop your fighting! This battle is over!"

Several of the dark soldiers heard his exclamation, and although they did not want to surrender, they ceased their fighting nevertheless. As more Concurians realized that their fellow fighters had halted their melees, the armies from Arcadia and the unified towns held their ground, not pressing their battles any further. Finally, all men stopped fighting and an eerie calm permeated the area.

Harrison seized the moment. Lowering his blade, he stepped forward and said, "My fellow warriors, we are not here to overrun you, but to liberate you."

A Concurian soldier took exception to the young warrior's remark. "You invade our city, our way of life, and expect us to believe that you intend to save us? I'd rather die than allow you to advance any further!" Several Concurians cheered at their comrade's statement.

"I understand your apprehension," started Harrison before the Concurian soldier interrupted him.

"Do you?" said the same man in black. "What if we invaded your city?"

Harrison could feel his sense of diplomacy waning. Taking a different line of reasoning, he asked, "Do you enjoy living under Lord Hammer's sword?"

Several of the Concurians exchanged glances, hearing the name of their superior, unsure if they should go against him.

"He treats us well, gives us a place to live, a job to do," said the Concurian, trying his best to convince himself and his fellow warriors.

"And if you go against him?" pressed Harrison. "Is there justice?"

The Concurian lowered his head, knowing there was not. "This is our way of life! This is how we choose to live!"

The young warrior did not believe the man's statement, and felt that the soldier did not either. "Your parents, your families, are they safe?"

An uncomfortable silence befell the area. No one dare speak, for they knew anything else said could result in unwanted imprisonment or death of their loved ones.

"That's what I thought," said Harrison. The young warrior knew the time was ripe to change the allegiance of these men. "Do you know that Lord Hammer has sequestered Meredith, your First Lady, in his mansion?"

Again, the Concurians exchanged curious glances. Harrison continued. "We wish to liberate and allow her to rule Concur, to make things right again, and to have this fine city become part of the unified land. And after that is accomplished, we will all leave."

"What will become of us, those who had been loyal to Lord Hammer?" asked the Concurian.

"Pledge your allegiance to Meredith, protect her and your new city, and you will have freedom." Harrison paused. "But, those who remain loyal to Nigel will be handled appropriately."

"Handled appropriately?" said the Concurian, an eyebrow arched. "What does that mean?"

"Meredith and her advisors will decide what to do with those who do not wish to take this golden opportunity. It will not be for us to decide."

Brendan approached the young warrior while the platoons of Concurian soldiers pondered their fate.

"You know, I might lie down my arms to you, Harrison," said the elder warrior in jest. "That was a wonderful speech; one I think the Concurians cannot refuse."

An angry rider gazed at the chaos in the distance. Lord Hammer did not appreciate an attack on his sovereignty and the fact that foreign invaders had infiltrated his city incensed him even more.

"Sir, how should we proceed?" asked an anxious general from atop his steed.

Nigel had ridden with his top soldiers to the South Gate in hopes of thwarting an attack from the Arcadians, only to find that Bracken Drake had other plans. Lord Hammer had not anticipated the strength of the Arcadian's ultimate weapon or the intensity of Allard's spell. Making a snap decision, Nigel elected to flee the area of certain destruction and take his chances on another battlefield. Now, he watched as two large invading forces sandwiched scores of his soldiers into a confined area close to the West Gate.

The Concurian governor panned the immediate area, finding a hundred or so loyal fighters. Not enough to defeat Harrison and Bracken, thought the dark lord. Most of his other men had either perished, defected, or were scrambling to save their lives.

"Assemble the archers," started Nigel, "and have them shoot flaming arrows in that direction." Lord Hammer motioned toward the growing mass of soldiers to the west.

"But, sir, we have men of our own over there," protested the soldier. "We might mistakenly hit them if we go forward with your plan."

Nigel continued his stare, his mind made up. "So be it."

The general maintained a blank gaze, before turning and shouting, "Ignite your arrows and fire into that mob!"

Less than a minute later, glowing projectiles hurtled through the air and began to hit their mark on unsuspecting soldiers, foreign and Concurian alike. Lord Hammer liked what he saw.

Taking control, he pointed at the mass of soldiers and yelled, "Fire!" A second volley of arrows flew toward their targets again.

Harrison, in the midst of trying to turn the Concurian troops, watched in horror as men all around him began to fall to the ground, their bodies igniting from the flaming projectiles. Taking his bewildered gaze before him, the young warrior searched for the origin of his new dilemma.

Before he could get a fix on his situation, a soldier shouted, "Lord Hammer is attacking us!"

Harrison sought the man with the exclamation, realizing that he too was Concurian. Taking advantage of the moment, the young warrior said, "You see, he doesn't care about you or the rest of his men! Your loyalty for him is over!"

Another volley of arrows forced everyone in the immediate area to seek cover, though no shelter existed. Harrison instinctively ducked and shielded his head, before a horrific scream jolted him. An arrow had penetrated the upper torso of the man before him, its fiery payload igniting the man's clothing.

The young warrior raced to the Concurian and attempted to pat out the flames, but the fire had enveloped the soldier's body. The flaming monster stumbled aimlessly, shrieking in terror. Harrison watched in horror for a few more seconds before the man dropped to the ground, his motionless corpse ablaze, never to rise again.

A burning rage, hotter than any flame that hurtled toward his ever-growing army, began to consume the young warrior. Gritting his teeth, he looked in the distance and found Concur's lead man in black atop his steed, watching the scene unfold before him.

Unleashing his fury, Harrison pointed his battle-axe in the direction of Lord Hammer and called to his troops. "Charge them!"

All the men around the young warrior — Concurian and Unified army alike — yelled at the top of their lungs and raced in Lord Hammer's direction.

Just as Harrison began his charge toward his adversary, a firm hand grabbed the young warrior's arm, forcing him to stop.

"Just what do you think you're doing?" exclaimed Brendan.

Harrison, his eyes still filled with rage, said, "I'm going to kill that man!"

"No, you're not!" said the elder warrior. "You're going to get yourself killed!"

The young warrior stopped, while soldiers rushed by his position. "Now is the time, Brendan! We have the manpower to overtake him!"

"That we do," said the Aegean warrior in an eerily calm voice. "Have the armies surround him. Force him to surrender."

"He'll never surrender!" said Harrison, amazed that his mentor would even suggest such a wild scenario.

"Exactly," said Brendan with a wry smile. "Give him the option, and when he rejects your proposal, then we can kill him."

Lord Hammer glared at the foreigners who rushed his position. "Prepare for battle!" barked the dark leader.

One of Nigel's generals positioned next to his superior swallowed with fear. "Sir, they greatly outnumber us!"

The Concurian leader glared at his subordinate. "Don't tell me the obvious!"

The fighter concurred with a single nod, then yelled to his bowmen, "Fire into the crowd!"

Seconds later, a deadly volley of flaming arrows whistled through the air and hit their marks on advancing Unified soldiers. Moments later, another round of projectiles also hit their targets.

Though the attacks dropped many men, the foreigners kept charging. Lord Hammer knew he had no way of winning this battle and resigned himself to the fact that he had to incorporate his secondary plan.

"Everyone, fall back to the mansion!" commanded Nigel, yanking on his horse's reins, pulling the beast in the opposite direction. The hundred or so loyal soldiers did likewise.

Nigel's steed galloped toward the awaiting structure. As it did, the Concurian leader passed scores of townspeople who pondered the fate of their city. Ahead in the distance, Lord Hammer witnessed another unfortunate turn of events – the breach of the East Gate. Plumes of colored smoke rose into the morning sky, signaling yet another defeat to his beloved city.

The Governor gritted his teeth and swallowed his pride, knowing that the two women who remained prisoner in his palatial complex held the key to his freedom.

CHAPTER 31

Ȣ

Marissa and Adrith followed Lance away from the Governor's complex and through the streets of Concur with Gelderand and Swinkle in tow. No one in the group worried about the flow of soldiers who passed them by.

"Where are they going?" asked the young cleric to Gelderand.

"If I had to venture a guess, I would say the mansion," answered the mage.

Swinkle felt a hollow feeling in his heart, sensing that the residence's prisoners would soon become the cornerstone of the next battle.

"Where are *we* going?" asked the younger man.

"To seek the creator of the explosion," said Gelderand, analyzing the city's landscape with a careful eye. Up ahead, the two females halted and waited for the men to catch up with them.

The magician came to a stop and stood next to the women, never taking his eyes from the city's activities. From his vantage point, buildings and shops lined the central road with townsfolk and soldiers clashing before him.

"Can you explain what we should be looking for?" asked Marissa, her round, green eyes unsure of their plan.

"Look for someone out of place," said Gelderand. "Specifically, a wizard as myself."

Marissa glanced at Adrith with a hint of concern in her eye. Both warriors then took their gaze to the streets, finding nothing out of the ordinary in the rather chaotic scene.

Adrith spoke up next, saying, "Trying to find a magician in this mess is going to be ..."

"There!" shouted Gelderand, interrupting the young girl and pointing to someone in the distance. "That's them!"

All eyes focused on where the mage pointed. Diagonally across from them, about fifty yards away, ran two robed figures, one carrying a large staff.

Swinkle squinted, trying to get a better fix on the people. "Who are they?"

Gelderand stood tall, a strange calm overtaking his body. "I think I know. We must run after them. Let's go!" The small group then made haste to catch up to the fleeing people.

Nigel and his contingent of men reached the mansion first. With precious little time, the Governor dismounted his horse and barked his last orders.

To the closest general, he yelled, "I'm going inside. Lock this place down and don't allow anyone but Harrison to enter the premises!"

The soldier saluted and scurried to enforce his superior's orders. With the foreign armies converging on the building, Lord Hammer rushed inside his domicile and bolted the doorway. His sentries gave him curious stares, their anxious eyes conveying their true feelings.

Lord Hammer pointed to the secure entranceway. "No one comes in!" he shouted to his guardians. "Secure all doors into this place! Now!"

The men ran off to handle their task while Nigel bolted up the spiral staircase.

Harrison's Unified army, along with the Arcadians, stormed the compound from the west, while the Forge Brothers pressed forward from the east. Without issuing a command, Bracken Drake guided his men around the southern side of the complex, isolating the structure from the rest of the city.

The young warrior proceeded to the front of his soldiers and gestured for them to hold their ground. Likewise, all of the other platoons followed Harrison's lead and encircled the mansion from fifty yards away.

Harrison scanned the area, figuring that no more than two hundred Concurians loyal to Lord Hammer stood in their way. The young warrior searched for Nigel himself, but could not see him in the immediate area.

"The bastard's holed up inside his own mansion," said Brendan, advancing to Harrison's position. "What's your next move?"

The young warrior pondered the situation. He had more than enough force to storm the building, but that would put Meredith and Tara at great risk. If Nigel was inside, which Harrison more than assumed, then he must be with the women right now, waiting for a final confrontation. Nothing else made sense other than that scenario.

Harrison locked his gaze on Brendan. "I must go inside and negotiate Meredith and Tara's release."

The elder warrior smirked. "Is that so? You're just going to stroll in and everything's going to be all right?"

"I'm figuring that's what must happen next," said the young warrior, trying to hide his fraying nerves. "Remember, you and the others assured me that if we can take Nigel alive, we would. This is our chance."

Brendan grimaced and looked away, knowing that he had agreed to those very terms, but had secretly hoped to take down Nigel in an epic battle with the Aegean victorious.

Before Harrison could enact his plan, the remaining leaders of the Unified army joined their comrades. The Forge Brothers left their men to defend the north and east areas of the mansion, while Bracken Drake's army secured the south. Now, all members of the liberation team stood before Concur's most important building.

Octavius Forge took the lead. "Glad to see that you're all still alive," he said, making eye contact with his fellow equals. Taking his gaze to Harrison, he said, "It looks like you've gotten your wish. The rat's nested in his mansion."

"Let it be known," started Bracken, "that the Arcadians are willing to storm the building at your command, Harrison."

The young warrior was about to respond to the Arcadian, but stopped when he saw a small contingent of fighters weaving through the crowd of armored men. A wide smile graced Harrison's face upon recognizing the group.

"You don't think we're going to let you go through this alone, do you?" said Murdock with a sly smile. Pondle and Kymbra trailed the ranger, followed by a robed figure. All three nodded in Harrison's direction, acknowledging the young warrior.

"Am I glad to see all of you!" exclaimed Harrison, happy to know that his friends were safe and ready to continue with the battle.

"Where's Swinkle and Gelderand?" asked Harrison with concern.

"We left them in the stables along with Marissa and Adrith," said Kymbra. "I'm sure they're safe." The young warrior smiled and nodded, agreeing with the female warrior.

"So," said Bracken, bringing the focus back to the situation at hand, "what is our next course of action?"

For the first time, Harrison felt the weight of the world on his shoulders. Before him stood the most decorated leaders of the land, all waiting to hear what the young warrior had in mind. Furthermore, in all likelihood an enraged Nigel Hammer awaited the young warrior with two very important hostages in his possession. How am I going to succeed, he lamented to himself.

"I suggest you think this through very carefully," said Brendan, offering his advice and breaking into the young warrior's thought processes.

Harrison heeded his mentor's advice and pondered the situation in his head for a long moment.

"They're heading toward the water!" said Gelderand through ragged, gasping breaths.

The small posse had followed Allard and his apprentice through the frenzied city, tracking him to Concur's large harbor. The group stopped fifty yards from Allard's position, trying to figure out the meaning of the magician's actions. They all watched as the dark wizard waded into the harbor after motioning for his apprentice to remain on the shore. Next, the mage jammed his staff into the water.

"What's he up to?" asked Marissa, her brow furrowed in confusion.

Just then, the wizard began to churn the staff in the water and, as he did, wispy clouds began to form high above his position.

"Look!" exclaimed Adrith, pointing at the scene that began to unfold before them. In the direction that the woman had indicated, the thin clouds began to darken and swirl.

Upon seeing the new phenomenon, Gelderand's eyes widened and his mouth dropped open in shock. "He wouldn't …" mumbled the mage in disbelief.

Swinkle witnessed Gelderand's reaction. "Please, Gelderand, tell us what this man is trying to do!"

"He's attempting to destroy the city," said the magician, never removing his stare from the scene. Gelderand took purposeful steps toward the harbor. "We must stop him now!"

Not bothering to look back at his friends, the elder man walked directly toward his adversary, wielding a mighty staff of his own.

"Where are you going?" lamented Marissa, but the girl received no answer. The female warriors then focused their attention on Swinkle.

The young cleric shook his head, then said, "Follow him!"

Catching up to the elder man, the three people allowed the mage to remain in the lead. Lance scurried by their side, completing the not-so-intimidating show of force.

Allard's apprentice saw the approaching group first and alerted his superior. The wizard motioned with his head, signaling his young magician to handle the intruders.

When Gelderand and his friends advanced to within a hundred feet of their position, the man thrust a hand in their direction and yelled, "Proceed no further or face the consequences!"

Gelderand came to a halt, gesturing for his friends to do likewise. Without looking back, he said in a hushed tone, "Allow me to handle this situation. I don't know about this person, but the man in the water possesses formidable magical abilities."

"What are you going to do?" asked Swinkle with concern.

"I have not figured that out yet," said Gelderand, and with that comment, he proceeded to leave his friends behind and move closer to the other magicians.

After some thought, Harrison knew exactly how he needed to proceed with his current predicament. With an air of confidence, he said, "I have to believe that Meredith and Tara are still alive and both are being held captive inside the mansion. Therefore, we will not storm the complex; I'll go in alone."

Octavius shook his head and Caidan threw his hands up into the air, both Forge Brothers in obvious disagreement with the young warrior's plan.

"You can't be serious," lamented Bracken.

"Why don't we allow Harrison to further outline his strategy," said Brendan, allowing his protégé a way to communicate his plan.

The young warrior nodded, then began with his reasoning. "It's a given that Nigel will not surrender, and he knows that we know that. He also understands that we want the women alive. I think I can convince him to hand over the ladies … and give him a way to bow out gracefully."

"And how is that?" said Caidan with more than a tinge of sarcasm in his voice.

"I can't say for sure, but I'll know what to do when I get inside there."

"I have an idea," said a monotone voice from behind the men. Thoragaard stepped forward, continuing, "I will accompany you into the mansion."

Harrison shook his head. "No. Nigel will never allow for that."

"Agreed, but if he cannot see me, he will not know I am there."

"What do you mean, 'if he cannot see you'?"

"There is always another way to handle the situation. A simple illusion shall suffice."

"I think we should go, too," said Murdock. "There are enough men to handle any uprisings, but going in alone is not a good idea."

The illusionist concurred. "I can accommodate Kymbra and your friends, too."

Harrison faced Thoragaard. "Just what are you proposing?"

"Think of it as an invisibility haze," said the wizard. "Something that will distort the guards' eyes."

The young warrior pondered Thoragaard's proposal. If anyone could make that trick work, it would be him, thought Harrison. He then turned his attention to the battlefield leaders.

"I think I know what Nigel's thinking," said the young warrior.

Octavius folded his arms across his chest. "Enlighten us."

"Nigel must already have a plan in place to vacate his city," started Harrison. "It only makes sense. Why else would he run back to a place that can be completely surrounded?"

"Because he's an arrogant bastard, that's why," said the elder Forge. "He's waiting for us to attack and he's using those innocent women as bait."

Harrison agreed with Octavius' reasoning. "I agree, but something's telling me there's more to his actions."

"He's going to be pretty upset about losing his city," added Caidan.

"All the more reason for his bargaining stance," said the young warrior. "But I must deal with him. He's waiting for me."

"What do you want us to do while you're inside with Nigel?" asked Brendan, accepting the young man's fate with the simple question.

"Hold your ground, and don't allow anyone to enter the mansion until I return with Tara and Meredith."

"And how long shall we wait?" asked Brendan. Everyone else looked on, waiting for the answer.

Harrison shook his head, unsure. "I'll leave that decision to you. Just please allow me the opportunity to make this situation right."

Brendan drew a heavy sigh and glanced to his equals. Octavius and Caidan shook their heads, reluctantly accepting the news, while Bracken shrugged in unenthusiastic compliance.

"Do what you feel you must," said Brendan, "but we're not going to wait a lifetime while you negotiate with Nigel. In the end, it'll be our call to storm the residency."

"I understand," said Harrison. "Now, let's figure out how we're going to reveal our desires to the Concurians."

The main group of liberators then went about discussing the task of relaying their intentions to Lord Hammer.

Gelderand kept a wary eye on the man in front of him while he stared at the wizard in the water. Swinkle, Marissa, and Adrith, along with Lance, waited in anxious anticipation of what might happen next.

"My good sir," said Gelderand in the wizard's direction, "what are you trying to prove?"

Allard took his gaze to Gelderand and, upon seeing his face, flashed a wicked smile. "Well, well, well, if it's not Gelderand the Great! You've decided to finally leave your little village of Tigris, I see!"

"Allard?" said Gelderand, his eyes wide in shock. "I'm not at all surprised to see you here today!"

Gelderand tried to suppress his emotions concerning Allard, not wishing to reveal his true feelings to the dark wizard. The magician recalled the time, many years ago, when he had set out to uncover the Ancient Scrolls of Arcadia. While trekking near the Empire Mountains, Gelderand and his friends encountered a large platoon of men that included Allard the Magnificent, his namesake at the time. Allard's band of warriors overmatched Gelderand's team and forced them to divulge all of the secrets that they had uncovered. After days of torture and imprisonment, the leaders of Allard's squad had extracted as much information about the elusive scripture as they could from Gelderand's party and left them to die. Fortunately, three of the men, including Gelderand, survived the ordeal. Gelderand then returned to his residence in Tigris where he took on a greater mission – Tara's caretaker. However, he never forgot the man who now stood before him.

Allard continued to steady his staff, swirling clouds turning darker above him with every passing second. "You should have remained in your quaint village."

Gelderand gazed at the sky. "Why are you doing this, Allard? What possible reward could Nigel Hammer have offered to you?"

"That is none of your business," said the dark wizard, avoiding the questions.

Gelderand watched as the clouds began to gather high above Allard's head, twisting into the shape of a funnel. With concern in his voice, the mage said, "You must stop this, Allard, before it's too late."

"I'm doing my part for Concur," said Allard, struggling to keep his staff in the water.

Gelderand, a six and a half foot staff in his own hand, took a step toward Allard. The dark wizard's apprentice tried to halt his progress.

"Not another step," said the younger man.

"I will only ask you to move aside once," said Gelderand, continuing his advancement with a firm grip on his weapon.

Allard's apprentice clasped his hands together and began to mumble something inaudible. Gelderand, recognizing that the young man was preparing a spell, took the opportunity to try to stop him. The older man, still a bit apprehensive about using his magical device with powers still unknown, maneuvered his staff before him, then flicked his wrist, forcing the wooden rod toward the younger wizard. The staff's head transformed into that of a dragon and in a split second, the beast roared and spewed fire toward the unsuspecting man.

The Concurian halted his chant and tried to defend himself, but the scorching wave of heat more than startled him. Flames ignited his dark blue robe, and he used his bare hands in an attempt to pat out the blaze.

Noticing the young man's vulnerable state, Marissa and Adrith sprinted from their position and forced the magician into the water, where they dunked him to extinguish the flames. The two warriors then apprehended Allard's apprentice, twisting his arms behind his back and guiding him out of the harbor.

Swinkle, witnessing the whole scene from the shore, waited for the women to bring the man to dry ground before aiding with his wounds. With Allard's apprentice detained, Gelderand proceeded to advance toward his primary target.

Allard had witnessed the event, but paid little attention; rather he continued his current task. With a gaze upward, both wizards noticed that a perfectly formed funnel cloud began its slow descent to the ground.

"It's all but over now," said Allard. "Soon this city will be flooded and your pathetic insurrection will be over."

Gelderand positioned his weapon to strike again. "Allard, stop this insanity! Are the deaths of thousands of innocent Concurians worth your position in Lord Hammer's ranks?"

For the first time, Allard felt a pang of doubt. His relationship with Nigel was tempered, at best. Moreover, he knew he could not trust him. However, over the years Lord Hammer remained the only person who could deliver the promise of armies, supplies, and money that allowed him to scour the land for any relic he wished to find.

Pushing Gelderand's comment to the back of his mind, Allard said, "It's too late. So be it."

The magician frowned, hoping that his plea could sway the dark wizard's mind. Gelderand gripped his staff tighter and wondered if the next flick of his wrist would yield another formidable beast. The magical item he had uncovered as part of the Treasure of the Land had intrigued him, but its random nature made his threats veiled at best. However, the current situation forced him to trust in the weapon's powers.

Gelderand pointed the staff in Allard's direction, yielding another creature's form at the wooden tip. The Concurian watched his nemesis's actions before laughing aloud.

Maintaining his grip on his own magical weapon, Allard shouted, "Is that a nice furry rabbit you have ready to attack me?"

Gelderand glanced at the critter resting at the staff's point. The mage strained his eyes and determined that the creature's fur had more of a coarseness associated with it, rather than a rabbit's fur coating. He then slowly lifted the weapon and, as he did, sharp quills protruded from under the soft-looking coat.

Allard witnessed the weapon's transformation, his eyes widening at the sight of the projectiles pointed in his direction.

Gelderand flicked his wrist again and this time the porcupine shot its quills toward the defenseless wizard.

A volley of fifty quills, one foot in length, hurtled through the air and hit their mark, easily penetrating the human's tender skin. Allard howled in pain as projectile after projectile pierced his body; each had a barbarous tip lodging it in place.

Gelderand watched the dark wizard release his grip on his staff and fall into the water. The mage's eyes then focused on a still ominous sight - Allard's weapon remained in place, summoning the dark funnel cloud to its point.

While the Unified Army's leadership pondered how they would approach Lord Hammer's mansion, Caidan Forge took his gaze to the skyline behind his friends.

His eyes round, the Argosian pointed into the distance, saying, "Look at what's happening over there!"

Harrison and the others swiveled their heads in the direction Caidan pointed, each one sporting the same shocked expression.

"What in the world?" said Harrison, unsure of the new phenomenon.

Black clouds were beginning to swirl near Concur's harbor, rotating tighter and forming a definable funnel cloud.

"That's not natural!" exclaimed Bracken. "We need to investigate this before something bad happens!"

"What about Nigel?" asked Harrison. The young warrior had finally entered the walled city, persuaded scores of Concurians to join their cause, and surrounded the government complex with his Unified Army. Now, a strange occurrence hindered his next step.

"We'll take care of this situation," said Octavius, taking his line of sight to Caidan and Bracken. "You two need to handle entering that mansion and bringing Lord Hammer out."

"Octavius is right," said Brendan, weighing in his thoughts. "Take as many men as you need and leave the rest to surround the building."

The elder Forge nodded in the Aegean's direction, then started pointing at platoons of men. "Make haste to the harbor! Go, now!"

The men Octavius indicated turned on their heels and started to run to the opposite side of the city. Bracken then ordered Arcadian troops to help with the new mission. Leaving more than enough men behind to aid Harrison's cause, Octavius, Caidan, and Bracken then proceeded to follow their men.

Harrison and Brendan held their ground, watching roughly five hundred soldiers race toward the northern part of the city. The elder Aegean broke the tension.

"Time to concentrate on our task," said Brendan.

The young warrior looked over at Thoragaard and his friends. Addressing the illusionist, he asked, "How should we proceed?"

"Send over a few men to the mansion and tell them that we wish to speak to Nigel alone," said Thoragaard. "That will at least initiate the dialogue process."

"We'll relay the message," said Murdock, jerking his thumb in Pondle's direction.

"I'm going, too," said Kymbra, glaring at the ranger for leaving her out of his plans.

The young warrior smiled. "I was hoping that I didn't have to ask you to do this."

"You should know me by now," said Murdock with a smile. "What do you want us to tell Nigel? Surrender or die?"

Harrison raised his palms in the ranger's direction. "No! We're not going to give him ultimatums just yet!"

Murdock smirked. "I'm joking. You need to calm down a bit, Harrison."

The young warrior nodded, flashing a sheepish smile. "Just tell those sentries that we want to have proof that Tara and Meredith are alive and well. Once that's confirmed, we'll take the next step."

"And that is?"

"We'll talk about the terms of their release."

The ranger gave his friend a single nod. "Easy enough." Taking his gaze to Pondle and Kymbra, he said, "Ready to go?"

Both fighters nodded yes. "We'll be back soon," said Murdock. With a wave of his hand, the trio proceeded to leave the army behind and made their trek to Lord Hammer's compound.

Harrison watched the three people depart, while his thoughts drifted to Tara. The young warrior envisioned her blue eyes, soft skin, and blond hair and, at that moment, realized just how much he loved and missed her. With his heart pounding, the young warrior waited as his friends performed their task.

CHAPTER 32

¤

The rumbling sound of approaching footsteps began to permeate the area. Swinkle, Lance, and everyone else near the harbor turned their heads to see platoons of men storming their position. Meanwhile, even though he had neutralized Allard, Gelderand knew that he had not completed his task just yet.

The magician watched the dark wizard howl in pain from the deadly quills, trying to keep his head above water at the same time. All the while, Allard's staff continued to summon the funnel cloud to the ground.

Gelderand dropped his own rod and sprinted into the cool waters, heading straight for the ailing mage. At the same time, members of the Unified Army reached their location.

Swinkle witnessed the confused expressions on the faces of the soldiers before recognizing the Forge brothers. "Octavius! Caidan!" yelled the young cleric as he approached the leaders.

"Please tell me what's going on here!" said Octavius, flanked by his brother and Bracken Drake.

"Can we stop whatever is about to happen?" asked the Arcadian.

"I don't know what Allard is planning," started Swinkle, who turned and glanced at the funnel cloud, "but I don't like what I see."

"Whatever's happening seems to be caused by that stick," said Caidan, pointing to the magical item.

Octavius concurred with a nod and pointed to three soldiers. "Pull that thing out of the water!" The three men heeded their superior's order and rushed into the awaiting harbor.

"Are you sure that's a good idea?" asked Bracken, but before anyone could say otherwise, the three men tried to grab the staff.

As they made contact with the weapon, a bright flash emanated from the wooden object, violently repelling the men from the stationary item. To everyone's horror, the dark cloud continued its downward spiral like an evil finger from the heavens above.

Gelderand witnessed the soldiers' failed attempt at destroying the staff. Having prevented Allard from drowning, the mage waded over to the men who floated in the water. Upon reaching them, he found all three dead. A pit forming in his stomach, the magician waded back to Allard.

Shaking, cold, and in pain, Allard did his best to remain standing. Gelderand searched for a place devoid of quills to lay his hands on the wizard. Finding open spots near his shoulders, Gelderand grabbed Allard and stared into his eyes.

"You must stop this madness now!"

Allard tried to push the pain out of his mind. "Or what?"

Gelderand suppressed his desire to force this man's head under the water for good. Glancing upwards, the magician found that the tornado had almost reached its landing point.

"Stop this violent act and I'll remove the quills from your body," said Gelderand.

The mage then placed a hand on one of the quills near Allard's shoulder blade, applying pressure. The barb twisted deeper into the wizard's body, bringing tears to the man's eyes, the pain excruciating.

"Stop!" screamed Allard. "I'm begging you!"

"Revoke this spell!" Gelderand pushed a bit harder, dropping the man to his knees.

"I'll break the spell if you take me to the mansion," said Allard.

Gelderand crinkled his brow. "The mansion? Why there?"

"If I'm going to be handed over to anyone, it must be Meredith, not Nigel."

The magician pulled his nemesis out of the water and back onto his feet. Moving his face to within inches of Allard's, Gelderand said, "Break the spell and you will have your wish."

"You'll remove the quills, too?"

"Stop this tornado before it destroys everything!"

Unbeknownst to Gelderand, Allard smirked, getting the very wish he had hoped to bargain for. Shuffling gingerly toward the pole, the wizard placed two hands on the staff and began to mumble to himself.

All eyes watched as the waterspout swirled closer to the targeted endpoint. Allard suppressed his pain and strained to get the words out of his mouth. Suddenly, bolts of electricity erupted from the wizard's hands, ran up the staff and into the sky, zipping past the approaching funnel and into the darkening cloud cover. Bright flashes appeared in all directions, followed by a violent crash of thunder. Pounding rain then began to soak the area.

Gelderand watched with baited breath as Allard continued his chant. He gazed up at the tornado, its funnel spinning faster, and at that moment a hollow feeling coursed through his body as he wondered if Allard had reneged on his deal.

Seconds later, another flash erupted from the dark wizard's position, this time sending electricity toward the evil finger. The surge brought howling winds along with it, which in turn neutralized the approaching funnel, disrupting its downward descent and causing it to recoil back into the black clouds. Allard stopped his chant and rested his weary head on the stationary pole, his task complete. Rain continued to pound the area.

Gelderand came to Allard's side and, determining that he had indeed negated the evil spell, maneuvered the exhausted individual away from the staff. As Allard waded toward the shore, Gelderand retrieved his own staff, as well as his adversary's magical item, and kept them both close.

Swinkle, along with the others, waited for the men to leave the cool waters and reach dry land.

"What shall we do with him?" asked the young cleric over the din of the rain, while Octavius, Caidan, and Bracken corralled their men.

"We need to remove these quills before he dies on us," said Gelderand.

Allard's soaked body shivered, and with each shake, shooting pains darted throughout him. "A blanket, please," he said through ragged breaths.

The young cleric retrieved the item from his pack and draped it over the broken man's shoulders.

Allard made eye contact with the young cleric, and in a shallow voice, said, "Thank you."

Before Swinkle could begin attending to the dark wizard, a woman wearing a cloak similar to his approached. "Brother Swinkle," started Sister Martel, "might your brethren help with your cause."

The young cleric gazed back wide-eyed. "Will the soldiers suffer if you cease your prayer in order to help me?"

The Robusite smiled. "We have attained our goal. Pious has watched us succeed in entering this city, providing assistance to these brave men. Our services are complete; we can now assist you."

Swinkle smiled back, realizing that his brothers and sisters from Robus indeed influenced the outcome of the battle. "I would be honored to work with you, Sister."

As Swinkle set about instructing his fellow clerics in regards to healing Allard, as well as any other soldier with wounds, the Unified Army leaders stopped them in their tracks.

Octavius brought his focus on Gelderand. "Fine job, my good sir, but he's our prisoner now," said the warrior, moving toward Allard.

Gelderand furrowed his brow. "I promised him that he would meet Meredith, and she would decide his fate."

"Not until Meredith is liberated," said the elder Argosian, extending his hand in an attempt to grab the wizard.

Gelderand blocked Octavius' effort. "A valid point, but I also promised to remove the quills. It is a pledge I intend to keep."

"Fine," said the Argosian leader, "but as soon as you're finished healing him, he becomes our prisoner. And, there's no negotiating that point."

Gelderand took a moment to think, the only sound being the pounding rain. "Only until we liberate Meredith."

Octavius gestured for twenty of his soldiers to surround the robed men and Robusite clerics. "We'll discuss that with Harrison and the rest of the leadership." Making eye contact with his men, the Argosian said, "Accompany these magicians and," pointing at Allard, "don't let this man out of your sight."

Gelderand accepted his fate for now, acquiescing his position to Octavius, and joined the procession of fighters, clerics, and prisoners to the Governor's mansion.

Several minutes passed before Murdock, Pondle, and Kymbra returned with their valuable news. "No one enters the mansion except you," said the ranger, pointing at Harrison. "Lord Hammer's orders, or so his guardians say."

Harrison had anticipated this move on Nigel's part. Turning to face Brendan, the young warrior said, "Then I must appear to go in alone." All eyes then focused on Thoragaard.

"My illusion will work," he began in his monotone way, "just be sure that the doorway remains open long enough to let us enter."

Murdock shook his head. "I don't like the sounds of this. You're making it seem too easy."

"I have to agree," said Harrison. The young warrior motioned with his head in the complex's direction. "Plus, the soldiers will be watching us and track our every movement."

Thoragaard raised a hand. "We shall file within the ranks of our soldiers, I will enact the spell, then we will follow you to the building."

Brendan remained skeptical. "Your bodies will still occupy space, no?"

"That is true," answered the magician.

"Then it's possible for Nigel's sentries to impede your progress."

"That is also true."

The Aegean leader shook his head. "This is too risky. If Nigel's men sense we're planning something, they'll react."

Thoragaard shrugged. "It is a risk we must take."

"And just what do you hope to accomplish by being inside with Harrison?"

"To aid in apprehending Nigel, liberate Meredith, and give freedom back to Concur's people."

Brendan smirked. "You know Nigel as well as I do; he won't relinquish control that easily."

"That's why I must be the person to speak with him," said Harrison. Taking his attention to the illusionist, he said, "Thoragaard, do what you must to prepare your spell. I want to leave as soon as we can."

The mage nodded, then gestured for the others to follow him into the ranks of the soldiers. When he felt that he had infiltrated the men enough, he motioned for Murdock, Pondle, and Kymbra to huddle together.

"I will remain invisible at all times, but you must stay close together throughout this spell or you will be seen," said Thoragaard.

"How close do you mean?" asked Pondle with concern. The last thing they needed was for Concurian soldiers to foil their plan before it had time to gel.

"No more than ten feet away from me, in any direction," said the magician.

"Can we draw our weapons?" asked Murdock, recalling that Gelderand's ring allowed the wearer to remain invisible until he removed his weaponry.

"Yes, but all sounds will still be audible."

Pondle squinted. "Can others sense our presence?"

"Yes."

Murdock gazed at the large double doors that acted as the entrance into the mansion. "How are we all going to squeeze through that doorway without being detected?"

"We'll just be careful," said Kymbra, getting tired of hearing all of the negative possibilities. "Thoragaard, do what you must and tell us how to proceed."

The illusionist placed himself in the middle of the small grouping, then muttered something aloud. Seconds later, a translucent sphere engulfed him and the startled trio, extending to a ten-foot radius from the mage. Another few seconds passed and all disappeared from view.

"Harrison," said Thoragaard's voice from apparent nothingness, "lead us to Lord Hammer's mansion."

The young warrior glanced at Brendan, who nodded, indicating that it was indeed time to leave. Harrison took a moment to reflect on the journey that had brought him to Concur. He and his friends laid his brother to rest, trekked across the countryside to spread the good news about their discovery of the Treasure of the Land, formed a unified alliance with the villages and towns, and now stood on the precipice of completing his goodwill mission.

However, Nigel Hammer had different ideas. Imprisoned in the structure before him, his love Tara and the heir apparent to the great walled city, Meredith, awaited the young warrior's visit. The time had finally come.

Harrison met Brendan's anxious gaze. "I'm ready to finish what I have started. The end of Nigel Hammer's reign starts now."

With determination in his eye, the young warrior began his march to the governor's complex, followed by a quartet of invisible friends.

Lord Hammer paced inside his master bedroom, frequently sending a menacing glare at the two women who watched his every move. A sudden knock at the door stopped him in his tracks.

"What is it?" hissed Nigel, his head cocked toward the portal.

"I have important information for you, sir," said the voice from the other side.

The Concurian leader unlocked the door and exited the room, leaving Meredith and Tara behind to wonder at the importance of the visit.

"Sir," began the sentry, "Harrison Cross has sent an envoy to understand the terms of our discussions. The guards sent them away with the message that only Harrison is allowed to enter the building."

Lord Hammer nodded. "Has he arrived?"

"Indications are that he is on his way."

Nigel turned away in thought. A moment later, he turned back to the sentry and said, "I'm counting on you when the time comes. You'll be handsomely rewarded for your loyalty."

The soldier stood tall, shoulders back, his chest out, proud. "It is my honor to serve you, sir."

"Has anyone seen Allard?"

"Last report placed him at the harbor in the north end of the city."

Lord Hammer glared at his sentry, a scowl on his face. "Something has gone wrong. There should be more chaos, not just rain."

"I'm sure there's a reasonable explanation, sir," said the sentry, hoping to put his superior at ease.

"Escort Harrison to this room when he arrives," said Nigel. "Him and him alone."

"It will be done, my lord," said the soldier.

Nigel then returned to his room of seclusion, latching the door behind him.

Harrison made his cautious approach to the governor's mansion, knowing that his invisible friends trekked close behind. About a hundred Concurian soldiers stood before the young warrior, blocking his way to the building. As he advanced closer, the men slowly moved out of his way, all the while keeping a close eye on this intruder.

The young warrior recalled the time when he had visited Concur's pristine complex only several months ago. At that time, he had searched for clues to the Sacred Seven Rooms, which Meredith relayed to him. He envisioned her dark hair and radiant blue eyes, as well as the pain that she harbored in her soul. Now, along with his love, the First Lady awaited her liberation and Harrison was not about to let her down.

Harrison and his unseen friends walked up the staircase that led to the entranceway. Again, guardians with weapons drawn stood before him. Just as the young warrior reached the top stoop, several Concurians swarmed to his position.

The young warrior raised his hands. "I'm here to speak with Lord Hammer!" Harrison's eyes darted and his heart raced, wondering how the sentries had not detected his friends with their swift maneuvers.

"We're taking your weapons," snarled a guard, while another removed Harrison's battle-axe and other assorted blades from his person.

"Don't do anything stupid," barked a third sentry. "You'll see the governor soon enough."

When the soldiers had taken all of his weaponry, two guards pushed him forward toward the double doorway. Two more guardians blocked his final hurdle into the complex.

The guard to Harrison's left said, "Someone will escort you to Lord Hammer." The man stepped closer to the young warrior, his face inches from Harrison. "If you try to harm Lord Hammer in any way, you will be killed."

The man let his comment linger for a moment before gesturing to his comrade to open the large, wooden doors.

Thoragaard witnessed the portals opening and moved forward. Kymbra followed, but the guards' actions hindered Murdock and Pondle's advancement. Knowing that they had to maintain their tight configuration, the ranger made an ill-advised move.

A sentry at the top of the stairs felt his body shoved. A quizzical expression graced his face as he searched for the reason. Taking a step in Harrison's direction caused the man to cross Murdock's path, forcing the ranger and Pondle to stop in their tracks. A second later, the Concurians' actions breached their minimum distance threshold. All eyes stared at the two men and attractive female who appeared out of nothingness.

"What is the meaning of this?" shouted a guard, and without a moment to spare, soldiers swarmed the intruders' position.

The two guards who had blocked the main entrance shoved Harrison inside the mansion, while the other soldiers apprehended Murdock, Pondle, and Kymbra. Thoragaard remained unseen.

The lead guardian ordered the doorway shut, then pointed to the adjacent room off the main foyer.

"Take them in there and bind them," he ordered in regards to Murdock, Pondle, and Kymbra. "When you're finished with that, secure them away."

Five sentries heeded their superior's orders, and the lead man brought his attention back to Harrison.

"You're coming with me," said the Concurian as he led the young warrior toward the spiral staircase.

Harrison could only wonder what would happen to him now and, furthermore, he had no idea of Thoragaard's whereabouts.

Brendan witnessed the sudden turn of events and tempered his desire to storm the complex.

"What shall we do, sir?" asked an anxious soldier, observing the same scene.

The Aegean gritted his teeth. "Nothing," he said. "Harrison's on his own now."

Before he could put more thought into the matter, a cadre of soldiers approached his position. Brendan turned to face the men who had investigated the phenomenon on the other side of Concur, the Aegean happy to see the faces of their leaders.

"Is Harrison inside the mansion," asked Bracken, reaching his equal.

"That he is," answered Brendan, taking his gaze to the structure. Changing the subject, he asked, "Did all go well?"

Octavius Forge heard the question and responded, "For us, yes." He gestured over to the limp man, full of quills that Gelderand and Swinkle held up. "Him, not so much."

"What in the world happened?" asked Brendan with wide eyes.

"Let's just say he lost the battle of wizards," said Caidan with a smirk. "But, he's still responsible for the rain."

The Aegean looked over the broken man, then called to Gelderand, "Can you heal him? I have a feeling that he's going to be an important bargaining chip later."

The mage made eye contact with Swinkle, who nodded yes. "We will do our best," said Gelderand.

Satisfied with the magician's answer, Brendan brought his focus back to the mansion and in a loud voice said, "Now we wait."

CHAPTER 33

¤

Two of Lord Hammer's guards forced Murdock, Pondle, and Kymbra into the study off the main foyer and one of them pushed the ranger to the floor.

"Just what do you think you were trying to accomplish?" shouted a sentry. "Sneaking into the governor's mansion under a veil of secrecy to boot!"

The man then took his heavy foot and kicked the defenseless human in the ribs. Murdock buckled and winced in pain.

"That's uncalled for!" said Kymbra in the ranger's defense. "You've captured us already; there's no need to beat us!"

Another Concurian grabbed Kymbra's forearm and swiveled her to face him. "We make the rules, woman! Keep your mouth shut and we'll see what happens."

The female warrior was not about to let the guardian get the best of her. Jerking her arm from his grip, she said, "Take your hands off me!" Kymbra then instinctively reached for her weapon. Two guards saw her actions and pounced on the woman, preventing her from using her sword.

"Bad idea!" yelled the sentry in front of her, unsheathing his blade in the process. The man then used the butt of his weapon to strike Kymbra on the side of her head. The force of the blow rendered her unconscious.

Pondle came to Kymbra's defense, but his efforts proved futile as well. More of Lord Hammer's men grabbed the thief, using their fists to deliver punch after punch to the overmatched halfling.

Another soldier grabbed Murdock from the floor, lifting him to his feet. Several men then began to beat him as well. After a short time, all three intruders lay bloody and motionless on the floor.

The lead guardian ordered his men to stop. Gesturing to one of his comrades, he said, "Bind and lock them away."

As his men heeded his task, the leader noticed bloodstains on the flooring and finely woven carpet. "Fetch someone from the mansion's staff and have them clean this mess. You know how Lord Hammer likes his things."

Another man ran off to perform that task, while sentries dragged Murdock, Pondle, and Kymbra to their new holding place.

Lord Hammer's men hurriedly ushered Harrison up the spiral staircase and to the second floor. One of the guards leaned hard on the young warrior, telling him, "Lord Hammer will learn about your misconception."

"That wasn't my intent!" lamented Harrison.

"Tell that to Lord Hammer!"

As Nigel's men led Harrison further into the mansion's depths, the young warrior found more soldiers milling about the second floor. He has the girls very well protected, thought the young warrior. The sentry forced Harrison to an abrupt halt, interrupting his thinking.

A couple of doorways away stood two sentries. The man controlling Harrison beckoned one to come over. "Tell Lord Hammer that Harrison Cross has arrived and that he tried to sneak others into the complex with him."

The guard nodded once and departed for the room. Knocking, he said, "Sir, might I have a word with you."

The young warrior heard a muffled voice say, "Come in."

Harrison's heart pounded for he knew the ramifications of this very important visit. The love of his life, along with the next ruler of Concur, awaited his arrival just a few yards away while Nigel Hammer remained firmly in his path. After what seemed like an eternity, the guardian exited the room, glanced at his comrade, and gestured with his finger to bring Harrison to the doorway.

Upon reaching the entrance, the guard clenched his teeth and told Harrison, "If you so much look at Lord Hammer the wrong way, we'll storm the room and apprehend you."

The young warrior swallowed and nodded in concurrence. The guard, determining that Harrison understood his demands, opened the door and allowed the young warrior to enter the room.

Harrison took a step forward and the door behind him slammed shut, the guard locking the portal in the process. The young warrior had anticipated a conflict, but he was not ready for what stood before him.

Nigel, clad in his black armor, clutched Tara against his body, a knife planted against her pale throat. Tears formed in the young maiden's eyes, the sudden contrast of fear over the current situation and joy at seeing Harrison overwhelming her. Meredith remained on the other side of the room, the course of events tapping her resolve.

Lord Hammer broke the uncomfortable silence. "So nice to see you again, Harrison." Squinting and focusing on the young warrior's striped eyes, he asked, "Is that color now called Resistance blue?"

The young warrior brushed off Nigel's comment. Squinting, he pointed and said, "Release her!"

"You're not in any position to make demands!"

"There's an army surrounding your mansion as we speak and if I don't return, they'll storm the compound."

"Tara will be dead well before they could make it to this room," said Nigel in a cold tone. "We have much to talk about, like why you didn't come alone?"

Harrison raised his palms. "That was a mistake," he lied. "I didn't know they were following me."

"Well, you should have!" barked Nigel, pressing the blade a bit tighter, causing Tara to gasp.

"Please, take the knife away from her throat. She has nothing to do with us anyway."

Nigel furrowed his brow. "Nothing at all? Did you not send her into my city to infiltrate my people! To send a message to her!" Lord Hammer pointed the dagger in Meredith's direction, before returning it to Tara's soft skin with a rapid jerk.

Harrison shook his head, realizing that he was losing the argument. Spreading his arms wide, he said, "All right, I'm guilty of that. It's my fault, not Tara's or Meredith's."

"Don't even bring that traitor into the conversation." Nigel scowled at the mention of his woman's name. "You're lucky that I've allowed both of them to live for so long."

Harrison knew the time for diplomacy had come. "Be that as it may, we need to figure out where we go from here."

"Precisely," said Lord Hammer. "Remove your people from my city and I'll let Tara go."

Meredith had sat patiently, allowing the dialogue between the two men to take shape, but upon hearing the governor's demand, she said, "Nigel, you can't be serious! You've lost the battle! Let Tara go before you do something foolish!"

Lord Hammer glared at the First Lady. "I don't lose, Meredith!"

"And you're not going to win, either!"

Harrison took the moment to gaze at Tara, seeing the fear in her eyes, the sadness in her soul, and the longing to be in his arms, safe from danger.

"Nigel, take me as your prisoner and let the women go free."

Lord Hammer smirked. "Nice try, boy, but Meredith is the one who holds the most weight in this room as far as my people are concerned." Letting his glare linger another moment, he repeated, "Pull back your army."

Murdock's head pounded and his wrists ached. Gathering his bearings, he found himself with his hands bound behind his back and laying against Kymbra. The ranger wiggled himself away from the unconscious female warrior, noticing that someone had bound her as well.

The ranger squinted, searching the small, dark room for signs of life. He maneuvered to the right and gasped, a sharp pain piercing his side. His newfound wound throbbed and he almost passed out from his anguish. Gathering himself, he took care in attempting his task again.

Kymbra lay on the ground next to him. To the ranger's left, a few feet away, rested Pondle, not moving either. Just like Murdock, all members of the party had their hands tied behind their backs.

The ranger gazed over his right shoulder to the small window that shed a sliver of light through its closed shutters. Using the small beam as best he could, he discovered that he lay in a small supply room. He then figured the time had come to try to awaken his friends.

"Pondle," called Murdock, a shade above a whisper. The thief did not respond. Frustrated, the ranger brought his attention to the woman on the ground next to him.

"Kymbra," he whispered again, to no avail.

Realizing that calling his friends would be fruitless, he carefully moved his body near Kymbra's and pushed against her backside. Still, the woman remained motionless.

His frustrations getting the better of him, Murdock attempted to shove Kymbra harder, only to find himself losing control of his body, and he slumped on top of the warrior. The sudden jolt woke the woman from her haze.

The female fighter twisted her neck over her shoulder, finding Murdock gazing back at her.

Woozy, she said, "What happened?"

"I'm not sure," said Murdock. "Pondle's over there." The ranger used his head to point in the opposite direction.

Kymbra instinctively tried to rise, but found her hands bound and was unable to move. She then noticed Murdock's proximity to her.

With a huff, she said, "Get off me!"

"Trust me, if I could I would," said the ranger, wincing as he tried to maneuver away from Kymbra. Panting, he stopped his futile attempt.

"I think one of my ribs is broken," said Murdock. "I need to find Swinkle."

The blonde warrior took her gaze about her surroundings. After gathering as much of the information that the room presented her, she said, "We must still be in the mansion."

Murdock nodded. "I think you're right. The floors aren't made of stone like the prison ones are."

"The question is where are we?" Kymbra raised her upper body off the floor, allowing Murdock to slip off her.

"Hey!" said the ranger. "What do you think you're doing?"

The female did not remove her stare from the closed door. "We need to know what's behind that portal."

"I'm sure it's guarded!" said Murdock. "We need to remove our bonds before doing anything else."

"You're right." Kymbra gestured with her head to the pantry supplies. "I think we're near the kitchen area."

"Probably," answered the ranger with a nod. "What do you think happened to Harrison and Thoragaard?"

Kymbra shook her head. "I don't know." She then maneuvered to a sitting position and away from Murdock, leaving only her back to him.

"Try to get over to me," said the woman. "If we put our backs against one another, we might be able to work on each other's bonds."

Murdock understood exactly what Kymbra meant. "Good idea!"

The ranger squirmed against the floor until he reached the wall. He tried to rotate into the proper position, but instead winced and slipped into Kymbra's backside.

Exasperated, the woman spun her head around as far as it could go and said, "What in the world are you doing back there?"

"This injury hurts a lot more than you think," said Murdock.

Tapping into his inner strength, he blocked the pain from his mind and spun around, wiggling close to Kymbra, their backs touching.

"We're in place," said the female, "try to release my bonds and I'll do the same to yours."

Murdock's fingers searched for Kymbra's twine, but instead he felt her hands. To his surprise, he found them soft and inviting.

"Stay on task," said Kymbra.

The ranger closed his eyes and shook his head, concentrating on the binding and not her touch. Murdock carefully searched the rope, finding a bulge.

"I got the knot!" he exclaimed. "Move a little closer to the left so that I can use both hands." Kymbra obliged.

The ranger fondled the twine, trying to loosen the knot in the process. After a couple minutes of fidgeting with the binding, Murdock succeeded in untying Kymbra's rope.

After Murdock relaxed the fastenings enough for Kymbra to wiggle her hands free, she quickly removed the twine. The woman rolled her wrists in an attempt to loosen her muscles, then went to freeing Murdock. A minute later, both hostages were liberated.

"Untie him," said Kymbra in reference to Pondle. "I'll investigate our surroundings."

Before the female warrior could commence her search, she heard several muffled groans from behind the doorway. She stared at Murdock with wide eyes, neither one sure what just happened beyond the portal. Then, without any resistance, the door to their temporary shelter opened.

Kymbra beamed when she saw the face of their liberator. "Thoragaard!" she exclaimed. "We were wondering what had happened to you!"

The illusionist put everyone at ease with a wave of his hand. "Is everyone all right?"

"Not really," said Murdock, favoring his side. "We're all beat up pretty bad. That typically happens when you're left to fend for yourself."

"I am sorry about leaving you vulnerable," said the mage, "but I could not compromise my position."

"We could've been killed!" said the ranger, scowling at the magician. Thoragaard nodded, accepting the fact that Murdock did not appreciate his actions.

Wincing, the ranger bent down to shake Pondle. "Wake up!"

A moment later, the thief began to squirm, then tried to jump to his feet. His head still throbbing, Pondle stumbled and fell to one knee.

"What happened to us?" he asked to no one in particular.

"That is irrelevant now," said Thoragaard. "Soldiers have taken Harrison upstairs and I presume that he is speaking with Lord Hammer now."

"We need to help him," said Murdock, knowing all too well the dangers of being in an enemy compound.

"First, we must find the room where they are holding him and the ladies."

The ranger smiled. "Second floor, three doors down on your right." Murdock witnessed the mage's look of surprise and said, "We did our fair share of reconnaissance. I'm positive of their location."

"He's right," chimed Kymbra. "Gelderand used his cat to find their exact position. He also saw Tara and Meredith, and they appeared fine."

"Then we must hurry," said Thoragaard. "It is not out of the realm of possibilities for Lord Hammer to do something rash."

"Like hanging innocent people," sneered Murdock.

"Precisely."

Pondle, who had kept quiet for the time being, added his thoughts to the conversation. "Just what do you have in mind for us to do?"

Thoragaard pointed a finger in the air. "This is my intent. We must secure the mansion while Nigel is preoccupied with Harrison. If we can do that, then we can allow the Unified leaders access to the complex."

"Your intent?" said Murdock, not allowing the simple play on words to pass him by.

"The possibility does exist for things to go wrong, but I believe it is the best course of action."

The ranger glanced at Pondle, a smile appearing on both of their faces. Murdock, feeling that the diplomatic angle had long worn out its welcome, said with a smirk, "Give us the details and we'll make sure everything goes right."

While Thoragaard explained his intentions, Pondle went about gathering the weaponry used by the now incapacitated sentries. Finding only two swords, the thief handed one to Murdock and the other to Kymbra. Upon further examination, he found a dagger attached to one of the guard's belts, which he took for his own. Armed and ready for confrontation, the small group left the confines of their former cell behind and ventured deeper into the mansion.

"The armies aren't going anywhere," said Harrison, sensing an impasse in any dialogue with Lord Hammer.

"Then we have quite the dilemma," responded Nigel. "What is your next move?"

The young warrior had struggled with this problem ever since they embarked on their journey from Aegeus. Harrison knew that Nigel would never surrender, but he had promised Swinkle that he would give the Concurian leader every chance to relinquish control of his city without the use of force. However, swaying Nigel to his manner of thinking had proven more than difficult.

"I'm asking you for your surrender," said Harrison.

"My *surrender*?" snarled Nigel, holding the knife a tad tighter near Tara's throat. "That, boy, will never happen!"

The young maiden's chest heaved as she tried to hold back her tears. Harrison watched with a heavy heart, unable to help his love and running out of ideas for Nigel. To his surprise, an answer came from one of the women.

"Place Nigel into my custody," said Meredith. "What happens to him should be a Concurian matter and not one for the foreigners to judge."

Both Harrison and Lord Hammer's eyes met Meredith's. "I would agree to that," said the young warrior.

Nigel tried to keep his rage in check. Though he had not figured on his adversaries releasing him into his woman's custody, the idea was not a bad one. Meredith doesn't have the backbone to do anything rash, he rationalized. Furthermore, it would make his escape that much easier.

"And how would you handle your quaint little prosecution?" asked the dark lord, bitterness in his voice. "What courts would I be subjected to? And for what charges?"

"All that will be settled later," said the First Lady, rising from her seat. "For now, please let Tara go."

Nigel glared at Meredith. "Are you going to imprison me until you figure out your plan?"

The woman spread her arms wide. "What would you do if the roles were reversed? Actually, you've locked me and Tara away for well over a month already, haven't you?"

Lord Hammer pondered the arrangement. Meredith was right, he had sequestered the women for quite some time, and the only logical situation for Meredith would be to lock him away as well. But, for how long? Any length of time in the prison system he created would be unacceptable.

"Think harder," said Nigel. "I won't let anyone hold *me* hostage!"

Thoragaard performed his invisibility cloak once again to hide him and the others from detection. The illusionist had watched Lord Hammer's sentries attack, bind and lock away Kymbra, Murdock, and Pondle in an oversized closet. Waiting until the appropriate time, he surprised the two guards posted in front of the prisoners' doorway and rendered them unconscious. Now, he hoped his magic would allow them to reach Harrison before it was too late.

From inside their invisible shield, Thoragaard said, "Remember, we have the element of surprise right now. Sentries are on high alert while Harrison is in the mansion. Be quiet and follow my lead."

The foursome left the confines of the small hallway and began to head deeper into the mansion. Pondle, bringing up the rear, knew he was best suited for covert operations. Analyzing his surroundings, the thief surmised that the soldiers had taken them to a room off the kitchen, an area not heavily guarded.

Thoragaard reached the end of the corridor and peeked his head around the corner. He then raised a palm to his friends behind him, signaling them to stop.

In a whisper, the mage relayed, "The kitchen lies ahead of us and sentries are mingled in with the mansion staff. We must get to the second floor." Thoragaard raised a finger in the air.

"Remember, we are invisible to them. Stay close together and do not make a sound."

The magician waved his anxious team forward, each person moving as quietly as possible with their unfamiliar weapons drawn.

The ranger nearly lost his breath upon entering the kitchen. Lord Hammer's guardians had started to gather the staff, unaware that intruders had invaded their space. Four armed sentries mingled on the opposite side of the room, explaining to the nervous servants that foreigners now surrounded the building. Looks of shock and anxiety flashed across the staffers' faces, unsure of the next course of action.

Murdock felt a hand grab his arm from behind. His heart pounding, the ranger swiveled his head, finding Pondle pointing to the four figures, then to the doorway behind him. Murdock nodded, understanding the information his friend conveyed; they needed to pass the guards and enter the adjoining hallway.

The small procession kept their backs against the wall, trying their best to remain unseen. Murdock brought his eyes to the concerned man behind a large wooden carving table. The butcher began to remove his smock and readied himself to leave the area.

He really can't see me, thought the ranger, maintaining his stare on the man. His momentary lack of focus caused him not to see a low hanging fixture, which he bumped with his head. The iron candleholder jiggled, causing its flame to move and wax to drip.

The butcher, already in a heightened apprehensive state, stared at the fixture. The ranger witnessed the man frown, wondering if he had really seen the holder move. Deciding that he had not, the man brought his attention back to his fellow servants.

Murdock exhaled anxiously, knowing that he had spared the group for the time being. Maneuvering toward the exit took on a new challenge since the armored men near the doorway waved the kitchen staff forward, not allowing enough spacing for the party members to pass. With precious time ticking away, Thoragaard raised a hand to stop their procession, then he did the unthinkable.

Making a subtle hand gesture, the mage ended his spell, allowing everyone in the room to see them. Members of the mansion staff gasped and pointed at the intruders, while the sentries focused on their newfound enemy. Even Thoragaard's accomplices stared wide-eyed at the magician.

A sentry took the initiative, pointed his sword, and said, "Stay right there and don't move!" The man's comrades also unsheathed their weapons and began to advance on their new targets.

Thoragaard shifted his eyes, taking in his surroundings in the time it took for the soldiers to begin their advancement. Understanding the gravity of what he planned to do next, the mage looked to his friends and said, "Cover your ears and yell at the top of your lungs!"

Kymbra, Murdock, and Pondle did as instructed while Thoragaard clasped his hands together over his mouth, closed his eyes, and mumbled aloud. The befuddled Concurians stopped their approach upon hearing the foreigners' shouts.

The magician took only seconds to cast his spell and, upon completion, flew his hands open. A shockwave permeated the room, knocking over everyone and everything in the immediate area. All of the room's occupants dropped to the floor howling in pain, including Thoragaard's people.

Knowing that his latest trick would cause others to come looking for the source of the commotion, the illusionist dropped to his knee and shook his friends.

"Get up now!" said Thoragaard, knowing every second lost meant a greater chance of Lord Hammer's men capturing them.

Kymbra rose to one knee and shook her head. Murdock, favoring his injured side, used the wall to help get to a standing position. Pondle righted himself, though he teetered and felt dizzy. Noticing the fallen soldiers, the thief grabbed one of their swords that lay harmlessly on the floor.

"Stay close together," said Thoragaard. "We're going to become invisible again."

The illusionist cast his spell, making the foursome disappear from view. A moment later, the small group stepped over the strewn bodies that howled in agony as their hands clutched their ears and proceeded out of the kitchen area.

A tremor shook the bedroom, causing furniture to move and small objects to sway back and forth. The people taking residence in the room also felt the shudder.

Nigel squinted at Harrison. "Tell me, boy, was that sound another part of your negotiating strategy?"

Harrison did not know what had caused the crashes from below, but he knew it involved his presence in the mansion. That and Lord Hammer's annoying use of the word "boy" in regards to him began to take a toll on his nerves.

"No one should be in the mansion," said Harrison. "I made my intentions clear to the other leaders."

"Why should I trust you?" reiterated Lord Hammer, taking a second to gaze down at the blonde head that trembled in his arms. "As I recall, you left me to die before you ventured into the Seven Rooms."

Harrison remembered leaving Nigel behind, instructing the lions that guarded the area to allow him safe passage.

"Yet you're here today," said the young warrior. "I kept my word."

"You left me with a pride of lions!" said Nigel, his agitation level rising.

Harrison crinkled his brow, then said, "I always wondered what happened after we left you behind."

"Let me enlighten you," hissed Lord Hammer. "Those beasts wouldn't allow me to move an inch for hours on end, snarling at me, roaring to keep me in place!"

The young warrior listened to the older warrior's tale with great anticipation for he had hoped that the beasts would keep to their word. Nigel continued.

"Then, after several hours of hell, the walls began to crumble and the earth started to rise." Lord Hammer paused. "The temple area eventually breached the earth, depositing me and those beasts into the middle of the Dark Forest.

"If that wasn't enough, your furry friends felt obligated to escort me out of the woods and to the plains of Gammoria. They then left me for good."

Harrison cocked his head. "They did just what I had asked."

"I had no provisions!" screamed Nigel, terrifying the girl he held hostage. "I had little water! For two weeks, I trekked across my land, wary of the beasts that occupied the territory, wondering if I would survive.

"But I tell you this … The only thing that kept me going was knowing that I would get my revenge on you!"

"Will she be my revenge?" asked Lord Hammer with a wicked smile, pressing the knife tighter to Tara's throat. The young maiden tried not to squirm, her eyes bulged, her breath came in short bursts, anxious.

Harrison raised a palm to Lord Hammer. "Please, don't hurt her."

The disturbance in the kitchen did not go unnoticed. Concurian sentries rushed in the direction of the screams, which also happened to be where Thoragaard and the others now stood, albeit invisible to the naked eye. The illusionist glanced at his friends, placing a finger to his lips, signaling them to remain quiet.

A hallway ventured away from the food preparation room and led deeper into the mansion. The small posse, adhering to their tight configuration, pressed their backs against the wall while five armored men ran past their position.

Murdock saw the intensity in their eyes and knew certain death loomed if they failed on their mission. Pondle, acutely aware of the gravity of their situation, grabbed his friend's forearm, encouraging him to press forward.

Thoragaard took the opportunity to slip into the hallway while the Concurians assessed their state of affairs. The illusionist understood that they needed to get to the second floor and, having prior knowledge of the mansion's layout, knew the route they needed to take.

The group continued their journey down the corridor, which led to a larger room. The ballroom, used to house elaborate mansion events, proved the perfect avenue to remain hidden in plain view. Mansion staffers and sentries alike could easily gaze into the area and surmise that the intruders were definitely not in there, or so it seemed. However, Lord Hammer's men had gathered the mansion staff in the spacious area, assigning them a place to congregate with the building under siege.

Thoragaard made eye contact with his friends, relaying the message to be careful. Before them stood seven servants and three guardians - and the exit that led to the foyer. The staffers appeared nervous, unsure at all of the commotion. The sentries remained on alert.

Murdock, not one to keep quiet for so long, swiveled his head to Pondle, raising his eyebrows twice as if to say, "This will be easy."

The group found themselves in the middle of the ballroom, traversing the area in single file, when two soldiers entered from the kitchen.

"They're invisible!" yelled one of the men, wielding his sword, gazing wildly about the room.

Staffers gasped while the three sentries rushed to guard the other exit. The men who had entered the room blocked the way back to the kitchen.

Thoragaard stopped in his tracks, signaling for his friends to do likewise. While he pondered their predicament, the remaining three guards emerged from the food preparation area, joining their comrades. For several uncomfortable seconds, no one said a word. Then, using hand signals, the sentries relayed the message for their fellow soldiers to start combing the room, one step at a time.

Murdock glanced at Pondle, his heart pounding and eyes wide. The thief shook his head, unsure what Thoragaard had in mind. The magician watched as the Concurians began their search.

Examining their surroundings, Thoragaard determined that the room was square, one hundred feet by one hundred feet. Two large chairs, one for Nigel and the other for Meredith, sat on a raised platform away from the wall in the middle of the room, while tables and chairs surrounded an area reserved for dancing, singing, and any other form of entertainment.

The sentries worked their way around the room, starting with the tables that surrounded its outskirts. Kymbra, her sword drawn, touched Thoragaard's sleeve. The mage found his warrior's blank stare gazing back, before she shrugged, raising her empty palm to the sky. The illusionist pursed his lips, reluctant to give his next command. A second later, he made a throat-cutting gesture across his neck.

Kymbra's eyes opened wide. Thoragaard, out of tricks, signaled that they would have to fight their way out of the room. Murdock and Pondle witnessed the gesture, and both of them clenched the hilts of their weapons tighter, ready to fight.

Lord Hammer's men continued their sweep. Finding no one hiding around the room's perimeter, the men began converging toward the open floor space. The adventurers witnessed the guards' new maneuvers and huddled close together, their backs against one another, weapons poised, waiting to strike.

With each passing second, their comfort zone shrunk as Lord Hammer's soldiers came ever closer. Thoragaard moved to the center of the floor, his friends doing likewise. Still unseen, the magician took in his surroundings one final time.

Glancing from side to side while remaining motionless, Thoragaard found one man guarding each exit to the ballroom, while three men converged on their position. The staffers remained huddled near the foyer exit, wondering what might happen next.

The three Concurians took cautious steps toward one another, some twenty feet apart from their respective positions. A few seconds later, they cut their distance to the group in half.

Thoragaard, knowing that the time to fight had come, yelled, "Now!"

The Concurians stood still for a brief moment, startled from the command from seemingly nowhere. Then, springing from thin air, Kymbra, Murdock, and Pondle attacked the sentry closest to their position. Having the element of surprise on their side, each fighter connected with their initial blow.

Staffers screamed in horror, while the Concurians did their best to defend themselves. Murdock, his side searing in pain, slashed at his adversary again, delivering only a glancing blow. Pondle and Kymbra faired better, dropping their opponents to the ground.

The Concurian battling Murdock raised his blade and swept it across the ranger's midsection. Murdock's leather armor absorbed most of the blow, but his balance, compromised from his injured side, caused him to tumble.

Pondle, seeing his friend's dire state, rushed over, lowered his shoulder, and rammed the attacker. The guardian stumbled, fell, and a moment later felt the cold, steel blade of Kymbra's weapon. The man's blood spilled and he never rose again.

Lord Hammer's servants screamed in horror and ran from the function room, while the remaining sentries yelled for reinforcements. Thoragaard knew they needed to head for the foyer, which led to a spiral staircase and eventually to the second floor. He also knew that their covert operation ended in this very room. Harrison was now on his own.

Lord Hammer tossed Tara aside, the girl bouncing off the soft bed covering. Meredith gathered the terrified girl, hugging her tight and stopped her from crying.

Nigel secured his dagger, then unsheathed his sword and pointed it at Harrison. "Join the women," he said, motioning with his weapon.

The young warrior raised his hands, surrendering his position, not wanting to give this unstable man a reason to harm the ladies. He then maneuvered closer to Tara and Meredith, wary of Nigel's sword. Harrison found himself next to Tara. He could feel her nervous energy and wanted nothing more than to hold her in his arms, to comfort her, to feel her body close to his own. Instead, he remained focused on Nigel and the glint of his blade.

"You have failed, Harrison," snarled Nigel, bringing the point of his sword to the young warrior's face. "There's no turning back for me or you now."

"Don't be foolish, Nigel!" exclaimed Harrison. "We can work something out!"

"You came to me without a plan, boy," hissed the Governor. "I'm going to make it out alive."

"You have no chance! How do you possibly believe that you can escape our blockade?"

Nigel knew he could not, yet he did not envision himself dying in a rage of anger. He did not care to have his name etched in Concur's history books as the leader who fought to his death, hoping to bring salvation to the people of Concur; he cared little for the townsfolk. What he cared about the most was scouring the land for its riches, imposing his will on others, showing them how a real leader looked and acted. With his rule of Concur all but over, he knew he needed to make his demands clear, right now.

"Listen, and listen good, boy," said Nigel. "I want to be escorted away from this city, along with Allard, with no strings attached. No one following, no prison time, no nothing!" Lord Hammer continued to point his sword inches from Harrison's face.

"I don't think I can offer that," said the young warrior.

Lord Hammer frowned, releasing his stern grip on his weapon a tad. In an overly condescending tone, he said, "But, Harrison, isn't that the noble thing to do?"

The young warrior thought hard about his predicament. Had he not told the elders that he would give Nigel every opportunity to relinquish his power and if he did, to adhere to his wishes? Harrison could hear Swinkle's voice resonate in his head; did Nigel not give you the opportunity to do the right thing?

Dropping his head, Harrison said in a low voice, "I will agree with Meredith's wishes, no matter the consequences."

Lord Hammer's body tensed, infuriated by this foolish boy's response. "I'm through *negotiating,*" he said. Raising his blade, Lord Hammer gripped his long sword as tight as he could and prepared to strike the defenseless warrior.

Before he could administer the deathblow, a raven, black as night with sparkling green eyes, flew through the open window, landed on the sill, and squawked at the top of its lungs. Nigel hesitated, startled at the sudden appearance of the bird.

In the time that Lord Hammer took to collect his bearings, Tara mumbled something under her breath. Gathering all the strength in her petite body, she uttered the words to her spell and flung her hands in Lord Hammer's direction. A bright flash of white light permeated the area, rendering the Concurian governor blind. He recoiled, dropped his weapon, and moved to shield his eyes, as the raven cawed once from the sill.

Harrison took the unforeseen opportunity to charge the Concurian leader, ramming his shoulder into the older man's chest, driving him to the ground. Nigel, still blinded by Tara's spell, wildly threw punches into the air, hoping to connect with the young warrior, but instead hit nothing.

Lord Hammer incapacitated for the time being, Harrison brought his gaze to the floor, searching for the elder man's sword. Meredith, closest to the elusive object, kicked the weapon toward Harrison, who snagged the sword and tightly gripped its hilt.

"Get away from him!" said Harrison to the women. Meredith and Tara heeded the young warrior's command and scurried closer to the bed. Harrison positioned himself in front of the fallen warrior and, mimicking Nigel's actions, pointed the sword at him.

"Stay on the ground and you'll be spared," said Harrison.

Lord Hammer, seeing only shadowy figures, slowly sat up. "It's best that you kill me, boy, but I know that you won't." Nigel flashed Harrison a wide, toothy grin, playing on the young man's emotions. "I'm now a blind, defenseless soul and your righteousness prevents you from striking me."

"All I need is a reason and your blood will spill," said Harrison through clenched teeth. The young warrior brought his gaze to the quivering women, then back to Nigel, his blood simmering. "Don't test me."

The sudden course of events also brought a new set of circumstances for Harrison. The door to the makeshift prison cell flew open and two sentries rushed in with weapons drawn. The young warrior moved closer to Lord Hammer, placing the tip of his sword on Nigel's chest.

"Stop where you are!" commanded Harrison, causing the men to halt their advancement. "Move any closer and your leader dies. Drop your weapons and push them over to Meredith. If you do so, maybe she will have mercy on your souls."

The two men exchanged anxious stares, then looked upon their leader, who lay on the floor, incapacitated. The sentry on the right placed his sword on the floor and did as Harrison instructed.

Gazing at Meredith, the guard said, "It will be an honor to serve you, Milady." He then bowed in her direction.

The sentry next to him, shocked at his comrade's actions, took an extra moment to decide his fate, but in the end, he found himself pushing his sword across the floor to the First Lady, too.

The first man, his gaze still fixed on Meredith, asked, "Shall I bind him?"

Meredith, for the first time since Harrison entered the room, began to feel the ramifications of the moment. Standing tall, she said in a forceful tone, "Yes. Be sure that he does not escape. And, I want you to find Allard and do the same."

The sentry approached his former superior, grabbing him under his armpits and lifting him off the floor. He then gestured with his head for his comrade to help him, which he did.

"You are both marked men," said the blind leader, while the guards placed Nigel's hands behind his back. Taking thick twine from their packs, the two men secured Lord Hammer. The Governor of Concur had now become the first prisoner of the new regime.

Nigel's sight began to return, and he sought the young man who had orchestrated his fall. Glaring at Harrison, he said, "This is far from over, boy." He then swiveled his head in Tara's direction. "Had I known that your woman was a witch, I would have handled her differently."

The young maiden moved from her position and took two purposeful steps to Lord Hammer. With all her might, she slapped the deposed leader across the face.

"You're a wicked, wicked man," said Tara, her eyes focused, memories of Justin in her head. "Remember those innocent souls you killed in the square? I hope you suffer a similar fate."

Nigel locked his gaze on the young maiden, unfazed. "Don't get your hopes up," he snarled. "Meredith doesn't have the resolve to do that." Lord Hammer then flashed his familiar wicked smile.

"Now do you, sweetheart?"

The First Lady inhaled deeply, trying to control her fury. She then addressed the guardians. "Use the platform in the town's center," she began, "and make preparations to hang both him and Allard." Nigel's eyes widened, shocked at the turn of events.

"Plan for tomorrow at high noon," finished Meredith with a coldness in her voice that no one had ever heard before.

Lord Hammer's eyes stayed round. "You can't be serious! You're a weak person! You'll never go through with this!"

Meredith approached Nigel, bringing her face close to his. In a steady voice, she said, "You overran a peaceful city, erected hideous walls to keep us from leaving, and made living here unbearable.

"Furthermore, you murdered my father and destroyed my family!" Meredith's voice rose ever so subtly. "I've bided my time with you, being the loyal woman, waiting for this day, and now the day has come. I'm through with you and anyone aligned with you!"

The First Lady glared at the sentries. "Make it known throughout the ranks of Concurian soldiers that I will spare their lives if they pledge their support to the New Concur. If not, imprison them and we'll deal with their executions later."

Both guards nodded.

"Yes, ma'am," said the first soldier. "Where shall we hold him?"

"Put him in the darkest, dankest cell you can find," answered Meredith, glaring at Nigel once again.

Harrison, surprised at Meredith, asked, "Do you want more time to think this over? We have more than enough force to keep him from escaping."

The raven-haired woman said, "I made up my mind a long time ago. Consider my statements the first order of business for this new city."

With the turmoil in the room over, the black bird hopped from its position on the windowsill to the floor. From there, the raven transformed into a beautiful, red-haired woman.

Harrison's mouth fell agape. "Fallyn!"

With teary eyes, the Aegean woman said, "Harrison, forgive me for my actions." She then brought her gaze to Tara, saying to her, "This was all my fault. I should have never listened to Gareth."

The young warrior checked his rage, not allowing it to breach the surface and cloud his judgment. "If you're truly sorry, go and tell the others to storm the mansion now," said Harrison with conviction. "Tell them where we are and that we have a prisoner."

Fallyn nodded, then dropped her head in shame. Seconds later, the woman morphed back to the shape of a raven and flew out the open window to fulfill her task.

Before anyone could truly comprehend Fallyn's transformation, the sounds of scuffling and clashing weapons emanated from outside the room. Everyone held their ground, unsure of what might happen next. A moment later, two people entered.

"Thoragaard!" said Meredith, rushing to the illusionist, wrapping her arms around him. Kymbra followed the magician into the room as well.

The mage noticed Lord Hammer's condition and smiled. "It's all over."

Meredith pulled back, beaming. "Almost."

More shuffling came from beyond the room before Murdock and Pondle entered it as well. A huge smile graced Harrison's face.

"Am I glad to see you two!" exclaimed the young warrior.

"The bastard's ours now!" said Murdock, glaring at Nigel.

"Good work, Harrison." Pondle placed a hand on his friend's shoulder.

The young warrior's demeanor changed to one of concern. "Where are Swinkle and Gelderand?"

"With Adrith and Marissa," said Kymbra, sheathing her sword.

"Lance?"

"He's with them, too."

Harrison sighed in relief.

More heavy footsteps began to rumble about the mansion, as did shouts and screams. The young warrior's body began to feel at ease; his allies were storming the complex. A moment later, scores of striped-eyed soldiers scoured the mansion, securing the area for Meredith and her loyal subjects.

The two sentries who had guarded the First Lady's room each grabbed one of Lord Hammer's arms and escorted him toward the doorway.

Nigel, never one to let someone else get the last word, turned to Meredith. "Mark my words, woman; you're going to regret this." He then glared at Harrison and said, "That goes for you, too. We'll meet again."

The young warrior allowed the Concurian to get the last word as he watched the men guide him through the doorway and lead him to his awaiting cell. With Nigel's imminent threat neutralized, Harrison focused on the true object of his desire.

Tara had anxiously waited for the situation to resolve itself and, now that it had, she rushed to Harrison. The young warrior met her halfway across the room, threw his arms around his love, and kissed her passionately. Tears streamed down Tara's face.

"I've missed you so much," said the young maiden, sniffing.

"I'll never let this happen again," lamented Harrison. "I should have never let you go." He traced the line of tears down her soft cheek, then gently moved a lock of hair from her brow.

"I was so scared," said Tara. "He was so cruel."

"Nigel will never hurt you again or anyone else for that matter," said the young warrior, wiping the tears from Tara's face. Gazing at his love, he said, "I love you more than you can imagine."

The young girl smiled wide, tears welling again in her eyes. "I love you so much, too!" Standing on tiptoe, she reached up to run her fingers through his hair.

After another kiss, Harrison said, "It's time to get out of this place. There's still a lot more to do."

The young warrior took Tara's hand and led her toward the doorway. Murdock and Pondle gave their friend an approving smile, the ranger patting him on the back as they walked by.

Meredith, a broad smile gracing her face as well, stopped the couple. "Harrison, I just wanted to thank you for all that you have done do make this day a reality. I'll always owe you a debt of honor."

"I told you that I'd come back some day to help you and your cause," said the young warrior, wrapping his arms around Meredith to give her a hug. "You're going to make such a great leader."

"I will do my best," said Meredith, squeezing the young warrior back.

After separating, Harrison gestured with his free hand, "After you, Milady."

Meredith took one more look around her room, knowing that it would no longer be a place for her to sleep. She would gut her sleeping quarters after tomorrow's events and did not know or care what would become of it beyond that.

Harrison and Tara then followed Meredith, Thoragaard, and Kymbra out of the bedroom with Murdock and Pondle bringing up the rear.

Taking his gaze to Tara, the young warrior said, "There are people who are dying to see you." Harrison reached for her, the young maiden graciously receiving his kiss.

Everyone breathed a sigh of relief upon exiting the elaborate holding area. With the day's final actions behind them, the Unified Army had finally liberated Concur.

CHAPTER 34

¤

A controlled chaos awaited Harrison and Tara when they exited the mansion. Unified army soldiers had helped usher Lord Hammer, along with his loyalists, toward the prison just a few blocks away. The young warrior searched the throngs of armored men, searching for his friends. A sudden bark alerted Harrison to the first of them.

"Lance!" said the young warrior as the little dog came bounding out from the crowd. Harrison dropped to one knee and rustled with the canine's fur. Lance jumped repeatedly with excitement.

"Look who I've brought back."

Tara bent down to address the happy dog as well. Lance rushed to her side, pushing his head against her legs, doing his best to get as near to her as possible.

"I've missed you, too," said the young maiden with a little laugh, scratching the dog's ears as well.

Tara noticed a figure moving closer to her. Lifting her gaze, she saw Gelderand approach, a smile beaming across his face.

"Uncle!" exclaimed the young maiden with delight as she jumped to her feet and threw her arms around the magician. "I'm so happy to see you!"

Gelderand hugged his niece hard. "I thought I had lost you forever."

"I never gave up hope," said Tara, tears of happiness welling in her eyes.

The mage brought his attention to the man next to the young girl. "Well done, Harrison."

The young warrior nodded once, saying, "It was a group effort. I couldn't have done anything without the help of all of you."

"You could say that again," came the voice from behind Harrison. Murdock sauntered toward the gathering, along with Pondle and Kymbra. "Don't you forget that!"

"Believe me, I won't," said Harrison with a smile.

Swinkle, along with Marissa and Adrith, approached the delightful scene, while maintaining their watch on their prisoner.

"Good to see you again, Harrison," said the young cleric, before taking his gaze to Tara, "and it is very good to see you, too."

The young maiden left her uncle's arms and surprised Swinkle with a big hug as well. "I've missed you all."

"You won't have to worry about that ever again," said Harrison. "That I promise."

Tara finished her hug with Swinkle, then took the young warrior's hand, gripping it tight. "I'm going to hold you to that promise," she said, gazing up at him.

Escorting a sickly man, several soldiers, followed by the Robusite clerics, broke the young couple's trance. One of the fighters addressed Harrison. "Sir, what shall we do with him?"

The young warrior took a moment to look over Allard's injured body. Puncture wounds littered his torso and he could tell that the man stood before him in obvious pain.

Harrison stared at Swinkle. "What happened to him?" he asked, shock in his voice.

"Gelderand's weapon surprised us all," said the young cleric, then motioning with his head toward Allard, "especially him."

The young warrior leaned closer to Swinkle and whispered, "Will he survive?"

"Gelderand, my fellow clerics, and I carefully removed the quills that impaled his body. After that, we prayed over his injured areas." Swinkle shrugged. "It is the best that we can do."

Satisfied with the information he received, Harrison brought his eyes to the soldier. "Take this man to the prison and keep him in a cell next to Lord Hammer. Meredith has plans for them tomorrow."

The fighter saluted. "Yes, sir!" The men then heeded their superior's orders and took Allard away.

In the throngs of people that congregated around the governor's mansion, Harrison found several prominent people heading in his direction. Brendan Brigade approached the young warrior, followed by the Forge Brothers and Bracken Drake.

The Aegean extended his hand. "Well done, Harrison," he said with a smile. "You've apprehended Lord Hammer and liberated Concur."

"I can't take all the credit," said the young warrior, embarrassed that a man he looked up to for so long would bestow such an appraisal on him.

"Don't be modest, young man," added Bracken. "Because of you, the Concurian people now have a chance to be part of a greater purpose."

"And you," Octavius Forge pointed at Tara, "did more than anyone could have asked for. Your name will go down in the history books as well." The young maiden blushed, accepting the warrior's accolades.

"Today's just the first step in a long process," said Harrison. "We need to help Meredith restore order, get her people to accept her as their leader, aid in the reconstruction of their city …"

Brendan raised a hand. "All in due time, Harrison." With a laugh he added, "You didn't expect everything to happen overnight, did you?"

Harrison looked down. "I suppose not."

Murmurs and hushed voices stopped the impromptu meeting. Most people around the area turned their attention to the mansion's entranceway. Harrison did likewise.

The young warrior watched an elegant figure exit the building, a robed man standing by her side. Soldiers, Concurian and Unified alike, removed their helmets and bowed as Meredith left the confines of her building and headed in Harrison's direction.

The young warrior and his fellow army leaders bowed to Concur's new leader. "Gentleman," started Meredith, "I want to thank you all for coming to my city's aid. This day was a long time coming, but I knew it would eventually arrive. I just wish that my father was still alive to witness the new Concur."

"Meredith," said Harrison, "there is still much to do."

The new Concurian leader raised a hand, stopping the young warrior's speech. "That is for another day. Today, I want to walk freely through my hometown, just like I did when I was a child."

"Milady," said Brendan, "though we might have defeated Lord Hammer, the city's streets are still quite unsettled and the town has sustained much damage."

"I need to see everything for myself," said Meredith. "I must connect with my people."

"Then allow all of us to walk with you," said Harrison, extending his hand toward his friends and fellow leaders. "No one will harm you while we're by your side."

Meredith smiled. "I would like that very much." The Concurian woman signaled them to wait. "But first, I need to speak with members of my staff."

The First Lady called a soldier and asked him to find her main servant. Shortly thereafter, Percival appeared from the mansion, a puzzled look on his face.

"Milady, what may I do for you?"

"Prepare a gala event for tomorrow evening," Meredith began, "and be sure to have enough food to feed everyone."

The servant crinkled his brow. "Everyone? How many guests should I expect?"

"I'm opening the mansion to all Concurian citizens. They have the right to see who governs them and they should partake fully in this most glorious day."

Percival's eyes widened. "All of our townspeople? I don't think we have that much food to even consider an event of this magnitude!"

Meredith smiled. "They will understand and I think our citizens will surprise you. Be sure to have entertainment as well." Waving her hands in Percival's direction, the woman said, "Go off, you have a lot of preparing to do!"

"To say the least, Milady," said the servant with exasperation in his voice. "I will do my best." The frail man then departed to begin his arduous task.

Meredith turned her attention to the armored men before her. "Please, let's take a stroll around the city."

As the small group started their trek, Harrison and Tara positioned themselves beside Meredith. "That is a very noble thing you are doing," said the young warrior.

"My people deserve it. Nigel repressed them for years and it's the least I can do." The Concurian woman focused on the young couple.

"I want both of you, and all your friends, to be my personal guests," said Meredith. "You will dine with me at the head table."

Harrison raised his eyebrows. "That is most generous of you. We gladly accept!"

"And," the dark-haired beauty said with a smirk, "I'll be sure to reserve a room in the mansion for you two. I'm sure you need some alone time."

The young couple blushed, before gazing into each other's eyes. The anticipation of being alone together caused their hearts to pound.

"We look forward to that as well," said the young warrior, unable to contain his smile. "Thank you, again."

The group then continued their trek from the mansion complex and wandered further into the heart of Concur. More and more townsfolk joined the group as they realized that Meredith was the person of interest in the procession. Cheers erupted as word spread of Meredith's journey through the city.

The Concurian woman smiled and waved to the townspeople, her eyes becoming teary. Leaning toward Harrison, she said, "You see, this is the most glorious day in our town's history."

A cadre of soldiers escorted Lord Hammer through the prison compound to the secluded Death Row paddock. The lead guardian halted the procession at the entranceway to the hallowed corridor. He then removed a key from his belt, unlocked the metal portal, and swung it open.

"You two," said the leader, pointing to two guards, "bring Lord Hammer to his cell. Everyone else remain here."

The two guards grabbed Lord Hammer by his arms, one on each side, and moved him forward. The one-time Concurian leader grimaced as he walked down the dank corridor before the lead guardian commanded him to stop in front of cell five. The man unlocked this portal as well, then swung the door open.

"Your new home, sir," snarled the guard as the other two fighters tossed their old superior into the jail cell.

The lead Concurian gestured to the chamber across the hall. "Prepare that one for Allard." The two men did as commanded and began to ready the small room.

While his men tended to their chores, the lead soldier addressed Nigel. In a hushed tone, he began, "Sir, forgive my actions, but I must appear as if I'm heeding Meredith's orders." Nigel gave a single nod in understanding.

"I have handled all arrangements," continued the guardian, darting his eyes to the men across the hall, making sure that they continued their task. "Your plan will commence tomorrow at noon."

"Be sure that Allard is ready for his assignment," said Nigel in a low hiss.

The soldier lowered his eyes, ready to deliver bad news. "He was injured while trying to create the funnel cloud."

"What do you mean, *injured*?"

"He's hurt quite badly, sir, but still alive."

Lord Hammer pondered this news. His only means of escaping the city he once ruled hinged on Allard being able to perform the next part of his plan.

Nigel looked into the soldier's eyes. "You manned the doorway leading to Meredith's chamber."

The man stood tall. "I did indeed, sir."

In an unprecedented move, Lord Hammer asked, "What is your name?"

The fighter appeared taken aback, since the former governor never cared to know the names of his soldiers. "My name is Seth, sir."

"Thank you, Seth. You will be handsomely rewarded in our new regime." Nigel paused. "Has Allard prepared you?"

"That he did," said the guard with a nod. "You need not worry." Lord Hammer huffed and looked away.

The two guards completed their task across the corridor and returned to their leader. "The cell is ready for Allard, sir."

"Excellent," commented Seth. He then slammed Lord Hammer's door shut, locking it in the process. Peeking through the small barred window, he snarled, "Enjoy your last day!"

Seth then motioned for his men to leave their prisoner and move out of Death Row.

An hour later, three former Concurian soldiers escorted Allard to his holding place. Lord Hammer rose from the cell's floor and peered through his barred window.

"You three," he snarled, "release me from this place!"

One of the guardians peered over. "You don't direct us anymore," he said, before slamming Allard's portal shut and locking it. The soldier then motioned for his comrades to leave Death Row.

"You'll be sorry for this!" barked Nigel in a fury. The former governor's outburst did not faze the soldiers who exited the corridor, closing the door behind them with a resounding thud.

Lord Hammer hung his head, feeling the weight of defeat descend on his shoulders. Pausing a moment to gather his thoughts, he finally said, "Allard, can you hear me?"

The magician did not respond right away, but when he did, his voice came in shallow whispers. "A fine mess ... we find ourselves in."

Nigel scowled, not caring for his current environment. "Be that as it may, have you secured our getaway?"

The older man again took a moment to speak. "I have ... performed the necessary spell ... if that's what you mean."

"I have my men in place," said Lord Hammer, nodding to reassure himself. "They won't fail us."

"Where ... will they lead us?"

"Through the South Gate," said Nigel, reiterating the plan he had solidified with his loyal soldiers. "Your magic blew a hole through the gates. An army could rush through the opening."

"Did one not … rush through?" Allard laughed, before coughing.

Nigel did not care for the reference, picturing the red-uniformed Arcadians storming his city. Changing subjects, he asked, "How are you feeling?"

"Awful." Allard coughed again.

Lord Hammer did not care for the current condition of the only man who could truly orchestrate his escape from this hellhole. "Will you be able to perform your next spell?"

"I need … rest," said the magician. "I should be … better tomorrow."

"Should be?" snarled Nigel. "If you can't perform, we're both dead!"

"Point taken." Allard paused. "I need rest, Nigel."

Lord Hammer nodded, taking his gaze to the cell's stone floor. "Get some sleep," he said in a low hiss. "Our lives are on the line tomorrow."

CHAPTER 35

¤

Thin shards of sunlight woke Lord Hammer from a dismal night's sleep. The former Governor of Concur stretched his back, stiff from lying on the stone flooring. Judging by the sun's position, he figured the day had approached mid-morning. Knowing that Meredith had plans for him a short time from now, Nigel rose from the ground and approached the locked doorway.

Lord Hammer peered through the small barred window in search of Allard. At first glance, it appeared that the magician had vacated his cell.

"Allard!" called Nigel, hoping for a response. "Allard, can you hear me?" The Concurian feared that his only chance at escape had perished in the holding cell across the hall.

"I hear you, Nigel," said a heavy, tired voice.

"You need to wake up," said the former leader. "They'll be coming for us soon!" Lord Hammer waited for a response, but instead heard the moaning of an injured man.

Allard rose to a standing position, holding the bars on his window. The mage peered across the aisle with an ashen face and sunken eyes.

"Our escape will be a challenge today," said the magician.

Lord Hammer did not care for Allard's statement. "We did not come this far just to fail now!" With his anger rising, Nigel continued, "Do what you must to regain your strength!"

"It's not that easy, Nigel." Allard drew a heavy sigh. "Quills littered my entire body. I am very sore."

Lord Hammer tried to show empathy, but failed miserably. Taking a moment to gather his thoughts, he said, "Will you be able to perform your task today?"

The mage cocked his head. "I will do everything in my power to ensure our survival."

Nigel did not say another word; instead, he nodded, sat back down on the ground, and waited for the inevitable.

Less than an hour later, a cadre of soldiers entered Death Row. Nigel heard the metal portal open at the end of the corridor and jumped to see who had entered the area. He recognized the first person he saw.

Seth led the other Concurians to their former leader's cell, then held up a hand, signaling for them to stop their procession.

"Give me a moment with Lord Hammer," he said to his men. The Concurian unlocked and entered the holding area.

The soldier approached his former leader and, speaking in a whisper, said, "All is set. Do as I say."

Seth backed away from Nigel and said with a loud voice. "Your day of reckoning has arrived!" Upon hearing their leader's outburst, the other Concurians congregated outside Lord Hammer's cell.

"Prepare this man for his death!" Seth stepped aside and ordered the others to handle Nigel.

"What, no last meal?" said Lord Hammer with a hiss.

"We didn't want to waste good food on a man who's about to die," said one of the soldiers, while another bound Lord Hammer's hands. After securing his bonds, the men placed a black hood over Nigel's head. Across the hall, soldiers performed a similar act on Allard.

Lord Hammer felt a hand on his back, forcing him forward. Next, two soldiers grabbed him by the arms and led him down the hallway. Though he could not see Allard, he figured his former faithful subjects guided the mage down a similar path.

For the first time in his life, Nigel truly felt nervous. Lord Hammer never allowed others to dictate important personal events, but today his life rested in the hands of those who he felt lay far beneath him. The heavy covering caused droplets of perspiration to sting his eyes. He knew that his loyalists had enacted their makeshift plan, but a nagging feeling of doubt permeated his soul.

In less than thirty minutes, he would know if his preparations would save his life.

The impromptu staging erected by Lord Hammer's men just a couple of days earlier stood ready for use once again. A large crowd had gathered under the noontime sun to witness the most pivotal event in Concur's history.

Meredith, flanked by Thoragaard on her right and Harrison on her left, had made the solemn journey to her town's epicenter. The evening before, she had dined with the military leaders. To their surprise, she had rebuffed their calls for remorse in the handling of Nigel Hammer.

Harrison, harking Swinkle's sentiments about purity and decision-making, had hoped to sway Concur's First Lady, but alas, her bitterness toward Nigel and the revenge she so desperately sought for her father proved to be an unwavering force. Now, the young warrior waited for his longtime adversary to enter the Town's Square.

The group, including Harrison's friends and the Unified Army leaders, waited with great anticipation for Concurian Resistance soldiers to march Nigel to his final stand. Their wait did not last long.

To the right of where they stood, Harrison noticed that many people in the crowd turned to get a better look at the approaching mass of soldiers. As they grew nearer, the young warrior determined that the soldiers were escorting two hooded figures, presumably Nigel and Allard. Harrison brought his gaze to Meredith, who stared stoically ahead, not bothering to look in the prisoner's direction.

The young warrior felt a soft tug on his sleeve. "She's really going to hang them," said Tara with concern. Though she loathed Nigel, the young maiden did not care to witness another gruesome event like the one that stole poor Justin's life.

"It's what she feels she must do," said Harrison, his own feelings mixed.

As the seconds ticked by, the crowd became angrier as more people realized that their hated dictator walked before them.

"Kill him now!" shouted one man.

"Hang him slowly," cursed another, while townsfolk moved closer to the staging area. Soldiers formed a perimeter around Meredith and the others, not allowing the crowd to get any closer.

Concurian fighters led the prisoners up the wooden staging amidst taunts and shouts from the mob. Moments later, the once-loyal soldiers positioned Nigel and Allard on the trap door, then moved away.

Lord Hammer's newest ally took over the proceedings. Seth removed Nigel's hood, then Allard's. Upon seeing their faces, the crowd grew louder, anticipating the inevitable.

Nigel gazed upon his people, a pit in his stomach. Though he could care less for their individual lives, he did feel a sense of pride knowing that he had ruled over such a large populace. Furthermore, no one had ever attacked his sovereignty from within, and only with the help of many diverse armies of the land, no other regime dared to enter his domain.

Nigel's henchman walked over to Allard first and placed a noose around his neck; the mob cheered. He did the same to Nigel, whispering as he performed the act, "Make a break for the South Gate and don't look back." Lord Hammer offered a subtle nod, then turned and looked straight ahead.

With the angry crowd growing more impatient, Seth threw up his hands and signaled for everyone to quiet down. After a minute of unrest, he had his fellow townspeople's attention.

"We must offer Lord Hammer a chance to say his final words," said the Concurian before gesturing to his former leader.

Nigel stared forward, his hands bound and a rope around his neck. These pathetic fools, he lamented to himself. They will pay for their ignorance!

"I gave you a safe city to live in, protection from enemies, and a means to make a decent life," snarled the dark lord. "And this is how you repay me? By sentencing me to death? Let it be known, I will have my vengeance some day."

Nigel brought his stare to the small group in front of the platform that included Meredith and Harrison. "You all will feel my wrath again!"

Stunned for a moment after Nigel's outburst, the crowd began to hiss and boo at their old leader. Lord Hammer delivered a slight smile, stared out over the crowd again, and remained silent.

Tara tugged on Harrison's sleeve. "What does he mean 'feel his wrath again'?"

The young warrior's brain churned. How could Nigel seek vengeance if he were dead? A sour feeling overtook his stomach as he shook his head and said, "I don't know. "

Sensing that Nigel would not speak again, Seth brought his focus to Meredith. "Milady, I will wait for your mark." The Concurian then walked over to the lever that held the fate of the two men who awaited death.

Meredith raised her hand high, staring at Nigel. Lord Hammer refused to look at the black-haired woman; instead, he gritted his teeth and gazed ahead. Without a drop of remorse, Meredith lowered her arm to the ground, and as she did, Seth pulled the lever. With everyone's eyes glued on the falling men, the Concurian discreetly left the staging.

Lord Hammer felt the floor underneath his feet disappear and sensed his body dropping at an incredible rate. Seconds later, he heard the snap of the twine before his body came crashing to the ground.

Nigel rolled and maneuvered to a kneeling position. Laughing, the Concurian placed his bound hands before him, then pulled. The twine gave way, reducing the bindings to flimsy strings.

Allard's panicked voice broke him from his trance. "Hurry! Help me find the bag!"

The two prisoners patted the ground around them, searching for the elusive object. A second later, Allard found a brown cloth sack and said, "I've got it!"

The magician made haste in opening the sack and pouring two gold rings into his hand. "Put this on!" Allard handed one of the objects to Nigel.

Lord Hammer quickly secured the ring on his finger, then peered at Allard. "Is this going to work?"

"Yes!" Allard waved in the direction behind Nigel. "We're invisible now! Run that way!" Lord Hammer kept his head down, wary of hitting it on the underside of the platform, and began his escape from the gallows.

Before following his leader, Allard had one more trick to perform. With the angry crowd confused at not seeing their former leader swaying dead, the mage used all the remaining strength that he could muster to summon a final chant. Waving his hands toward the base of the platform, the magician recited his spell and, when finished, three huge fireballs flew from his fingertips. After completing his task, he, too, ran in Nigel's direction.

Harrison watched with wide eyes as the stage exploded with a mighty crash. Flames engulfed the wooden structure, sending people running away from the burning platform and soldiers attempting to extinguish the blaze.

"Where did they go?" yelled Harrison in disbelief. The young warrior panned repeatedly, searching for the two men who should be dead by now. He found no sign of them.

Meredith brought a hand to her open mouth, shocked at the scene that had transpired before her. "This can't be happening," she lamented, not wanting to believe the strange twist of fate. Thoragaard moved closer to Meredith, unsure of the events that had just transpired.

The young warrior stood in front of the First Lady and held her arms. "Meredith, I'm going to find them." He then turned to his love.

"Tara, keep her safe." The young maiden, trying her best to keep her composure, nodded.

Lowering his gaze and pointing a finger downward, the young warrior ordered, "Lance, stay with Tara and Meredith." The canine barked once in affirmation and huddled next to the women.

Before Harrison could start his search, platoons of soldiers encircled their small group in an effort to protect their new leader. While the young warrior struggled to think, a welcome sight interrupted him.

"That bastard's not going to get away with this!" exclaimed Murdock. Pondle, Swinkle, and Gelderand joined the ranger. Seconds later, Kymbra and her two cohorts entered the mix.

"Which way did he go?" asked Harrison amidst the ensuing chaos.

"This was not a spur of the moment action," said Kymbra. "They planned this all along! We need to act now!"

"He must have soldiers helping him," said Harrison. "Watch for unusual movements."

The small group brought their individual gazes all about the immediate area, searching for a sign. Moments later, Marissa grabbed Kymbra's arm and pointed. The lead female looked in the direction her friend indicated, sensing something out of place.

Pointing to the right of the staging, she exclaimed, "Why are those men heading toward the South Gate?"

Harrison and the others thought back to the battles that had ensued the previous day, recalling the battering that the great walls surrounding Concur had sustained, and came to a logical conclusion.

"The South Gate is destroyed!" said the young warrior. "That's the only accessible way out of the city!"

Harrison immediately searched for Brendan and the other leaders, finding them close to Meredith. Pushing his way through the crowd, he approached the elder Aegean.

"Brendan, he's going to leave the city through the south entrance," said Harrison.

The elder warrior swiveled his head in that direction, witnessing an unusual amount of Concurian soldiers scampering that way.

"You're right," said Brendan. "Go after them! I'll relay the message to the other leaders and we'll divert our armies to the south."

The Aegean then made eye contact with Octavius, Caidan, and Bracken. "We need to get Meredith back to the mansion!" Brendan then commanded all soldiers around him. "Everyone, make haste to the South Gate and take your orders from Harrison!"

Without a moment to spare, the liberator leaders summoned men from their troops, surrounded the First Lady and Thoragaard, and ushered them toward the government complex.

The young warrior, feeling better about Meredith's situation, waved his friends onward, and within seconds, the small platoon and scores of fighters streamed toward the South Gate.

Two invisible men raced through the crowd, bumping into townspeople, startling them in the process. Their stealth defense intact, the duo continued running away from the chaos and toward the southern part of the city. Nigel stopped at the corner of a building and turned around to locate Allard. The mage staggered ten paces behind Lord Hammer.

Allard finally reached Nigel's position where he bent over and tried to catch his breath.

"I hope you're having fun," said Nigel, not happy to be using magic and trickery to save his life.

"We need … to find the horses," said the mage through ragged breaths.

Lord Hammer scanned the immediate area. In the distance, an inferno raged where the platform once stood; townsfolk and soldiers alike ran about in chaotic fashion. From his position, the Governor's mansion sat two hundred yards behind him with the prison complex a quarter mile away from that.

"Our steeds await us at the prison compound," said Nigel. "Let's go!"

Allard stood tall, his body sweaty and his face white. "We cannot waste any more time."

Lord Hammer took his cue from Allard and continued toward their next destination. As he ran through the city streets, he passed dozens of people — no one saw him. A sly smile graced Nigel's face, sensing that he now had the upper hand even though everyone in town was on high alert to find him.

Steering away from the government compound took a few extra minutes, but Lord Hammer and Allard eventually reached the prison complex unscathed.

Again through ragged breaths, the magician said, "Locate … your people."

Nigel panned the area in search of a familiar face. At first, he saw no one sympathetic to his cause, but a few moments later, he recognized a welcome sight. Six soldiers, each leading two horses apiece, emerged from the complex's entranceway.

Allard tugged on Nigel's sleeve. "Those are for us."

Lord Hammer nodded and began to advance in the horses' direction. The magician stopped him. "You can't just walk up to them! You're invisible, remember?"

Nigel pointed a finger in Allard's face. "Good point. How should we proceed?"

The mage knew that if they removed their rings, everyone would be able to see them, which could also mean unnecessary problems for the two.

Allard took a moment to watch the men parading the steeds. After they passed by, another soldier appeared from the entrance. The magician recognized this man immediately.

"That one there!" exclaimed Allard, pointing at the Concurian. "You know him!"

Lord Hammer smiled. "That I do. Follow me."

Nigel made haste in advancing to the leader's position. "Seth!" called Lord Hammer. The Concurian stopped in his tracks, shifting his eyes in an attempt to find the person who called out his name.

Nigel walked right up to the fighter. Standing no more than three feet away, Lord Hammer again said, "Seth." He then removed his ring, allowing the soldier to see him for a brief moment, before placing it back on his finger and disappearing again.

"Lord Hammer! Follow me! And, hurry!" said Seth, motioning for the invisible people to tag along. The Concurian knew that he needed to commence with the next part of their plan, having no time to waste.

Seth took several hurried steps in the direction of his soldiers before calling out, "Halt your procession!"

The six men stopped the horses' advancement and waited for their leader. Seth examined the steeds and, choosing the pair in the middle of the group, said, "Keep them steady!"

The Concurian leader then pointed to the horses and called out to apparently no one, saying, "Take those two."

Lord Hammer and Allard approached the steeds, each one mounting their own animal. The six soldiers watched the horses shift their weight, surprised to feel someone on their backs.

"Don't use the reins," said Seth to the invisible riders. "Hug the horses by the neck. Holding the reins will only draw suspicion to your steeds." Nigel and Allard heeded the Concurian's order.

"Who'll be following us to the South Gate?" said Lord Hammer. Upon hearing their true leader's voice, the six soldiers stood at attention.

Just before Seth could answer Nigel's question, a bell began to ring in the town square. "They're coming now! Race through the South Gate, then head for the desert. Your loyal subjects will rendezvous with you outside the city walls."

Seth then turned his attention to his men. "Drop those lead ropes."

The soldiers heeded their superior's command. With the bell tolling in the background and chaos erupting throughout the city, the Concurian started to yell at the animals, smacking their hindquarters, scaring them into running away.

Nigel and Allard took Seth's actions as their cue to start their dash to the South Gate. A minute later, the two men could see the shattered remains of the southern exit.

Sprinting past the governor's complex and prison compound, Harrison and the others headed south. Instead of encountering resistance, he found scores of Concurian soldiers streaming away from them.

Murdock raced to the young warrior's position, grabbing him by the arm. "Nigel's gone, Harrison!" The two men stopped in their tracks.

"He can't just disappear!" lamented Kymbra through heavy breaths.

"He didn't," said Pondle, taking a closer look at the ground. The thief pointed to the hoofmarks in the soil. "They're on horseback!"

"We'll never catch up to them now!" said Murdock, glaring into the distance.

Negative thoughts raced through the young warrior's mind. How could Nigel just disappear? One moment he stood on the platform with a noose around his neck and the next minute he was gone. With that thought swirling in his head, two robed men finally reached the small group.

Gelderand drew a heavy sigh, his body aching from the unwanted exercise. "Allard has employed a magical tactic."

Harrison shook his head. "They're invisible, aren't they?"

"I knew that the moment we lost sight of them in the town's square," said the mage.

"How do we even see them?"

The magician fumbled with a small sack attached to his belt. A moment later, Gelderand removed the gold ring and slid it onto his finger, disappearing in the process.

"I will be able to see them, if they truly are invisible," said the unseen person. Gelderand removed the magical object. "However, I need to be close enough to observe them."

Harrison made a quick glance to the South Gate. Knowing Gelderand could not run faster than he could, the young warrior said, "Give me the ring and I'll chase after them."

The mage handed Harrison the gold object, which he placed on his finger, disappearing in the process. "Keep heading for the South Gate," said the young warrior to his friends, beginning his quest again.

Along with Unified Army soldiers, the small group maintained their sprint toward the southernmost part of Concur. With each passing step, it became apparent that Lord Hammer had foiled Meredith's plot to do away with him.

Harrison's lungs yearned for more air, and even though he began to outpace his friends, there was no way that he could possibly catch up to galloping horses. Turning a corner, the young warrior found himself dashing down the main road that led to what used to be the South Gate. Ahead in the distance, Concurian soldiers dispersed into the open countryside, along with twelve steeds without riders.

Squinting at the horses, Harrison tried his best to focus on the riderless animals. The dirt and dust that the steeds kicked into the air hindered his vision, but a moment later, he found what he had sought.

Anyone else who gazed at the galloping beasts would think that someone had spooked the animals, causing the majestic horses to run in fear. However, Harrison saw two men clutching their animal's neck, holding on for dear life.

The young warrior's heart quickened and he started rushing in their direction once again. After less than a minute, Lord Hammer and Allard outdistanced the sprinting human ten paces to his one. Gasping and almost out of breath, Harrison stopped in his tracks, knowing he could not possibly keep pace with the horses. Frustrated and dejected, the young warrior stared at the escaping men, then removed the ring from his finger.

Murdock, Pondle, and Kymbra saw Harrison first, halting to a standstill. "Why are you stopping?" asked the ranger, trying to catch his breath.

The young warrior maintained his stare at the galloping animals. "I see them," he said in a defeated tone, pointing to the rightmost steeds. "They're exiting the city."

"Which way?" asked Murdock, not knowing the direction the fugitives had headed. Gelderand and Swinkle finally caught up to the rest of the group and congregated around Harrison's position.

"We have to keep moving!" said Murdock, exasperated. The ranger watched as the horses dispersed in different directions, disappearing into the Concurian countryside.

Murdock brought his focus to the people surrounding him. "If we can get the Arcadians and their horses, we can definitely catch them!"

Harrison's voice remained calm. "Forget it, Murdock."

"What?" said the ranger, his brow crinkled in confusion. "We're going to let that bastard get away?"

"We can't catch them," said Harrison. "Like it or not, he's gone."

"But the horses," lamented Murdock, but to no avail. Taking his gaze to Concur's gaping wound, the ranger sighed, knowing deep down that Harrison was right.

"By the time we saddle up the Arcadians, Nigel will be long gone," said Harrison. "We need to report our findings to Meredith, then she can decide what she wants to do next."

"Harrison, we have succeeded," said Swinkle, offering his support. "Concur is now rid of Lord Hammer and Meredith has assumed power."

The young warrior smiled. "Let's go back to the mansion."

Several soldiers witnessed the small group's actions. "Sir, shall we chase after them?"

Harrison shook his head. "No. Secure the South Gate and don't allow anyone entrance. You'll get more orders later."

"Yes, sir!" said the fighter with a salute before heeding his superior's command.

The young warrior then gestured for the group to begin their return march to the mansion. Though the circumstances of the day had changed, one fact remained – Lord Hammer no longer ruled Concur.

By the time Harrison and his friends arrived back at the mansion, soldiers loyal to Meredith had surrounded the complex. The young warrior knew he needed to give the First Lady an update on the current situation.

Allowed to pass through the guard's blockade, the small posse climbed the main staircase where two sentries permitted them entrance through the vast double doors. Inside, Harrison could hear loud voices discussing a most delicate problem. As he walked down the corridor, he also noticed Tara in the background. The young maiden saw Harrison and she felt a heavy burden lift from her shoulders.

"Milady, we need to secure your city," said Bracken, trying to convince Meredith to his manner of thinking.

"He'll come back!" said Meredith, in reference to Lord Hammer. "He's relentless!" Thoragaard took a step closer to the First Lady, resting his hands on her shoulders in an effort to calm her.

"Not if we can provide a perimeter defense around Concur," said Brendan in a soothing voice. "He has lost many men who were loyal to him. He's down to a manageable force."

"We can handle him now," added Octavius, his brother nodding in agreement.

The First Lady brought a hand to her forehead, thinking. She then noticed Harrison's group enter the foyer and waved them over.

"Did you find Nigel?" asked Meredith, hoping for better news.

Harrison pursed his lips. "He escaped through the South Gate. We tried to pursue him, but he rode on horseback and we couldn't catch him being on foot." The young warrior's friends, including Kymbra and her partners, formed a semi-circle around the land's decorated fighters.

"So he's just gone?" said Meredith, who took her wide-eyed gaze to the leadership group hoping for a negative answer.

"Like I said, Milady," started Bracken, "all the reason to let Lord Hammer go and secure your city."

The young warrior took a step in Meredith's direction. Taking her hands, he said, "Meredith, Nigel is an arrogant man, but he's no fool. We defeated him and he won't be coming back any time soon. He knows that would be suicide."

Meredith sighed. "Then what should we do?"

"Listen to these men," said Harrison, taking his gaze to his fellow leaders. "They're doing what's right for you and Concur."

The dark-haired woman took a moment to digest Harrison's comments and after she did, nodded.

"All right," she began, bringing her focus to the men who surrounded her. "I'm allowing you to secure my city for the time being. However, I want my loyal army to eventually assume control of Concur. Do I make myself clear?" The army leaders all nodded.

"Good. Please perform that task now," finished the First Lady.

"What are your plans after that?" asked Brendan.

Meredith smiled. "The party must go on. Though the circumstances are not what I had expected, the fact still remains that my people must know that I am in charge.

"My staff will prepare a gala event for all citizens of Concur. It's time to spread the word."

"It shall be done, Milady," said Brendan with a bow. Turning to his fellow leaders, he said, "Let's begin securing this city."

"I'm expecting all of you to be at the mansion tonight," said Meredith. "This is a glorious day!" The army leaders gave the First Lady a nod, then proceeded to embark on protecting the metropolis.

The Concurian woman turned her attention to Harrison and his friends. "I want everyone to stay in the mansion tonight."

Harrison smiled, then reached his hand in Tara's direction. The young girl gladly obliged, grabbing her mate's hand and squeezing it tight.

Focusing on the First Lady again, Harrison said, "That's most generous of you, Meredith."

"Consider yourselves distinguished guests of Concur," said the Concurian woman, a smile beaming across her face. "I owe you my life, Harrison."

"No, you don't," said the young warrior. "I made a promise that I would return someday and I'm happy that I did."

The First Lady embraced Harrison. Whispering in his ear, she said, "I always knew that you would. Thank you."

Releasing her hug, she continued, "I'll have my servants prepare a special room for you two." Meredith gazed at the young couple. "You've been separated for far too long."

Both young people blushed. "You don't have to do that, Meredith, really."

"Nonsense," said the Concurian. "You'll awaken to a beautiful view of the harbor."

"Thank you once again," said Harrison. Changing the subject, he said, "We need your signature on the Unification Treaty, in order for Concur to join the other villages in the land."

"We'll have that ceremony before the big event tonight," said Meredith. "For now, all of you freshen up and get some well-deserved rest. Consider this compound your home for the remainder of your stay. The festivities will start in a few short hours."

Guards and mansion staffers then escorted Harrison and his friends to their respective rooms, while Meredith and Thoragaard tended to their city's immediate needs. For the first time in months, everyone involved with the reuniting of the land felt more at ease and waited with anticipation for the night's events to commence.

CHAPTER 36

¤

Harrison and his friends enjoyed the confines of Concur's regal palace. Meredith's staff made sure that the adventurers all had a place to rest, clean up, and eat before the night's festivities.

The young warrior took some of the time to speak with Meredith and the Unified Army leaders to discuss how to present the signing of the Unification Treaty. Though Harrison had solicited the signatures from other town dignitaries after presenting them with their share of the Treasure of the Land, he knew that having Meredith sign the document was a much more prestigious event.

After an hour of deliberation, they all agreed on the format of the historic signing. With that matter settled, Harrison bid everyone good-bye and returned to one of the most majestic rooms of the mansion.

The young warrior opened the door to a massive bedroom adorned with paintings, artifacts, and tapestries that all ended with a set of double doors that led to a private patio. Harrison heard Tara in the adjacent bathroom, preparing for the night's events. He noticed a carafe of red wine resting on a table next to the elaborate bedding and he poured two glasses of the crimson liquid.

While his love continued in the washroom, Harrison took his goblet and proceeded out to the terrace. From his vantage point, the Concurian harbor loomed a mile away, its calm waters reflecting the late afternoon sun. The young warrior gazed about the city, still fresh with destruction and despair, but knew that he had helped usher a new era to the Concurian townspeople. He took a sip of the fine wine, allowing the alcohol to begin its mind-altering process. The sound of someone walking from behind broke his concentration.

Harrison turned to see the most radiant woman he had ever set eyes on. Tara leaned against the door jam, holding a goblet of wine. A beige skirt, hanging low on her hips, and a white blouse completed her outfit. Gold earrings adorned the young maiden's ears and a necklace with a single sparkling diamond graced her neck.

Taking two steps towards Harrison, she said, "Meredith gave me some fresh clothes to wear." She nervously played with the gemstone that lay on her chest.

The young warrior could hardly catch his breath. "You're absolutely breathtaking," he said. Placing his wine on the terrace railing, he rushed to embrace her.

Tara looked deep into Harrison's eyes. "I love you so much."

"I love you more," said the young maiden's mate. Then their lips joined. "I couldn't stand to be away from you another minute."

"You won't have to ever again," said Tara.

The couple then separated and gazed into each other's eyes. Harrison raised an eyebrow. "Do you want to skip the festivities?"

Tara blushed, arching an eyebrow of her own. "I would love to, but you know we can't do that now."

Harrison smiled. "We've waited so long."

Tara sighed and looked down, her heart pounding. "I know, but nighttime will come soon enough." She then gazed back at Harrison with a sly smile.

"Did I mention that I love you?" said Harrison, unable to contain his grin.

"I think it's time to head downstairs," said Tara before taking a sip from her goblet.

Harrison drew a heavy sigh, not wanting to leave the beautiful sight before him. Alas, he knew Tara was right. "I suppose we should." The young warrior lowered his head to place his lips on Tara's once again, kissing her deeply.

As the couple separated, the young warrior again was smitten with Tara's beauty. "I know I've said this already, but you look stunning."

"Thank you," said Tara, playing with her jewelry. "Meredith has such nice things. I feel like a princess!"

Harrison looked at her without saying a word. Instead, he took in Tara's wholesomeness, knowing the intense love he felt for her now. With the Battle of Concur behind them, he could finally concentrate on his true love - Tara.

The young maiden took Harrison by the hand and led him away from the patio. "Time to make more history," she said.

"That we will."

Downstairs in the mansion, staff hurriedly prepared for the gala event while an important group of people congregated in the function room.

Harrison and Tara walked hand in hand into the grand ballroom. Meredith and Thoragaard sat in two large regal chairs situated across the room, a large oak table placed before them. Around the table sat members of the Unified Army and the Robusite clerics, as well as their friends. On the opposite side of the ballroom, staffers were erecting a staging while others arranged long tables and chairs in the main area.

"It's about time you two showed up," said Murdock with a smile.

Harrison pulled out a chair for Tara, then sat in one next to her. "I'm sorry we're late. Did we miss anything?"

"We were about to finalize the plans for the armies in Concur, as well as to sign the treaty," said Meredith. She then turned her attention to the unified leadership.

"You say that your people can help repair our city and provide protection during that time?"

"All the villages throughout the land will help restore Concur back to prominence," said Brendan. "Aegeus is behind your rule and welcomes Concur into the new order."

"As does Argos." Octavius smiled.

"And Arcadia," added Bracken.

Sister Martel and her clerics also agreed to help the Concurians. "Robus will pray for your city's resurrection and provide hands to help its restoration."

"We'll even help reconstruct the great walls that surround this city," said Brendan.

Meredith raised her palms. "On the contrary, I would like to see these walls come down."

All eyes shifted amongst the parties seated at the table. "Um, of course," said Brendan, taken aback by the First Lady's request. "It might take a little longer, but we certainly can bring these walls down."

"They have become Concur's most recognizable feature," started Meredith, her eyes staring at the table before her. "And I hate the very sight of them. Nigel erected the walls to feign protection for his people; in reality, he didn't want anyone to leave."

"I think it's a brilliant idea," said Harrison, adding to the conversation. "Think of it as a new start for Concur."

"Precisely," said the Concurian with a smile. "As for the treaty …" Meredith brought the parchment nearer in order to read it better. "By signing my name, I'm pledging Concur's allegiance to be part of the new order, correct?"

"Yes," said Harrison, knowing how close he was to getting humanity unified. "And you'll need to choose a representative for the Legion of Knighthood."

"Oh, that's easy," said Meredith. "Thoragaard will be the perfect person for that role."

The illusionist showed an uncharacteristic look of surprise. "Meredith, I am honored, but this is a big decision. You should take your time and think this through."

"Nonsense! You've been instrumental in seeing our plans come to fruition," said the dark-haired women. "You put your life on the line for Concur many times and this is your reward."

"I am humbled, Milady," said the mage with a nod. "I accept."

Meredith was about to sign her name with a quill pen when she noticed an important aberration. Turning to Bracken Drake, she said, "Why hasn't Arcadia pledged their support to this cause?"

The Arcadian leader shifted in his seat. "Milady, Arcadia is not ready to join this alliance in all facets. We feel that we can remain self-sufficient, but Arcadia will pledge its support to help those in need, like we did for Concur."

The Concurian raised an eyebrow. "I feel your justifications are wrong, though Concur is indebted to you. I can only hope that you change your mind in the future."

"We will constantly reevaluate our situation," said Bracken.

Meredith, satisfied with the Arcadian's response, added her historic name to the Unification Treaty. She then rolled the parchment and handed it to Harrison.

"Thank you, Meredith," said the young warrior, accepting the scroll. "We have the first of many artifacts belonging to Concur for you."

Harrison motioned for Swinkle to retrieve the messenger falcon. The young cleric presented the bird of prey to Meredith, who accepted the animal with a wrinkled brow.

"This is a treasure?" she asked, while gazing at the falcon perched atop Swinkle's forearm.

"It's a special bird," said Harrison. "Each town and village has one unique to their dwelling. It's a way to communicate throughout the land."

Meredith smiled in feigned appreciation. "Concur thanks you for this wonderful gift." She then waved over a member of her staff to take the bird away. The falcon squawked as a male servant did his best to accommodate his superior's request.

The First Lady, comfortable with the plans for Concur, its acceptance into the new allegiance, and the handling of the living gift, decided the time had come for a celebration.

"I want everyone to enjoy themselves tonight," started Meredith and gave her head servant, Percival, a nod. The frail man knew just what the dark-haired woman wanted. A moment later, staffers delivered carafes of fine wine and flagons of ale to the leader tables.

"I wish for everyone to enjoy the comforts of Concur," said Meredith. Raising her chalice, she said, "A toast to our new alliance."

Everyone raised their flagons and goblets, toasting Meredith and her city's resurrection. After taking a sip of wine, Meredith continued.

"It is now time to invite all of the citizens of this fine city to partake in some of Concur's riches, if only for a day." The First Lady called to her servant.

"Percival, open the main doors to the mansion, begin serving food and drink to our people, and have the minstrels start their songs!"

"I am happy to do so," said Percival, who then bowed to his new leader before going off to perform his task.

Moments later, Harrison smelled the aroma of freshly cooked food. The young warrior could not recall the last time he had a homemade meal, let alone any kind of celebration to go along with it.

"This is going to be a lot of fun," said Tara with a girlish smile. "I'm hoping tonight will erase the bad memories that this building holds for me."

"This will be a most special night," said Harrison. "I assure you." The young warrior reached beneath the table to hold her soft hand.

Across from them, four musicians began to play a song. Everyone turned to face the men who sang in perfect tune. Harrison leaned closer to Tara, saying in a soft voice, "Their melodies are fantastic and their voices are flawless."

Tara listened in amazement. "I've never heard such beautiful music."

Just as the minstrels began to play, random people began to enter through the double doorway on the opposite side of the room. Servants guided them to seats at the long tables, and servers brought them food and drink.

Members of the serving staff carried silver-colored pails filled with Cornish hens and piled the diminutive birds on awaiting plates along with fresh vegetables, soup, and an assortment of pastries and bread. The townspeople could not believe what they saw, having grown accustomed to the oppressive rule of Lord Hammer. Never in their lifetimes had their former leader given them anything for their hard work, yet Meredith showed them love and compassion. Word of the festivities at the mansion began to spread at a feverish rate.

As the night proceeded, Harrison and his friends enjoyed the fine wine and ale that Meredith's staff so happily served. Swinkle, who had not forgotten what the effects of wine did to him in this very mansion a short time ago, caught the young warrior's attention.

"Look around us," started the young cleric, taking his gaze about the room, "I would say that we fulfilled the ancient kings' hope of uniting humanity."

Harrison and the others scanned the room likewise. The young warrior looked upon Arcadian soldiers conversing with Concurians loyal to Meredith, while local townsfolk chatted with fighters from other villages. Swinkle was right; he and his friends had helped unite the land, if only for this day.

"I'm very proud of what we accomplished," said Harrison.

"We all are," added Murdock. "I didn't think we'd get this far, at least not this fast."

"It took a lot of convincing, and a lot of hard work."

"We should be proud of ourselves," said Gelderand. "The kings sent us out on a monumental task and we succeeded. There is still much to do, but we can build off this day and be happy to know that others throughout the land believe in us and our cause."

"Having a large army along with us to help hand out pieces of the Treasure of the Land didn't hurt either," said Murdock with a smirk.

Harrison laughed. "That's true!"

Swinkle continued with his line of reasoning. "The kings also said that we needed to find the remaining pieces of the Talisman of Unification. We need to visit Moradoril and his elven brothers."

The young warrior allowed his friend's comments to sink in. Though they could rejoice today, they still had unfinished business to handle. "We'll worry about that later, Swinkle." Harrison noticed a familiar face heading toward their table.

A young girl with brown hair approached Meredith. "Milady, I'm so glad to see you're all right!"

"Catherine!" exclaimed the First Lady, who jumped from her seat and embraced her handmaiden. "I'm so happy to see you!" She patted a seat next to her, signaling for the girl to sit down.

"I was so worried when I didn't hear from you again," said Meredith.

"The guards told me that I couldn't enter the mansion anymore," said the young girl with a hint of remorse. "I did what you asked of me, but I never found out what had happened to you." Catherine's eyes began to water.

"After that awful ceremony in the Town's Square, I could only hope that Lord Hammer would spare you."

Meredith hugged her handmaiden again. "Everything is better now," she said before pulling away, "and I want you to come back to work in the mansion."

A smile lit Catherine's face. "Really? I would like that very much!"

"Come by tomorrow and tell Percival that I sent you here to work." Meredith then shifted her eyes in Swinkle's direction. "Look who else has come back."

The young girl peered in the same direction, her eyes finding the young cleric. Catherine swiveled her head, her eyes round. "That's Swinkle!"

Meredith stood from her position. "Let's say hello, shall we?"

The young girl could hardly refuse and followed the First Lady. Swinkle saw the two women coming and immediately turned away, his face changing to a lovely shade of red.

"Swinkle," said Meredith, "I think you remember Catherine?"

The young cleric faced the women, his gaze stopping at the young girl. "Um, yes, I do," fumbled the nervous boy. "It is so nice to see you again." Catherine smiled and gave him a nervous nod.

"Why don't you two catch up on things," said Meredith, taking the opportunity to leave the young couple alone. She then went back to her chair at the end of the table. Catherine took a seat next to the young cleric.

Swinkle had trouble looking the girl in the eye. After several uncomfortable seconds of silence, he finally said, "I'm so ashamed of what happened the last time I saw you."

The young girl placed a hand on his forearm. "Don't be! I wasn't upset at you. You just had a little too much to drink."

"A little," said Harrison, overhearing the conversation. "If that's what you want to call it!"

Swinkle tried to diffuse the situation. "That will not happen again." He gestured toward the table, full of goblets and chalices of wine and ale, yet none belonged to him. "I am not partaking of any alcohol tonight."

At that time, a servant asked if Catherine would like something to drink. She happily accepted a chalice of the forbidden liquid. "I am," she said with a sly smile. Swinkle turned red yet again.

As the night continued, more minstrels took the stage, people danced to the music, and everyone consumed part of the abundance of food and drink. Harrison and Tara enjoyed their time with their friends, Swinkle caved to desires of alcohol and started to slur his speech with Catherine, and Murdock and Kymbra became cozier as the night went on. Pondle commiserated with Adrith and Marissa, while Gelderand entered intense philosophical discussions with Sister Martel and her brethren. Even Lance and Rufus played with local children who had attended the event with their parents.

With it getting late, Tara, snuggled next to Harrison, gazed up with her big blue eyes and said, "I'm going to go back to our room. Meet me up there in a little while."

The young warrior watched as Tara rose from her chair, kissed him on the cheek, and left the party behind.

Sitting with an arm around Kymbra, Murdock witnessed the young maiden's actions and said, "I wouldn't wait too long. She might fall asleep!"

Kymbra, slightly intoxicated herself, whispered something in the ranger's ear, then left the others as well. A curious look graced Murdock's face before he chugged the rest of his ale and wiped his mouth on his sleeve.

"She told me to follow her." The ranger shrugged, then went after the tall, blonde-haired woman.

Harrison smirked at his friend, having never seen this side of the ranger in the past. Before reuniting with Tara, the young warrior made a point to speak with Meredith one more time.

The First Lady saw Harrison approaching and patted a chair next to her, signaling for him to sit by her side.

"Enjoying yourself?" asked Meredith, a wide smile on her face and eyes narrow as slits. The young warrior knew the wine was taking its toll on the new Concurian leader.

"I certainly am."

"Where's that beautiful woman of yours?"

"She went back to our room."

The Concurian woman raised an eyebrow. "And you've kept her waiting?"

"I wanted to thank you once again for your hospitality, not only for me and my friends, but for all of the people who fought so hard for your freedom."

Meredith closed her eyes and smiled, trying her best to sit without wobbling. "I'll always be in debt to you; this function is the least I could do." She then changed the conversation.

"You really love Tara, don't you?"

The question surprised Harrison. "Um, yes, I do very, very much."

"She's very smart and tougher than she lets on."

The young warrior smiled just thinking about his love. "She's more than I could ever ask for."

"You know," started Meredith before sipping from her silver chalice, "I had hoped that you would come back for me some day."

"Well, I did come back to save you."

Meredith shook her head, then cast her eyes to the table. "No, you came for Tara. I was a byproduct of your liberation."

Harrison placed his hand under her chin and lifted her head. He then stared into her sad eyes. "I came for both of you," stated the young warrior with conviction in his voice.

"My heart broke when I let Tara convince me that she could take on her mission, and it shattered when I heard that Nigel imprisoned both of you. I made a pledge a while ago to help liberate you if the opportunity rose. When it did, I made sure that you would not suffer anymore."

A single tear of happiness rolled down Meredith's cheek. "Go to your woman, Harrison. She loves you so much and you deserve to be together."

"Will you be all right?"

"I will," said Meredith, wiping her tear away. "Go." She gestured for Harrison to leave. The young warrior leaned over and kissed Meredith on the cheek, then left her behind and began his trek upstairs.

CHAPTER 37

¤

Harrison left the main function room and began his journey to meet his love. People littered the mansion's corridors, most conversing with their friends and acquaintances while holding a goblet or chalice in their hand. Many times, the young warrior needed to excuse himself and squeeze between members of the crowd.

After a few minutes, he reached the base of the spiral staircase that led to the building's sleeping quarters. Two guards manned the area, preventing unauthorized people from going upstairs. As Harrison approached the stairs, one of the guards recognized him.

"Have a good evening, sir," said the sentry, extending his arm toward the staircase, allowing him to pass.

"Thank you," said Harrison and proceeded to the second floor.

The young warrior hastened his step, finally reaching his bedroom. Inside, Tara had arranged candles in strategic positions, illuminating the area with a soft yellow glow. She left the doorway leading to the terrace slightly ajar, allowing a gentle breeze to blow through the opening, rippling the curtains and causing the candles to flicker. The sweet aroma of perfume filled the room.

Harrison's heart began to pound with anticipation, the romantic atmosphere overloading his senses. The young warrior brought his focus to the bed where he found Tara waiting for him. She lay on her side, gazing at him seductively. Soft down blankets covered the young maiden up to her midsection; the diamond from her necklace sparkled between her bare breasts.

"I'm glad you didn't stay downstairs much longer," said Tara, a glint in her eye.

"Me, too," said Harrison as he fumbled with his clothes. A moment later, he joined his love beneath the coverings.

"I've been waiting for this night for so long," said the young warrior, taking Tara in his arms, pulling her against him.

"So have I," said the young maiden before giving him a passionate kiss. Another light breeze blew through the open doorway, fluttering the candles, dancing shadows on the wall. Harrison pulled the blankets tighter, keeping them both warm.

The young couple then gave into their desires, becoming one, and releasing their passions for each other until the wee hours of the night.

A glint of sunlight woke Harrison from a deep, sound sleep. He found his arms wrapped around Tara's sleeping body, her shallow breaths raising her chest ever so slightly. He buried his face in her soft, blonde hair and kissed her on the head. The young maiden stirred and snuggled closer to him.

The young warrior watched his love sleep a few minutes longer, loving her more with every passing second. Though he felt a total bliss, a nagging feeling overcame him. Having sharp warrior instincts, he knew better than to just let the sensation pass.

Sweeping the room with his eyes, he found the candles extinguished, Rufus curled and asleep at the end of the bed, Lance snoring on the floor, and a light breeze flowing through the terrace doors. Nothing unusual there.

Harrison craned his neck in search for another blanket, while trying not to wake Tara. Finding one draped over the footing of the bed, the young warrior wiggled away from his love. Tara curled up in Harrison's vacated spot, clutching his pillow and pulling it against her.

His mate comfortable, the young warrior snatched the covering and wrapped it around his torso. Being as quiet as possible, he tiptoed to the patio entranceway and stepped outside.

Concur was quiet, a nice change from the brutal happenings that had occurred over the past few days. Harrison gazed out over the city, taking a deep breath of the cool, sea air. The sun had risen above the waterline without a cloud to hinder its ascent. Down below, the streets were empty, too early for the townsfolk to begin their day.

The young warrior still had an unsettling feeling, but nothing had presented itself. Harrison pushed the sensation to the back of his mind, keeping it for his subconscious to process, and leaned against the terrace railing. He closed his eyes and allowed the morning sunlight to warm his face.

"Are you trying to run away from me already?" said the sweetest voice he had ever heard.

Harrison opened his eyes and found Tara approaching from their bedroom. The young maiden had wrapped herself in the blankets from their bed. Joining him on the terrace, she snuggled against him and accepted a kiss.

"Not on your life," said the young warrior.

"You're up early," said Tara, her brow furrowing. "Is something wrong?"

Harrison shook his head, unsure. "I just had a strange feeling, but everything seems to be in place. I didn't want to worry you over nothing."

"You could have awakened me, you know."

The young warrior smiled and traced the curve of her jaw with a light touch. "I planned on doing that when I came back in."

Tara reached for her man's hand, using her other to keep her blanket from falling to the floor. Flashing him a seductive smile, she said, "Why don't you come back to bed?"

"That sounds like a very good idea." But before the young maiden could lead Harrison to the double doors, the young warrior felt the need to look back. Tara witnessed Harrison's actions.

"Harrison?"

The young warrior stood still for a second, gazing into the distance. At first, he thought he was mistaken, that the speck he saw in the sky was nothing more than a sea gull or hawk searching for its morning meal. However, the creature grew larger the closer it came to the shore.

Tara looked up at Harrison, then followed his line of sight. She, too, saw something in the air and squinted to get a better look.

"What is it?" she asked, her concern level rising.

"I'm not sure, but it's heading right for us." The young warrior positioned Tara behind him, the young maiden peering around Harrison's muscular torso.

A moment later, both young people could clearly see a bird of prey heading in their direction. Harrison's eyes widened when the raptor approached to within two hundred feet of their position.

"Well, I'll be ...," said the young warrior, recognizing the creature.

"Is that what I think it is?" asked Tara, remembering the gift that Swinkle had offered to Meredith the night before.

"It's one of the messenger falcons!" said Harrison. A moment later, the bird perched on the railing.

Harrison peered at the collar around the falcon's neck where a velvet pouch awaited the young warrior. He carefully removed the band from the bird's neck and opened the bag to see a small parchment. The young warrior unfurled the note and he read it with wide eyes.

"What does it say?" asked Tara with anticipation.

Harrison hesitated with his answer, shocked at what the note stated. Then he read verbatim, *Scynthians are overrunning the city! Buildings are burning! We need your help now!* The young warrior stared into nothingness after he finished the letter, his mind churning.

Tara frowned and her heart began to race. "What city did this message come from?"

The young warrior asked, "What is your name?" The bird responded with a single squawk.

The young maiden struggled with her anxiety. "Well?"

Harrison continued to stare straight ahead. "Arcadia."

The young warrior pulled his mate close with one hand, feeling her warm body next to his, while his mind raced with a thousand thoughts. He then spun Tara around in order to hold her tightly in his arms. The young maiden rested her head against Harrison's broad chest.

"What does this mean?" said Tara, her voice barely a whisper.

"It means we still have a lot of work left to do," said Harrison, his heart heavy. The young warrior then placed a hand under Tara's chin and lifted her head. He found a single tear rolling down her right cheek.

"You're going to leave me again, aren't you?" said Tara.

Harrison felt a heaviness form in his chest. His warrior instincts told him in what direction he would go, but his heart yearned for the woman in his arms.

"I made a promise that I would never leave you again, and I intend to keep that promise," said the young warrior. "But we need to alert the others."

Tara could feel the turmoil churning in his soul. She sniffed once and nodded. "I know."

Harrison leaned down to her and the two engaged in a passionate kiss. When they parted, the young couple gazed out over the terrace again. Both of their eyes widened, for flying toward them were three more falcons.

The young warrior pulled his mate closer and stood tall. Humanity's fragile alliance had barely taken hold and now a potential conflict with a bitter enemy stood on the horizon. Without saying a word to each other, the young couple waited in anticipation for the remaining birds to arrive.

Epilogue

A light mist clung to the cool, early morning air. King Holleris could see his breath as he blew into his hands, trying to keep them warm while he waited for Finius to complete his final task.

The regal man had spent the past six months changing his body back to its original form. Finius had reattached his severed head, but the scars from that wound would never disappear. However, the barbs connecting his skull to the rest of his body were gone, replaced with his own flesh and muscle tissue. His body ached all the time, and a persistent pain shot from the base of his skull to radiate throughout his upper body every time he moved his head from side to side. Better than death, he rationalized many times.

Standing outside their modest cabin, tucked away from the rest of the world in a thick forest of the Empire Mountains, King Holleris watched the gangly figure approach.

Rubbing his hands together, the king asked, "Do we really need to settle here, Finius?"

The ancient warlock's brow scrunched. "We need to keep away from everyone until the time is right. Surely, my lord, you must understand this?"

King Holleris fully understood the rationale of being anonymous, for now. "I do, Finius, but it's so damn cold in this range!"

Finius flashed a sly smile, full of chipped teeth. "Cold is but a state of mind." The mage waved his superior over. "Follow me, my lord. My work is complete."

The man in black exhaled deeply, a grin overtaking his face. "You have worked hard; harder that I thought you were capable of, Finius. Show me our creation."

The two men ventured away from their homestead and plodded through a few inches of fresh snow, entering deeper into the coniferous forest. Pine needles and cones littered the immediate area, and the sound of rushing water filled the otherwise quiet woodland setting. A few minutes later, the unusual couple reached their destination.

The king focused on the obvious object that contrasted with the vegetation of the dense, tall pine trees. Situated near a coldwater stream stood a deciduous tree that resembled a grand willow, in likeness to the ones that were found in thick marshlands. This plant, however, boasted an abundance of fruit that bent its branches low to the ground.

"Tell me again, Finius, when will our minions be ready?"

The wizard peered up at one of the pods. Shaped like a teardrop, the clear casing housed a living being, albeit not ready for harvesting. "All in due time, my lord," said Finius, reaching up to feel the membrane that encased the creature.

"Their covering is still too thick," added the warlock.

King Holleris gazed at the pod as well. Its dark contents stirred, sensing a force outside the protective casing, unhappy at the mage's touch. The unborn beast opened its eyes, stared at the king, then blinked twice. The regal man held his breath for a moment, surprised at their creation's extent of development.

Exhaling, King Holleris said, "And they will do what we say, act as we think?"

Finius brought his gaze to the man in black. Nodding, he answered, "That they will."

Content with the magician's answer, the king clasped his hands behind his back, standing tall. "We're still on track with our timeframe, correct?"

"Yes. The Shethar will be ready to perform their first task in a couple of months."

King Holleris smiled. "Our first test subjects will be most surprised."

Finius flashed a sinister smile as well. "Indeed they will."

The two men then spent the next few minutes inspecting their evil creation before returning to their cabin and continuing with their wicked plans.

Made in the
USA
Middletown, DE